高等学校商务英语系列教材　　　　　　　　总主编　杨翠萍

新编

商务英语听说教程

Business English Listening & Speaking

第2册

教师用书
Teacher's Book

主　编　周　淳　刘鸣放
编　者　周　淳　戴红珍　余　晓
　　　　汪玉枝　刘鸣放　杨翠萍

清华大学出版社
北京交通大学出版社
·北京·

内 容 简 介

本教程是与《新编商务英语听说教程学生用书》第 2 册配套的教师用书，主要内容包括与各单元主题相关的背景材料及听力部分的文字材料和练习答案。

本教程可供高等学校经贸和商务英语专业的学生使用，同时也可作为具有相应英语水平的商务工作者及商务英语爱好者的参考书。

图书在版编目（CIP）数据

新编商务英语听说教程教师用书. 第 2 册 / 周淳，刘鸣放主编. —北京：清华大学出版社；北京交通大学出版社，2010.12

（高等学校商务英语系列教材 / 杨翠萍总主编）

ISBN 978 – 7 – 5121 – 0003 – 9

Ⅰ. 新…　Ⅱ. ① 周…　② 刘…　Ⅲ. 商务 – 英语 – 听说教学 – 高等学校 – 教学参考资料　Ⅳ. H319.9

中国版本图书馆 CIP 数据核字（2010）第 204152 号

责任编辑：张利军　　特邀编辑：易　娜

出版发行：清 华 大 学 出 版 社　邮编：100084　电话：010 – 62776969　http://www.tup.com.cn
　　　　　北京交通大学出版社　邮编：100044　电话：010 – 51686414　http://press.bjtu.edu.cn
印 刷 者：北京瑞达方舟印务有限公司
经　　销：全国新华书店
开　　本：185 × 260　印张：15.25　字数：495 千字
版　　次：2011 年 1 月第 1 版　　2011 年 1 月第 1 次印刷
书　　号：ISBN 978 – 7 – 5121 – 0003 – 9/H·191
印　　数：1 ～ 3 000 册　定价：26.00 元

本书如有质量问题，请向北京交通大学出版社质监组反映。对您的意见和批评，我们表示欢迎和感谢。
投诉电话：010 – 51686043，51686008；传真：010 – 62225406；E-mail：press@bjtu.edu.cn。

前　言

　　《新编商务英语听说教程》是针对高等学校经贸和商务英语专业的学生、具有相应英语水平的商务工作者及英语爱好者编写的基础课系列教材。本教程突破了传统的教材模式，综合考虑了高等学校经贸、商务英语专业学生的特点，力求把经贸和商务知识的传授与英语听说技能的培养结合起来。

　　本教程从学生的实际水平出发，始终遵循"学用结合，重在运用"的原则。本教程循序渐进，通过内容丰富、专业面广、程度适宜、趣味性强的商务材料，促使学生积极参与有关商务实践的听说活动，在提高其口语表达能力的同时，了解商务活动的各个主要环节，拓宽视野，获取新知识。

　　为适应商务英语听说教学紧扣时代脉搏、满足社会需求的发展趋势，本教程编写人员在听取汇总来自语言教学专家、商务专业人士和教学一级的广大师生等多方面的意见及建议的基础上，结合国外相关教学领域最新的研究成果，在内容的编排、材料的选择、题型的设计和结构的完善等方面进行了大量的创新性探索。

　　本教程精选了24个商务活动中最常用的主题，采用全新的结构，分两册编排，使其更具系统性和可操作性。本教程在单元主题的择取和确立上兼顾了社会需求、专业培养目标、学生的认知程度和语言技能。本教程设计了 Preliminary Listening、Pre-listening、Listening、Speaking、Further Listening 和 Home Listening 等教学模块，力求突出教材的专业性、商务性及练习的多样性、趣味性和实用性等特点。

　　《新编商务英语听说教程》分两册，每册12个单元，按主题编排各单元的内容。每册配有相应的教师用书和录音光盘。各单元的基本构成如下。

　　1. Preliminary Listening：该部分以"spot dictation"的形式对单元主题（unit topic）进行概括性的介绍，旨在导入单元主题并让学生对单元主题有初步的认识和了解，激发学生进一步学习的兴趣和积极性。

　　2. Listening & Speaking：该部分为每个单元的主体构成部分，围绕单元主题对学生进行听与说的综合训练。该部分含两个结构基本相同、内容相对独立的教学模块：Section A 和 Section B。每个教学模块均具有其独立的且与单元主题紧密关联的副主题（sub-topic），并配有相关的一揽子听说活动。这样的编排化整为零，模块交替，听说结合，师生互动，既保证了教学内容的丰富性和多样性，也便于教师根据自己的实际需求，灵活机动地组织课堂教学。因此，本教程在借鉴国外同类教材先进经验的基础上，更好地兼顾了教学的灵活性和系统性，弥补了通常按主题定单元所编写的教材在教学系统性方面的缺陷。

Section A 和 Section B 主要包含以下内容。

（1）Pre-listening：针对听力材料中出现的热点问题提问，以导入后续的听说活动。

（2）Listening：分成对话（conversation）和语篇（passage）两部分对学生进行针对性的听力训练。每部分分别配有两项练习，一项侧重培养学生捕捉细节信息的能力，另一项侧重培养学生对信息进行整体把握和综合归纳的技能。

（3）Speaking：围绕教学模块的副主题（sub-topic）设计的综合性的口语活动。活动的形式多样，有小组讨论、看图说话、班级辩论、个案讨论、角色扮演等，旨在培养学生对英语语言和单元所涉及的商务文化背景知识的综合运用能力。

3. Further Listening：该部分按照特定的商务场景编排了相互关联的 5 个短篇（如电话留言、语音信息、财经新闻简报等）听力练习，帮助学生进一步熟悉真实场景下的商务活动及办公用语。

4. Home Listening：该部分安排了相关财经新闻报道一篇，突出了商务英语的时效性和在日常生活中的实用性。

《新编商务英语听说教程》的编写是以 6 学时完成一个单元为基础的，教师也可根据学生的实际情况灵活使用本教程。

本教程由华东师范大学联合上海对外贸易学院、上海立信会计学院、上海理工大学、上海外国语大学院等院校编写而成。虽然本教程是在全体参编教师多年的教学实践与研究的基础上产生的，但仍可能存在不妥之处和有待进一步完善的地方，欢迎各位专家、同仁及使用本教程的广大师生批评指正。

编　者
于华东师范大学
2011 年 1 月

2

 Contents

目录 Contents

Unit 1

Marketing

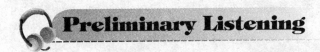
Dictation

Listen to the following short paragraph and fill in the blanks with what you hear.

The average consumer would probably define marketing as (1) <u>a combination of advertising and selling</u>. It actually includes a good deal more. Modern marketing is most simply defined as activities that (2) <u>direct the flow of goods and services</u> from producers to consumers. It encompasses, however, a broad range of activities including (3) <u>product planning, new-product development, organizing the channels</u> ... In advanced industrial economies, marketing considerations play a major role in determining corporate policy. Once primarily concerned with increasing sales through (4) <u>advertising and other promotional techniques</u>, corporate marketing departments now focus on credit policies, product development, (5) <u>consumer support, distribution, and corporate communications</u>. Marketers may look for outlets through which to sell the company's products, including (6) <u>retail stores, direct mail marketing, and wholesaling</u>. Marketing is used both to (7) <u>increase sales of an existing product</u> and to (8) <u>introduce new products</u>.

Listening & Speaking

SECTION A **Marketing Mix**

Pre-listening ▶▶

Background Information

1. Role of marketing

The role of marketing in the success of a business has only recently been recognized. In earlier years, marketing was viewed as not much different from selling. Many companies' focus was on the products sold, and the major emphasis of marketing was on maximizing profitability by generating sales volume through advertising and personal selling. They believed that with enough effort and expense, almost any product could be sold by high-powered selling and aggressive advertising. As time went by, a number of firms recognized that they needed to increase marketing efficiency to equal production efficiency and capabilities. They had gradually become aware that good sales techniques could no longer compensate for mistakes that resulted in producing the wrong products, and that the satisfaction of particular customer needs was essential for success. Essentially, the marketing concept focuses all the activities of the organization on satisfying customer needs by integrating these activities with marketing to accomplish the organization's long-range objectives.

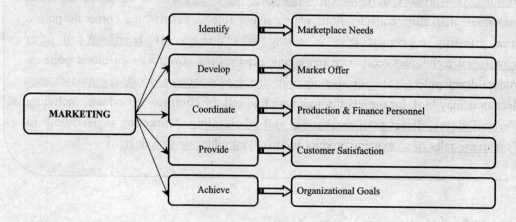

2. Marketing mix

The term *marketing mix* refers to the four major areas of decision making in the marketing process that are blended to obtain the results desired by the organization. The four elements of the marketing mix are sometimes referred to the four Ps of marketing. The marketing mix shapes the role of marketing within all types of organizations, both profit and nonprofit. Marketing managers make numerous decisions based on the elements of the marketing mix, all in an attempt to satisfy the needs and wants of consumers. Although some marketers have added other Ps, such as personnel and packaging, the fundamental dogma of marketing typically identifies the four Ps of the marketing mix as referring to:

❑ Product — an object or a service that is mass produced or manufactured on a large scale with a specific volume of units. A typical example of a mass produced service is the hotel industry. Typical examples of mass produced objects are the motor car and the disposable razor.

❑ Price — the amount a customer pays for a product. It is determined by a number of factors including market share, competition, product identity and the customer's perceived value of the product.

❑ Place — the location where a product can be purchased. It is often referred to as the distribution channel. It can include any physical store as well as virtual stores on the Internet.

❑ Promotion — all of the communications that a marketer may use in the marketplace. Promotion has four distinct elements — advertising, public relations, word of mouth and point of sale. Advertising covers any communication that is paid for, from television and cinema commercials, radio and Internet adverts through print media and billboards. Public relations are where the communication is not directly paid for and includes press releases, sponsorship deals, exhibitions, conferences, seminars or trade fairs and events. Word of mouth is any apparently informal communication about the product by ordinary individuals, satisfied customers or people specifically engaged to create word of mouth momentum.

Broadly defined, optimizing the marketing mix is the primary responsibility of marketing. By offering the product with the right combination of the four Ps marketers can improve their results and marketing effectiveness. Making small changes in the marketing mix is typically considered to be a tactical change. Making large changes in any of the four Ps can be considered strategic. For example, a large change in the price, say from $129.00 to $39.00 would be considered a strategic change in the position of the product. However a change of $129.00 to $131.00 would be considered a tactical change, potentially related to a promotional offer.

3. Internet marketing

Overview: Internet marketing is a component of electronic commerce and has become popular as Internet access is becoming more widely available and used. It ties together both the creative and technical aspects of the Internet, including design, development, advertising and marketing. Internet marketing methods include search engine marketing (both search engine optimization and pay per click advertising), banner advertising, e-mail marketing, affiliate marketing, interactive advertising, and email advertising.

Business models: Internet marketing is associated with several business models. The main models include business-to-business (B2B) and business-to-consumer (B2C). B2B consists of companies doing business with each other, whereas B2C involves selling directly to the end consumer. A third, less common business model is peer-to-peer (P2P), where individuals exchange goods between themselves. Internet marketing can also be seen in various formats. One version is name-your-price (e.g. Priceline.com). With this format, customers are able to state what price range they wish to spend and then select from items within that price range. With find-the-best-price websites (e.g. Hotwire.com), Internet users can search for the lowest prices on items. A final format is online auctions (e.g. Ebay.com) where buyers bid on listed items.

Benefits: Some of the benefits associated with Internet marketing include the availability of information. Consumers can log onto the Internet and learn about products, as well as purchase them, at any hour. Companies that use Internet marketing can also save money because of a reduced need for a sales force. Overall, Internet marketing can help expand from a local market to both national and international marketplaces. And, in a way, it levels the playing field for big and small players. Unlike traditional marketing media (like print, radio and TV), entry into the realm of Internet marketing can be a lot less expensive. Furthermore, since exposure, response and overall efficiency of digital media is much easier to track than that of traditional "offline" media, Internet marketing offers a greater sense of accountability for advertisers.

Limitations: Limitations of Internet marketing create problems for both companies and consumers. Slow Internet connections can cause difficulties. If companies build overly large or complicated web pages, Internet users may struggle to download the information. Internet marketing does not allow shoppers to touch, smell, taste or try on tangible goods before making an online purchase. Some e-commerce vendors have implemented liberal return policies to reassure customers. Germany for example introduced a law in 2000 that allows any buyer of a new product over the internet to return the product on a no-questions-asked basis and get a full return. Another limiting factor, particularly with respect to actual buying and selling, is the adequate development (or lack thereof) of electronic payment methods like e-checks, credit cards, etc.

Security concerns: For both companies and consumers that participate in online business, security concerns are very important. Many consumers are hesitant to buy items over the Internet because they do not trust that their personal information will remain private. Recently, some companies that do business online have been caught giving away or selling information about their customers. Several of these companies have guarantees on their websites, claiming customer information will be private. Some companies that buy customer information offer the option for individuals to have their information removed from the database (known as opting out). However, many customers are unaware that their information is being shared and are unable to stop the transfer of their information between companies. Encryption is one of the

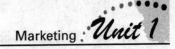

main methods for dealing with privacy and security concerns on the Internet.

4. Affiliate marketing

Affiliate marketing is an Internet-based marketing practice in which a business rewards one or more affiliates for each visitor or customer brought about by the affiliate's marketing efforts. The Affiliate Marketing industry has four core players at its heart: the Merchant, the Network, the Publisher and the Consumer. Eighty percent of affiliate programs today use revenue sharing or cost per sale (CPS) as a compensation method, nineteen percent use cost per action (CPA), and the remaining programs use other methods such as cost per click (CPC) or cost per mille (CPM). Merchants favor affiliate marketing because in most cases it uses a "pay for performance" model, meaning that the merchant does not incur a marketing expense unless results are accrued. Some businesses owe much of their success to this marketing technique, a notable example being Amazon.com. Amazon launched its associate program in July 1996. Amazon associates could place banner or text links on their site for individual books, or link directly to the Amazon home page. When visitors clicked from the associate's website through to Amazon and purchased a book, the associate received a commission. Amazon was not the first merchant to offer an affiliate program, but its program was the first to become widely-known and serves as a model for subsequent programs. Affiliate marketing has grown quickly since its inception.

5. Canon

Canon Inc. has ranked as one of the world's leading manufacturers of electronics, principally optical electronics, since the late 1970s. This multinational manufacturer of film, video, television, and X-ray cameras and a wide range of increasingly sophisticated office equipment was established by Goro Yoshida and Saburo Uchida as the Precision Optical Research Laboratories. Registering the Canon trademark for its products in 1935 the company produced its first 35-millimetre camera, the Kwanon. In 1947 the company changed its name to the Canon Camera Co., intending to unify its brand and image as a platform for penetrating Western export markets. In 1969 Canon was taken up as the corporate name. Takeshi Mitarai, the company president from 1942 to 1974, did much to ensure the company's foundations for future success. Year in and year out one of the top three companies receiving US patents, Canon has a history of innovation that has brought it a leadership position in copiers, laser and ink-jet printers, fax machines, scanners, multifunction devices, film-based and digital cameras, and camcorders. Canon has been involved in an important alliance with Hewlett-Packard Company (HP) since 1985 whereby Canon produces laser printers that are sold by HP under the HP LaserJet brand; approximately one-fifth of Canon's total revenues are derived from this partnership. Canon still manufactures the majority of its products in Japan, while also operating manufacturing subsidiaries in the United States, Germany, France, Taiwan, China, Malaysia, Thailand, and Vietnam along with a manufacturing joint venture in Korea. Fully 73 percent of the firm's revenues are generated outside Japan, with the Americas and Europe accounting for about 30 percent each.

Canon has been keen to promote itself through sponsorship, as with its official sponsorship of the 1984 Olympic Games in Los Angeles, through a commitment to active recycling policies in the following decade, and the exhibition of its products, technological prowess, and visions of the future as at the Canon Expo 2000 seen in New York, Paris, and Tokyo.

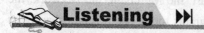 **Listening** ▶▶

Conversation

Tapescript

Jim Daniels started his online business with just $300. Six months later he was earning enough to quit his day job and his "web income" is now well into six figures a year. In this interview with Julia Caron, Jim will show you how to make a living online, right from the comfort of your own homes.

Julia: Jim, I know you started back in 1995, and how long did it take you to start successfully achieving your marketing objectives?

Jim: Actually, it was February 1996 when I got started. I worked part-time on my computer each night when I got home from my regular job. But by May I started seeing some decent income. By November that same year I was making more on my PC working from 7 to 12 PM than I was making 40 hours a week on my job. So that's when I made up my mind and went full time online. It was scary at first, but I'm glad I did it.

Julia: Surely, you are lucky you did it. Jim, if I were just starting my online venture, what key elements do you think would bring me success?

Jim: First of all, you need a hot selling product or service. If you can develop your own, that is the best road to take. And while you're doing that, jump into affiliate marketing. You can do really well if you select the right programs. Even with my own products now I still pull in $70,000 to $80,000 a year from affiliate programs. Number two is a professional site of your own. Even if you plan to promote mostly affiliate programs, you need a site of your own. That's a big key to long-term success online.

Julia: Jim, most marketers just starting out have a limited budget. If someone had only $200 a month, where would they get the best bang for their money?

Jim: Simple. Find medium-sized magazines and buy top sponsorship ads. As long as they choose magazines that are read by a good percentage of the readership they will get traffic and make sales. If they do not, something is wrong with their sales letter or site.

Julia: One last question, Jim. The pop-up script that I used from your *Make a Living Online Member Site* has increased my subscriber base considerably. Other than e-books and free reports where else could one find subscribers for their magazine?

Jim: Yeah, that baby doubled my sign-up rate since the day I added it to my site too. I now get 5,000 subscribers a month easily. As far as other places to get subscribers, consider joint ventures with other publishers in your industry. I've teamed up with a few other publishers over the years and it always works well. As long as they get about the same number of subscribers each month or week you can simply do a cross-recommendation on your signup process and you'll both benefit.

I. Listen to the conversation and decide whether the following statements are true or false. Write T for true and F for false in the brackets.

1.(T)   2.(F)   3.(F)   4.(T)   5.(T)   6.(F)   7.(F)   8.(T)   9.(F)   10.(T)

II. Listen to the conversation again and complete the following notes with what you hear.

The Key to E-marketing Success

The road leading to achievement of marketing objectives:

▢ In Feb. 1996: starting to (1) <u>work part-time on the computer at night</u>
▢ By May 1996: starting to (2) <u>make some decent income online</u>
▢ By Nov. 1996: starting to (3) <u>make more money online than laboring 40 hours a week on the regular job</u> and deciding to go full time online

The elements bringing success to online-venture starters:

▢ (4) <u>A hot selling product or service</u>
  ✓ the best road to take: (5) <u>developing your own product or service</u>
  ✓ in the meantime, (6) <u>taking affiliate marketing programs</u>
▢ (7) <u>A professional site of your own</u>

The way to start out with a limited budget:

▢ To find (8) <u>medium sized magazines</u>
▢ To buy (9) <u>top sponsorship ads</u>

The sources of magazine subscribers:

▢ E-books
▢ Free reports
▢ (10) <u>Joint ventures with other publishers in the industry</u>

Passage

Tapescript

The Marketing Mix describes the specific combination of marketing elements used to achieve an organization's or individual's objectives and satisfy the target market. The mix depends on a number of decisions with regard to four major variables: product, place, promotion, and price.

Product decisions involve determining what goods, services, and ideas to market, the level of quality, the number of items to sell, the innovativeness of the company and the packaging. They also include features such as options and warranties, the level and timing of research, and when to drop existing offerings.

Place decisions include whether to sell through intermediaries or directly to consumers, how many outlets to sell through, whether to control or cooperate with other channel members, supplier selections, determining which functions to assign to others, and identifying competitors.

Promotion decisions include the selection of a combination of selling tools, whether to share promotions and their costs with others, how to measure effectiveness, the image to pursue, the level of customer service, and the choice of media, such as newspaper, television, radio and magazine. They also include the format of messages and advertisement timing throughout the year or during peak periods.

Price decisions include determining the overall level of price, the range of prices, the relationship between price and quality, the emphasis to place on price, how to react to competitors' prices, when to advertise prices and how prices are computed.

When developing a marketing mix, product, place, promotion, and price decisions must be compatible with the desires of the selected target market and with the company's resource capabilities.

Canon, a leading manufacturer of cameras and other products, is one of many firms that apply the marketing-mix concept well. Canon uses distinctive marketing mixes for different target markets, such as beginners, serious amateurs, and professional photographers. For beginners, Cannon offers very simple cameras with automatic focus and a built-in flash. These cameras are sold through all types of retailers, including discounters and department stores. Advertising is concentrated on television and general magazines. These cameras retail for under $100. For serious amateur photographers, Canon offers relatively advanced cameras with superior features and a number of attachments. These cameras are sold via camera stores and finer department stores. Advertising is concentrated on specialty magazines, with some television advertising. These cameras retail for several hundred dollars. In sum, Canon markets the right products in the right stores, promotes them in the right media, and has the right prices for its various target markets.

I. Listen to the passage and choose the best answers to the questions you hear.

1. Which of the following is NOT among the PRODUCT decisions?   (D)
2. What is PLACE in the Marketing Mix mainly about?   (C)
3. Which of the following is NOT mentioned as a choice of PROMOTION media in the passage? (B)
4. Which of the following is NOT categorized as a PRICE decision?   (D)
5. What can be concluded from the passage?   (C)

II. Listen to the passage again and complete the following notes with what you hear.

The Marketing Mix & Canon

What to Know about Marketing Mix

☞ The marketing mix is defined as a combination of marketing elements used to (1) <u>achieve an organization's or individual's objectives</u> and (2) <u>satisfy the target market</u>.

☞ What marketing mixes to use is determined by (3) <u>the desires of the selected target market</u> and (4) <u>the company's resource capabilities</u>.

Marketing Mixes Used by Canon

Target / 4Ps	For Beginners	For Serious Amateur Photographers
Product	offering (5) <u>simple cameras with automatic focus and a built-in flash</u>	offering (6) <u>relatively advanced cameras with superior features and a number of attachments</u>
Place	selling through (7) <u>all types of retailers, including discounters and department stores</u>	selling through (8) <u>camera stores and finer department stores</u>
Price	retailing for (9) <u>under $100</u>	retailing for (10) <u>several hundred dollars</u>
Promotion	concentrating advertisement on (11) <u>television and general magazines</u>	concentrating advertisement on (12) <u>specialty magazines, with some television advertising</u>
In conclusion	Canon markets (13) <u>the right products in the right stores</u>, promotes (14) <u>the right products in the right media</u>, and has (15) <u>the right prices for its various target markets</u>.	

SECTION B **Marketing Strategies**

Background Information

1. International marketing considerations

International marketing occurs when companies plan and conduct transactions across international borders in order to satisfy the objectives of both consumers and the company. While company managers may try to employ the same basic marketing strategies used in the domestic market when promoting products in international locations, those strategies may not be appropriate or effective. Company managers must adapt their strategies to fit the unique characteristics of each international market. Unique environmental factors need to be explored by company managers before going global. The first factor to consider in the international marketplace is each country's trading system. All countries have their own trade system regulations and restrictions. Common trade system regulations and restrictions include tariffs, quotas, embargoes, exchange controls, and non-tariff trade barriers. The second factor to review is the economic environment. There are two economic factors which reflect how attractive a particular market is in a selected country: industrial structure and income distribution. Industrial structure refers to how well developed a country's infrastructure is while income distribution refers to how income is distributed among its citizens. Political-legal environment is the third factor to investigate. For example, the individual and cultural attitudes regarding purchasing products from foreign countries, political stability, monetary regulations, and government bureaucracy all influence marketing practices and opportunities. The last factor to be considered before entering a global market is the cultural environment. Since cultural values regarding particular products will vary considerably from one country to another around the world, managers must take into account these differences in the planning process.

2. Marketing effectiveness

Improved marketing effectiveness can be achieved by employing a superior marketing strategy. By positioning the product or brand correctly, the product/brand will be more successful in the market than competitors'. On the other hand, by improving marketing execution, marketers can achieve significantly greater results without changing their strategy. At the marketing mix level, marketers can improve their execution by making small changes in any or all of the 4Ps without making changes to the strategic position. At the program level marketers can improve their effectiveness by managing and executing each of their marketing campaigns better. Whether it's improving direct mail through a better call-to-action or whether it is editing website content to improve its organic search results, marketers can improve their marketing effectiveness for each type of program. Understanding and taking advantage of how customers make purchasing decisions can help marketers improve their marketing effectiveness too. Groups of consumers act in similar ways leading to the need to segment them. Based on these segments, they make choices based on how they value the attributes of a product and the brand, in return for price paid for the product. Consumers build brand value through information, which is received through many sources, such as advertising or word-of-mouth. There are many factors outside of our immediate control that can impact the effectiveness of our marketing activities. These can include the weather, interest rates, government regulations and many others. Understanding the impact these factors can have on our consumers can help us to design programs that can take advantage of these factors or mitigate the risk of these factors if they take place in the middle of our marketing campaigns.

3. Logo design

Logo design is commonly believed to be one of the most difficult areas in graphic design. It's not just an image. It is the face of an organization, which is the visual representation of a brand. For brand continuity, and because of the expense involved in changing it, a "good" logo is expected not to be too trendy, but ideally to last many years before needing a redesign. A "good" logo:

❑ is distinctive, and is not subject to confusion with another logo among customers;

❑ is clearly and instantly recognizable, in different contexts;

❑ usually includes a brand name;

❑ evokes an emotional response;

❑ associates the brand with positive qualities, in line with the target audience's needs.

For certain brands, bold use of primary colors, especially red and yellow, is used to draw attention. This is especially important for logos that are used in signage along roads, where the objective is to attract customers to the immediate location. e.g. *McDonalds*, *Denny's*, etc. When designing a logo, practices to encourage include:

❑ using few colors;

❑ avoiding gradients as a distinguishing feature;

❑ producing alternatives for different contexts;

❑ not using the face of a (living) human being;

❑ avoiding culturally sensitive imagery, such as religious icons or national flags, unless the brand is committed to being associated with any and all connotations such imagery may evoke.

4. Footstar & THOM McAN®

Footstar Inc. is principally a specialty retailer conducting business in the discount and family footwear segment through its Meldisco business, and in the branded athletic footwear and apparel segment through its Footaction and Just For Feet businesses. The retailer's Meldisco division operates leased footwear departments in about 5,800 US stores and offers shoes under private labels as well as licensed brands Everlast, Route 66, and Thom McAn. Since 1922, the THOM McAN® brand has represented classic fashion, top-quality leather shoes and accessories for the whole family. The quality of THOM McAN® footwear is apparent in the earmarks of the brand — comfortable, flexible outsoles that make each step a comfortable step; padded insoles and a comfortable sock that cushions the foot; and fashionable yet breathable leather constructions that represent the latest styles and colors. The THOM McAN® brand of leather footwear for the family is available in Kmart stores nationwide, select Wal-Mart stores and all Shoe Zone stores.

5. NIKE

NIKE Inc. is engaged in the design, development and worldwide marketing of footwear, apparel, equipment and accessory products. The Company sells its products to retail accounts and through a mix of independent distributors, licensees and subsidiaries in over 120 countries around the world. NIKE's athletic footwear products are designed primarily for specific athletic use, although some of its products are worn for casual or leisure purposes. The Company creates designs for men, women and children. Running, basketball, children's, cross-training and women's shoes are the Company's top-selling product categories. NIKE also markets shoes designed for outdoor activities, tennis, golf, soccer, baseball, football, bicycling, volleyball, wrestling, cheerleading, aquatic activities, hiking and other athletic and recreational uses.

 **Listening** ▶▶|

Conversation

Tapescript

Michelle Ross is the creator of *ceogo.com*, a website devoted exclusively to CEO news and information. Roy Young spoke with her recently about what marketers can do to have influence at the very highest level of an organization.

Young: In general, how do you believe that CEOs think about the marketing function?

Ross: I believe that they think about marketing their products, services and overall corporate brand frequently. Unfortunately, many companies focused too heavily on Wall Street and forgot about communicating with their customers. CEOs today should better understand the importance of marketing themselves to a portfolio of audiences.

Young: Is it true that CEOs rarely come out of the marketing function?

Ross: There are very few of them. Finance and operations are the top two most common functions among Fortune 500 CEOs. Marketing and sales come out as a distant third and fourth. The next generation of CEOs will probably have more marketing experience because it will be part of everyone's job to listen to and communicate with various audiences.

Young: You talked in your book about the importance of the first 100 days for a CEO. How does marketing fit in during this critical period?

Ross: A CEO's first 100 days should be spent listening to employees and earning their trust and respect. In a sense, the CEO is marketing himself or herself because without employee support little can be accomplished.

Young: Then in what ways has the Internet changed the CEOs?

Ross: Technology has changed everything. CEOs can use technology to communicate with employees, customers and all stakeholders in real time. We have been examining how companies can use their CEOs to more effectively market themselves. Some company websites have a CEO letter welcoming prospective recruits. Other companies use their websites to catalog CEO speeches and presentations.

Young: So, the Web should be considered a reputation-management tool?

Ross: Yes, but the vast majority of companies does a poor job of managing. Absolutely websites should not be overlooked as marketing tools. Media and financial analysts frequently check company websites when rumors or crises are spreading. A lack of information is equivalent to a lack of comment for these influential visitors.

Young: One of the frustrations that marketers have is that ROI tends to be short term and not long term. Another way to think about it is that a new CEO is usually swept in by the time the long-term results come rolling in. Then companies start all over again. Is that the reality?

Ross: Reality is that too many people are in their jobs for the short term, and marketing is a long-term process. However, I do think senior marketers and chief marketing officers will have an easier time in the future because more CEOs will have marketing experience in their backgrounds and will understand how good marketing drives results.

Young: That's an optimistic point of view.

Ross: Hope I am right.

I. Listen to the conversation and choose the best answers to the questions you hear.

1. According to Michelle, what should today's CEOs attach more importance to?   (A)
2. How does marketing fit in the first 100 days for the CEOs in Michelle's eyes?   (B)
3. Which of the following is NOT true about the changes brought by the Internet to CEOs?   (C)
4. When will media and financial analysts frequently check a company's website?   (B)
5. Why is Michelle optimistic about the future of marketing?   (C)

II. Listen to the conversation again and decide whether the following statements are true or false. Write T for true and F for false in the brackets.

1. (F) 2. (T) 3. (T) 4. (F) 5. (F) 6. (T) 7. (F) 8. (T) 9. (T) 10. (F)

Passage

Tapescript

Blue is for boys. And pink is for girls. Among many Canadians and US citizens these color associations are so ingrained that they seem to be instinctive. On store shelves, boxes of disposable diapers designed for male infants are often colored blue. Those for baby girls, similarly, are in pink boxes.

In fact, there's nothing natural or instinctive about these associations. Much of the rest of the world, for example, associates yellow with females. And in many countries, red is the predominant masculine color.

The point is that marketers educated in the United States and Canada find to their deep chagrin that they have been blind to the traditions of other cultures. Nike Inc. knows that only too well. The company recently recalled 38,000 basketball shoes after its flame-design logo drew protests from Muslims. The logo was said to resemble the Arabic word for Allah.

Indeed, Nike is not the first shoe manufacturer to have such problems. A riot in Bangladesh a few years back is said to have been a result of the resemblance of the Thom McAn shoe logo to the word Allah. Neither Nike nor Thom McAn intended to put the word Allah on their products; they simply failed to recognize how their graphics resembled the word for God.

Actually, Nike and Thom McAn, with their emphasis on feet, ran afoul of another cultural tradition. In the Arabic world, the foot is considered unclean. And to show the sole of one's foot to another person is an insult. Imagine how Muslims felt when they saw shoes, something that comes in contact with an unclean body part apparently decorated with the name of Allah!

There are at least two other important points about marketing to the Muslim world that should be kept in mind: Islam proscribes the drinking of alcohol and the eating of pork; and dogs and the unclothed human body are culturally objectionable.

Finally, global marketers need to recognize that Muslim populations exist not only in the Middle East, but throughout much of Africa and Asia as well. Indeed, the most populous Islamic nation in the world is Indonesia in Southeast Asia. It has almost 200 million citizens, 87% of whom are Muslim. Islam also is one of the fastest-growing religions in North America, where there are now some 6 million Muslims.

Marketers may feel that the demands of various religions and cultural traditions are a burden. However, as Nike discovered, even when a community is a minority, its opposition can still affect a corporation's public image and purse strings.

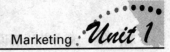

I. Listen to the passage and choose the best answers to the questions you hear.

1. What is the typical masculine color in America?　(B)
2. Why did Nike Inc. recall 38,000 basketball shoes recently?　(D)
3. What can be said about Thom McAn?　(B)
4. Where is the most populous Islamic nation located?　(C)
5. Which of the following statements is true according to the passage?　(A)

II. Listen to the passage again and answer the questions briefly according to what you hear.

1. What incurred protests from Muslims about Nike's products?
   Nike's flame-design logo which was said to resemble the Arabic word for Allah.
2. Why did Muslims feel insulted when they saw the Nike and Thom McAn shoe logos?
   In the Arabic world, the foot is considered unclean. Of course Muslims will feel insulted when they saw shoes, something that comes in contact with an unclean body part apparently decorated with the name of Allah.
3. What is the most populous Islamic nation in the world? And how many Muslim citizens does it have?
   Indonesia. It has about 174 million Muslim citizens.
4. What is thought to be offensive to Muslims?
   Showing the sole of one's foot to another person, drinking alcohol, eating pork, dogs and the unclothed human body.
5. What would be the consequence if marketers turn a blind eye to the traditions of other cultures?
   Their corporate public image would be affected and extra commercial cost would be generated.
6. What lesson can be learned from the Nike and Thom McAn cases?
   Marketers should take various religions and cultural traditions into their marketing considerations.

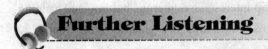

Short Recordings

Tapescript

Item 1

NEW YORK — J. M. Smucker Co. said Monday it was buying International Multifoods Corp. for about $500 million to add an array of highly popular baking mixes and other food brands to its product line-up. Smucker, whose product base includes such iconic brands as Jif peanut butter and Smucker's ice cream toppings, said it would pay $25 per share in a mix of stock and cash for

International Multifoods, based in Minneapolis. Smucker anticipates the acquisition will boost its prominence in the baking aisle, and it expects it to add to its fiscal 2005 earnings.

Smucker J. M. Company operates principally in the manufacturing and marketing of branded food products on a worldwide basis, although the majority of the Company's sales are in the United States. Smucker's distribution outside the United States is principally in Canada, Australia and Brazil, although products are exported to other countries as well.

International Multifoods Corp. produces consumer and commercial baking mixes (including Pillsbury cake mixes), frozen batters, and doughs for in-store and food service baking operations. In Canada its Robin Hood Multifoods unit produces the Number 1 brand of consumer flours and baking mixes (Robin Hood) and a leading brand of pickles and condiments (Bick's). It also sells hot cereals (Old Mill, Purity, Red River).

Item 2

ATLANTA — Coca-Cola Co. Wednesday named Don Knauss to lead its business in North America, a critically important but struggling market, which accounts for about 30 percent of the soft drink firm's revenues. Despite a reputation as one of the soft drink maker's best operators, Knauss faces a stiff challenge. In the past year, the Atlanta-based company has cut more than 1,000 jobs in North America, where it has been pinched by an economic slowdown and tough competition from chief rival PepsiCo. Inc.

Coca-Cola Co. manufactures, distributes and markets nonalcoholic beverage concentrates and syrups, including fountain syrups, in markets across the world. It manufactures and sells non-alcoholic beverages, primarily carbonated soft drinks, and a variety of non-carbonated beverages. Coca-Cola also manufactures and distributes juices and juice drinks and certain water products such as Dasani. In addition, it has ownership interests in numerous bottling and canning operations. Finished beverage products bearing its trademarks are sold in more than 200 countries worldwide.

Item 3

NEW YORK — Battered toy retailer Toys R Us Inc. is expected to announce a restructuring next week that could include selling some of its weaker toy stores and focusing more on its burgeoning baby business, industry experts say. The New Jersey-based retailer last month posted a 4.9 percent drop in same-store sales at US toy stores during the key holiday period, and said the toy selling environment was "extremely difficult." Meanwhile, sales at its Babies R Us stores rose 3.6 percent during the period.

TOY is a retailer of children's products. As of 2003, TOY operated 1,595 retail stores, consisting of Kids R Us children's stores, Babies R Us infant stores and educational specialty stores.

Same-store comparisons measure the growth in sales, excluding the impact of newly opened stores. Generally, sales from new stores are not reflected in same-store comparisons until those stores have been open for fifty-three weeks. With these comparisons, analysts can measure sales performance against other retailers that may not be as aggressive in opening new locations during the evaluated period.

Item 4

DETROIT — General Motors Corp. has added new sales incentives to spur demand after its US sales fell more than 15 percent in June, dealers said Tuesday. GM, the world's largest automaker, has cut lease payments on some vehicles by as much as $1,500 to boost sales. GM also extended an offer to buy out the remaining months on lease contracts for consumers whose lease expires before March next year if they buy a new GM vehicle. Dealers also expected the automaker to announce new cash rebates and interest-free loans soon.

General Motors Corp., founded in 1908, has been the global automotive sales leader since 1931. GM today has manufacturing operations in 32 countries and its vehicles are sold in 192 countries. GM's global headquarters are at the GM Renaissance Center in Detroit. GM's automotive brands are Buick, Cadillac, Chevrolet, GMC, Holden, HUMMER, Oldsmobile, Opel, Pontiac, Saab, Saturn and Vauxhall.

Item 5

SAN FRANCISCO — Google Inc., the No. 1 Web search provider, announced several enhancements to its services Tuesday, as new research showed Internet users are turning to more than one Web search provider when seeking information. Software firm Microsoft Corp. is spending millions of dollars to build its own Web search product and media services company Yahoo is integrating search technology from its recently acquired companies. The average searcher in the United States searched 28.4 times in December and no single search engine captured all of that activity.

Microsoft Corporation develops, manufactures, licenses & supports a range of software products, including scalable operating systems, server applications, worker productivity applications and software development tools.

Yahoo Inc. is a global Internet communications, commerce and media company that offers a branded network of services to millions of users daily.

I. In this section, you will hear five short recordings. For each piece, decide what action each company took or will take to boost its business.

1. J. M. Smucker	C	A. Cost reduction	
2. Coca-Cola	B	B. Senior management change	
3. Toys R Us	H	C. Company acquisition	
4. General Motors	F	D. Brand expansion	
5. Google	E	E. Service improvement	
		F. Sales promotions	
		G. Image enhancement	
		H. Company restructuring	

II. Listen to the five recordings again and decide whether the following statements are true or false. Write T for true and F for false in the brackets.

1. (F) 2. (F) 3. (F) 4. (T) 5. (F) 6. (T) 7. (T) 8. (F) 9. (T) 10. (F)

Home Listening

Business News

. . . .

Tapescript

India is asking Asian countries to resist a potential backlash in developed nations as Western companies move technology jobs to India and other low-cost destinations.

India's Communication and Information Technology Minister Arun Shourie wants Asian countries to work out a common strategy to counter growing public concern in Britain and the United States about job losses overseas.

In recent years, multinational companies have been moving work such as customer support, software research, design and development to cheaper destinations. More than half of all Fortune 500 companies say they are expanding their development centers outside Western countries.

Much of this work is flowing into countries such as India, China and the Philippines, where skilled technology workers are available for cheaper wages.

In Britain, the flight of jobs has sparked heated debate and protests by labor unions. Several states in United States are considering legislation to protect local jobs.

India is worried by what it sees as an emerging protectionist trend.

Mr. Shourie says Western countries should not expect developing countries to open their markets if they erect barriers against outsourcing.

Officials from countries such as Israel and China also say there should be no attempts to restrict the international flow of jobs in a world trying to liberalize trade rules.

The head of India's National Association of Software and Service Companies, Kiran Karnik, says India is anxious to protect the advantages offered by its skilled and cheap workforce.

"Whereas some countries have natural comparative advantages in goods, some countries like India have advantages in services, and in the process of negotiations in places like WTO we should make sure these interests are balanced," he said.

Mr. Karnik also says more jobs will be created in Western countries as outsourcing helps companies save money.

"And if anything, the process of outsourcing is one that increases efficiency, and brings in more profits so that they can be reinvested in creating other jobs and growth opportunities," he added.

Western companies have hired nearly 200,000 Indian workers in recent years to handle much of their customer support and software operations. The figure is expected to increase to one million by 2008.

Listen to the business news report and decide whether the following statements are true or false. Write T for true and F for false in the brackets.

1. (T) 2. (F) 3. (F) 4. (F) 5. (T) 6. (T) 7. (F) 8. (F)

Unit 2

Advertising

Dictation

● ●

Listen to the following short paragraph and fill in the blanks with what you hear.

Advertising is the (1) <u>paid, non-personal promotion</u> of a cause, idea, product, or service by an identified sponsor attempting to (2) <u>inform or persuade a particular target audience</u>. Advertising has evolved to take a variety of forms and has permeated nearly (3) <u>every aspect of modern society</u>. Every major medium is used to deliver the message: (4) <u>television, radio, movies, magazines, newspapers, the Internet, and billboards</u>. Advertisements can also be seen (5) <u>on the seats of grocery carts</u>, on the walls of an airport walkway, and the sides of buses, or heard (6) <u>in telephone on-hold messages</u> — nearly anywhere (7) <u>a visual or audible communication</u> can be placed. Advertising clients are predominantly, but not exclusively, for-profit corporations seeking to (8) <u>increase demand for their products or services</u>.

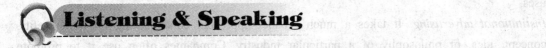

Listening & Speaking

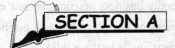

SECTION A   **Advertising Media**

Pre-listening ▶▶

Background Information

1. Forms of advertising

Advertising can take a number of forms, including comparative, cooperative, direct-mail, informational, institutional, outdoor, persuasive, product, reminder, point-of-purchase, and specialty advertising. Most companies are successful in achieving their goals for increasing public recognition and sales through these efforts.

Comparative advertising. Comparative advertising compares one brand directly or indirectly with one or more competing brands. This advertising technique is very common and is used by nearly every major industry. One of its drawbacks is that customers have become more skeptical about claims made by a company about its competitors because accurate information has not always been provided, thus making the effectiveness of comparison advertising questionable. In addition, companies that engage in comparative advertising must be careful not to misinform the public about a competitor's product. Incorrect or misleading information may trigger a lawsuit by the aggrieved company.

Cooperative advertising. Cooperative advertising is a system that allows two parties to share advertising costs. Manufacturers and distributors, because of their shared interest in selling the product, usually use this technique. Cooperative advertising is especially appealing to small storeowners who, on their own, could not afford to advertise the product adequately.

Direct-Mail advertising. Catalogues, flyers, letters, and postcards are just a few of the direct-mail advertising options. Direct-mail advertising has several advantages, including detail of information, personalization, selectivity, and speed. But while direct mail has advantages, it carries an expensive per-head price, is dependent on the appropriateness of the mailing list, and is resented by some customers, who consider it "junk mail."

Informational advertising. In informational advertising, which is used when a new product is first being introduced, the emphasis is on promoting the product name, benefits, and possible uses.

Institutional advertising. It takes a much broader approach, concentrating on the benefits, concept, idea, or philosophy of a particular industry. Companies often use it to promote image-building activities, such as environment-friendly business practices or new community-based programs that they sponsor. Institutional advertising is closely related to public relations, since both are interested in promoting a positive company image to the public.

Outdoor advertising. Billboards and messages painted on the side of buildings are common forms of outdoor advertising, which is often used when quick, simple ideas are being promoted. Since repetition is the key to successful promotion, outdoor advertising is most effective when located along heavily traveled city streets and when the product being promoted can be purchased locally.

Persuasive advertising. It is used after a product has been introduced to customers. The primary goal is for a company to build selective demand for its product. For example, automobile manufacturers often produce special advertisements promoting the safety features of their vehicles. This type of advertisement could allow automobile manufacturers to charge more for their products because of the perceived higher quality the safety features afford.

Product advertising. It pertains to non-personal selling of a specific product. An example is a regular television commercial promoting a soft drink. The primary purpose of the advertisement is to promote the specific soft drink, not the entire soft-drink line of a company.

Reminder advertising. It is used for products that have entered the mature stage of the product life cycle. The advertisements are simply designed to remind customers about the product and to maintain awareness. For example, detergent producers spend a considerable amount of money each year promoting their products to remind customers that their products are still available and for sale.

Point-of-Purchase advertising. It uses displays or other promotional items near the product that is being sold. The primary motivation is to attract customers to the display so that they will purchase the product. Stores are more likely to use point-of-purchase displays if they have help from the manufacturer in setting them up or if the manufacturer provides easy instructions on how to use the displays.

Specialty advertising. It is a form of sales promotion designed to increase public recognition of a company's name. A company can have its name put on a variety of items, such as caps, glassware, gym bags, jackets, key chains, and pens. The value of specialty advertising varies depending on how long the items used in the effort last.

2. Advertising media selection

Once a company decides what type of specific advertising campaign it wants to use, it must decide what media to carry the message. A company is interested in a number of areas regarding advertising, such as frequency, media impact, media timing, and reach.

Frequency. Frequency refers to the average number of times that an average consumer is exposed to the advertising campaign. In a crowded and competitive market repetition is one of the best methods to increase the product's visibility and to increase company sales. The more exposure a company desires for its product, the more expensive the advertising campaign.

Media impact. Media impact generally refers to how effective advertising will be through the various media outlets (e.g., television, Internet, print). A company must decide, based on its product, the best method to maximize consumer interest and awareness. Before any money is spent on any advertising media, a thorough analysis is done of each one's strengths and weaknesses in comparison to the cost. Once the analysis is done, the company will make the best decision possible and embark on its advertising campaign.

Media timing. Another major consideration for any company engaging in an advertising campaign is when to run the advertisements. For example, some companies run ads during the holidays to promote season-specific products. The other major consideration for a company is whether it wants to employ a *continuous* or *pulsing* pattern of advertisements. Continuous refers to advertisements that are run on a scheduled basis for a given time period. The advantage of this tactic is that an advertising campaign can run longer and might provide more exposure over time. Pulsing indicates that advertisements will be scheduled in a disproportionate manner within a given time frame. The advantage with the pulsing strategy is twofold. The company could spend less money on advertising over a shorter time period but still gain the same recognition because the advertising campaign is more intense.

Reach. Reach refers to the percentage of customers in the target market who are exposed to the advertising campaign for a given time period. A company might have a goal of reaching at least 80 percent of its target audience during a given time frame. The goal is to be as close to 100 percent as possible, because the more the target audience is exposed to the message, the higher the chance of future sales.

3. Internet advertising formats

In conventional media, ads' format is generally fixed in the basic pattern such as 30 or 60 seconds spots of TV commercials and 30-sheet poster of outdoor. The Internet relatively supports more various formats for ads. Looking into Internet ads format will help us understand and assess how the Internet differs from traditional media as an advertising medium.

Banners. Banner ads are those rectangular-shaped graphics, usually located at the top or bottom of a web page. Targeting gives advertisers the opportunity to filter messages to selected audiences based on certain criteria. It supports the most powerful feature of the Internet as an advertising medium: the ability to indicate the exact composition of an advertisement's audience.

Interstitials and pop-ups. Interstitials are full-screen ads that run in their entirety between two content pages, while pop-ups appear in a separate window on top of content that is already on the user's screen. Pop-up ads that interrupt the user's flow of work may be perceived as less favorable than interstitial ads that run in between the user's activity.

Sponsorships. In traditional media vehicles including outdoor, most sponsorships tend to be simple and are limited to brand name identification or the brand name and a brief slogan. On the other hand, online sponsorships also can appear as part of the content of a web page, or as part of a list of sponsors. In addition, online sponsorships can be interactive, so that a click of the mouse sends a visitor to the homepage of the sponsor.

Hyperlinks. A hyperlink is to allow users to link to another web site by simply clicking on the hyperlink. There are some similarities to online sponsorships in that they have less space than other ad formats, and are generally embedded in the content itself. A difference is that the number of hyperlinks on web page is not limited.

4. Internet advertising features

Followings are the summarized features of Internet advertising.

Easy to access. Internet advertisements are accessed on demand 24 hours a day, 365 days a year.

Low Cost. Costs are the same regardless of audience location. Distribution costs are low (just technology costs), so it costs the same to reach millions of consumers as to one.

Direct response. Advertisers can reach variously segmented consumers who are able to purchase their products or services on the spot.

Interactivity. The Internet allows customers to communicate directly with you. Advertisers can get to gain customers' information on their consuming behavior and preference. Most pages even offer online ordering on the spot. That cuts down on the number of steps that need to occur between the time the customer makes the decision to buy and the actual purchase.

Tracking. By using Internet technology, advertisers can measure exactly message audiences. Response (click-through rate) and results (page views) of advertising are immediately measurable.

Diverse style. Internet relatively supports more format for ads, some of which we do not find in traditional media. Also, using multimedia makes ads more creative, attractive and compelling.

Immediacy. Online advertising message can reach consumers just prior to purchasing. It is able for consumers to know in great detail on how and why they buy.

Flexibility. The Internet allows advertisers to change their messages frequently. Advertising and content can be easily and frequently updated, supplemented, or changed. It allows advertisers to easily offer audiences updated information.

Accuracy. Consumers primarily access ads because of interest in the content, so advertisers can gain more accurate data on their consumers, and market segmentation opportunity is large.

5. Brand loyalty

Brand loyalty has been proclaimed by some to be the ultimate goal of marketing. It refers to the degree to which a consumer repeatedly purchases a brand. For advertisers to achieve their ultimate goal of brand loyalty, the consumer must perceive that the brand offers the right

combination of quality and price. Many factors influence brand loyalty, such as consumer attitudes, family or peer pressure, and friendship with the salesperson. The advertiser must consider all such factors. Brand loyalty is stronger on established products than on new products.

 **Listening** ▶▶|

Conversation

Tapescript

Interviewer:	Today with us is Mr. Rayman, the president of a major advertising agency in New York. Mr. Rayman, let's start with a fairly simple question: What is advertising?
Mr. Rayman:	Well, advertising differs from other forms of sales promotion. It can be defined as non-personal commercial messages designed to inform both established and potential customers. Traditionally, all advertising was classified either as direct-action advertising or as institutional advertising.
Interviewer:	Direct-action advertising and institutional advertising, what do they really mean?
Mr. Rayman:	Direct-action advertising is designed to sell a firm's products or services, while institutional advertising is designed to promote a firm's name. Thus, the statement "Raincoats are on sale today at $9.95" is an example of direct-action advertising, and the claim "Our employees subscribe to the United Fund 100 percent" is an example of institutional advertising.
Interviewer:	I see.
Mr. Rayman:	Modern business practices have further divided these two types of advertising into distinct approaches. For instance, primary-demand advertising seeks to increase the total demand for certain products without distinguishing specific brands. Brand advertising promotes the use of a particular brand among competing products. Comparative advertising points to the advantages of the advertiser's product over competing products. Institutional advertising also can take a wide variety of forms. For example, when a large corporation sponsors a symphony concert or underwrites a program for educational television, it basically is using institutional advertising.
Interviewer:	The word advertising reminds me of a lot of things such as television, radio, newspapers, magazines, etc. Are there any other advertising media available?
Mr. Rayman:	In planning an advertising program, we can choose from a large assortment of

media. There are many others such as outdoor billboards, specialty advertising, public transportation vehicles, yellow pages of telephone directory, direct mail, internet, catalogs, samples, leaflets, and so on.

Interviewer: Specialty advertising?

Mr. Rayman: Yeah, specialty advertising. It refers to calendars, matchbooks, telephone pads, etc.

Interviewer: Oh，I see now. But here comes another question: How do people choose different advertising media?

Mr. Rayman: It obviously doesn't pay for a local, one-unit department store to advertise on national television. Likewise, it usually is not practical for a neighborhood variety store to advertise in a large metropolitan newspaper. In deciding which media to use, advertisers must consider two questions: Does the advertising medium cover the market? What is the cost per reader or listener in the market? In considering these basic questions, we can see why Ford, General Motors, and Chrysler can afford the huge costs of national television advertising. We can also see that local department stores cannot benefit proportionately from national television advertising to justify the expense.

Interviewer: Is it true that there are no such things as the best or the most effective when choosing advertising media?

Mr. Rayman: Absolutely. Different media have different advantages. For instance, the yellow pages of the telephone directory is an effective way to promote goods or services for which customers prefer to check sources by telephone first. Direct-mail advertising has been so overdone that its effectiveness has been impaired. Such promotion must be well prepared or it will be tossed into the nearest wastebasket. Still, direct mail offers the advantages of being selective in coverage, relatively inexpensive, and more flexible.

I. Listen to the conversation and choose the best answers to the questions you hear.

1. Which type of advertising is designed to increase sales for certain products without giving information about particular brands?   (C)
2. Which of the following does NOT fall into the category of direct-action advertising?   (B)
3. Which type of advertising is employed if a large sportswear corporation sponsors a tennis tournament?   (B)
4. Which of the following is NOT mentioned in the conversation as one of the advantages of direct-mail?   (D)
5. Why do local merchants and small firms seldom use national television advertising to promote sales?   (D)

II. Listen to the conversation again and complete the following notes with what you hear.

About Advertising

Types of advertising:
❑ Direction-action advertising
    ✓ (1) <u>primary-demand advertising</u>
    ✓ (2) <u>brand advertising</u>
    ✓ (3) <u>comparative advertising</u>
❑ (4) <u>Institutional advertising</u>

Variety of advertising media:
❑ Television, Radio, Newspaper, Magazines
❑ (5) <u>Outdoor billboards</u>
❑ Specialty advertising
    e.g.   (6) <u>calendars, matchbooks, telephone pads</u>
❑ (7) <u>Public transportation vehicles</u>
❑ (8) <u>Yellow pages of telephone directory</u>
❑ Direct mail
❑ (9) <u>Internet</u>
❑ And others
    e.g. (10) <u>catalogs, samples, leaflets</u>

Selection of advertising media:
Questions to consider in selecting appropriate advertising media
❑ (11) <u>Does the advertising medium cover the market?</u>
❑ (12) <u>What is the cost per reader or listener in the market?</u>

Passage

Tapescript

    Of other methods of promotion directed at consumers, people are most likely to be aware of advertising because it is so visible and widespread. Over the last several years, advertisers have had to respond to criticism and consumers' doubts about the usefulness of advertising and about its truthfulness and costs. According to one study, although more than 60 percent of the consumers interviewed said advertising is becoming more informative, 58 percent believed advertising makes false claims and is misleading; 61 percent felt advertising should be more closely regulated by the government.

Some companies often spend considerable sum of money on advertising. Many critics suggest that if advertising expenditures were reduced, companies could afford to sell their products to the public at lower prices. Other critics emphasize another way in which advertising increases costs. Expensive nationwide advertising campaigns, when successful, can develop brand loyalty for a few brands. This loyalty can be so strong as to make it extremely difficult for newcomers, especially smaller companies, to enter the field. As a result, a few large companies can dominate the market, charging higher prices than they could in a more competitive situation. Many experts contend that these criticisms are unjustified and that advertising stimulates demand so that higher levels of production are possible. As a result, the unit cost is reduced.

Does advertising inform? Almost everyone agrees that advertising performs useful informational functions. By advertising, a seller can inform a potential buyer of his existence, line of goods, and prices. Such advertising can reduce the time and effort spent by consumers in seeking out goods and services. It lets them know in advance what is available and where it can be bought. The advertising message itself must be clear, informing the customer why the product is unique, better than the competitor's in terms of cost, availability, reliability, and/or quality. The message must also signal a call for action by the potential customer — to buy at a discounted price before a set date or respond before inventory is exhausted, for example. Advertising also performs a less obvious informational function: the dollars spent by advertisers subsidize the media we rely on for information and entertainment. An estimated 55 to 60 percent of the cost of periodicals, 70 percent of the cost of newspapers and 100 percent of the cost of commercial radio and TV broadcasting are paid for by advertising.

Although advertising does inform, it is not a panacea for promotion. It cannot sell a poor product or service, a product for which there is little or no demand, or one that is over-priced.

I. Listen to the passage and choose the best answers to the questions you hear.

1. Which of the following statements is NOT true according to the study on advertising?   (C)
2. When is advertising likely to push prices upward?   (B)
3. Financially speaking, which of the following media benefits most from advertising?   (D)
4. According to the passage, which of the following products cannot be promoted by advertising?   (B)
5. What can be concluded from the passage?   (A)

II. Listen to the passage again and complete the notes with what you hear.

Public attitude towards advertising:

Among the consumers interviewed,

- ❑ more than 60 percent said advertising (1) <u>is becoming more informative</u>.
- ❑ 58 percent believed advertising (2) <u>makes false claims and is misleading</u>.
- ❑ 61 percent felt advertising (3) <u>should be more closely regulated by the government</u>.

Pros and cons of advertising:

Negative: Advertising increases costs

- ❑ (4) <u>Advertising expenditures</u> push companies to sell products at higher prices.
- ❑ (5) <u>Brand loyalty</u> developed from expensive nationwide advertising campaigns makes it difficult for (6) <u>newcomers to enter the field;</u> the consequent market domination enables a few large companies to (7) <u>charge higher prices</u> than they could in a more competitive situation.

Positive: Advertising reduces the unit cost

- ❑ Advertising stimulates demand and thus enables (8) <u>higher levels of production</u>.

Informational functions of advertising:

- ❑ informing a potential buyer of (9) <u>a seller's existence, line of goods, and prices</u>
- ❑ informing consumers in advance of (10) <u>what is available and where it can be bought</u>
- ❑ informing the customer (11) <u>why the product is unique</u> or better than the competitor's
- ❑ subsidizing the media we rely on for (12) <u>information and entertainment</u>

SECTION B **Advertising Techniques**

Pre-listening ▶▶

Background Information

1. What makes a good advertisement

In general, a good advertisement:

- must stop the reader from turning the page. An ad has 5-to-10 seconds to jump off the page and grab the reader's attention.
- works like a good salesperson, telling potential customers what a product will do for them.
- is built on a concept or idea. The reader must instantly recognize the concept being communicated.
- sells a product's benefits rather than its features. People decide what to buy based on what the product will do for them, not for what ingredients it has.
- has a sense of urgency. It tells the reader to do something.
- promotes the name of the store while it visually creates an image for the store.
- speaks to a specific group of people it is trying to reach.
- provides all the facts a reader needs without providing too many.
- is well organized in its layout. The orderly division of space makes it easier for the eye to read.
- conveys its message simply. It is believable and honest.
- is distinctive. Ads must be different, instantly recognizable and sell the store in addition to the merchandise.
- attracts a reader's eye. Using the basic principles of design as they relate to layout: proportion, balance, contrast, movement and unity.
- remembers who the customer is and what would make that customer buy.
- is news. Readers believe advertising in newspapers is as important as the rest of its content. The interactivity of a newspaper causes readers to seek out good advertising.
- limits its use of typefaces. A good rule of thumb is to use no more than three typefaces in an ad. This reduces the feeling of an ad being too busy or cluttered.
- sells answers to consumer's current needs. Advertising sells to people's wants not just to their needs. People need a car but want a Mercedes. They need clothing, but they want Polo.

2. The Federal Trade Commission (FTC)

The FTC is an independent federal agency created in 1915, whose main goals are to protect consumers and to ensure a strong competitive market by enforcing a variety of consumer protection and antitrust laws. These laws guard against harmful business practices and protect the market from anti-competitive practices such as large mergers and price-fixing conspiracies. The FTC deals with complaints that are filed regarding unfair business practices such as scams, deceptive advertising and monopolistic practices. It reviews these complaints to determine if businesses are in fact engaging in harmful practices. The FTC is also responsible for reviewing mergers in the market to ensure that they do not hurt competition in the market and potentially harm consumers. Generally speaking, the FTC does not have the ability to directly enforce its rulings, but it can go to the courts to have them enforced.

3. Advertising puffery

Puffery refers to promotional statements and claims that express subjective rather than objective views. For instance, a diner advertisement promoting the "world's best cup of coffee" would classify as puffery. That claim would be almost impossible to substantiate, and no reasonable consumer would take such exaggeration at face value. Puffery often uses the superlative form of a word, like "best" or "greatest". Puffery might also exaggerate the advertised effects of a product. However, a company making a superlative claim such as "cheapest" or "safest" usually has to substantiate such competitive claims. Merchants must exercise extreme caution when making statements about the quality, condition, or facts about their products or services.

 **Listening** ▶▶|

Conversation

Tapescript

Interviewer: Ben was just 19 when he started his first business, a Web marketing and advertising firm geared towards teenagers that eventually grew into two offices and 10 employees. Now 26, Ben is launching his third venture, again with teenagers as his target audience. Ben, is there any main advertising mistake you see young entrepreneurs making over and over?

Ben: The main thing I see is, just not knowing who their customers are, not knowing whom they're directing to, and not knowing what they want. You can buy ads online, just a general ad that will appear on any site that's not that expensive. But if you do that, you don't know who your customers are and you're just doing blind ads. If you don't know who your customers are, then there's absolutely no way to reach them.

Interviewer: How can young entrepreneurs figure out whom their marketing should target?

Ben: They should first develop a marketing and advertising plan. They should really research who their customers are and see what they're doing. If they're targeting teenagers, they have an advantage because they know how they get their information: They know teenagers don't really click on online ads, that they look more at magazines, and that they like getting fliers handed out to them.

Interviewer: Do you think it's easier for young entrepreneurs to go after customers of their own age?

Ben: That was one of my advantages when I ran my Internet company because I targeted teenagers. It was easy, because all I ever thought about was, "This is how I get my information." I knew what wasn't going to work for my customers because it wouldn't work for me.

Interviewer: Sometimes, though, experts warn against basing your strategies too much on yourself. Do you think that may be a problem, if entrepreneurs take for granted that, "I do everything this way, so all 19-year-olds must be like me"?

Ben: You can't just rely on one source. If you market to teenagers and you're marketing based on yourself, your research is based on just one person and that won't work because the teenage demographic is very big and very different and very diverse. You have to base your research on a larger target group.

Interviewer: How do you determine how much money and time you should put into your marketing and advertising?

Ben: It really depends on what kind of business you have. For some businesses, advertising is not that important. But if you're a consumer company that's just released a new product, you're probably going to have to dedicate 40 or 50 percent of your budget to marketing and advertising.

Interviewer: Do you think Internet advertising is the most effective way for young entrepreneurs to market their businesses?

Ben: For young entrepreneurs, absolutely, because the reason why Internet marketing works so well is that you don't have to spend much money and you pay only for results. When people use a search engine, they're specifically looking for your product. From there, you only pay when somebody actually comes to your site and does business with you. It really minimizes your risk because if you buy an ad in a magazine or on TV, there are no guarantees. But if you buy an ad on a search engine, you're getting a guarantee that someone's going to visit your site. Then it's up to you to make the sale or not. If you find you have a lot of people coming to your site and you can't make a sale, there's something wrong on your end and you'll have to do research to find out why people aren't buying.

I. Listen to the conversation and choose the best answers to the questions you hear.

1. How many businesses has Ben operated so far? (C)
2. What may young entrepreneurs benefit from when they are targeting customers of their own age? (B)
3. According to Ben, what determines the money and time you should put into your marketing and advertising? (A)
4. Which of the following advertising media guarantees your messages reaching the target audience? (C)
5. What can be concluded from the interview? (D)

II. Listen to the conversation again and answer the following questions with what you hear.

1. How old was Ben when he started his first business? And what kind of business is it?
   Ben was just 19 when he started his first business. It is a Web marketing and advertising firm geared towards teenagers.

2. What does Ben see as the main advertising mistake young entrepreneurs are repeatedly making?
   They do not know who their customers are, who they're directing to, and what their customers want.

3. According to Ben, how do teenagers usually get their information?
   Teenagers often get messages from magazines or fliers rather than online ads.

4. According to Ben, how can young entrepreneurs avoid doing blind ads?
   They should develop marketing and advertising plan, and research their target market.

5. When young entrepreneurs market to their peers, why are they warned against basing their strategies too much on themselves?
   People are different and diverse so they are advised to base their research on a larger target group instead of merely on one source.

6. When should a consumer company commit a large proportion of its budget to marketing and advertising?
   When it has just released a new product.

7. Why is Internet advertising said to be the most effective way for young entrepreneurs to market their businesses?
   It's a relatively cost-effective way to reach the specifically targeted audience.

8. What does Ben suggest if a lot of people are visiting your site but not buying?
   You have to do research and find out why people aren't buying.

Passage

Tapescript

Advertising can legally include opinions and exaggerations which may be misleading. These "legal lies" are called puffs, because they puff up a product's qualities and make it seem better than it really is. So we should learn how to spot advertising puff.

Advertising is controlled by law. The Federal Trade Commission (FTC) regulates the content of advertisements and decides on what the manufacturer can and cannot say about its products. You as a consumer can protect yourself from misleading ads by learning how to recognize them.

Misleading advertising often presents the seller's opinion as if it were fact. "Zado's Cola is the finest soft drink." "Ace Cars give you the most comfortable ride in town." When you see advertisements like this, ask yourself, "Who says so?" This is the type of advertising puff that reflects an opinion. The words "finest" and "most" show that a judgment is being made. That is a personal opinion, not a statement of fact. Of course the Zado Company thinks their cola is the finest. They want you to think so too, so you'll buy it.

Some advertising puffs try to connect an unrelated quality to a product. For example, beauty and popularity are often linked with perfume, cars, mouthwash, or toothpaste. This kind of advertising is called "image making". Will you really meet nicer people if you drive a Panther automobile? Will people think you are sexier if you brush your teeth with Sparkle Toothpaste? Of course not. When you see these advertisements, remember that very few products will automatically make you a better or happier person.

Some advertising puffs describe the product accurately but are still misleading. For instance, a leading burger does weigh a quarter of a pound. The statement is true: the hamburger does weigh a quarter of a pound — before cooking. Since it is purchased after being cooked, this claim may be classified as a puff. Check the frozen food aisle in your supermarket. A frozen pie is labeled as a "nine-inch pie". This statement is true if you measure the pie from the outside of the rim on one side to the outside of the rim on the other side. The actual body of the pie is only. 7.5 inches. If you buy a standard nine-inch pie plate for making your own pies, you'll see that the nine-inch measurement is for the inside of the pie.

You should always question the claims made by any advertisement. Ask yourself: Will the product really do all of these things? Is it really the best? Who says so?

I. Listen to the passage and answer the following questions with what you hear.

1. What is the passage mainly about?
   Learning how to spot advertising puffs.

2. What is the characteristic of advertising puffs?
   They puff up a product's qualities. / They make the product seem better than it really is.

3. Can the manufacturer say anything about its products? Why or why not?
   No, they can't. Because the FTC regulates the content of advertisements.

4. What are "image-making" advertisements?
   They are the ads which try to link an unrelated quality to a product.

5. What is the actual body size of a frozen pie labeled as "nine-inch pie" in the supermarket?
   The actual body size of the pie is only 7.5 inches.

6. How should we measure a pie if we want to know its actual body size?
   From the inside of the rim on one side to the inside of the rim on the other side.

II. Listen to the passage again and complete the notes with what you hear.

Advertising Puffs

Ways of protection from misleading ads:

☐ FTC regulates the content of advertisements and decides on:

(1) <u>what the manufacturer can and cannot say about its products.</u>

☐ Individual consumer can protect himself from misleading ads by:

(2) <u>learning how to recognize them.</u>

Types of advertising puffs:

☐ (3) <u>Advertisements that contain the seller's opinion only.</u>

☐ (4) <u>Image making advertisements.</u>

☐ (5) <u>Advertisements that seem to be facts but not exactly so.</u>

Ways to spot advertising puffs by questioning:

☐ (6) <u>Will the product really do all of these things?</u>

☐ (7) <u>Is it really the best?</u>

☐ (8) <u>Who says so?</u>

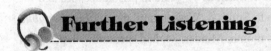

Further Listening

Short Recordings

Tapescript

Item 1

NEW YORK — Burger King Corp., the world's second-largest hamburger chain, said Friday Chief Executive Brad Blum has left the company due to strategic differences with the board of directors. In a statement, privately-held Burger King said its senior management team would oversee the business until a new CEO is found. Blum became CEO of Burger King, which ranks behind No. 1 hamburger chain McDonald's Corp., in January of 2003. Burger King has struggled financially in recent years, with at least 20 percent of its roughly 7,900 restaurants losing money, and at least three of its 10 largest franchisees filing for bankruptcy protection in recent years.

Burger King Corp.   In 1954, James McLamore and David Edgerton opened the first Burger King restaurant in Miami; selling 18 cent broiled hamburgers and milk shakes. Today Burger King restaurants serve chicken nuggets, salads, a breakfast menu and kids meals. In 1998, the company opened its 10,000th location in Sydney, Australia.

Item 2

ATLANTA — Coca-Cola Co. CEO Doug Daft, who has been dogged by government probes, disappointing sales and an anemic stock price, will retire at the end of 2004, the world's largest soft drink maker said Thursday. Atlanta-based Coca-Cola said President and Chief Operating Officer Steve Heyer, who in December took control of operations in the huge North American market, would be a strong internal candidate to take over as chairman and chief executive. Sluggish sales of Coke's soft drinks and other products, particularly in the No. 1 market of North America, taxed Daft's tenure as CEO and kept a lid on the stock price he had been hired to revive.

Coca-Cola Co. is a manufacturer, distributor and marketer of soft drink concentrates and syrups. It also markets and distributes juice and juice-drink products.

Item 3

NEW YORK — James Joseph Minder, chairman of handgun maker Smith & Wesson Holding Corp., resigned after a published report revealed he had spent as much as 15 years in prison decades ago for armed robberies. Minder's convictions were unknown to Smith & Wesson until the *Arizona Republic* newspaper reported Minder's criminal past earlier this month. Minder, 74, had spent time in prison in the 1950s and 1960s for a string of armed robberies and an attempted prison escape, according to the *Republic*. Minder also told the paper that he turned his life around after finishing his prison sentence in 1969. He said he has spent his professional career trying to help kids.

Smith & Wesson Corp. is a producer of handguns, law enforcement products and firearm safety and security products

Item 4

WILMINGTON — Newspaper tycoon Conrad Black testified in his legal battle with board members of Hollinger International Inc. on Friday that they pushed him into resigning and agreeing to repay disputed compensation. Black, who is accused of lining his pockets with millions of dollars in unapproved payments, has denied the company's contention that he collected improper payments during his tenure as chairman and chief executive of the company.

Hollinger International Inc. has filed a separate lawsuit in Chicago federal court accusing him and several associates of collecting more than $200 million in improper payments, altering company records and misleading board members about the compensation.

HLR, through its subsidiaries, is a publisher of English-language newspapers in the US, UK, Canada and Israel.

Item 5

NEW YORK — Credit Suisse Group said Thursday its co-CEO John Mack will leave the investment bank amid a management shake-up and corporate restructuring. John Mack is a Wall Street veteran, who became known for his penchant to cut costs, which earned him the name "Mack the Knife". He went to Credit Suisse after a power struggle at investment bank Morgan Stanley. John Mack led a dramatic turnaround at CSFB — delivering a $1.4 billion profit last year, enhancing its reputation by resolving major regulatory challenges and strengthening the franchise in key areas for future growth. In addition, the company said it will restructure with investment banking and wealth and asset management under Credit Suisse First Boston, retail and corporate banking under Credit Suisse and insurance under its Winterhur unit.

Credit Suisse First Boston (CSFB) is a leading global investment bank serving institutional, corporate, government and high net worth clients. Its businesses include securities underwriting, sales and trading, investment banking, private equity, financial advisory services, investment research, venture capital and asset management. It operates in more than 68 locations across more than 33 countries on five continents. It is a business unit of Zurich-based Credit Suisse Group, a leading global financial services company.

I. In this section, you will hear five short recordings. For each piece, decide why the chief of each company resigned or will resign from his position.

1. Burger King	F	A. Criminal record
2. Coca-Cola	H	B. Management reorganization
3. Smith & Wesson	A	C. Accounting fraud
4. Hollinger	G	D. Armed robberies
5. Credit Suisse	B	E. Corporate internal strife
		F. Conflict with the board
		G. Defalcation practices
		H. Substandard performance

II. Listen to the five recordings again and choose the best answers to the questions you hear.

1. Which of the following statements is NOT true about Burger King Corp.?　(C)

2. What did Coca-Cola Company expect to achieve when it appointed Doug Daft its CEO?　(B)

3. What can be learned about James Joseph Minder, chairman of Smith & Wesson Holding Corp.?
　(A)

4. What is NOT included in the accusations of Hollinger International Inc. against Conrad Black?　(D)

5. What resulted in John Mack's ouster from Morgan Stanley?　(B)

Home Listening

Business News

Tapescript

A Washington based Institute for International Economics says that five years after a major financial crisis the restructuring of South Korea's industrial conglomerates is only partially complete. Barry Wood reports that the reckless financial dealings of the chaebols contributed to South Korea's late 1990s financial meltdown.

Former Duke University business professor Edward Graham says despite significant reform in some areas, the chaebols are still too big and too powerful. The new South Korean president has promised to crack down on the practices of the chaebols. This week the government said it is investigating possible illegal securities transactions by the chaebols.

At the time of the 1997 crisis, the biggest conglomerates or industrial holding companies were Hyundai, Samsung, Daewoo, LG, and SK, In 1999, Daewoo was permitted to fail or go bankrupt, with its auto manufacturing assets being sold off. South Korea's financial crisis occurred when the central bank was unable to stand behind the short-term debts of the chaebols which had expanded aggressively and piled up a huge volume of debt.

Mr. Graham says the finances of the remaining chaebols are still questionable. He says South Korea's industrial economy is still lacking in transparency. Off balance sheet operations similar to those which contributed to the collapse of the Enron energy trading company in Texas are common in South Korea.

Mr. Graham says it may be a good idea to break up the chaebols. He says South Korea still has a relatively weak financial system and the reforms that have been made are only half-complete. He says it is not true that South Korea has followed the Chinese example and fully opened its previously closed economy to foreign direct investment. He says while there was some opening in the aftermath of the crisis, foreign investment has recently leveled off at relatively low levels.

South Korea's economy registered stunning economic growth rates in the 1980s and early 1990s. Ten percent annual growth was not unusual. After the crisis, the economy contracted by eight percent in 1998 but growth resumed by 1999.

Listen to the business news report and decide whether the following statements are true or false. Write T for true and F for false in the brackets.

1. (T)   2. (F)   3. (F)   4. (F)   5. (T)   6. (F)   7. (T)   8. (T)   9. (F)   10. (F)

Unit 3

Branding

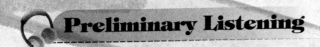

Preliminary Listening

Dictation

Listen to the following short paragraph and fill in the blanks with what you hear.

A brand is (1) <u>a name, logo, slogan, and/or design scheme</u> associated with a product or service. Brand recognition and other reactions are created by the use of the product or service and through (2) <u>the influence of advertising, design, and media commentary</u>. A brand is (3) <u>a symbolic embodiment of all the information</u> connected to the product and serves to (4) <u>create associations and expectations</u> around it. A brand often includes a logo, fonts, color schemes, symbols, and sound, which may be developed to (5) <u>represent implicit values, ideas, and even personality</u>. Branding provides identity to the product. A number of advantages can be attributed to branding. These include identification, (6) <u>effective use of marketing mix variables</u>, (7) <u>consistency in product quality</u>, (8) <u>aid in communication with the consumers</u>, consumer trust in the products, and the like.

Listening & Speaking

SECTION A   **Brand Positioning**

Background Information

1. Branding

Branding provides identity to the product and can be accomplished in a number of ways. Firms may use brand names, trade names, corporate identification marks, service marks, or a combination of these to identify their products or services. A number of advantages can be attributed to branding. These include identification, effective use of marketing mix variables, consistency in product quality, aid in communication with the consumers, consumer trust in the products, and the like. Certain guidelines should be born in mind when selecting brand names. Brand names should reflect product benefits, should be easily recognized and recalled. In developing brand names, a thorough understanding of what the product is, its benefits and its competitive stance is a must. Legal protection given to a brand name is called a trademark.

2. Brand value

Brand value measures the total value of the brand to the brand owner, and reflects the extent of brand franchise. A brand can be an intangible asset, used by analysts to rationalize the difference between a company's "book value" and market value. For example, the market value of a company can far exceed its tangible assets (physical assets owned by the company, such as stock or machinery), and its brand value can account for some of the difference. Up to 85 percent of a company's market value might be intangible (for example know-how, existing client relationships). Sometimes tangible assets may account for less than five percent of a company's market value, for example in the case of Coca-Cola or Microsoft. Brand value, especially in the case of consumer product brands, may arise out of customer loyalty. Brand value may also arise in terms of staff retention benefits (e.g. the ability of the company to attract and retain skilled and/or talented employees offering competitive salaries). Brand value can be negatively influenced. For example, in 1999 Nike's brand value was estimated at US$8 billion . Facing media exposure and consumer

boycotts over supply chain issues, Nike's brand value declined in following two years to US$7.6 billion , and rose back to US$9.26 billion in 2004 after Nike addressed its supply chain issues.

3. Brand image

Brand image refers to qualities that consumers associate with a specific brand, expressed in terms of human behavior and desires, but that also relates to price, quality, and situational use of the brand. For example: a brand such as Mercedes-Benz will conjure up a strong public image because of its sensory and physical characteristics as well as its price. This image is not inherent in the brand name but is created through advertising.

Listening ▶▶

Conversation

Tapescript

Mr. Johnson, the Marketing Director of a beverage company, is giving a presentation about the performance and trend of four brands of drinks manufactured by his company.

Mr. Johnson: We all know that there have been some major changes in our market over the last ten years, and we can expect further changes over the next ten years. I'd like to present our brand performance over the last ten years and also anticipate the trends we predict over the next ten years.

I'm not going to talk for long — just long enough to give you an overview of developments so that we can discuss the implications. Do interrupt me if you've got any questions or comments. So let's start by looking at our brand performance over the last ten years. Well, the actual market share of our four products has changed radically; the Power Coke has fallen dramatically from 74% to 42% — here on this line graph; the Koo Tea has rocketed from only 12% to 35%, reflecting the weight of publicity directed towards the health-conscious fad. The other two branded products are Magi Water and LAF Milk Drink. It's interesting to see that Magi Water has risen from 5% to 13% — a significant rise considering initial consumer resistance to this type of water. And finally, the LAF Milk Drink has remained pretty stable, just increasing by 1%. So the two bigger winners of the decade are Koo Tea and Magi Water, and the big loser, the Power Coke.

Now what's really important is the likely trends over the next ten years for these brands. If you look at this graph, beyond this line we've plotted the anticipated trends over the next ten years. We forecast that the Coke will decline more

> gradually over the next five years to around 40% and then fall a further 2% by the end of the 10-year period; the Koo Tea …
>
> **Participant A:** Excuse me, can I just ask how you account for this decline?
>
> **Mr. Johnson:** Er … if you don't mind, I'll come to that in a moment. Just to complete the picture, the Koo Tea should continue to rise steadily to 40% over the next five years and then level off around this figure for the next five years. We expect Magi Water to continue rising moderately so that at the end of this period this brand will represent a significant 20%. Finally we project a fairly marked decline for the LAF Milk Drink as consumer awareness of the sugar content of these drinks increases. We forecast an eventual fall to just 2% by the end of the period.
>
> Right, now let me come back to your question: why do we expect these trends? Well, one critical factor …

I. Listen to the conversation and choose the best answers to the questions you hear.

1. What is the job title of Mr. Johnson?   (C)
2. Which brand of drinks was resisted by consumers at the initial stage?   (C)
3. Which brand of drinks experienced a loss of market share over the last decade?   (B)
4. What accounts for the decline of the LAF Milk Drink over the next decade?   (D)
5. Which of the following is not covered in the presentation?   (C)

II. Listen to the conversation again and match each of the brands with an appropriate line in the chart below.

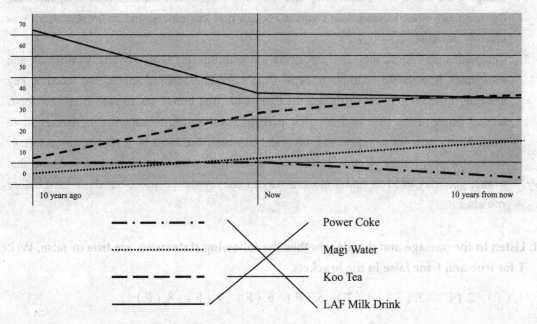

Passage

Tapescript

Competitive brand positioning is hard work. Many brands falter sooner than they should; some don't even make it out of the gate. Here are five pitfalls to watch out for.

1. Companies sometimes try to build brand awareness before establishing a clear brand position. You have to know who you are before you can convince anyone of it. Many dot-coms know this pitfall well. A number of them spent heavily on expensive television advertising without first being clear about what they were selling.

2. Companies often promote attributes that consumers don't care about. The classic example: for years, companies that sold analgesics claimed their brands were longer lasting than others. Eventually, they noticed that consumers wanted faster relief more than sustained relief.

3. Companies sometimes invest too heavily in points of difference that can easily be copied. Positioning needs to keep competitors out, not draw them in. A brand that claims to be the cheapest or the hippest is likely to be leapfrogged.

4. Certain companies become so intent on responding to competition that they walk away from their established positions. General Mills used the insight that consumers viewed honey as more nutritious than sugar to successfully introduce the Honey Nut Cheerios product-line extension. A key competitor, Post, decided to respond by repositioning its Sugar Crisp brand, changing the name to Golden Crisp and dropping the Sugar Bear character as spokesman. But the repositioned brand didn't attract enough new customers, and its market share was severely diminished.

5. Companies may think they can reposition a brand, but this is nearly always difficult and sometimes impossible. Although Pepsi-Cola's fresh, youthful appeal has been a key branding difference in its battle against Coca-Cola, the brand has strayed from this focus several times in the past two decades, perhaps contributing to some of its market share woes. Every attempt to reposition the brand has been followed by a retreat to the former successful positioning. Brand positioning is a tough task. Once you've found one that works, you may need to find a modern way to convey the position, but think hard before you alter it.

I. Listen to the passage and decide whether the following statements are true or false. Write T for true and F for false in the brackets.

1.(T) 2.(F) 3.(T) 4.(T) 5.(F) 6.(F) 7.(F) 8.(F)

II. Listen to the passage again and summarize the five pitfalls in brand positioning in the chart below.

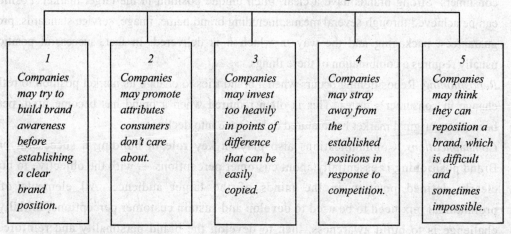

The Pitfalls of Brand Positioning

1	2	3	4	5
Companies may try to build brand awareness before establishing a clear brand position.	Companies may promote attributes consumers don't care about.	Companies may invest too heavily in points of difference that can be easily copied.	Companies may stray away from the established positions in response to competition.	Companies may think they can reposition a brand, which is difficult and sometimes impossible.

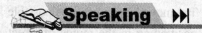

Speaking ▶▶

Discussion

1. — F	2. — D	3. — E	4. — H
5. — B	6. — G	7. — A	8. — C

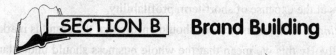

SECTION B   **Brand Building**

Pre-listening ▶▶

Background Information

1. Brand building

Seven main factors are identified in building successful brands.

Quality. Quality is a vital ingredient of a good brand. Statistically higher quality brands achieve a higher market share and higher profitability than their inferior competitors.

Positioning. Positioning is about the position a brand occupies in a market in the minds of consumers. Strong brands have a clear, often unique position in the target market. Positioning can be achieved through several means, including brand name, image, service standards, product guarantees, packaging and the way in which it is delivered. In fact, successful positioning usually requires a combination of these things.

Repositioning. Repositioning occurs when a brand tries to change its market position to reflect a change in consumer's tastes. This is often required when a brand has become tired, perhaps because its original market has matured or has gone into decline.

Communications. Communications also plays a key role in building a successful brand. Brand positioning is essentially about customer perceptions — with the objective to build a clearly defined position in the minds of the target audience. All elements of the promotional mix need to be used to develop and sustain customer perceptions. Initially, the challenge is to build awareness, then to develop the brand personality and reinforce the perception.

First-mover advantage. In terms of brand development, by "first-mover" we mean it is possible for the first successful brand in a market to create a clear positioning in the minds of target customers before the competition enters the market. However, being first into a market does not necessarily guarantee long-term success. Competitors — drawn to the high growth and profit potential demonstrated by the "market-mover" — will enter the market and copy the best elements of the leader's brand.

Long-term perspective. This leads to another important factor in brand-building: the need to invest in the brand over the long-term. Building customer awareness, communicating the brand's message and creating customer loyalty takes time. This means that management must "invest" in a brand, perhaps at the expense of short-term profitability.

Internal marketing. Finally, management should ensure that the brand is marketed "internally" as well as externally. By this we mean that the whole business should understand the brand values and positioning. This is particularly important in service businesses where a critical part of the brand value is the type and quality of service that a customer receives. Think of the brands that you value in the restaurant, hotel and retail sectors. It is likely that your favorite brands invest heavily in staff training so that the face-to-face contact that you have with the brand helps secure your loyalty.

2. Niche market

Niche market, also known as a target market, is a focused, targetable portion (subset) of a market sector. By definition, then, a business that focuses on a niche market is addressing a need for a product or service that is not being addressed by mainstream providers. A niche market may be thought of as a narrowly defined group of potential customers. A distinct niche market usually evolves out of a market niche, where potential demand is not met by any supply. Such ventures are profitable because of disinterest on the part of large businesses and/or lack of awareness on the part of other small companies. The key to capitalizing on a niche market is to find or develop a market niche that has customers who are accessible, that is growing fast enough, and that is not owned by one established vendor already.

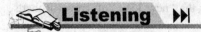 Listening ▶▶|

Conversation

Tapescript

Mr. Edwin Roberts, Business Development Manager of Trevor-Roberts Associates, talked about his company's re-branding strategies at a recent interview.

Interviewer: Tell me a little about Trevor-Roberts Associates. What do you do?

Edwin: We are a consulting firm with the aim to help organizations enable their individuals to achieve their career and life goals. For organizations, we understand their needs first and then help them develop a career management process to assist their employees. For individuals, we help them to become more employable and achieve their goals by expanding their career options and helping them find their ideal work or life balance.

Interviewer: Recently you made some changes to your company image and marketing direction. Why did you do this?

Edwin: For the first 7 or so years of the company's existence, we have labeled ourselves as "Human Resource Consultants" and later "Human Resource Professionals". After speaking to some of our clients, there seemed to be confusion between what they thought we did and what we actually specialized in. It was this confusion in the marketplace as to our niche field that prompted a change in our marketing direction.

Interviewer: What were the main changes that you implemented?

Edwin: The first and most major change was a new branding strategy. This involved dropping the old slogan and implementing a more accurate slogan of "Career Architects". To match this we had a graphic designer revamp our logo and corporate colors on our brochures, letterheads, business cards, website, etc. We also decided to upgrade our offices and invested in an architect who helped redesign our office to address a few key problems we had.

Interviewer: In your opinion what was the most important aspect of the change to get right?

Edwin: The most important aspect is communicating to everybody, especially clients, as to why we were undertaking this transformation. This was especially important to retain our credibility and leverage off our existing reputation. Regardless of how flashy one's offices or logo look, if people do not perceive that you have the expertise to fit your "new look" then it can amount to a very expensive mistake.

Interviewer: What were the risks involved with undertaking the "new look" of Trevor-Roberts Associates?

Edwin: Surprisingly very few. We were already well established in the market place with a loyal clientele so re-branding only further reinforced in their minds our specialty and knowledge of the careers field.

Interviewer: What has been the reaction to date from clients? Have you had any feedback from competitors?

Edwin: The reaction of our clients and potential clients has been extremely positive. In particular, they have been impressed by the focus on our new branding exhibits as well as the values of our organization that we have strongly communicated.

Interviewer: What is your advice to other firms considering a similar shift in corporate image and marketing direction? Are there any specific pitfalls to be aware of?

Edwin: My advice is to make sure that your marketing plans align with your strategic direction. If there is a seamless integration between where you want to be and how you plan to get there, then your marketing will work.

Interviewer: Any other comments?

Edwin: Invest in experts. Bring in experienced people to help you with your strategy, marketing and branding efforts — they are well worth the investment. Be very cautious of costs. We undertook our transformation over a period of about a year to ensure that our cash flow was not overly affected.

I. Listen to the conversation and choose the best answers to the questions you hear.

1. What line of business is Trevor-Roberts Associates in?   (A)

2. What is the main purpose of Trevor-Roberts Associates' new branding strategy?   (D)

3. Which of the following is included in Trevor-Roberts Associates' new branding strategy?   (D)

4. How do Trevor-Roberts Associates' clients perceive the transformation?   (C)

5. What can be concluded from the interview?   (D)

II. Listen to the conversation again and complete the notes with what you hear.

Company name: *Trevor-Roberts Associates*

Scope of business:
❑ At organizational level:
  helping organizations (1) <u>develop career management process to assist employees</u>
❑ At individual level:
  a. helping employees (2) <u>become more employable and achieve their goals by</u>
  <u>expanding their career options</u>
  b. helping employees (3) <u>find their ideal work/life balance</u>

The company has labeled itself:
❑ first as (4) <u>"Human Resource Consultant"</u>
❑ later as (5) <u>"Human Resource Professionals"</u>
❑ now as (6) <u>"Career Architects"</u>

Reason(s) for change:
(7) <u>There has been confusion in the marketplace as to the company's niche field/</u>
  <u>specialization.</u>

Changes made:
a. (8) <u>dropping the old slogan and implementing a new one</u>
b. (9) <u>revamping the logo and corporate colors on company brochures, letterheads, business</u>
  <u>cards, website, etc.</u>
c. (10) <u>upgrading and having an architect redesign company offices</u>

The most important aspect of the change:
(11) <u>Communicating to everybody, especially clients, as to why the transformation was</u>
  <u>taken</u>

Reactions from clients: (12) <u>extremely positive</u>

Advice for those considering similar transformation:
a. (13) <u>To make sure that marketing plans align with strategic direction</u>
b. (14) <u>To invest in experts</u>
c. (15) <u>To be cautious of costs</u>

Passage

Tapescript

When you think of marketing, you think of marketing to your customers. But another "market" is just as important: your employees, the very people who can make the brand come alive for your customers. Why is internal marketing so important? Because it's the best way to help employees make a powerful emotional connection to the products and service you sell. We've found that when people care about and believe in the brand, they're motivated to work harder and their loyalty to the company increases.

Unfortunately, in most companies internal marketing is done poorly, if at all. While executives recognize the need to keep people informed about the company's strategy and direction, few understand the need to convince employees of the brand's power. What's more, the people who are charged with internal communications — HR professionals, typically — don't have the marketing skills to communicate successfully. Information is doled out to employees in the form of memos, newsletters, and so on, but it's not designed to convince them of the uniqueness of the company's brand. The marketing department might get involved in while to tell employees about a new ad campaign or branding effort. But the intent usually is to tell people what the company is doing, not to tell them the ideas. We've found that by applying some principles of consumer advertising to internal communications, leaders can guide employees to a better understanding of, and even a passion for, the brand vision.

The goal of an internal branding campaign is to create an emotional connection to your company. You want the connection to influence the way your employees approach their jobs, even if they don't interact with customers. You want them to have the brand vision in their minds. How do you do that? You need to plan and execute a professional branding campaign to introduce and explain the messages and then reinforce them by weaving the brand into the fabric of the company.

Top executives should first answer some key questions: What do employees think of the company? What do we want them to think? What will convince them of this? And why should they believe us? Once these questions have been answered, the work of creating communications materials can begin. To be effective, these materials must be as creative and eye-catching as the materials you deliver to an external audience. This is a task of persuasion, not information, and dry, lifeless materials will quickly be shelved.

When it comes to delivering the message, it's tempting to send out a memo, a video, or a package of colorful materials and consider it done, but there's no substitute for personal contact from the organization's highest levels. For large, geographically diverse organizations, the company intranet can be a superb facilitator of interaction. Indeed, we've found that in companies that do not use intranets for candid dialogue, employees inevitably turn to external Web sites to complain about the company. But don't let the Web become a substitute for face time and corridor chat. Remember, it is a truth of business that if employees do not care about their company, they will in the end contribute to its demise. And it's up to you to give them a reason to care.

I. Listen to the passage and choose the best answers to the questions you hear.

1. How are companies doing currently in terms of internal marketing?　(A)
2. Which department is usually in charge of internal marketing in a company?　(B)
3. What mainly accounts for the failure to implement successful internal marketing in most companies?　(C)
4. What is an indispensable form of delivering the messages to employees?　(D)
5. What can be concluded from the passage?　(B)

II. Listen to the passage again and complete the following statements with what you hear.

1. Marketing to your employees is as important as marketing to your customers because <u>internal marketing is the best way to help employees make a powerful emotional connection to the products and service you sell</u>.
2. If employees care about and trust the brand, <u>they're motivated to work harder and their loyalty to the company increases</u>.
3. Internal marketing is done poorly in most companies because:
   a. few executives <u>understand the need to convince employees of the brand's power</u>;
   b. people who are charged with internal communications <u>don't have the marketing skills to communicate successfully</u>.
4. Employees can develop a better understanding of, and even a passion for, the brand vision if <u>some principles of consumer advertising are applied to internal communications</u>.
5. By means of internal branding campaigns, companies want to create an emotional connection to <u>influence the way their employees approach their jobs</u> and want their employees to <u>have the brand vision in their minds</u>. To achieve this goal, a professional branding campaign needs to be planned and executed to <u>introduce and explain the messages</u> and then reinforce them by <u>weaving the brand into the fabric of the company</u>.
6. To implement a successful internal branding campaign,
   <u>a. some key questions should be addressed by top executives first;</u>
   <u>b. communications materials should be created, which are creative, eye-catching and meant to persuade rather than inform;</u>
   <u>c. messages should be delivered through company intranet, or better, by personal contact from the organization's highest levels.</u>

Further Listening

Short Recordings

Tapescript

Item 1

NEW YORK — Avon Products Inc., the world's largest direct seller of cosmetics, said Wednesday its quarterly profit rose 35 percent, as foreign markets flourished and representatives' sales jumped. The New York-based company's net income in the second quarter rose to $232.3 million, or 49 cents per share, compared with $171.5 million, or 36 cents per share a year earlier. Sales rose 13 percent to $1.84 billion. Excluding the impact of foreign currency exchange, sales rose 12 percent. Avon said the sales growth was driven by a 17 percent increase in sales of beauty products, with all major categories delivering double-digit gains. Active representatives rose 11 percent, with all geographic regions showing increases.

Avon Products, Inc. is a global manufacturer and marketer of beauty and related products. The Company's products fall into three product categories: Beauty, which consists of cosmetics, fragrances and toiletries; Beauty Plus, which consists of fashion jewelry, watches, apparel and accessories, and Beyond Beauty, which consists of home products, gift and decorative products and candles. Avon's business primarily consists of one industry segment, direct selling, which is conducted worldwide. The Company's segments are based on geographic operations in four regions: North America, Latin America, Europe and the Pacific.

Item 2

LONDON — HSBC Holdings PLC's first-half profit rose by more than half, surpassing market expectations and boosting its shares, as the global bank benefited from last year's purchase of US lender Household International. Pretax profit for the six months ended June 30 rose 53 percent to a record $9.37 billion from $6.11 billion a year earlier, the world's third-biggest bank by market value said Monday. Its bad-debt charge also came in lower than forecast. US consumer finance business Household contributed $1.9 billion to first-half pre-tax profit, compared with $536 million in the three months after HSBC bought it last year.

HSBC Holdings PLC is the UK's largest banking company; it also owns The Hongkong and Shanghai Banking Corporation, France's CCF, and 62% of Hong Kong's Hang Seng Bank. HSBC has more than 8,000 offices in about 80 countries, providing consumer and business banking services, asset management, investment banking, securities trading, insurance, and leasing. US operations, which include HSBC USA and joint venture Wells Fargo HSBC Trade Bank, got a boost with the purchase of consumer lender Household International. HSBC also bought Bank of Bermuda as well.

Household International, acquired in 2003 by megabank HSBC Holdings, is the #2 consumer finance firm in the US, behind Citigroup. Its primary subsidiaries, Household Finance and Beneficial, make secured (home equity) and unsecured consumer loans, mostly to lower-middle-income and working-class customers. Household International is one of the largest issuers of MasterCard and Visa credit cards, providing co-branded and private-label credit cards such as The GM and AFL-CIO Union Plus cards. The company also offers auto loans and various insurance products targeted to the under-insured.

Item 3

NEW YORK — Northrop Grumman Corp. said Thursday quarterly net earnings soared 44 percent on stronger demand for surveillance and battleship equipment. The third largest US defense contractor raised its outlook for the year, sending shares higher. Northrop Grumman shares jumped to $56.15 in early trading, from their Wednesday close at $53.70. The Los Angeles-based builder of warships and intelligence gathering systems posted second-quarter net earnings of $295 million, or 81 cents per share, compared with $205 million, or 54 cents per share, a year ago. Northrop reported income from continuing operations of $289 million, or 79 cents per share, compared with $207 million, or 55 cents per share, for the same period of 2003.

Northrop Grumman Corporation provides products, services and solutions in defense and commercial electronics, nuclear and non-nuclear shipbuilding, information technology, mission systems, systems integration and space technology. As prime contractor, principal subcontractor, partner or preferred supplier, Northrop Grumman participates in many defense and commercial technology programs in the United States and abroad. The majority of the Company's products and services are ultimately sold to the United States Government, which accounted for 86.7% of total revenue in 2003.

Item 4

NEW YORK — Hilton Hotels Corp. on Wednesday reported higher second-quarter earnings as increased business travel boosted occupancy at its high-end urban hotels. The company raised its full-year outlook. The Beverly Hills, California-based company said profits rose to $75 million, or 19 cents per share, from $54 million, or 14 cents per share, a year earlier. Hilton, best known for its high-end flagship hotels, also owns brands such as Hampton Inn and Embassy Suites. Hilton said it now expects full-year earnings per share in the middle to high end of the 50-cent range. The company also raised its 2004 revenue outlook to about $4.17 billion from $4.16

billion.

Hilton Hotels Corporation is engaged, together with its subsidiaries, in the ownership, management and development of hotels, resorts and the franchising of lodging properties. As of December 31, 2003, its system contained 2,173 properties, totaling over 348,000 rooms. The Company's hotel brands include Hilton, Hilton Garden Inn, Doubletree, Embassy Suites, Hampton, Homewood Suites by Hilton and Conrad.

Item 5

AMSTERDAM — Europe's biggest insurer, ING, trumped market expectations with a 38 percent rise in second-quarter group core profit on Thursday, fueled in part by a hearty performance in banking operations. The Dutch financial services group, Europe's No. 1 insurance firm by market capitalization, posted core profit of 1.605 billion euros, well ahead of a consensus estimate of 1.15 billion. Operating net profit in banking alone rose 65.4 percent to 670 million euros with much of the increase from the wholesale business, where results were supported by a sharp decline in risk costs and continued growth in commissions and other income.

ING Groep N.V. (ING) is a global financial institution of Dutch origin that offers banking, insurance and asset management to more than 60 million clients in more than 50 countries. The Company consists of a spectrum of businesses that serve their clients under the ING brand. Its segments, which are based on the management structure of the Company, are ING Europe, ING Americas and ING Asia/Pacific. It primarily offers retail and wholesale financial services. On the retail side, the strategy focuses on retail wealth accumulation and financial protection, such as retail banking, asset management, asset gathering, life insurance and pensions and private banking.

I. **In this section, you will hear five short recordings. For each piece, decide what mainly contributes to the profit increase of each company.**

1. Avon	C	A. Tax refund
2. HSBC	G	B. Brand Loyalty
3. Northrop Grumman	E	C. Overseas sales
4. Hilton	D	D. Business travel
5. ING	F	E. Military demand
		F. Banking business
		G. Company acquisition
		H. Customer satisfaction

II. Listen to the five recordings again and complete the following notes with what you hear.

Company	Fact Sheet of Profit Increase
Avon Products Inc. the world's largest <u>direct seller of cosmetics</u>	❑ Avon's <u>quarterly profit</u> rose 35 percent. ❑ Avon's net income in the second quarter rose to <u>$232.3 million</u>, or 49 cents per share, compared with <u>$171.5 million</u>, or 36 cents per share a year earlier. ❑ Avon's sales rose 13 percent to <u>$1.84 billion</u>. ❑ Avon's sales growth was driven by a 17 percent increase in sales of <u>beauty products</u>, with all major categories delivering <u>double-digit gains</u>.
HSBC Holdings PLC the world's <u>third-biggest bank</u>	❑ HSBC's first-half profit rose by <u>more than half</u>. ❑ HSBC's pretax profit for the six months ended June 30 rose 53 percent to a record <u>$9.37 billion</u> from <u>$6.11 billion</u> a year earlier. ❑ Household contributed $1.9 billion to first-half pre-tax profit, compared with <u>$536 million</u> in the three months after HSBC bought it last year.
Northrop Grumman Corp. the third largest <u>US defense contractor</u>, builder of <u>warships and intelligence gathering systems</u>	❑ Northrop Grumman's <u>quarterly net earnings</u> soared 44 percent. ❑ Northrop Grumman shares jumped to <u>$56.15</u> in early trading, from their Wednesday close at <u>$53.70</u>. ❑ Northrop Grumman posted second-quarter net earnings of <u>$295 million</u>, or 81 cents per share, compared with <u>$205 million</u>, or 54 cents per share, a year ago. ❑ Northrop reported income from continuing operations of <u>$289 million</u>, or 79 cents per share, compared with <u>$207 million</u>, or 55 cents per share, for the same period of 2003.
Hilton Hotels Corp. best known for its <u>high-end flagship hotels</u>	❑ Hilton's profits rose to <u>$75 million</u>, or 19 cents per share, from <u>$54 million</u>, or 14 cents per share, a year earlier. ❑ Hilton raised its 2004 revenue outlook to about <u>$4.17 billion</u> from <u>$4.16 billion</u>.
ING A Dutch <u>financial services group</u>, Europe's No. 1 <u>insurance firm</u>	❑ ING posted core profit of <u>1.605 billion</u> euros, well ahead of a consensus estimate of 1.15 billion. ❑ ING's operating net profit in banking alone rose <u>65.4 percent</u> to 670 million euros with much of the increase from <u>the wholesale business</u>, where results were supported by <u>a sharp decline in risk costs</u> and <u>continued growth in commissions</u> and other income.

Home Listening

Business News

Tapescript

A leading human-rights group says the Angolan government cannot account for more than $4 billion in missing oil revenue, nearly 10 percent of the country's gross domestic product.

New York-based Human Rights Watch released a report on Tuesday that says profits from the state-run oil company suspiciously disappeared from government coffers between 1997 and 2002.

Angola is Africa's second largest oil exporter. Its $17.8 billion in oil revenue during that same period made up 85 percent of the government's total earnings.

Arvind Ganesan is director of the Human Rights Watch business program. He says Angolan officials refused to give international aid auditors an accounting of the missing funds, at a time when millions of Angolans have no access to hospitals or schools.

"After they had looked at everything the government had spent its money on, it found that in total over six years about $4.2 billion had been spent, but for no definable purpose, and when they asked the government and the institutions within the government for an explanation for how this money was spent, they were either not forthcoming or unwilling to provide that information."

Mr. Ganesan also says that even though a 27-year civil war ended two years ago, the absence of fighting has not led to any improvement in the lives of most Angolans. He says nearly one million Angolans are still homeless and 7.4 million children are malnourished.

"While the government is asking the international community for more money, they need to account for what happened to this money that disappeared since it's roughly equal to how much was spent on life security and social programs and humanitarian aid. While we wouldn't say that the international community should cut off Angola, they should clearly require that the government account for its own revenues and expenditures and make it clear how it's spending its money."

The International Monetary Fund has so far refused to enter into a formal aid program with Angola because of what it says is the lack of transparency of its accounting practices.

Some analysts say Angola is rapidly becoming a major oil-exporter, and will be able to produce as much oil as Kuwait by 2010.

Listen to the business news report and choose the best answers to the questions you hear.

1. What does Human Rights Watch refer to in the news report?   (C)

2. How much does Angola's gross domestic product come to?   (D)

3. What did Angolan government say in explanation of the missing funds?   (B)

4. Which of the following is true about Angola?   (B)

5. What can be inferred from the news report?   (A)

Unit 4

Sales

2. How much does Angola's gross domestic product com...
3. What did Angolan government say in explanation of...
4. Which of the following is true about Angola? (B)
5. What can be inferred from the news? (A)

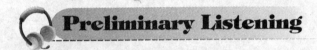

Preliminary Listening

Dictation

Listen to the following short paragraph and fill in the blanks with what you hear.

Sales are the activities involved in providing products or services in return for (1) <u>money or other compensation</u>. It is an act of (2) <u>completion of a commercial activity</u>. The "deal is closed" means the customer has consented to the proposed product or service by (3) <u>making full or partial payment</u> to the seller. The primary function of professional sales is to (4) <u>generate and close leads</u>, educate prospects, fill needs and (5) <u>satisfy wants of consumers</u> appropriately, and therefore turn (6) <u>prospective customers</u> into actual ones. The successful questioning to understand a customer's goal, the (7) <u>further creation of a valuable solution</u> by communicating the necessary information that encourages a buyer to achieve his goal (8) <u>at an economic cost</u> is the responsibility of the sales person or the sales engine (e.g. internet, vending machine, etc).

Listening & Speaking

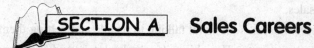

| SECTION A | Sales Careers |

Pre-listening ▶▶

Background Information

1. A career in sales

How would you like a job with enough autonomy to make you feel that you are your own boss? How would you like a career that lets you learn something new every single day? That's what a career in sales can offer you. Many leading sales professionals are motivated by the three "Is." Some choose the profession for the *Impact* they have on their community, their clients or their families. Others choose it for the *Independence* and, yet for others, it is the *Income* potential (getting paid for what you're worth). Whether it is one of these reasons or another, sales professionals ultimately have great more control of their lives, personally, professionally and financially. The best part of a career in Sales is that it is undefined. It is hard to describe your typical day as a salesperson because every day is different. One day you are on the Internet researching prospective clients and, along the way, learning a great deal about a company and, perhaps, a new industry. The next few days may be spent calling these prospective clients and then an entire week may be in face-to-face sales calls. On other days, you are writing up sales-call reports and preparing proposals for clients. Some sales positions allow you to work out of your home office, others require traveling, and still others will allow you to do both. Sales is actually the process of problem solving for a potential buyer or enhancing his/her business. Salespeople develop the skills to discover needs and solve problems. Contrary to the viewpoint often held by people who don't understand selling, the most successful salespeople sell by asking questions, not delivering a "spiel" or "talking someone into something they don't need." The old cliché is that a good salesperson can sell sand in the desert. However, the successful salesperson doesn't follow this mentality, but will walk away from a potential order because his/her product/service doesn't help the potential buyer. Good salespeople sell what customers really need.

2. Basic skills successful salespeople should have

Techniques and methods of sales are teachable to anyone who has the desire to learn, however, there are a few natural skills that are of great benefit if they already exist within those that want to be successful in sales.

Effective communicator. Sales is all about talking to people and getting them to understand what you are trying to communicate. The ability to speak clearly and in a manner that is easy to understand is a must.

Ability to listen. Along with speaking, a great salesperson knows when to stop talking and listen. They never cut someone off while they are talking, because in doing so they would fail to hear a key element in identifying what that person's needs might be.

Ask great questions. Salespeople are naturally inquisitive and know that in order to isolate what the real need or desire is in the buyer, they need to ask questions that will lead them to the answer. They naturally ask questions because they have a desire to help solve the problem.

Well organized. Sales people have a keen ability to break things down into smaller steps and organize a plan of action. They know how to analyze what their goal is and in what order the steps need to be to reach that goal.

Self-starter and self-finisher. A successful salesperson moves forward on their own. They never need anyone to tell them when it is time to go to work because they know that if they do not work they will not earn. They are also very persistent to finish what they start.

Positive self-image. Having the attitude that they can do just about anything that they put their mind to is usually very common among sales people. They do not cower from meeting or talking to people or trying something new. They rarely allow negatives to affect what they are trying to accomplish because they know who they are and what they are capable of doing.

Well-mannered and courteous. The best sales people are very well mannered. People are attracted to those that respect them and mutual respect is fundamental in building lasting relationships with people, including buyers.

Naturally persuasive. Another very common inherent skill with great salespeople is that they are very persuasive or know how to get what they want. They focus on what they want and they are persistent to keep chipping away until they get what they want. They almost never give up or give in.

3. Pareto Principle

（帕累托法则，又称为 80/20 效率法则，帕累托定律、最省力法则或不平衡原则、犹太法则。）

The Pareto principle (also known as the 80-20 rule, the law of the vital few and the principle of factor sparsity) specifies an unequal relationship between inputs and outputs. Business management thinker Joseph M. Juran suggested the principle and named it after Italian economist Vilfredo Pareto, who observed that 80% of income in Italy went to 20% of the population. The principle states that, for many phenomena, 20% of invested input is responsible for 80% of the results obtained. Put another way, 80% of consequences stem from 20% of the causes. This principle serves as a general reminder that the relationship between inputs and outputs is not balanced. For instance, the efforts of 20% of a corporation's staff could drive 80% of the firm's profits. In terms of personal time management, 80% of your work-related output could come from only 20% of your time at work. The Pareto Principle can be applied in a wide range of areas such as manufacturing, management and human resources.

Listening ▶▶|

Conversation

Tapescript

Mrs. Norman:	Hello, Mr. Pride, my name is Karen Norman and I'd like to talk with you about how to save your company executives' time. By the way, thanks for taking time to talk with me.
Mr. Pride:	My pleasure. Then, what's on your mind, Mrs. Norman?
Mrs. Norman:	As a busy executive, you know time is very precious. Nearly everyone would like to have a few extra minutes each day and that is the business I'm in, selling time. I'm not joking. While I can't actually sell you time, I do have a product that is the next best thing ... the Dyno Electric Cart — a real time-saver for your executives.
Mr. Pride:	Well, I guess you are perfectly right — everyone would like to have some extra time. However, I don't think we need any golf carts.
Mrs. Norman:	Our Dyno cart is more than a golf cart. It is an electric cart designed for use in industrial plants. It has been engineered to give comfortable, rapid transportation in warehouses, plants, and across open areas.
Mr. Pride:	Er ... I guess they probably cost too much for us to use.
Mrs. Norman:	First of all, they only cost $2,000 each. With a five-year normal life, that is only $400 per year plus a few cents for electricity and a few dollars for maintenance. Under normal use and care, these carts only require about $100 of service in their five-year life. Thus, for about $50 a month, you can save your key people a lot of time.
Mr. Pride:	It would be nice to save time, but I don't think the management would go for the idea.
Mrs. Norman:	This is exactly why I am here. Your executives will appreciate what you have done for them. You will look good in their eyes if you give them an

opportunity to look at a product that will save them both time and energy. Besides, saving time is only part of our story. Dyno carts also save energy and thus keep you sharper toward the end of the day. By the way, Mr. Pride, would you want a demonstration today or Tuesday?

Mr. Pride: How long would your demonstration take?

Mrs. Norman: I only need one hour. When would it be convenient for me to bring the cart in for your executives to try out?

Mr. Pride: There really isn't any good time.

Mrs. Norman: That's true. Therefore, the sooner we get to show you a Dyno cart, the sooner your management group can see its benefits. How about next Tuesday? I could be here at 8:00 and we could go over this item just before your weekly management group meeting. I know you usually have a meeting Tuesdays at 9:00 because I tried to call on you a few weeks ago and your secretary told me you were in the weekly management meeting.

Mr. Pride: Well, we could do it then.

Mrs. Norman: Fine, I'll be here. Your executives will really be happy.

I. Listen to the conversation and choose the best answers to the questions you hear.

1. What does Mrs. Norman, the salesperson try to sell? (C)

2. What position does Mr. Pride most likely hold in his company? (A)

3. What is the Dyno cart designed for? (C)

4. When will the product demonstration be conducted? (D)

5. Which of the following is NOT mentioned as one of the Dyno cart's benefits? (A)

II. Listen to the conversation again and decide whether the following statements are true or false. Write T for true and F for false in the brackets.

1. (T) 2. (F) 3. (F) 4. (F) 5. (T) 6. (T) 7. (F) 8. (F) 9. (T) 10. (T)

Passage

Tapescript

People often think of sales careers because they have heard that salespersons can earn good salaries in selling their products. They probably think anyone can sell. These people have not considered all of the facts. A sales job has high rewards because it also has many important responsibilities. Companies do not pay high salaries for nothing. A sales career involves great challenges that require highly qualified individuals.

To a salesperson, love of his job means love of selling. A successful salesperson is an individual who loves selling, finds it exciting, and is strongly convinced that the product being sold offers something of great value.

To be successful, a salesperson should be willing to work hard, work smart and then work some more. He/she usually has to sacrifice some time with his/her family to make sales calls, presentations, etc. The harder he works, the luckier he gets.

To be successful, a salesperson should have a higher desire for success. He wants to excel. The need to achieve involves persistence. With persistence often comes the ability to go beyond normal limits.

Salespeople credit a positive attitude toward their companies, products, customers, themselves, and life as major reasons for their success. Procrastination is their greatest enemy. To succeed, they should be enthusiastic, confident, and constantly think of themselves as successful. Sure, salespeople have times when things do not go as they wish. Yet their positive mental attitude helps overcome periodic problems.

To succeed, a salesperson never stops learning. He learns through study, such as reading which does not end after college. Many professionals have extensive personal libraries. In other words, successful salespeople are those who place great emphasis on being thoroughly knowledgeable in all aspects of their business, for they know knowledge is power while enthusiasm pulls the switch.

A successful salesperson knows how to guard his/her time. He knows the Pareto principle very well, which is named after the 19th-century economist, Vilfredo Pareto, who found that in any human activity, the biggest results usually arise from a small number of factors. A successful salesperson defines the specific results that practically guarantee success. Then they ruthlessly arrange daily priorities to invest 80 percent of their time behind the 20 percent of work with the greatest results payout. Time is limited and effective time management is a must.

A successful salesperson is a good listener who asks questions to uncover the prospect's needs and then listens as the prospect answers and states his needs.

A successful salesperson respects his/her customers and is ready to serve them all the time.

A successful salesperson knows very well that it is an important component of being successful that he is in shape to deal with today and tomorrow. He/she believes that his status of body and soul directly influence his/her performance level.

I. Listen to the passage and decide whether the following statements are true or false. Write T for true and F for false in the brackets.

1. (T)   2. (T)   3. (F)   4. (F)   5. (T)   6. (F)   7. (F)   8. (T)   9. (F)   10. (T)

II. Listen to the passage again and complete the following notes with what you hear.

What makes a successful salesperson

A successful salesperson

☐ loves (1) <u>his/her job or selling</u>;

☐ is willing to (2) <u>work hard, work smart and then work some more</u>;

☐ has (3) <u>a higher desire for success</u>;

☐ is enthusiastic, confident, and constantly (4) <u>thinks of himself/herself as successful</u>;

☐ never stops learning and places great emphasis on (5) <u>being thoroughly knowledgeable in all aspects of his/her business</u>;

☐ knows (6) <u>how to guard or manage his/her time effectively</u>;

☐ is (7) <u>a good listener</u> as the prospect answers and states his needs;

☐ respects his/her customers and is ready to (8) <u>serve them all the time</u>;

☐ knows the importance of staying in shape and believes his/her (9) <u>status of body and soul</u> directly influence his/her (10) <u>performance level</u>.

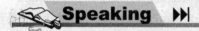 **Speaking** ▶▶

Discussion

For Teachers' Reference

You should not have checked any boxes.

1) Despite all of the training we have had telling us that "Good questions deserve good answers", one of the most common and most damaging mistakes that many salespeople make, day in and day out, is providing in-depth answers before they know why their prospect asked the question. Doing that usually lowers the odds that a sale will happen and most often falls into the category of "Unpaid Consulting". If you sometimes catch yourself answering too many questions too soon, reprogram your self-talk with the core belief that says "The intent of their question is always more important than my answer".

2) There are really only four possible outcomes to any sales call. A real "Yes". A real "No". A real "Future". And a "Let's Pretend". And you know which one is completely unacceptable ...

the "Let's Pretend". Real No's happen usually because for some reason there is just not a fit. Everyone is not a prospect.

3) Most salespeople never achieve their true potential, or even fail, not because they can't sell, but because they won't. And unfortunately, most often, they never even recognize those hidden weaknesses that are causing the frustrations and the failures and preventing them from consistently doing what they know is right.

4) Selling is not telling. People buy for personal, compelling and emotional reasons. Educating should be saved for the presentation. Unpaid consulting is not only unprofitable; it also greatly reduces the odds of actually closing the sale.

5) Many of the traditionally trained salespeople still believe that asking a prospect for the order is somehow better than helping them to discover that they may truly find a win-win outcome with your solution. If you do it right, the only close you'll ever need to use is "What do we need to do next?".

6) Right idea, but a bad way to ask the question. Most times when a salesperson asks, "Are you the decision-maker?", it hooks the prospect's ego. And along with it, the answer, "Of course I am." The A-Player salesperson learns to start with questions about the prospect's decision-making process first, and gets down to the who questions later.

SECTION B   Sales Techniques

Pre-listening ▶▶

Background Information

1. Key to great sales presentations

If your business depends on selling products or services to other companies, then you and your staff need to make great sales presentations. Here's how to make presentations that show prospective clients exactly what your company can do for them.

Rehearse. Rehearse every aspect of your presentation. Read in front of a mirror to practice eye contact. Practice varying the pace of your reading and the tone of your voice. Rehearse in front of a friend or colleague who can offer constructive criticism. Rehearse for more advice on how to hone your presentation to perfection.

Know your audience. Tailor your presentation to your prospective clients. To do that, consider what they are likely to need from you. Use terminology they will understand and make sure you are familiar with their business jargon. That will help you to establish common ground with them.

Be honest. If you don't know the answer to a question, don't try to answer it. There's nothing wrong with admitting uncertainty. At the same time, be sure to play up your strengths — including the ability to learn what you must to serve the client's needs.

2. Components of a sales presentation

The introduction. Begin by thanking your prospective clients. Let them know that you are glad to be there and convey how enthusiastic you are about the things you can do for their business. If you had help in preparing your proposal, give a quick word of thanks and acknowledgment to the people who assisted you.

The body. Offer a clear, concise and convincing description of the benefits you can provide to your prospective clients. Be specific and offer concrete examples. Highlight your expertise, the methods you would use to apply it and the benefits that will result from choosing your company.

The conclusion. Summarize the body of your talk. Once again, highlight the likely benefits of doing business with your company. Thank everyone in the audience.

The Q&A. Offer the opportunity to clarify any points in the body of your talk and emphasize again your company's strengths. Try to anticipate important questions before your talk so you can formulate answers. Restate questions so everyone in the audience can hear them, then keep your answers brief and to the point. Remember: If you can't answer a question, don't try.

3. Sales presentation methods

There are four sales presentation methods most usually used by salespeople in the business world: memorized, formula, need-satisfaction and problem-solution selling methods. The basic difference between the four methods is the percentage of the conversation controlled by the salesperson. In the first two selling techniques, the salesperson normally has a monopoly on the conversation while the rest allow for greater buyer-seller interaction.

The *memorized presentation* is also called the canned sales presentation in which the salesperson does 80 to 90 percent of the talking and occasionally allows the prospect to respond to predetermined questions. He/she concentrates on discussing the product and the benefits, concluding the pitch with a purchase request. This method can be used where time is short and the product is simple, for example, in door-to-door or telephone selling of books, cooking utensils and cosmetics. However, it requires the salesperson to ask for the order several times, which may be interpreted by the prospect as high-pressure selling.

The *formula presentation*, often referred to as the persuasive selling presentation, obtains its name from the salesperson using attention, interest, desire, and action procedure of developing and giving the sales presentation. It is effective in repeat purchase or when you know or have already determined the needs of the prospect.

The *need-satisfaction presentation* is designed as a flexible, interactive sales presentation, the most challenging and creative form of selling. It consists of two phases: the need-development phase and the need-fulfillment phase, also called the need-awareness phase and the need-satisfaction phase. It may be the most appropriate method when information needs to be gathered from the prospect as is often the case in selling industrial products.

The last method, the *problem-solving sales presentation* method is a customized one, which involves an in-depth study of a prospect's needs. It can be used in selling highly complex or technical products such as insurance, industrial equipment, accounting systems, office equipment and computers.

4. Steps in the selling process

The selling process has six key steps. Virtually every sales interaction will follow these steps, whether it lasts several minutes or several months.

Step One: Prospecting. Finding qualified prospects for your products or services is the natural first step in the sales process. Once you've identified prospects, you'll want to learn all you can before you approach them. "Fact finding" will help you:

❑ determine your sales approach and plan your sales calls;

❑ determine which products and services best suit particular prospects;

❑ uncover reasons why you should not pursue some prospects, saving you valuable time and resources.

Step Two: The Initial Contact. When the prospect initiates the contact, prospects will visit you during normal business hours if you have a store or business location. If you do not have a store, they might contact you by phone, mail, email, or through your Web site to request information, ask questions and/or to make a purchase. When it is you who initiate the contact, one of the most common initial contacts is a "cold call", which refers to a contact made with prospects who have not indicated they desire the call. These tips may help you turn cold calls into warm prospects.

❑ First, determine your objective and the purpose of your call. Your purpose may be to make an appointment, to inform, to question, to talk to a certain person, to sell, etc. Additionally, determine if you want to close the sale on the first call or simply pave the way for a later call or sales presentation.

❑ Try to do a little homework before the call. If you know someone who may have insight or information about the prospect, call him or her.

❑ Send a fax or mail some information prior to the cold call and make reference to the information in the call.

❑ When you're ready to make the call, make sure you have all the materials you need at hand. For example, if the purpose of your call is to make an appointment, have your appointment book open and a working pen or pencil in front of you.

❑ State your purpose quickly — within 15 seconds.

❑ Get prospects interested by asking questions that make them think.

Step Three: Presentation. Many sales people feel the most exciting part of the sales process is presenting products or services to prospects. A few tips about sales presentations are listed below.

❑ Don't be afraid to be excited about your product. If you're not, your prospect certainly won't be.

❑ During the presentation part of your sales process, focus on benefits of your products and services. Benefits are different from features, which are characteristics such as size, color and functionality. Benefits answer the customer's question: "What's in it for me?" Benefits are what cause people to buy.

❑ Set objectives for sales calls. Write the objectives on index cards and keep the cards handy to make notes as you think of items to add.

❑ Be on time for sales appointments. If you are unavoidably delayed, call before the appointment to let the prospect know your estimated time of arrival.

❑ Be prepared for your call. Have your sales kits, sales tools and answers ready.

❑ Be relaxed during sales calls. If you're tense you might make prospects uncomfortable, which is a state that's not conducive to buying.

❑ Let prospects talk 90 percent of the time; they'll tell you how to sell to them. You just need to listen.

❑ Use testimonials. Your best selling tool is a reference from a satisfied customer.

❑ Don't be afraid to ask for the business.

❑ Invite prospects to interact with products. For example, encourage customers to try a watch on, operate a device or smell the bubble bath.

❑ Limit the choices during a sales presentation. Most experts advise sales people to show prospects only three options at a time. Too many options may prove overwhelming and prospects won't choose anything!

❑ Adapt your sales presentation to your prospect. For example, a travel agent would provide different types of information about a cruise package to a couple going on their first cruise rather than to a couple that has been on dozens of cruises.

❑ Rate yourself after sales calls. Determine what you did well and what you need to improve upon. Develop action steps for improvement.

❑ Follow up, follow up, and follow up. It often takes five to 10 exposures to get a sale.

Step Four: Handling Objections. During the sales process, you'll probably meet a familiar obstacle: the objection. Objections are prospects' statements about why they don't plan to buy your product or service. It may be a statement such as, "I don't need that service right now." or, "I already buy those products from ABC Company." Don't be afraid of an objection; it's simply part of the sales process. In fact, objections oftentimes are a signal that the sale is progressing and you're getting closer to "yes". Objections are oftentimes a prospect's way of saying: "I'm not convinced yet; but I could be!" Anticipate objections. Rehearse answers to standard objections. Learn to ask questions of prospects to drill down to their real objections.

Step Five: Closing the Sale. Although you should never be shy about "asking for the business," prospects will probably give you some signals when they are ready to become customers. Familiarize yourself with the following readiness signals.

❑ Asking about availability such as, "How soon can someone be here?"

❑ Asking specific questions about rates, prices or statements about affordability.

❑ Asking about features, options, quality, guarantees or warranties.

❑ Asking positive questions about your business.

❑ Asking for something to be repeated.

❑ Making statements about problems with previous vendors; they might be seeking reassurance from you that you won't pose the same problems.

❑ Asking about follow-up service or other products you carry.

❑ Requesting a sample or asking you to repeat a demonstration for them or for others in their company or family.

❑ Asking about other satisfied customers. You should have a list of satisfied customers ready to give to prospects who ask.

❑ You might try these techniques to help prospects make the decision to buy.

❑ Offer an added service, such as delivery.

❑ Offer a choice, such as "would you prefer the blue or green one?"

❑ Imply that you have the sale with positive statements such as: "I'll have it gift-wrapped and delivered for you."

❑ Offer an incentive such as a 10 percent discount for purchases made now.

❑ Create an urgency because the item is the last one in stock.

❑ Lead the customer through a series of minor decisions that are easier to make rather than one large decision. For example, a travel agent may get to "yes" through a series of questions such as: "Would June or July be best for travel? Would you prefer a five-day or seven-day cruise?"

❑ Don't give up too soon. Learn to understand prospects' buying styles; some people take longer than others to make a decision.

Step Six: Follow-Up and Service after the Sale. Some sales people believe that follow-up after the sale is just as important as making the sale. That's when your relationship with a customer really takes hold. Relationship marketing during the sales process allows you to make additional use of your initial investment of time and money spent selling to each customer. Good follow-up and service after the sale will:

❑ establish and maintain your good reputation;

❑ build goodwill among customers and in the community;

❑ and most importantly, generate repeat and referral business.

Listening ▶▶

Conversation

•••

Tapescript

Salesperson:	This is a beautiful old building, Mr. Bell. Have you been here long?
Buyer:	About 10 years. Before we moved here, we were in one of those ugly glass and concrete towers. Now you wanted to talk to me about office security.
Salesperson:	Yes, Mr. Bell. Tell me, do you have a burglar alarm system at present?
Buyer:	No, we don't. We've never had a break-in here.
Salesperson:	I see. Could you tell me what's the most valuable item in your building?
Buyer:	Probably the computer.
Salesperson:	And is it fairly small?
Buyer:	Yes, amazingly, it's not much bigger than a typewriter.
Salesperson:	Would it be difficult to run your business without it — if it were stolen, for example?
Buyer:	Oh, yes, that would be quite awkward.
Salesperson:	Could you tell me a bit more about the problem you would face without your computer?
Buyer:	It would be very inconvenient in the short term for our accounts and records people, but I suppose we could manage until our insurance gave us a replacement.
Salesperson:	But without a computer, wouldn't your billing to customers suffer?
Buyer:	Not if we got the replacement quickly.
Salesperson:	You said the computer itself is insured. Do you happen to know if the software, I mean, the programs, your customers' files, is also insured?
Buyer:	I don't believe so; our insurance covers the equipment only.
Salesperson:	And do you keep backup records somewhere else — in the bank, for example?
Buyer:	No, we don't.
Salesperson:	Mr. Bell, in my experience, software isn't left behind after a theft. Wouldn't it be a serious problem to you if that software were taken?
Buyer:	Yes, you're quite right, I suppose. Redevelopment would certainly cost a lot. The original programs were expensive.
Salesperson:	And even worse, because software development can take a long time, wouldn't that hold up your billings to customers?
Buyer:	We could always do that manually.

Salesperson:	What effect would that have on your processing costs?
Buyer:	I see your point. It would certainly be expensive to run a manual system as well as being inconvenient.
Salesperson:	And if you lost your software, wouldn't it also make it harder to process customer orders?
Buyer:	Yes, I don't have much contact with that part of the business, but without order processing and stock control I'm sure we would grind to a halt in a matter of days.
Salesperson:	Are there any other items in the building that would be hard to replace if stolen?
Buyer:	Some of the furnishings. I would hate to lose this antique clock, for example. In fact, most of our furnishings would be very hard to replace in the same style.
Salesperson:	So, if you lost them, wouldn't it hurt the character of your office?
Buyer:	Yes, it would be damaging. We've built a gracious and civilized image here, and without it we would be like dozens of other people in our furnishing business — the glass and concrete image.
Salesperson:	This may sound like an odd question, but how many doors do you have at ground level?
Buyer:	Let me see … uh … six.
Salesperson:	And ground level windows?
Buyer:	About 10 or a dozen.
Salesperson:	So there are 16 or 18 points where a thief could break in, compared with 1 or 2 points in the average glass and concrete office. Doesn't that concern you?
Buyer:	Put that way, it does. I suppose we're not very secure. How much is your industrial security system?

I. Listen to the conversation and choose the best answers to the questions you hear.

1. What does the salesperson sell?   (B)

2. Where is Mr. Bell's company located?   (C)

3. What line of business is Mr. Bell's company in?   (A)

4. Which of the following will be compensated for by the insurance company?   (B)

5. What can be learned from the conversation?   (B)

II. Listen to the conversation again and answer the following questions with what you hear.

1. Why does Mr. Bell fail to see the point in having a burglar alarm system at first?
   <u>There has never been a break-in in his office building.</u>

2. What is the most valuable item in Mr. Bell's office building?
   <u>The computer.</u>

3. According to Mr. Bell, who would suffer most without the computer?

<u>People doing accounts and records.</u>

4. What would be difficult to replace if stolen?

<u>Computer software (or: Computer programs, customers' files) and some of the office furnishings.</u>

5. Why would it be a serious problem to the company if the software were taken?

<u>Software redevelopment not only costs a lot of money, but also takes a long time, which would hold up billing customers and make it harder to process customer orders.</u>

6. What would be the disadvantages of processing customers' orders and bills manually?

<u>It would be expensive as well as inconvenient to run a manual system.</u>

7. How would the loss of some furnishing items affect the company?

<u>It would be damaging to the character/image of the office.</u>

8. What do you think of Mr. Bell, the buyer's consciousness of office security?

<u>Mr. Bell is not fully aware of the seriousness of the consequences of a possible office break-in.</u>

Passage

Tapescript

Prospecting is the first step in the selling process. A prospect is a qualified person or an organization that has the potential to buy your product or service. Prospecting is the lifeblood of sales because it identifies potential customers. The reasons that a salesperson must look constantly for new prospects are to increase sales and to replace customers that will be lost over time.

A prospect should not be confused with a lead. The name of a person or an organization that might be a prospect is referred to as a lead. Once the lead has been qualified, the lead becomes a prospect. As a salesperson, you can ask yourself three questions to determine if an individual or organization is a qualified prospect: (1) Does the prospect have the money to buy? (2) Does the prospect have the authority to buy? (3) Does the prospect have the desire to buy?

A simple way to remember this qualifying process is to think of the word MAD. A true prospect must have the financial resources, money or credit, to pay and the authority to make the buying decision. The prospect also should desire your product. Sometimes an individual or organization may not recognize a need for your product. It's a challenge for a salesperson to create a desire in the prospect for the product.

Locating leads and qualifying prospects are important activities for salespeople. Sources of prospects can be many and varied or few and similar, depending on the service or goods sold by the salesperson. Naturally, persons selling different services and goods might not use the same sources for prospects. A salesperson of oil-field pipe supplies would make extensive use of various industry directories in a search for names of drilling companies. A life insurance salesperson could use personal acquaintances and present customers as sources of prospects. A pharmaceutical salesperson would scan the local newspaper looking for announcements of new physicians and hospitals, medical office, and clinical laboratory openings, whereas a sales representative for a company such as General Mills or Quaker Oats would watch announcements of constructions for new grocery stores and shopping centers.

Frequently salespeople, especially new ones, have difficulty prospecting. The actual methods by which a salesperson obtains prospects may vary. Some most popular prospecting methods are listed here below.

The first method is cold canvassing, which is based on the law of averages. For example, if past experience reveals that 1 person out of 10 will buy a product, then if the salesperson contacts as many leads as possible, there would be a certain percentage of people approaching to buy the product.

The second method is called endless chain, which is also known as customer referral. Usually, a satisfied prospect tends to refer the salesperson to other customers. You must have heard that a satisfied customer is always the best advertising.

Picking up orphaned customers is also a good try. Sometimes, salespeople leave their companies and the customers they leave behind are orphaned. These orphans are great prospects.

Another commonly used method is to make prospect lists. Prepare a list of what your ideal prospect looks like and find out where you can most likely find the people who fit your prospect profiles.

And lastly, you can submit articles about your field or industry to journals, trade magazines, and newspapers. Convince the editor that you are an expert. Then you become the one people contact when they are ready to buy.

I. Listen to the passage and choose the best answers to the questions you hear.

1. What does prospecting in sales refer to?   (B)
2. How is a lead related to a prospect?   (D)
3. What challenge will a salesperson face in the process of qualifying prospects?   (B)
4. Which of the following is NOT true about the sources of prospects?   (B)
5. What can be concluded from the passage?   (B)

II. Listen to the passage again and complete the following notes with what you hear.

Prospecting in Sales

Reasons for constant prospecting:
- ❑ to (1) <u>increase sales</u>
- ❑ to (2) <u>replace customers that will be lost over time</u>

Questions asked to determine a qualified prospect:
- ❑ Does the prospect have (3) <u>the money</u> to buy?
- ❑ Does the prospect have (4) <u>the authority</u> to buy?
- ❑ Does the prospect have (5) <u>the desire</u> to buy?

Examples of varied prospect sources:
- ❑ An oil-field pipe salesperson may use:
  (6) <u>various industry directories</u>
- ❑ A life insurance salesperson may use:
  (7) <u>personal acquaintances</u> and (8) <u>present customers</u>
- ❑ A pharmaceutical salesperson may use:
  announcements of new physicians and hospital, medical office, and (9) <u>clinical laboratory openings</u> in local newspapers
- ❑ A sales representative for food companies may use:
  announcements of (10) <u>constructions for new grocery stores and shopping centers</u>

Common prospecting methods:
- ❑ Cold canvassing: contacting (11) <u>as many leads as possible</u>
- ❑ Endless chain: turning to (12) <u>a satisfied prospect</u> for other customers
- ❑ Orphaned customers: picking up customers left behind by (13) <u>salespeople who leave their companies</u>
- ❑ Prospect lists: preparing a list of prospect profiles and finding out (14) <u>where you can most likely find your ideal prospects</u>
- ❑ Get published: Getting articles published and becoming (15) <u>an expert that people contact when they are ready to buy</u>

Further Listening

Short Recordings

Tapescript

Item 1

PARIS — The world's biggest cosmetics group L'Oreal posted a 13.5 percent rise in 2003 profit on Friday, its 19th consecutive year of double-digit growth, helped by product launches and strength in emerging markets. The company, whose make-up and hair care products can be found on bathroom shelves around the world, said full-year net operating profit rose to €1.65 billion ($2.1 billion) from €1.46 billion a year ago. Last year, L'Oreal battled an economic slowdown and adverse currency movements, but its performance was helped by what Chairman Lindsay Owen-Jones called "spectacular progress" in emerging markets as well as by innovation, new products and tight cost controls.

L'Oreal is engaged in the cosmetics industry, as well as in the luxury goods and dermatological and pharmaceutical fields. L'Oreal's cosmetics products include hair color, skincare and sun protection products, makeup, perfumes and toiletries.

Item 2

SEATTLE — Coffee drinkers cashing in holiday gift cards helped fuel 13 percent sales gains at Starbucks cafes in February, the company said on Wednesday. Seattle-based the world's largest coffee shop chain, reported net revenues of $380 million for the four weeks ended Feb. 22, up 32 percent from the same period a year earlier. The same-store gains easily topped the company's long-standing forecast for average increases of 3 percent to 7 percent, thanks to a number of new strategies boosting brand loyalty and speeding customers through long lines. The Starbucks card, an increasingly popular prepaid purchase card, was a major driver behind the sales gains.

Starbucks Corporation purchases, roasts and sells high quality whole bean coffees, rich-brewed coffees, Italian-style espresso beverages, cold blended beverages and a variety of pastries.

Item 3

CHICAGO — Wal-Mart Stores Inc. said Monday it still expects to reach the high end of its February sales forecast, boosted by strong demand for clothes. On a recorded message covering sales through Feb. 21, Wal-Mart said men's, women's and girls' apparel were among the best-selling categories last week. Wal-Mart said its clothing inventory was lower than at the same time last year, and its early spring apparel sales were "encouraging". A year ago, weak clothing demand left the retailer with heavy stockpiles, which cut into profits. This year, unusually cold January weather across much of the United States helped Wal-Mart and other retailers clear out winter clothing supplies.

Wal-Mart Stores, Inc. operates discount department stores, warehouse membership clubs and superstores.

Item 4

NEW YORK — Luxury jeweler Tiffany & Co. said Wednesday its quarterly profit rose 24 percent, beating expectations, on sharp increases in holiday sales and strong demand for diamonds. Tiffany's net income in the fourth quarter was $110.4 million, or 74 cents a share, compared with $89.3 million, or 60 cents, a year earlier. Tiffany said holiday sales of the same store rose 16 percent in the United States and 10 percent worldwide. The figures came as the luxury goods sector enjoyed its best holiday season in four years, with a rebounding economy prompting consumers to spend more on high-end items. Tiffany shares closed at $37.12 on the New York Stock Exchange Tuesday.

Tiffany & Co. designs, manufactures, distributes and retails fine jewelry, timepieces, sterling silverware, china, crystal, writing instruments, scarves and ties.

Item 5

CHICAGO — Ketchup maker H.J. Heinz Co. said Tuesday that its fiscal third-quarter earnings rose as it rolled out a host of new foods to reinvigorate sluggish areas such as frozen foods. The company also said it eliminated some unprofitable products. The Pittsburgh-based company said it earned $202.2 million, or 57 cents a share, in its fiscal third quarter ended Jan. 28, compared with $151.6 million, or 43 cents a share, in the year-ago period. Revenue fell to $2.10 billion from $2.11 billion, as the benefit of the weak dollar in Europe and Asia, which boosts the value of overseas sales when they are converted into dollar, were offset by price reductions on some foods.

HNZ and its subsidiaries manufacture and market an extensive line of processed food products throughout the world, including ketchup & sauces/condiments, pet food, baby food, frozen potato products and low calorie products.

I. In this section, you will hear five short recordings. For each piece, decide which contributes most to the sales increase of each company.

1. L'Oreal	B	A. Price reduction
2. Starbucks	F	B. Growth in emerging markets
3. Wal-Mart	E	C. Sales promotion
4. Tiffany	D	D. Growth in holiday sales
5. H.J. Heinz	G	E. Demand for winter clothing
		F. Prepaid purchase card
		G. Product restructuring
		H. Customer service

II. Listen to the five recordings again and complete the following notes with what you hear.

1. L'Oreal, the world's (1) biggest cosmetics group, announced a 13.5 percent rise in 2003 profit on Friday, its 19th consecutive year of double-digit growth. In spite of (2) an economic slowdown and (3) adverse currency movements, L'Oreal's full-year net operating profit rose to €1.65 billion ($2.1 billion) from €1.46 billion a year ago, helped by (4) its progress in emerging markets as well as by innovation, new products and (5) tight cost controls.

2. Thanks to new strategies (6) boosting brand loyalty and (7) speeding customers through long lines, and above all, the popularity of the Starbucks card, Seattle-based the world's (8) largest coffee shop chain, Starbucks, reported net revenues of $380 million for the four weeks ended Feb. 22, up 32 percent from the same period a year earlier.

3. The (9) unusually cold January weather across much of the United States boosted strong demand for clothes and helped Wal-Mart and other retailers (10) clear out winter clothing supplies. Wal-Mart Stores Inc. expects to reach the high end of its February sales forecast and said that men's, women's and girls' apparel were among (11) the best-selling categories last week.

4. Due to (12) sharp increases in holiday sales and (13) strong demand for diamonds, luxury jeweler Tiffany & Co. saw its quarterly profit rise 24 percent. Tiffany's net income in the fourth quarter was (14) $110.4 million, or 74 cents a share, compared with (15) $89.3 million, or 60 cents, a year earlier. Tiffany shares closed at (16) $37.12 on the New York Stock Exchange Tuesday.

5. By (17) bringing out a host of new foods and (18) eliminating some unprofitable products, the Pittsburgh-based Ketchup maker H.J. Heinz Co. earned (19) $202.2 million, or 57 cents a share, in its fiscal third quarter ended Jan. 28, compared with (20) $151.6 million, or 43 cents a share, in the year-ago period.

Home Listening

Business News

Tapescript

South Korea's Central Bank cut the country's key interest rate this week by a quarter of a percentage point to 4 percent. The move is aimed at stimulating the economy, which is slowing due to weak consumption and the regional slump in travel and sales caused by Severe Acute Respiratory Syndrome.

JM Yun is head of research at the Korean Exchange Bank. He says the rate cut may not do much for the economy — because the problem is not a shortage of cash in the financial system.

"The sluggishness of the Korean economy lies not in the absence of money supply but in the shortage of demand."

South Korea officials say the country has lost at least 450 million dollars from a truck drivers' strike at the country's busiest port. The strike at Busan ended Thursday after the government agreed to reduce expressway tolls for drivers, and to use subsidies to cushion the effects of a fuel tax increase.

Japanese electronics giant Casio says it returned to profitability last year. The company posted a net profit of 49 million dollars in the year to March, reversing last year's loss of about 210 million dollars. Casio executives say cost cutting and a boost in demand for digital cameras and mobile phones helped lift the bottom line.

Yahoo Japan, the country's leading Internet portal, says its earnings doubled in the first quarter of the year. Net profits for April to June totaled $38 million, up eight percent from the previous quarter. The company attributes that performance to brisk growth in online advertising and auction businesses.

Vietnam Airlines has awarded ABN Amro and Citibank a 440 million dollar finance contract this week for the purchase of new aircraft. It is the first deal guaranteed by the US Export-Import Bank since the two countries signed a bilateral trade pact in July 2000.

Listen to the business news report and complete the notes with what you hear.

Asia Business Briefs	
South Korea	☹ In order to stimulate the economy which is slowing due to (1) <u>weak consumption</u> and (2) <u>the regional slump in travel and sales</u> caused by SARS，South Korea's Central Bank cut the country's key interest rate this week by a quarter of a percentage point to 4 percent.

continued

South Korea	☹ The interest rate cut may not do much for the economy because the sluggishness of the Korean economy lies not in (3) <u>the absence of money supply</u> but in (4) <u>the shortage of demand</u>. ☹ (5) <u>A truck drivers' strike</u> at the country's busiest port, Busan, ended Thursday after the government agreed to reduce (6) <u>expressway tolls for drivers</u>, and to use subsidies to (7) <u>cushion the effects of a fuel tax increase</u>.
Japan	☺ Thanks to (8) <u>cost cutting</u> and (9) <u>a boost in demand for digital cameras and mobile phones</u>, Japanese electronics giant Casio posted (10) <u>a net profit of 49 million dollars</u> in the year to March, reversing last year's loss of about 210 million dollars. ☺ Thanks to brisk growth in (11) <u>online advertising</u> and (12) <u>auction businesses</u>, Yahoo Japan, the country's (13) <u>leading Internet portal</u>, says its earnings doubled in the first quarter of the year.
Vietnam	☺ Vietnam Airlines has signed a finance contract with ABN Amro and Citibank this week for (14) <u>the purchase of new aircraft</u>, which is the first deal guaranteed by the US Export-Import Bank since the two countries signed (15) <u>a bilateral trade pact</u> in July 2000.

Unit 5

Negotiation

Listen to the following short paragraph and fill in the blanks with what you hear.

Negotiation is the process of two individuals or groups (1) <u>reaching joint agreement about differing needs or ideas</u>. It applies knowledge from the fields of (2) <u>communications, sales, marketing, psychology, sociology, politics, and conflict resolution</u>. Whenever an economic transaction takes place or (3) <u>a dispute is settled</u>, negotiation occurs; for example, when (4) <u>consumers purchase automobiles</u> or businesses negotiate salaries with employees. The (5) <u>effectiveness of various negotiation strategies</u> can vary based on cultural differences. In international negotiations, obstacles arise when negotiating teams possess (6) <u>conflicting perspectives, tactics, and negotiating styles</u>. Negotiators often assume that shared beliefs exist when, in reality, they do not. These cultural factors affect (7) <u>the pace of negotiations</u>, negotiating strategies, (8) <u>degree of emphasis on personal relationships</u>, emotional aspects, decision making and contractual and administrative elements.

Listening & Speaking

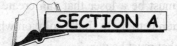

SECTION A Negotiation Basics

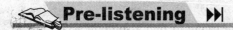

Pre-listening ▶▶

Background Information

1. The negotiation process

Negotiation refers to the process of bargaining that precedes an agreement. Successful negotiation generally results in a contract between the parties. Stages in the negotiation process are (1) orientation and fact finding, (2) resistance, (3) reformulation of strategies, (4) hard bargaining and decision making, (5) agreement, and (6) follow-up. For example, a consumer purchasing an automobile investigates price and performance, and then negotiates with an agent regarding price and delivery date. Resistance surfaces as pricing and delivery expectations are negotiated. Strategies are reformulated as the parties determine motivation and constraints. Key issues surface as hard bargaining begins. Problems surface, and solutions are created to counter pricing and delivery problems. After details are negotiated, the agreement is ratified. After the sale, the agent may follow up with the buyer to build a relationship and set the stage for future purchase and negotiation. The six stages of the process would be approached differently depending on where the negotiators reside on the style continuum. Negotiating is the process by which two or more parties with different needs and goals work to find a mutually acceptable solution to an issue.   Because negotiating is an interpersonal process, each negotiating situation is different, and influenced by each party's skills, attitudes and style. We often look at negotiating as unpleasant, because it implies conflict, but negotiating need not be characterized by bad feelings or angry behavior.   Understanding more about the negotiation process allows us to manage our negotiations with confidence and increases the chance that the outcomes will be positive for both parties.

2. Barriers to successful negotiation

Viewing negotiation as confrontational. Negotiation need not be confrontational. In fact effective negotiation is characterized by the parties working together to find a solution, rather than each party trying to WIN the contest of wills. Keep in mind the attitude that you take in negotiation will set the tone for the interaction. If you are confrontational, you will have a fight on your hands.

Trying to win at all costs. If you "win", there must be a loser that can create more difficulty down the road. The best perspective in negotiation is to try to find a solution where both parties "win". Try not to view negotiation as a contest that must be won.

Becoming emotional. It's normal to become emotional during negotiation that is important. However, as we get more emotional, we are less able to channel our negotiating behavior in constructive ways. It is important to maintain control.

Not trying to understand the other person. Since we are trying to find a solution acceptable to both parties, we need to understand the other person's needs and wants with respect to the issue. If we don't know what the person needs or wants, we will be unable to negotiate properly. Often, when we take the time to find out about the other person, we discover that there is no significant disagreement.

Focusing on personalities, not issues. Particularly with people we don't like much, we have a tendency to get off track by focusing on how difficult or obnoxious the person seems. Once this happens, effective negotiation is impossible. It is important to stick to the issues, and put aside our degree of like or dislike for the individual.

Blaming the other person. In any conflict or negotiation, each party contributes, for better or worse. If you blame the other person for the difficulty you will create an angry situation. If you take responsibility for the problem, you will create a spirit of cooperation.

3. Negotiation tips

Solicit the other's perspective. In a negotiating situation, use questions to find out what the other person's concerns and needs might be. You might try: What do you need from me on this? Or what are your concerns about what I am suggesting/asking? When you hear the other person express their needs or concerns, use listening responses to make sure you hear correctly.

State your needs. The other person needs to know what you need. It is important to state not only what you need but why you need it. Often disagreement may exist regarding the method for solving an issue, but not about the overall goal.

Prepare options beforehand. Before entering into a negotiating session, prepare some options that you can suggest if your preferred solution is not acceptable. Anticipate why the other person may resist your suggestion, and be prepared to counter with an alternative.

Don't argue. Negotiating is about finding solutions and arguing is about trying to prove the other person wrong. We know that when negotiating turns into each party trying to prove the other one wrong, no progress gets made. Don't waste time arguing. If you disagree with something, state your disagreement in a gentle but assertive way. Don't demean the other person or get into a power struggle.

Consider timing. There are good times to negotiate and bad times. Bad times include those situations where there is: a high degree of anger on either side, preoccupation with something else, a high level of stress, or tiredness on one side or the other. Time negotiations to avoid these times. If they arise during negotiations a time-out or rest period is in order, or perhaps rescheduling to a better time.

4. Negotiating desirable outcomes

You may not realize it, but you are involved in negotiation a good part of every day. Any negotiation — whether it involves settling on the price of a product or service, agreeing to the terms of a job offer, or simply deciding on a bedtime for your children — ends in one of five possible outcomes: (1) lose/lose, in which neither party achieves his goals; (2) lose/win or (3) win/lose, in which one party achieves his or her goals and the other does not; (4) no outcome or draw, in which neither party wins or loses; and (5) win/win, in which the goals of both parties are met.

The Win/Lose Outcome

In some negotiations, you will be the winner and the other party will be the loser. At first, it may seem that this is the ideal situation for you. But think about it. If you have ever lost a negotiation, you know the feeling is not pleasant. A significant problem with a win/lose outcome is that one person walks away with unmet needs and this person is unlikely to be willing to engage in future negotiations with the other party. Ultimately, this sets up the potential for a lose/lose outcome.

The Win/Win Outcome

The best outcome for almost all negotiations is win/win, when both parties walk away with a positive feeling about achieving their goals. Here are three keys to help you accomplish this ideal situation.

❑ Avoid narrowing your negotiation down to one issue. When you focus on just one issue, there can be only one winner. A common example is arguing over the price of something. To avoid creating a win/lose outcome, you can bring other factors into the negotiation, such as delivery fees, timing, quality, supplemental goods and services, and so on.

❑ Realize that the other party does not have the same needs and wants you do. If you think the other person's goals are exactly the same as yours (for instance, a "good" price, which may mean different things for the two of you), you will have the attitude that the other party's gain is your loss. With that attitude, it is virtually impossible to create a win/win outcome.

❑ Don't assume you know the other party's needs. Negotiators often think they know what the other party wants. Salespeople may assume that buyers want to pay the lowest possible price for a product. But many buyers have other needs that may influence their decision to buy. By asking questions, a skilled salesperson may find, for example, that a buyer's biggest concern is not that he or she pays the lowest price, but that his or her boss perceives the purchase decision as a good one. This knowledge allows the salesperson more negotiating room.

Listening ▶▶

Conversation

Tapescript

Bright Publications, a San Francisco-based company specializing in high-quality color art books, are currently looking for a suitable printer for their next series of books on 21ˢᵗ century world women painters. The series will comprise ten titles. The purchasing manager, Tony Davis, is going to negotiate to get the printing done. Before Tony contacts one of the printers, he is explaining to his boss on some of the competitive quotes he got from three companies.

Tony: Right, here are the three quotes I've got. First of all there's Parker's in Britain. They've quoted for the whole series, that is, $27,500 for all ten titles.

John: What if we use them only for one title?

Tony: I asked them about that, but they indicated that they're not interested.

John: Well, if they're not interested, we'll go somewhere else. How about the next?

Tony: There's a company based in Hong Kong, Conti, as they're called. They quoted $29,000 per title.

John: What about delivery?

Tony: If we have them produce the whole series, they'll deliver our books all free. If they only print one title, they'll charge us for delivery.

John: I see. Then who's the last one?

Tony: A company called Oriona in Italy.

John: Italy? I think that's a bit far away.

Tony: But they're very cheap. Only $21,000 per title.

John: Yes, but if something went wrong, what would happen then? We'd have to fly over there and it wouldn't be cheap at all. No, I'm not happy about that.

Tony flies to Hong Kong and meets the sales director of Conti, Ms. Yip.

Yip: As I mentioned to you on the phone, if we only print the first book in the series, we'll charge you for delivery, but if you give us the contract for the whole series, delivery will be free.

Tony: I understand that quite well. But, you see, if we gave you the contract for the whole series, it would be a big commitment for us. I mean, we don't know your work …

Yip: If you have reservations about that, we can give you plenty of testimonials and references.

Tony: Yes, but even if you have the best references in the world, it's still possible that something could go wrong and we would be left in a rather awkward situation then.

Yip: You may rest assured that nothing will go wrong. Besides, you must realize that if you give us your commitment for all the ten titles, we'll be able to give you a better price for the job.

Tony: That sounds encouraging. What if we gave you the contract for the first title, and if that was satisfactory, we could give you the contract for the next one then?

Yip: What if you gave us the contract for the first title then, and if that's satisfactory, you can give us the contract for the whole series?

Tony: I guess there's no problem about that. Then what about delivery?

Yip: In that way, we'll charge you for delivery on the first title and it'll be all free on the other titles.

Tony: How about charging us for delivery on the first title, but, if we gave you the contract for the whole series, you could credit us for that delivery charge?

Yip: OK. Can we complete the paper work now?

Tony: Ah, I'm afraid I've got another printer to see first, but I'll contact you next week.

Yip: As an added incentive, I'll offer you 5 per cent discount on the first title, if you sign the contract by the end of next week.

Tony: That would be interesting! I'll certainly come back to you at the beginning of next week.

I. Listen to the conversation and choose the best answers to the questions you hear.

1. What is Bright Publications looking for?   (C)

2. Which company quoted the lowest price?   (B)

3. Why does Bright Publications not consider Oriona as its printer?   (D)

4. Why does Tony Davis, the purchasing manager, refuse to give Conti the contract for the whole series?   (C)

5. What can be concluded from the conversation?   (A)

II. Listen to the conversation again and complete the following chart with what you hear.

The Preparation Phase

This is where you work out what you want and which is your priority.

Bright Publications cares most about (1)   ☐ price
(tick the correct option)   quality
                                                        ☐ printer's location

The Debating Phase

You try to find out what the other side wants. Say what you want, but do not say what your final conditions are. Try to find out in what areas the other side may be prepared to move.

Yip obviously wants to get the contract of (2) <u>printing the whole series of ten titles</u>.

Tony gets the message that (3) <u>printing price</u> and (4) <u>delivery charge</u> are the areas where Yip can make some compromise.

The Proposal Phase

This is the point at which you suggest some of the things you could trade. Be patient and listen to the other side's proposals.

If the printing job for the first title is satisfactory, Tony can give (5) <u>the contract for the rest of the titles</u> based on the condition that Conti (6) <u>will cover the delivery charge for the first title</u>.

When Yip offers to sign the contract right away, Tony says he will contact her next week because (7) <u>he has another printer to see</u>.

The Bargaining Phase

This is the part where you indicate what it is you will actually trade.

Yip prompts Tony to sign the agreement as early as possible by (8) <u>offering him 5% discount on printing the first title</u>.

Passage

Tapescript

It is often said that many aspects of our life involve negotiation. Teachers should negotiate lessons with their students. Parents should negotiate with their children about their allowance or holidays. In a working context, negotiations constantly occur between employers and employees on wages and conditions of service; between sales representatives and buyers on prices and contracts; between departments on resource allocation. Negotiations need not have a winner and a loser. In the sense that negotiation is about achieving a result which both sides can benefit from, or at least live with, then there is some truth in all of this.

As a negotiator, your aim should be actively to achieve the desired result or in simpler words — to do business! The essence of negotiating effectively lies in careful preparation, establishing a collaborative climate, and using skills of interpersonal communication, critical thinking and analysis.

Effective preparation is vital if you are to achieve the best results. Successful negotiators have broad and specific objectives and have planned how to achieve these before sitting down at the negotiating table. They can then be proactive and direct the negotiators towards achieving these objectives rather than being merely reactive to the other party's proposals. However, you should also be flexible. Try to identify clearly the areas of agreement, and potential areas of conflict where cooperation or compromise can be used to reach agreement.

The climate in negotiations has a major effect on progress to positive outcomes. Try to create the climate you want. It is formed in a very short time: seconds or minutes. It is affected by the past relationships between the parties, their present expectations, the attitudes, perceptions and skills they bring to the situation. It is affected by the context of the meeting, the location, the seating arrangements, the degree of formality. In the ice-breaking period you should strive to create a climate that is collaborative and businesslike. Friendly verbal communication and non-verbal cues (such as eye-contact) help enormously to create conditions for people to be motivated to collaborate.

The types of negotiating styles we can use can be described in two dimensions as direction and strength. Direction refers to the way we handle information. We can push: give information, make proposals, ignore other people's contributions, criticize, act as an irritator — all valid tactics dependent on the nature and context of the negotiation. Or we can pull: ask questions to obtain information, ask for suggestions, check for understanding, ask for clarification, state our feelings. Strength refers to the flexibility we use to move from our initial positions. We can act hard: we want to win at all costs, we will not concede or retract, will not accept offers — we aim high! Or we can act soft: we concede, we waver, we find it difficult to say no — we aim low. We may act hard on some issues and soft on others: this gives a clear indication of where our preferred outcome priorities lie.

I. Listen to the passage and complete the chart with what you hear.

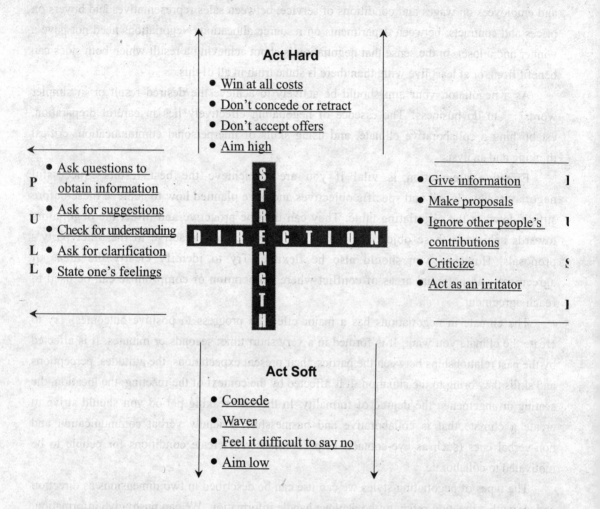

Act Hard

- Win at all costs
- Don't concede or retract
- Don't accept offers
- Aim high

P U L L

- Ask questions to obtain information
- Ask for suggestions
- Check for understanding
- Ask for clarification
- State one's feelings

STRENGTH

DIRECTION

- Give information
- Make proposals
- Ignore other people's contributions
- Criticize
- Act as an irritator

Act Soft

- Concede
- Waver
- Feel it difficult to say no
- Aim low

II. Listen to the passage again and complete the notes with what you hear.

Learn More about Negotiation

What to negotiate:

- ❑ Teachers negotiate with their students about lessons.
- ❑ Parents negotiate with their children about (1) allowance or holidays.
- ❑ Employers negotiate with their employees about (2) wages and conditions of services.
- ❑ Sales representatives negotiate with their buyers on (3) prices and contracts.
- ❑ Departments negotiate on (4) resource allocation.

Essence of successful negotiation:

- ☐ (5) <u>careful preparation</u>
- ☐ (6) <u>establishing a collaborative climate</u>
- ☐ (7) <u>using skills of interpersonal communication</u>
- ☐ (8) <u>critical thinking and analysis</u>

What makes successful negotiators:

- ☐ having broad and specific objectives
- ☐ (9) <u>having planned how to achieve their objectives</u> before sitting down at the negotiating table
- ☐ being proactive and directing the negotiators towards (10) <u>achieving desired objectives</u> rather than (11) <u>being merely reactive to the other party's proposals</u>
- ☐ being flexible
- ☐ trying to identify clearly the areas of agreement, and potential areas of conflict where (12) <u>co-operation or compromise can be used to reach agreement</u>

Factors affecting negotiation climate:

- ☐ (13) <u>the past relationships between the negotiating parties</u>
- ☐ (14) <u>the present expectations of negotiating parties</u>
- ☐ (15) <u>the attitudes, perceptions and skills</u> negotiators bring to the situation
- ☐ (16) <u>the context of the meeting</u>
- ☐ the location
- ☐ (17) <u>the seating arrangements</u>
- ☐ (18) <u>the degree of formality</u>

SECTION B   Negotiation Styles

Pre-listening ▶▶

Background Information

1. Negotiation styles

Two styles of negotiating, competitive and cooperative, are commonly recognized. No negotiation is purely one type or the other; rather, negotiators typically move back and forth between the two styles based on the situation.

On one end of the negotiation continuum is the competitive style. Competitive negotiation is used to divide limited resources; the assumption is that the pie to be divided is finite. Competitive strategies assume a "win-lose" situation in which the negotiating parties have opposing interests. Hostile, coercive negotiation tactics are used to force an advantage. Concessions, distorted communication, confrontational tactics, and emotional ploys are used. Skilled competitive negotiators give away less information while acquiring more information, ask more questions, create strategies to get information, act firm, offer less generous opening offers, are slower to give concessions, use confident body language, and conceal feelings. They are more interested in the bargaining position and bottom line of the other negotiating party, and they prepare for negotiations by developing strategy, planning answers to weak points, and preparing alternate strategies.

On the other end of the negotiating style continuum is cooperative negotiating. Cooperative negotiation is based on a win-win mentality and is designed to increase joint gain; the pie to be divided is perceived as expanding. Attributes include reasonable and open communication; an assumption that common interests, benefits, and needs exist; trust building; thorough and accurate exchange of information; exploration of issues presented as problems and solutions; mediated discussion; emphasis on coalition formation; and a search for creative alternative solutions that bring benefits to all players. The risk in cooperative negotiating is vulnerability to a competitive opponent. Cooperative negotiators require skills in patience; listening; and identification and isolation of cooperative issues, goals, problems, and priorities. Additionally, cooperative negotiators need skills in clarifying similarities and differences in goals and priorities and the ability to trade intelligently, propose many alternatives, and select the best alternative based on quality and mutual acceptability.

2. Cross cultural negotiation

Cross cultural negotiation is one of many specialized areas within the wider field of cross cultural communications. Cross cultural negotiation is about more than just how foreigners close deals. It involves looking at all factors that can influence the proceedings. There are three interconnected aspects that need to be considered before entering into cross cultural negotiation.

The basis of the relationship. In much of Europe and North America, business is contractual in nature. Personal relationships are seen as unhealthy as they can cloud objectivity and lead to complications. In South America and much of Asia, business is personal. Partnerships will only be made with those they know, trust and feel comfortable with. It is therefore necessary to invest in relationship building before conducting business.

Information at negotiations. Western business culture places emphasis on clearly presented and rationally argued business proposals using statistics and facts. Other business cultures rely on similar information but with differences. For example, visual and oral communicators such as the

South Americans may prefer information presented through speech or using maps, graphs and charts.

Negotiation styles. The way in which we approach negotiation differs across cultures. For example, in the Middle East rather than approaching topics sequentially negotiators may discuss issues simultaneously. The Japanese will negotiate in teams and decisions will be based upon consensual agreement. In Asia, decisions are usually made by the most senior figure or head of a family. In China, negotiators are highly trained in the art of gaining concessions. In Germany, decisions can take a long time due to the need to analyze information and statistics in great depth. In the UK, pressure tactics and imposing deadlines are ways of closing deals while in Greece this would backfire.

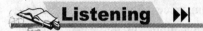

Listening ▶▌

Conversation

Tapescript

Hi-Cam's negotiating team, headed by Mr. Young, arrives at Teltron's head office to negotiate the joint venture for their VC10 and HB2 products with Teltron's CEO, Mr. Hamilton.

Mr. Hamilton:	So what I suggest, gentlemen, is that we get straight down to business.
Mr. Young:	All right. First of all, can I say that we see this only as an exploratory session, Mr. Hamilton? There are two main areas we'd like to clarify this morning. First, to decide the exact scope of the joint venture. And second, to identify the problems that might arise.
Mr. Hamilton:	Fine. We're ready when you are.
Mr. Young:	First of all, may we ask, how many production centers do you envisage and what will be their capacity?
Mr. Hamilton:	We see two centers. One in Europe and one in China. They will both have an annual capacity of 3,000 VC10 units and 20,000 HB2 units.
Mr. Young:	What is the total investment needed?
Mr. Hamilton:	Our present estimates put it at 17 millions for the VC10 and 40 millions for the HB2.
Mr. Young:	So, please, let me get this clear. Do these figures include all costs?
Mr. Hamilton:	They include all further R&D expenditure, plant and working capital costs, plus launch expenses.
Mr. Young:	All right. Have you carried out any cash flow forecasts for this project?
Mr. Hamilton:	Yes, we have. We've prepared some figures that I think are very relevant to this

discussion. They're in the documents here.

Mr. Young scans the documents briefly.

Mr. Hamilton: We're confident we can reach both the VC10 and the HB2 targets, Mr. Young. Let me tell you, we've done our homework on this.

Mr. Young: I'm sure you have. While we're on the subject of R&D, I'd also like to raise the question of patents. My question is, who will own the patents?

Mr. Hamilton: The basic patents will be held by Teltron.

Mr. Young: But part of our investment would be in further R&D. Is that correct?

Mr. Hamilton: That's correct. But what we'd be willing to do here is write off your R&D investment against a token fee to the joint venture.

Mr. Young: Excuse me, Mr. Hamilton. I don't understand.

Mr. Hamilton: I'm sorry. Let me explain. In normal circumstances, Teltron would charge a license fee to the joint venture for basic inventions. In this case, however, you'd be contributing to the development work. So although we'd keep the patents, the license fee would be nominal, say half a per cent.

Mr. Young: OK. Where would this further R&D work be carried out?

Mr. Hamilton: In the interests of continuity we feel that all R&D should remain in the Teltron parent company.

Mr. Young: But this would mean we have no say in the development of this product.

Mr. Hamilton: No. Let me reassure you, gentlemen. Teltron would guarantee full consultation during this phase of the project and ...

Mr. Young: I'm sorry to interrupt, but I want to get this quite clear. Your position is that both the R&D work and patents would remain in Teltron. Is that so?

Mr. Hamilton: Yes, sir. That's our current position.

Mr. Young: I'm afraid, Mr. Hamilton, that's probably as far as we can go for the moment.

I. Listen to the conversation and choose the best answers to the questions you hear.

1. What is not covered at the negotiation meeting?   (A)

2. Which of the following is true about the location and capacity of the production centers?   (C)

3. What is the total investment needed for the VC10 and HB2 products?   (D)

4. How will Teltron ensure its control over the R&D work?   (A)

5. What is Mr. Young most concerned about?   (B)

II. Listen to the conversation again and decide whether the following statements are true or false. Write T for true and F for false in the brackets.

1. (F)   2. (F)   3. (T)   4. (F)   5. (T)   6. (T)   7. (F)   8. (T)   9. (T)   10. (F)

Passage

Tapescript

Negotiations are complex because one is dealing with both facts and people. Negotiators must be aware of the general policy of the company in relation to the issues and they must be familiar with the organizational structure and the decision-making process.

However, awareness of these facts may not be sufficient to reach a successful outcome. Personal, human factors must be taken into account. The strategy adopted in negotiating is influenced by attitudes as well as by a clear logical analysis of the facts and one's interests. The personal needs of the actors in negotiating must therefore be considered. These can include a need for friendship, goodwill, recognition of status and authority, a desire to be appreciated by one's own side and, finally, an occasional need to get home reasonably early on a Friday evening. It is a well-known fact that meetings scheduled on a Friday evening are shorter than those held at other times. Timing can pressure people into reaching a decision and personal factors can become part of bargaining process.

Researchers who have studied the negotiating process recommend separating the people from the problem. This necessity to be hard on the facts and soft on the people can result in sometimes complex style of negotiating languages.

Language varies according to the negotiating styles. In negotiating you can use either a cooperative style or a competitive one. In the cooperative style, both parties can gain something from the negotiation without harming the interest of the other. This type of negotiation is likely to take place between companies when there is a long-standing relationship and common goals are being pursued.

Unfortunately, cooperative style negotiations without a trace of competition are rare. In most negotiating situations there is something to be gained or lost. In competitive negotiating, negotiators see each other as opponents. Knowledge of the other party's needs is used to develop strategies to exploit weaknesses rather than to seek a solution satisfactory to both sides. This style of negotiating may be appropriate in the case of one-off contracts where the aim is to get the best result possible without considering future relationships or the risk of a breakdown in negotiations. Needless to say, the language in this type of discussion may become hostile and threatening even if it remains formal.

In reality most negotiations are a complex blend of cooperative and competitive mode. Skilled negotiators are sensitive to the linguistic signals, as well as the non-verbal ones of facial expressions, gestures and behavior, which show the type of negotiating mode they are in.

I. Listen to the passage and choose the best answers to complete the following statements.

1. C   2. D   3. A   4. B   5. D

II. Listen to the passage again and answer the following questions briefly with what you hear.

1. What are the facts that negotiators must be aware of?

   The general policy of the company in relation to the issues, the organizational structure and the decision-making process.

2. What will influence the strategy to be adopted in negotiating?

   Attitudes as well as a clear logical analysis of the facts and one's interests.

3. What personal needs of the actors in negotiating must be taken into account?

   A need for friendship, goodwill, recognition of status and authority, a desire to be appreciated by one's own side and an occasional need to get home reasonably early on a Friday evening.

4. What do researchers who have studied the negotiating process recommend?

   Separating the people from the problem, that is, to be hard on the facts and soft on the people.

5. What is responsible for the sometimes complex style of negotiating language?

   The need to separate the people from the problem or to be hard on the facts and soft on the people in negotiating.

6. When is the cooperative style of negotiation likely to take place?

   When there is a long-standing relationship and common goals are being pursued between companies.

7. In what case is it appropriate to use the competitive style of negotiation?

   In the case of one-off contracts where the aim is to get the best result possible without considering future relationships or the risk of a breakdown in negotiations.

8. What will skilled negotiators be sensitive to? And why?

   The linguistic signals, as well as the non-verbal ones of facial expressions, gestures and behavior. Because they can show what type of negotiating mode negotiators are in.

Further Listening

Short Recordings

Tapescript

Item 1

NEW YORK — AT&T Corp. Wednesday told analysts it was planning to cut 8 percent of its workforce, or about 4,600 jobs, this year in a drive to cut costs. The nation's largest long-distance telephone company said the moves would save about $400 million this year, and leave it with about 57,000 employees. AT&T Senior Vice President and Chief Financial Officer Thomas Horton said the company cut 18 percent of its workforce in 2003 and saved $800 million.

AT&T provides voice, data & video telecommunications services, including cellular telephone & Internet services, to businesses, consumers and government agencies. AT&T is still the #1 long-distance telephone company in the US with 30.3 million long-distance customers.

Item 2

SEATTLE — Boeing Co. Friday said it would slow development work on an $18 billion US air refueling tanker deal and fire as many as 150 workers due to government reviews of the program. The No. 2 commercial jet maker and No. 2 Pentagon contractor spent $270 million preparing for the tanker program in 2003. Originally designed as a lease of 100 aircraft worth nearly $30 billion, the tanker deal has been repeatedly delayed, first over price concerns and later over ethical issues related to Boeing's hiring of a former Air Force procurement official.

Boeing Co. develops and produces jet transports, military aircraft and space and missile systems through 4 segments: commercial airplanes, military aircraft and missiles, space and communications.

Item 3

NEW YORK — Tyson Foods Inc., the nation's largest meat company, said Friday it will close its Jackson, Mississippi-based chicken processing plant later this year, cutting about 900 jobs. Springdale, Arkansas-based Tyson is in the midst of reducing its work force by about 5 percent, or nearly 6,000 jobs, as it invests roughly $70 million to further automate some of its facilities. The action should have a positive impact on earnings of about 4 cents to 5 cents per share beginning in fiscal 2005, the company said. Production at the plant will be scaled back in phases, Tyson said, and should be completed by July.

Tyson Foods Inc. is the largest meat processing company in the world, serving retail, wholesale, and food service customers in the US and more than 80 countries overseas. In addition to fresh meats, Tyson produces processed and pre-cooked meats, refrigerated and frozen prepared foods, and animal feeds. Don Tyson, son of the founder, controls 80% of Tyson's voting power.

Item 4

LOS ANGELES — Edgar Bronfman Jr.'s newly purchased Warner Music said Tuesday it will lay off about 1,000 people, or 20 percent of its work force, and combine parts of two labels in order to compete effectively in the consolidating marketplace. Bronfman, whose group closed on the $2.6 billion acquisition of Warner Music from Time Warner Inc. Monday, said in a statement that the "painful changes" were essential to help Warner Music remain competitive in a "rapidly evolving marketplace". Despite recent strides to make money from selling music online, the industry still faces rampant piracy and increased competition from other forms of entertainment. Industry insiders said they believed more trimming was likely at Warner Music.

Warner Music Group markets a variety of musical artists through its recording labels Atlantic Records Group and Warner Bros. Records. Its roster of more than 800 artists includes Green Day, Madonna, Faith Hill, and Red Hot Chili Peppers. It also owns stakes in several joint venture labels and owns 50% of music retailing club Columbia House. Its Warner/Chappell publishing unit holds the rights to more than a million songs. Warner Music Group has been purchased by a group led by Thomas H. Lee Partners and Edgar Bronfman, Jr., for $2.6 billion.

Item 5

NEW YORK — The ongoing restructuring at Vivendi Universal Games has claimed the jobs of 350 employees — nearly 40 percent of its US workforce — as the French media company shut down its third division in two months. The company on Monday informed workers at its Bellevue studios that the office would close within two months. The job cuts follow the May shutdown of a pair of longtime development studios. Papyrus Studios and Impressions Games both had solid track records in the industry but were closed last month because they had not been living up to corporate expectations.

Vivendi Universal Games (also known as VU Games) publishes best-selling video game titles for PC, console systems, and the Web. Games include The Simpsons: Hit & Run, The Hulk, Warcraft, and Crash Bandicoot. VU Games owns development studios such as Blizzard Entertainment, Fox Interactive, Knowledge Adventure, and Massive Entertainment. It also co-publishes and distributes games for partners including Interplay, InXile entertainment, and Mythic Entertainment.

I. In this section, you will hear five short recordings. For each piece, decide why each company decided to cut its workforce.

1. AT&T Corp.	D	A. Government supervision
2. Boeing Co.	H	B. Company acquisition
3. Tyson Foods Inc.	F	C. Company restructuring
4. Warner Music	B	D. Cost reduction
5. Vivendi Universal Games	C	E. Recession of economy
		F. Automation of facilities
		G. Decrease in market demand
		H. Suspension of an important deal

II. Listen to the five short recordings again and complete the table with what you hear.

Company	Workforce Cut Fact Sheet
AT&T Corp. *the nation's largest* (1) <u>long-distance telephone company</u>	To cut 8 percent of AT&T workforce, or about (2) <u>4,600</u> jobs, leaving it with about (3) <u>57,000</u> employees, as encouraged by the saving of $800 million from (4) <u>a cut of 18 percent of its workforce</u> in 2003.
Boeing Co. the No. 2 (5) <u>commercial jet maker</u> and No. 2 Pentagon contractor	To fire as many as 150 workers due to (6) <u>government reviews of an $18 billion US air refueling tanker program</u>, which has been repeatedly delayed, first over (7) <u>price concerns</u> and later over (8) <u>ethical issues</u> related to Boeing's hiring of a former Air Force procurement official.
Tyson Foods Inc. *the nation's* (9) <u>largest meat company</u>	To cut about 900 jobs at its Jackson, Mississippi-based (10) <u>chicken processing plant</u> later this year — a step in the midst of reducing its work force by about 5 percent, or nearly 6,000 jobs.
Warner Music *Entertainment*	To lay off about 1,000 people to help Warner Music (11) <u>remain competitive</u> in a rapidly evolving marketplace as the industry faces (12) <u>rampant piracy</u> and (13) <u>increased competition</u> from other forms of entertainment despite recent strides to make money from (14) <u>selling music online</u>.
Vivendi Universal Games *Video games*	To dismiss 350 employees at its Bellevue Studios within two months, following the last month's (15) <u>shutdown of two longtime development studios</u> for the reason that (16) <u>they had not been living up to corporate expectations</u>.

 **Home Listening**

Business News

Tapescript

A federal judge in the United States ruled that a sex discrimination case against Wal-Mart can be pursued as a class action lawsuit.

It would be the largest sex-bias lawsuit in history and the largest class action suit brought against a private US employer. The case was brought three years ago by six Wal-Mart female employees who claimed they were denied pay and advancement routinely offered to their male counterparts. Susan Medolo is one of the plaintiffs. She tells the NBC Today program that discrimination still continues at Wal-Mart.

"Definitely. I have a girl friend who has worked at the company over 15 years. And I won't give the exact number of years because they might find out who she is. And she is a cashier and she has been discriminated against. She is making less than $11 an hour."

Stephanie Odle, another plaintiff, was a manager at Wal-Mart in the 1990s. She says a male counterpart was being paid much more than she was being paid, on the grounds that he had a family to support. When she complained, she got a raise. She was grateful, she says, until she thought more about it.

"And then it took me a little while to realize. You know, he was making $20,000 more a year than you and you just got a $2,000 raise."

Wal-Mart denies the charges and will appeal the federal court ruling. It points to its hundreds of female managers. Wal-Mart's share price on the New York Stock Exchange has fallen for six consecutive days, in part because of concerns about the potential cost of the lawsuit. But consumer brand analyst Robert Passikoff says the case is unlikely to have much impact on Wal-Mart customers.

"The degree to which the corporation meets its legal obligations in terms of employment really only accounts for about three percent of overall customer loyalty in driving profitability for the brand."

This legal action against Wal-Mart is likely to take several years to resolve. The largest sex-discrimination case in the United States involved the US government branch that oversaw the Voice of America, which four years ago was found guilty of gender bias and had to pay 1,100 women $460,000 each. The case cost the US government $500 million.

Listen to the business news report and decide whether the following statements are true or false. Write T for true and F for false in the brackets.

1.（F） 2.（T） 3.（F） 4.（F） 5.（T） 6.（T） 7.（F） 8.（T） 9.（F） 10.（F）

Unit 6

E-commerce

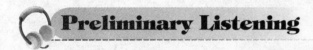
Dictation

Listen to the following short paragraph and fill in the blanks with what you hear.

E-commerce is the buying and selling of (1) <u>goods and services on the Internet</u>, especially the World Wide Web. When the Web first became well-known among (2) <u>the general public in 1994</u>, many people forecast that e-commerce would soon become a (3) <u>major economic sector</u>. However, it took about four years for security protocols to become (4) <u>sufficiently developed and widely deployed</u>. Subsequently, between 1998 and 2000, (5) <u>a substantial number of businesses</u> in the United States and Western Europe developed rudimentary web sites. Although a large number of "pure e-commerce" companies disappeared during (6) <u>the dot-com collapse in 2000 and 2001</u>, many "brick-and-mortar" retailers recognized that such companies had (7) <u>identified valuable niche markets</u> and began to (8) <u>add e-commerce capabilities to their web sites</u>.

Listening & Speaking

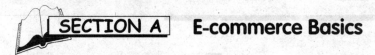

SECTION A | E-commerce Basics

Pre-listening ▶▶

Background Information

1. Electronic commerce

Electronic Commerce is exactly analogous to a marketplace on the Internet. Electronic Commerce (also referred to as EC, e-commerce, eCommerce or ecommerce) consists primarily of the distributing, buying, selling, marketing and servicing of products or services over electronic systems such as the Internet and other computer networks. E-commerce can apply to purchases made through the Web or to business-to-business activities such as inventory transfers. A customer can order items from a vendor's Web site, paying with a credit card or with a previously established "cybercash" account. The transaction information is transmitted to a financial institution for payment clearance and to the vendor for order fulfillment. Personal and account information is kept confidential through the use of "secured transactions" that use encryption technology. The emergence of e-commerce significantly lowered barriers to entry in the selling of many types of goods; accordingly many small home-based proprietors are able to use the internet to sell goods. Often, small sellers use online auction sites such as eBay, or sell via large corporate websites like Amazon.com, in order to take advantage of the exposure and setup convenience of such sites. Books are the most popular on-line product order — with over half of Web shoppers ordering books — followed by software, audio compact discs, and personal computers. Other on-line commerce includes trading of stocks, purchases of airline tickets and groceries, and participation in auctions.

2. Success factors in e-commerce

In many cases, an e-commerce company will survive not only based on its product, but by having a competent management team, good post-sales services, well-organized business structure, network infrastructure and a secured, well-designed website. A successful e-commerce organization must also provide an enjoyable and rewarding experience to its customers. The following factors go into making this possible.

❑ Providing an easy and secured way for customers to effect transactions.

❑ Providing reliability and security.

❑ Setting up an organization of sufficient alertness and agility to respond quickly to any changes in the economic, social and physical environment.

❑ Providing an attractive website. The tasteful use of color, graphics, animation, photographs, fonts, and white-space percentage may aid success in this respect.

❑ Streamlining business processes, possibly through re-engineering and information technologies.

❑ Providing complete understanding of the products or services offered.

❑ Providing value to customers.

❑ Providing service and performance. Offering a responsive, user-friendly purchasing experience, just like a flesh-and-blood retailer, may go some way to achieving these goals.

❑ Providing an incentive for customers to buy and to return. Sales promotions to this end can involve coupons, special offers, and discounts. Cross-linked websites and advertising affiliate programs can also help.

❑ Providing personal attention. Personalized web sites, purchase suggestions, and personalized special offers may go some of the way to substituting for the face-to-face human interaction found at a traditional point of sale.

❑ Providing a sense of community. Chat rooms, discussion boards, soliciting customer input and loyalty programs can help in this respect.

Naturally, the e-commerce vendor must also perform such mundane tasks as being truthful about its product and its availability, shipping reliably, and handling complaints promptly and effectively. A unique property of the Internet environment is that individual customers have access to far more information about the seller than they would find in a brick-and-mortar situation.

3. Product suitability in e-commerce

Certain products or services appear more suitable for online sales; others remain more suitable for offline sales. Many successful purely virtual companies deal with digital products, music, movies, office supplies, education, communication, software, photography, and financial transactions. Examples of this type of company include: Google, eBay and Paypal. Virtual marketers can sell some non-digital products and services successfully. Such products generally have a high value-to-weight ratio, they may involve embarrassing purchases, they may typically go to people in remote locations, and they may have shut-ins as their typical purchasers. Items which can fit through a standard letterbox — such as music CDs, DVDs and books — are particularly suitable for a virtual marketer, and indeed Amazon.com, one of the few enduring dot-com companies, has historically concentrated on this field. Products such as spare parts also seem good candidates for selling online. Retailers often need to order spare parts specially, since they typically do not stock them at consumer outlets; in such cases, e-commerce solutions in spares do not compete with retail stores, only with other ordering systems. Products less suitable for e-commerce include products that have a low value-to-weight ratio, products that have a smell, taste, or touch component, products that need trial fittings — most notably clothing — and products where color integrity appears important.

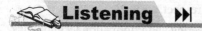

Listening ▶▶

Conversation

Tapescript

Interviewer:	Today we're very happy to have Mr. Sinton, the director of e-business solutions at Cisco here with us. Mr. Sinton, could you use an example to illustrate what electronic commerce is?
Sinton:	Electronic commerce refers to the use of electronic communications to complete a business transaction. For instance, every time we take cash from an automatic teller machine or pay for gasoline by a credit card through a card scanner, we're participating in e-commerce.
Interviewer:	I guess it is the Internet that makes all this possible, isn't it?
Sinton:	Exactly. The Internet is now opening new global commercial doors in ways that have stunned even its most ardent boosters. Every three months the industry analysts have to revise their estimates for the growth of Internet-based business.
Interviewer:	Oh, really. That's fantastic.
Sinton:	Yeah. We like to remind people that it took radio 38 years to reach the level of 50 million users. The personal computer took 16 years. Television took 13. It has only taken the Internet four years. Companies have to face the fact that movement toward the electronic age of information and commerce is inevitable. The only question is timing.
Interviewer:	It seems e-commerce is so pervasive in corporate life today that we bet firms like Cisco don't see e-commerce as a separate part of any business plan.
Sinton:	That's right. We consider e-business part of all we do. Having a separate organization for this domain would be counter to what we do. We have somebody at every office in charge of promoting e-commerce.
Interviewer:	Mr. Sinton, in what way has e-commerce transformed your company?
Sinton:	We launched Internet commerce applications in August 1996 to integrate our supply chain and make it easier to do business with Cisco. At that time, only 4%

of our bookings were received via the Internet. Today, those bookings have reached $21.5 million a day, equal to a $7.7 billion annual rate, and represent 70% of our business.

Interviewer: Like e-mail, e-commerce is money-saving, isn't it?

Sinton: Yeah. Internet integration will save Cisco $500 million a year. Part of the economies comes from being able to eliminate shipments of software packages which clients can now download from the Internet. It costs us $100 to ship each package of software. If you consider that 250,000 downloads were made by customers in November, we saved $25 million that month alone by not having to ship to them. Changes of this sort are making Cisco extraordinarily productive. Our sales run about $650,000 per employee, compared to $200,000 to $300,000 in companies with telephone-based systems.

Interviewer: Are the majority of commercial transactions done by e-commerce in the States currently?

Sinton: No, it represents only 5% of business activities in the United States. Besides, not all industries are suitable to make use of e-commerce. Certain industries — such as finance, travel and publishing — are particularly suited to take advantage of electronic channels of business.

Interviewer: Oh, I see. Thank you very much, Mr. Sinton.

I. Listen to the conversation and decide whether the following statements are true or false. Write T for true and F for false in the brackets.

1.(T) 2.(F) 3.(F) 4.(F) 5.(T) 6.(T) 7.(F) 8.(T)

II. Listen to the conversation again and complete the following notes with what you hear.

About E-commerce

Definition of e-commerce:

(1) using electronic communications to complete a business transaction

Examples of e-commerce in daily life:

(2) taking cash from an automatic teller machine

(3) paying for gasoline by a credit card through a card scanner

Pervasion of e-commerce in corporate life:

(4) considering e-commerce indispensable part of any business plan

(5) having somebody at every office in charge of promoting e-commerce

Growth of e-commerce at Cisco:

In August 1996, only (6) 4% of Cisco's bookings were received via the Internet. Today, the Internet bookings have reached (7) $21.5 million a day, equal to a (8) $7.7 billion annual rate, and represent (9) 70% of Cisco's business.

Major advantages of e-commerce for Cisco:

saving Cisco (10) $500 million a year

making Cisco (11) extraordinarily productive

Industries suited to e-commerce:

(12) finance, travel and publishing

Passage

Tapescript

The more I see of the Internet, the more enthusiastic I am. We're living through a period of dynamic change. America is ahead just now, with over 50 per cent of the population online. Britain is next, then Scandinavia and Japan, with the rest of Europe lagging surprisingly behind. But it won't be long before everyone catches up. In the third world especially, the Internet will be a liberating force that will power democracy and economic growth.

From the 1980s, American companies, eager to defend themselves from Japan and Germany, have got rid of bureaucracy and returned to the knife-edge of the market. On the knife-edge of the market some are going to bleed. One big innovation here is "frictionless selling" for cars, that is buying online rather than through a boasting salesman at a car dealership. I just bought my new car by telephone, which normally sells at 2 per cent more than what the dealer charges. I arranged finance and got just what I wanted — color, interior, engine size — in half an hour. That's great for me. But there are 25,000 — mostly family owned — car dealerships in the United States, and in the next century most will die. It's a transition that will surely be replicated many times over.

If there are losers who need protecting, there are also winners on a grand scale, many of whom from ethnic minorities. New technology attracts smart people who want to get rich from all over the world. Lots of separated rooms at Microsoft headquarters hold an Asian or Latino millionaire. And Yahoo was founded by Jerry Yang, who started by putting together a guide to cool websites as a bored graduate student at Stanford. He was under 30, was born in Taiwan, came to America with nothing, and his company is now worth tens of billions of dollars.

Telecom costs are falling towards zero, and computer costs aren't far behind; by next year we'll be able to store a terabyte of data for $10,000 — and not long ago the entire Internet was held to be a terabyte. The growth of the Internet in Africa, Asia and the Far East is putting these tools in everyone's hands. And I'm confident that if people get the chance to connect, they will quickly create wealth and opportunities across seven continents.

I. Listen to the passage and choose the best answers to the questions you hear.

1. What is the speaker's attitude towards the Internet?　(A)
2. What role will the Internet play in the third world?　(C)
3. Why have American companies got rid of bureaucracy since the 1980s?　(B)
4. What does the speaker mean when he says "on the knife-edge of the market some are going to bleed"?　(D)
5. What can we learn from the passage?　(C)

II. Listen to the passage again and complete the notes with what you hear.

The top five regions in the Internet market:
- 　(1) <u>America</u>
- 　(2) <u>Britain</u>
- 　(3) <u>Scandinavia</u>
- 　(4) <u>Japan</u>
- 　the rest of Europe

Features of online car purchases:
- 　Price: (5) <u>2 percent above the dealer's charge</u>
- 　Time needed to complete the purchase: (6) <u>in half an hour</u>

Founder of Yahoo:
- 　Name: (7) <u>Jerry Yang</u>

- 🖳 Birthplace: (8) <u>Taiwan</u>
- 🖳 Education: (9) <u>Stanford graduate student</u>
- 🖳 Worth of his company: (10) <u>tens of billions of dollars</u>

Future of the Internet growth:

- 🖳 Cost: (11) <u>will be falling</u>
- 🖳 Regions where Internet will grow: (12) <u>Africa, Asia and the Far East</u>

SECTION B   Online Shopping

Pre-listening ▶▶

Background Information

1. Consumer acceptance of e-commerce

Consumers have accepted the e-commerce business model less readily than its proponents originally expected. Even in product categories suitable for e-commerce, electronic shopping has developed only slowly. Several reasons might account for the slow uptake.

- ❑ Concerns about security. Many people will not use credit cards over the Internet due to concerns about theft and credit card fraud.
- ❑ Lack of instant gratification with most e-purchases. Much of a consumer's reward for purchasing a product lies in the instant gratification of using and displaying that product. This reward does not exist when one's purchase does not arrive for days or weeks.
- ❑ The problem of access to web commerce, mainly for poor households and for developing countries. Low penetration rates of Internet access in some sectors greatly reduce the potential for e-commerce.
- ❑ The social aspect of shopping. Some people enjoy talking to sales staff, to other shoppers, or to their cohorts: this social reward side of retail therapy does not exist to the same extent in online shopping.
- ❑ Poorly designed, bug-infested e-commerce web sites that frustrate online shoppers and drive

them away.

❑ Inconsistent return policies among e-tailers or difficulties in exchange or return.

2. Online shopping

Online shopping is the process consumers go through to purchase products or services over the Internet. An online shop, Internet shop, webshop or online store evokes the physical analogy of buying products or services at a bricks-and-mortar retailer or in a shopping mall. Online shopping is popular mainly because of its speed and ease of use. Some issues of concern can include fluctuating exchange rates for foreign currencies, local and international laws and delivery methods. An advantage of shopping online is being able to use the power of the Internet to seek out the lowest prices for items or services. For example if one is buying a digital camera he/she should enter "digital camera" into a search engine or a price search engine. Most price comparison services have the advantage of store ratings and reviews. Getting the lowest price is important but it is more important to make sure the merchant or store the customer is purchasing from is reputable.

Steps when buying online

❑ Browse product categories using a web browser.

❑ Put items into virtual shopping cart (or market basket).

❑ Just as in a physical store viewing the contents of the cart can be done at any time.

❑ Quantities of products can be changed or deleted.

❑ Checkout.

❑ Log in or register by choosing a username and a password.

❑ Enter personal data.

❑ Enter billing address.

❑ Enter shipping address (can be different from the billing address).

❑ Enter phone number.

❑ Enter e-mail address (usually optional).

❑ Choose means of payment.

❑ Choose delivery speed and method (post, courier and logistics service, etc.).

❑ Confirm order.

❑ After editing the personal data a confirmation page is displayed so that the online shopper can approve, change or abort the order.

❑ Logout.

Means of payment

Online shoppers commonly use their credit cards for making payments, however some systems enable users to create accounts and pay by alternative means, such as:

❑ Debit card;

❑ Various types of electronic money;

❑ Cash on delivery (C.O.D.);
❑ Check;
❑ Wire transfer/delivery on payment;
❑ Postal money order.

Once a payment has been accepted the goods or services can either be downloaded from the Internet or delivered to the consumer via traditional means.

3. Traditional shopping vs online shopping

Traditional Shopping

Identity. Customers can easily authenticate the identity of a merchant simply by walking into a bricks-and-mortar store. Stores can be members of a community and neighborhood; they can be part of customers' daily experience. There is a concreteness about a physical store that no amount of HTML will ever match.

Immediacy. Customers can touch and feel and hold the merchandise. A transaction that is face-to-face is usually unmediated: your communication with the merchant is not in the hands of a third party or technology (as with ordering by phone).

Value. The item at the center of the commerce transaction — the product, service, or property that is to be sold/bought — has some kind of value. Its price is determined and validated through the performance of the transaction. The seller agrees to a selling price, and the buyer agrees to a buying price. The value of an item, especially the relative value an item has for the buyer, is much easier to appraise if that item is close at hand.

Discourse. Customers can converse with the merchant face-to-face; unmediated conversation is basic to human communication. People want the feedback available from non-verbal behavior, which forms a large part of our judgment process.

Community. Customers can interact with other customers and gain feedback about the merchant from other customers, as well as by observing the merchant interacting with other customers.

Privacy. Customers can make purchases anonymously with cash; they usually don't have to give their name or address. They don't usually have to worry about what a store will do with their personal information. Privacy is often a measure of how much of his or her identity a buyer wants to invest in a transaction.

Online Shopping

Disadvantages. An online commerce customer faces mediation in every element and at every stage of the commerce transaction. Customers can't see the merchant, only the merchant's website; they can't touch the merchandise, they can only see a representation; they can't wander into a store and speak with employees, they can only browse HTML pages, read FAQs, and fire off email to nameless customer service mailboxes; they can't explore the store's shelves and product space, they can only search a digital catalog. A customer at an online commerce site lacks the concrete cues to comfortably assess the trustworthiness of the site, and so must rely on new kinds of cues. The problem for the online customer is that the web is new — to a large sector of the online audience — and online commerce seems like a step into an unknown experience.

Advantages. There are many advantages to shopping online, but probably the most notable one is convenience. The ability to find anything and everything you need without even leaving your home can be a great time saver. No longer do you have to make the trek to the grocery or discount store. You can order anything you want with the click of your mouse. Another thing to think about is that many online shops offer free shipping if you order over a certain amount. So, not only do you not have to pay for the gas to drive to the mall or store, you don't even have to pay the shipping cost for the items you order. You will never be able to match the selection of items that you will find online. You can find anything from books, music CD's, and DVD's to electronics, cameras, and computers. You will find a never-ending selection of clothes to choose from, in sizes to fit the entire family. Not to mention shoes in every style. Jewelry and accessories are available as well. The Internet is especially helpful when you are looking for an item that is hard to find. You can find any type of collectible or imaginable, like art prints, comic books, coins, dolls, games, and cards, just to name a few. Or maybe you are looking for a part for your car that your local auto parts store doesn't carry. You can likely find it online. Some websites allow you to search for the items you are looking for, and then compare the prices of these items from several different online shops in one place. This sure beats running all over town in search of the best deal.

 **Listening** ▶▶

Conversation

Tapescript

Interviewer:	Hot Hot Hot is a small shop specializing in fiery products of over 500 varieties from around the world. Business has been good for its owner, Monica. But it got better when one of her frequent customers convinced her to build a website. Monica, how many people visit your website each day?
Monica:	We have about a thousand to 1,500 visitors to the site every day, which, considering we only have a 300-square-foot shop, we could never possibly fit in here.
Interviewer:	Then how many actually order?
Monica:	About 1% of the people that visit the site, which is the same as direct mail.
Interviewer:	Monica, do you think people on the Web tend to order more?

Monica: Not really. But I think people on the Web tend to be adventurous anyway. People who might never have thought of ordering hot and spicy foods take the opportunity to do it. It's something that's never occurred to them, but it's something totally new.

Interviewer: Has a website enabled you to get more business?

Monica: We're indeed a very small shop. With the website, we get orders from all over the world. We have a guy from Germany who ordered for a friend in England. We have a guy from Guam who sends gifts to his family in the United States. That's something that small retail establishments like ours could never do in any other way.

Interviewer: How do you sell on the site?

Monica: Essentially we sell 150 hot sauces, which to someone who doesn't know anything about hot sauces would be 150 of the same thing. It was up to us to come up with the way of dividing them up, and arrange them in a logical pattern for them to follow. Otherwise you may spend a long time searching, and never find out the information you needed.

Interviewer: Then what do you exactly do in dividing them up?

Monica: Er, we divided them up in four logical ways. One would be by heat level. Another would be by place of origin. One alphabetical listing. And we had a lot of customers in the shop that ask us for sauces with no salt or no sugar or are 100% natural. So we set that up too.

Interviewer: What is the philosophy of the site?

Monica: I think that the Internet is a tremendously new place to do business. It's also a new medium. It's a totally new unexplored creative area for people. We happen to use it as a selling tool. You can see it used very creatively as an advertising tool, as a marketing tool, as a communications tool. I think it's really a fascinating new place for people to explore.

Interviewer: Do you have any suggestion to small businesses who are considering having a web presence?

Monica: Oh, yes. To start a business on the Internet, there are lots of things that you need to think about. For us, if you're selling something, you have to remember that you're now a worldwide company. You will be shipping overseas. You will get orders from overseas. You will need to be prepared to fully involve it in the rest of your business. Customers on the Net are much more likely to want to contact you than any sort of catalog business. Most catalog businesses have very little contact with their customers. But e-mail is easy. They can e-mail you questions. Customers feel more comfortable doing it. So you have to be prepared to spend a fair amount of time responding to them.

I. Listen to the passage and choose the best answers to the questions you hear.

1. What kind of shop does Monica run?   (C)

2. Why did Monica choose to have a web presence?   (D)

3. What is true about Hot Hot Hot?   (A)

4. Why does Monica arrange her products into different categories on the website?   (B)

5. What can be learned from the interview?   (D)

II. Listen to the conversation again and complete the notes with what you hear.

Hot Hot Hot

Hot Hot Hot is a small shop:

- specializing in (1) <u>fiery products of over 500 varieties</u>
- with a physical space of (2) <u>300 square feet</u>
- having (3) <u>a thousand to 1,500 people</u> visiting its website every day
- receiving orders (4) <u>from all over the world</u>

Hot Hot Hot categorizes its 150 hot sauces:

- by (5) <u>heat level</u>
- by (6) <u>place of origin</u>
- by (7) <u>alphabetical order</u>
- by content, with (8) <u>no salt or no sugar</u> or a 100% natural

Owners of Hot Hot Hot view Internet as:

- a new place for people to (9) <u>do business and to explore</u>
- a new medium for business
- a creative tool of (10) <u>selling, advertising, marketing and communications</u>

Suggestions by Hot Hot Hot owners:

To start a business on the Internet, be prepared to

- (11) <u>get orders from overseas and ship overseas</u>
- (12) <u>spend a fair amount of time responding to customers</u>

Passage

Tapescript

How would you like to do a week's worth of grocery shopping in 10 minutes? Rather than loading the kids into the car on shopping day, you can send them out to play and do your shopping from the comfort of your home. Thousands of busy people have traded their shopping carts for keyboards. Rather than fight the crowds in the downtown areas, they log on to the Peapod, an online shopping and delivery service.

Peapod is giving us a glimpse into the future of retailing. It is a pioneer in a rapidly expanding industry that is dedicated to enabling us to buy almost anything from PC. Peapod subscribers go shopping at the virtual grocery store by logging on to a system that lets them interactively shop for grocery items, including fresh produce, bakery, meat, and frozen products. Rather than running from aisle to aisle, you simply point and click around the screen for the item you want. Once online you can choose from over 20,000 items, or compare prices instantly to find the best deal, or check your subtotal at any time to stay within your budget, or create personal shopping lists to save time, or view images of products, or check out store specials, or view nutritional labels for products, sort products instantly by nutritional content, or choose a delivery time that fits your schedule.

Peapod's online shopping system is linked directly to its partner stores' computer systems. When you send your shopping list to Peapod, an order is transmitted to the nearest partner store. A professionally trained shopper takes your order and does your shopping for you. You can redeem your coupons when the delivery person arrives with your food.

The virtual supermarket is sure to change the way we shop. We can view items by category or by brand. We can even peruse the items on sale. We can request that items be arranged alphabetically, by brand, by price per unit, by package size, or, we can even request a listing by nutritional value. In the minds of the busy people who shop online, the cost of the service is easily offset by other savings, e.g. less spent on travel.

Online shopping is here to stay. The Peapod system has made life easier for a great many people. It has also saved them time and money. Working parents gladly trade shopping time for more time with the kids. Some people enjoy saving big on coupons and baby-sitting costs. Just about everyone saves money because the system encourages you to buy the product with the best per unit price.

I. Listen to the passage and decide whether the following statements are true or false. Write T for true and F for false in the brackets.

1. (F) 2. (F) 3. (T) 4. (F) 5. (F) 6. (T) 7. (F) 8. (F) 9. (F) 10. (T)

II. Listen to the passage again and complete the notes with what you hear.

Shopping at Peapod

How you shop at Peapod:

- to log on to a system that (1) <u>lets you interactively shop for grocery items</u>
- to (2) <u>point and click around the screen</u> for the item you want
- to send (3) <u>your shopping list</u> to Peapod, which is transmitted to (4) <u>the nearest partner store</u> where a professionally trained shopper (5) <u>takes your order</u> and (6) <u>does your shopping for you</u>
- to choose a delivery time that (7) <u>fits your schedule</u>
- to (8) <u>redeem your coupons</u> when the delivery person arrives with your food

Peapod allows you:

- to choose from over (9) <u>20,000</u> items, including (10) <u>fresh produce, bakery, meat, and frozen products</u>
- to compare prices instantly to (11) <u>find the best deal</u>
- to check your subtotal at any time to (12) <u>stay within your budget</u>
- to create (13) <u>personal shopping lists</u> to save time
- to view (14) <u>images of products</u> and (15) <u>nutritional labels for products</u>
- to check out (16) <u>store specials</u>
- to sort products instantly by (17) <u>nutritional content</u>
- to request that items be arranged (18) <u>alphabetically</u>, by (19) <u>brand</u>, by (20) <u>price per unit</u>, by (21) <u>package size</u>, by (22) <u>nutritional value</u>

How Peapod saves money for you:

- You enjoy saving big on (23) <u>coupons, baby-sitting costs</u>.
- You spend less on (24) <u>traveling</u>.
- You are encouraged by the system to buy the product (25) <u>with the best per unit price</u>.

Further Listening

Short Recordings

Tapescript

Item 1

SAN FRANCISCO — Intel Corp. said it is informing customers that it will miss its year-end target for delivering a high-speed Pentium 4 chip intended for desktop computers. It is the last in a string of delays reported by the world's largest chipmaker. Santa Clara, California-based Intel now expects to ship a Pentium 4 chip running at four gigahertz, or four billion cycles per second, in the first quarter, spokeswoman Laura Anderson said. "We're committed to putting our execution back on track in a way that makes the company even stronger," Ms Anderson said.

Intel, since its foundation in 1968, has become a legend. The world's leading semi-conductor manufacturer is over and above all known for its microprocessors, the "chips" which are found in 80% of the world's computers. Intel's activities are divided into three divisions, with the Architecture Business Group and its microprocessors accounting for more than 4/5 of its business. There is also the Networking and Communications Group for networks and their components, and finally the Wireless Communications and Computing Group which makes communications devices and instruments as well as mobile telephone, Flash memory, and embedded processors; Always at the cutting edge of research, Intel is constantly trying to push back the physical limits that electronic design sets.

Item 2

NEW YORK — IBM is moving to reduce the number of US workers it lays off due to the transfer of their work overseas, according to internal documents from the computer maker and comments from its executives. It is reported Thursday that IBM is taking more extensive steps to find jobs within the company for those whose work is being shifted to lower-wage countries. IBM now expects to lay off only 2,000 people out of the 5,000 whose jobs are being sent overseas. Finding new positions for affected employees is made easier because IBM is expected to add overall US and worldwide employment this year.

International Business Machines Corporation (IBM) is an information technology company. Its portfolio of capabilities ranges from services that include business transformation consulting to software, hardware, fundamental research, financing and the component technologies used to build larger systems. These capabilities are combined to provide business insight and solutions in the enterprise computing space. IBM's clients include many different kinds of enterprises, from sole proprietorships to large organizations, governments and companies, representing every major industry and endeavor. Organizationally, the Company's major operations consist of a Global Services segment; three hardware product segments: Systems Group, Personal Systems Group and Technology Group; a Software segment; a Global Financing segment, and an Enterprise Investments segment.

Item 3

NEW YORK — Dell Corp. surpassed rival Hewlett-Packard as the world's No. 1 maker of personal computers during the first quarter, thanks to stronger business buying, according to an industry report released Thursday. Dell's year-on-year growth surged 28 percent for the quarter with its global PC shipments nearing 7.7 million units versus 6 million units a year earlier. Its piece of the world market share pie inched up to from 16 percent in the fourth-quarter to 18.6 percent. HP slipped into second place as its market share declined to 15.6 percent in the first-quarter from 16.7 percent in the previous three months. Its total worldwide shipments rose 15.7 percent on a year-on-year basis to 6.4 million units.

Dell Inc. designs, develops, manufactures, markets, sells and supports a range of computer systems and services that are customized to customer requirements. These include enterprise systems (servers, storage and networking products, and workstations), client systems (notebooks and desktops), software and peripherals, and service and support programs. Dell also offers a portfolio of services that help maximize information technology, rapidly deploy systems and educate IT professionals and consumers. In addition, it provides financial services to its business and consumer customers in the United States. Dell markets and sells its products and services directly to its customers.

Item 4

NEW YORK — Apple Computer Inc. has introduced lower-priced versions of its iPod digital music player with longer battery life, positioning itself against rivals trying to use lower prices to undercut iPod sales. Apple said the new model iPod has up to 12 hours of battery life, compared with eight hours in previous models. The Cupertino, a company in California, best known for its Macintosh computer, has turned to digital music as it has failed to make major gains in the highly competitive PC market. But in digital music players, Apple also faces strong competition from Dell Inc. and Sony Corp. IPod claims a 50 percent market share in digital music players. Its sales almost tripled in the previous quarter.

Apple Computer, Inc. designs, manufactures and markets personal computers and related software, peripherals and personal computing and communicating solutions. Its products include the Macintosh line of desktop and notebook computers, the Mac OS X operating system, the iPod digital music players and a portfolio of software and peripheral products for education, creative consumers and business customers. The Company sells its products through its online stores, direct sales force, third-party wholesalers and resellers and its own retail stores. In addition to its own hardware and software products, the Company's retail stores carry a variety of third-party hardware and software products.

Item 5

Palo Alto — In step with a trend by printer companies to increasingly blur the line between printed and digital documents, Hewlett-Packard on Tuesday introduced three new printers that each integrate printing, scanning, copying, e-mailing and faxing, into a single unit. HP will also step up the promotion of its portfolio of purchase, lease, outsourcing options for financing and deploying the new HP printers. Since mainstream printers began arriving with their own IP addresses in volume last year, printer companies such as HP, Canon, Xerox, and others have each been evolving their printers into multifunction devices that can manipulate and send documents without the intervention of a PC.

Hewlett-Packard Company is a global technology company that operates six business segments: the Imaging and Printing Group (IPG), the Personal Systems Group (PSG), the Enterprise Systems Group (ESG), HP Services (HPS), HP Financial Services (HPFS) and Corporate Investments. IPG provides home and business imaging, printing and publishing devices and systems, digital imaging products, printer supplies and consulting services. PSG provides commercial personal computers (PCs), consumer PCs, workstations, a range of hand-held computing devices, digital entertainment systems, calculators and other related accessories, software and services. ESG offers servers, storage and software solutions. HPS provides a portfolio of information technology services. HPFS provides value-added financial lifecycle management services. Corporate Investments includes HP Laboratories and certain business incubation projects.

I. In this section, you will hear five short recordings. For each piece, decide what can be learned about each of the following high-tech companies.

1. Intel .... G	A. Regaining lead in PC market
2. IBM C	B. Missing production target
3. Dell .... A	C. Decreasing outsourcing-related layoffs
4. Apple .... E	D. Exploring new PC markets
5. Hewlett-Packard .... H	E. Unveiling new-generation products
	F. Replacing imperfect chips
	G. Postponing introducing new products
	H. Rolling out multifunction products

II. Listen to the five recordings again and decide whether the following statements are true or false. Write T for true and F for false in brackets.

1.（F） 2.（T） 3.（F） 4.（F） 5.（T） 6.（F） 7.（T） 8.（T） 9.（T） 10.（F）

Home Listening

Business News

Tapescript

Japan's central bank has issued a positive economic report, fueling hopes that a fragile economic recovery may be gaining speed.

Japan' central bank says the world's second largest economy could be picking up. The Bank of Japan has upgraded its monthly economic assessment for the first time in a year.

The report says exports, a key engine of growth, are showing a gradual improvement and that business sentiment among major manufacturers is recovering. BOJ Governor Toshihiko Fukui predicts that business investments will start to increase and says he also expects more economic activity in other spheres.

There have been other signs that Japan's troubled financial picture is brightening: stocks have rebounded strongly from a 20-year low set in April, and the economy grew one percent in the April to June quarter.

At the same time, however, the central bank remains cautious about Japan's long-term prospects. It notes that domestic demand is weak and consumer spending remains sluggish after three recessions in the last decade.

The number of corporate bankruptcies in Japan is falling. A study by a private research firm says bankruptcies declined nine percent in the first half of this year from the same period last year for a total of 8,984 cases.

The firm says job cuts and other strategies to improve profitability are behind the drop in figures. Despite the improvement, the number of failures is still very high.

The Japanese subsidiary of the US investment bank Merrill Lynch is introducing a new strategy. It is targeting the more than one million Japanese people who have at least $1 million in assets. About 17 percent of the world's dollar millionaires live in Japan, and Merrill is offering a series of new investment products to manage their assets. The financial services offered include insurance products as well as specially tailored stocks, bonds and mutual funds.

Merrill Lynch says it thinks more and more wealthy Japanese will look for alternatives to keeping their money in Japan's troubled banks, which are trying to shed billions of dollars in bad loans.

Listen to the business news report and complete the notes with what you hear.

Japanese Economy Shows Signs of Recovery

BOJ's Economic Report	Positive	☺ Japanese exports are showing (1) <u>a gradual improvement</u>. ☺ (2) <u>Business sentiment</u> among major manufacturers is recovering. ☺ BOJ has upgraded its (3) <u>monthly economic assessment</u> for the first time in a year. ☺ BOJ Governor predicts (4) <u>business investments will start to increase</u> and also expects (5) <u>more economic activity in other spheres</u>. ☺ Stocks have rebounded strongly from a (6) <u>20-year low set in April</u>. ☺ The economy grew one percent in (7) <u>the April to June quarter</u>. ☺ (8) <u>Corporate bankruptcies</u> declined nine percent in the first half of this year from the same period last year for a total of (9) <u>8,984 cases</u>.
	Negative	☹ (10) <u>Domestic demand</u> is weak and (11) <u>consumer spending</u> remains sluggish after three recessions in the last decade.
Merrill Lynch's New Strategy		☺ Whom to target — the more than one million Japanese people who (12) <u>have at least $1 million in assets</u>. ☺ What to offer — a series of new investment products, including (13) <u>insurance products</u> as well as (14) <u>specially tailored stocks, bonds and mutual funds</u>. ☹ Why — More and more wealthy Japanese will look for alternatives to (15) <u>keeping their money in Japan's troubled banks</u>, which are trying to (16) <u>shed billions of dollars in bad loans</u>.

Unit 7

Distribution

Dictation

Listen to the following short paragraph and fill in the blanks with what you hear.

In short, distribution describes all the logistics involved in (1) <u>delivering a company's products or services</u> to the right place, at the right time, for the lowest cost. In the unending efforts to realize these goals, (2) <u>the channels of distribution</u> selected by a business play a vital role in this process. Also known as marketing channels, distribution channels consist of a set of interdependent organizations — such as (3) <u>wholesalers, retailers, and sales agents</u> — involved in making a product or service (4) <u>available for use or consumption</u>. Like all aspects of operations and marketing, distribution offers a range of multifaceted options that can affect profitability. An effective distribution strategy must adequately (5) <u>serve the targeted customer segments</u>, (6) <u>minimize distribution costs</u>, (7) <u>maximize product volume</u> and (8) <u>gain a sustainable competitive advantage</u>.

Listening & Speaking

SECTION A   Delivery Services

Pre-listening ▶▶

Background Information

1. Delivery services

Virtually every business owner makes use of delivery services in their operations. For some companies, reliable, timely deliveries of parcels, letters, and documents are an essential element of their overall business practices. For others, delivery services are needed only occasionally to distribute contracts, business proposals, financial records, and other business materials. Today's business owners have a number of choices when it comes to delivery or courier services. These choices range from major international carriers such as Federal Express, Airborne Express, DHL Worldwide Express, the United Parcel Service to companies that provide regional services. Moreover, these options are relatively inexpensive, due to the fierce competition that characterizes the industry. As a matter of fact, delivery services have become so competitive that overnight and same day delivery services have been the norm for many business operations since the mid-1990s. As competition for delivery dollars has increased, so have the technological advances and innovations offered by delivery companies. These technological innovations are apparent in all facets of company operations, from the sophisticated operational equipment used to separate and track parcels to customer service operations that enable clients to utilize new technologies to monitor the location and status of every package.

2. Weighing Delivery Options

When selecting a delivery carrier, business experts urge companies to consider a wide range of factors. Shippers should look closely at what each parcel carrier can offer and decide how much real value each service brings to the shipper's business. Shippers should also take a close look at their own business and decide what their needs are. Specific considerations in this regard include the following.

- Are there alternative means of transporting the materials without incurring the expense of a delivery service? For example, some documents can be faxed for a fraction of the cost of physical delivery, and electronic mail can be used for many corporate communications.
- Does the service offer discounts to companies that drop off parcels at the carrier site?
- Does the delivery service charge fees based upon package size, in addition to package weight? This can be an important consideration if your company's parcels are of moderate size.
- What degree of parcel or document tracking capability does your company require? Companies that deliver materials to rural or remote locales typically look to major carriers offering universal coverage. In addition, businesses that ship time- or content-sensitive materials also typically enlist the services of companies like UPS or Federal Express, which can provide clients with detailed information on shipment data.
- What value-added services does the delivery company offer, and at what price?
- Do you want shipping data integrated into other operational aspects of your company, such as inventory management? Major carriers offer systems that can aid clients in this regard, although some experts warn that such arrangements can tie businesses to one carrier to the exclusion of others.
- Which delivery options are most cost-effective for your company? In today's fast-paced business environment, overnight delivery is immensely popular with small and large businesses alike, and same-day delivery guarantees have proven profitable for many regional carriers. But many letters and parcels simply do not have to be delivered in such short time spans. Savvy business owners often look to more economical two-or three-day delivery plans instead. These options provide shippers with time-definite guarantees at a fraction of the cost of same-day or next-day services.

3. FedEx

FedEx, whose full corporate name is FedEx Corporation, is a cargo airline, printing, and courier company offering overnight courier, ground, heavy freight, document copying and logistics services. FedEx is a syllabic abbreviation of the company's original name, Federal Express. The company was founded as Federal Express in 1971 by Fred Smith in Little Rock, Arkansas, but moved to Memphis, Tennessee in 1973 after Little Rock airport officials would not agree to provide facilities for the fledgling airline. The name was chosen to symbolize a national marketplace, and help in obtaining government contracts. In its advertising, the company made famous the line "Absolutely, positively" for their overnight service. Another slogan, "Relax, it's FedEx", is well recognized. Its major competitors include UPS, DHL, and TNT, in addition to post office organizations around the globe.

Listening ▶▶

Conversation

Tapescript

Interviewer:	FedEx is the world's largest express transportation company, spanning more than 211 countries, delivering 4.8 million packages each day, with a workforce of over 215,000 employees worldwide. Mr. Powell, what kind of educational qualifications and personality would enable one for a career at FedEx?
Mr. Powell:	People working for FedEx are very dynamic and are willing to change. We give equal emphasis to behavioral aspects of the candidates along with their educational qualifications.
Interviewer:	Great. Then at a junior level, what kind of training do you impart to your employees who come in direct contact with customers?
Mr. Powell:	Our customers expect professional and quality performance from us. To achieve 100% service satisfaction, FedEx has invested in training and development of all the employees. Employee training and development begins as soon as he starts his first assignment. Apart from a dedicated training and development department, career development of employees is a prime responsibility of every manager here. We give technical as well as soft skills training.
Interviewer:	I see. What kind of paymaster do you think FedEx is?
Mr. Powell:	Federal Express stands for competitive compensation and benefits packages. It believes in the "pay for performance" concept and incorporates it into the company culture. Compensation and benefits packages are designed considering skills and competency required for every job. Over and above compensation and benefits there are many merit incentives and reviews for the employees. To recognize individuals with exceptional performance, managers can use the Star or Super Star program to make a special payment to their top performers. Immediate rewards are given to employees who perform beyond their normal job responsibilities. This award is called "Bravo Zulu". "The Golden Falcon Award" recognizes unselfish acts that enhance customer service and are truly above and beyond the call of duty.

Interviewer: That's amazing. Then what kind of career growth can one expect from working in FedEx?

Mr. Powell: FedEx has a track record of being one of the Top 100 companies to work for in the US. It provides an environment where employees can grow. We have many programs developed to facilitate the growth of employees like: promotion/career progression policy, career development program and tuition refund program. FedEx provides financial assistance to employees who wish to obtain additional education or training in order to increase their competence in their current position.

Interviewer: Mr. Powell, could you tell us how effective your internal communication systems to record employee satisfaction or discontent are? And how often do you review your HR policies and amend them as required?

Mr. Powell: We believe in an open, communicative and creative work environment. To foster teamwork, constructive feedback is given through practices like: "Survey-Feedback-Action" and "Guaranteed Fair Treatment". The former is an online program, where the employees score their direct manager anonymously, the manager's boss and other general company performances. With the feedback, the managers are challenged to review their workgroups, opportunities for further development and create action plans for the coming year. The latter is a procedure designed to give employees an opportunity to have their concerns heard by management and ensure a fair evaluation of those concerns.

I. Listen to the conversation and choose the best answers to the questions you hear.

1. How many people work globally for FedEx, the world's largest express transportation company? (B)

2. Which award is given to reward those who perform beyond their normal job responsibilities? (C)

3. What are practices like "Survey-Feedback-Action" and "Guaranteed Fair Treatment" mainly designed for? (A)

4. Which of the following is true about employee training and development at FedEx? (C)

5. What can be inferred from the interview? (B)

II. Listen to the conversation again and complete the following notes with what you hear.

FedEx Profile

FedEx as a Paymaster:

Federal Express, a strong believer in the "(1) <u>pay for performance</u>" concept, offers:

❑ (2) <u>competitive compensation and benefits packages</u> that are based on skills and competency required for every job;

❑ (3) <u>many merit incentives and reviews</u> for the employees, including:

* *the Star or Super Star program* — a special payment to recognize (4) <u>individuals with exceptional performance</u>;

* *Bravo Zulu* — immediate rewards given to employees who (5) <u>perform beyond their normal job responsibilities</u>;

* *the Golden Falcon Award* — an award to recognize unselfish acts that (6) <u>enhance customer service</u> and (7) <u>are truly above and beyond the call of duty</u>.

Career Growth in FedEx:

Boasting a track record of being one of the Top 100 companies to work for in the US, FedEx provides

❑ an environment where (8) <u>employees can grow</u>;

❑ many programs developed to (9) <u>facilitate the growth of employees</u>, such as promotion/career progression policy, (10) <u>career development program</u> and (11) <u>tuition refund program</u>;

❑ financial assistance to employees who wish to obtain (12) <u>additional education or training</u> to increase their competence in their current position.

Internal Communication in FedEx:

In order to foster teamwork, FedEx adopts such practices to give constructive feedback as:

❑ "Survey-Feedback-Action" — an online program, where the employees anonymously (13) <u>score their managers and other general company performances</u>.

❑ "Guaranteed Fair Treatment" — a procedure designed to give employees an opportunity to (14) <u>have their concerns heard by management</u> and ensure (15) <u>a fair evaluation of those concerns</u>.

Passage

Tapescript

With the global economy speeding along at a breakneck pace, delivery services have become an integral and important part of day-to-day business. Just about any successful business, from restaurants, to supermarkets, wants reliable and quick delivery service with accurate tracking of shipments.

For the average individual, delivery services exist which can ship one or a few packages quickly. Anyone who has ever ordered an item off the Internet is familiar with how these services work. For businesses, there are many private delivery companies, and choosing the right one can make an essential difference in the survival of a company.

For businesses that deal with a lot of shipping needs, a delivery service should have an adequate facility that can store the items that would be shipped. The facility should be secure and well organized, so that items will be safe and easy to locate when shipping time arrives. The warehouse where the items are stored should have a good tracking system that follows the items from their origin to their destination.

The professionalism of the delivery service is important for business needs as well. Every business will have a different set of requirements regarding shipping details, and the service should be flexible enough to respond to those differing needs. A good service should be able to adapt so well that it acts as an extension of the company it serves.

Freight logistics has changed by leaps and bounds in recent years. Traditional hauling, though it shares a lot of its work with air and sea transportation modes, is still the number one method, both domestically and abroad. A modern logistics company is up to date, computerized, and incredibly efficient.

Delivery services are incredibly diversified. Small businesses and global corporations alike each have a lion's share of choices. Not only size, but also strategy and costs differ widely — making the right decision on which delivery services to use takes time, but will result in the gaining of an excellent and long-term business partner.

These days, few managers make the decision on which express delivery services to use without consulting the Internet. Comparing features, costs, and professionalism is the only way to enter into a contract. The latter, professionalism, is particularly important.

Every company that moves goods, whether raw or finished, needs to carefully consider their shipping needs in order to find the right delivery service. Some online research is the beginning of this process. Finalizing it means that you've landed an excellent and long-term partnership with an expediting service that both you and your customers can rely on.

I. Listen to the passage and choose the best answers to the questions you hear.

1. What makes delivery services an essential part of today's daily business?　(C)

2. To satisfy different shipping needs, what is expected of a good delivery service?   (A)

3. What is a particularly important factor in choosing delivery services?   (D)

4. What must be the first consideration of every company while choosing the right delivery service?   (B)

5. What can be concluded from the passage?   (C)

II. Listen to the passage again and answer the following questions with brief notes.

1. What delivery service does a successful business want?

   Reliable and quick delivery service with accurate tracking of shipments.

2. What can be of essential importance to the survival of a company?

   Choosing the right delivery company.

3. What do businesses that deal with a lot of shipping needs look for in delivery services?

   An adequate, secure, well-organized facility to store the shipping items; the professionalism of the delivery service.

4. Why should the facility for storing items be well organized?

   To make it easy to locate the items when shipping time arrives.

5. What is the use of a tracking system?

   To follow the shipping items from their origin to their destination.

6. What is a modern logistics company like?

   Up to date, computerized, and incredibly efficient.

7. How diversified are delivery services?

   Delivery services differ not only in size, but also in strategy and costs.

8. Why is it worth the time to make the right decision on which delivery services to use?

   Because it will result in the gaining of an excellent and long-term business partner.

SECTION B   Distribution Strategies

Pre-listening ▶▶

Background Information

1. Distribution channel

Traditionally, distribution has been seen as dealing with logistics: how to get the product or service to the customer. Frequently there may be a chain of intermediaries, each passing the product down the chain to the next organization, before it finally reaches the consumer or end-user. This process is known as the "distribution chain" or the "channel." A number of alternate "channels" of distribution may be available.

- Selling direct, such as via mail order, Internet and telephone sales.
- Agent, who typically sells direct on behalf of the producer.
- Distributor (also called wholesaler), who sells to retailers.
- Retailer (also called dealer or reseller), who sells to end customers.
- Advertisement typically used for consumption goods.

Distribution channels may not be restricted to physical products alone. They may be just as important for moving a service from producer to consumer in certain sectors, since both direct and indirect channels may be used. Hotels, for example, may sell their services (typically rooms) directly or through travel agents, tour operators, airlines, tourist boards, centralized reservation systems, etc.

2. Multiple channels of distribution

For many products and services, their manufacturers or providers use multiple channels of distribution. A personal computer, for example, might be bought directly from the manufacturer, either over the telephone, direct mail, or the Internet, or through several kinds of retailers, including independent computer stores, franchised computer stores, and department stores. In addition, large and small businesses may make their purchases through other outlets. Channel structures range from two to five levels. The simplest is a two-level structure in which goods and services move directly from the manufacturer or provider to the consumer. Two-level structures occur in some industries where consumers are able to order products directly from the manufacturer and the manufacturer fulfills those orders through its own physical distribution system. In a three-level channel structure retailers serve as intermediaries between consumers and manufacturers. Retailers order products directly from the manufacturer, and then sell those products directly to the consumer. A fourth level is added when manufacturers sell to wholesalers rather than to retailers. In a four-level structure, retailers order goods from wholesalers rather than manufacturers. Finally, a manufacturer's agent can serve as an intermediary between the manufacturer and its wholesalers, creating a five-level channel structure consisting of the manufacturer, agent, wholesale, retail, and consumer levels. A five-level channel structure might also consist of the manufacturer, wholesale, jobber, retail, and consumer levels, whereby jobbers serve smaller retailers not covered by the large wholesalers in the industry.

3. Benefits of intermediaries

Distributors act as intermediaries between manufacturers and retailers. They maintain a warehouse of merchandise, which is often purchased from many different manufacturers and then is sold (or distributed) among various retailers. If selling directly from the manufacturer to the consumer were always the most efficient way of doing business, the need for channels of distribution would be obviated. Intermediaries, however, provide several benefits to both manufacturers and consumers: improved efficiency, a better assortment of products, routinization of transactions, and easier searching for goods as well as customers.

The improved efficiency that results from adding intermediaries in the channels of distribution can easily be grasped with the help of a few examples. Take five manufacturers and 20 retailers, for instance. If each manufacturer sells directly to each retailer, there are 100 contact lines — one line from each manufacturer to each retailer. The complexity of this distribution arrangement can be reduced by adding wholesalers as intermediaries between manufacturers and retailers. If a single wholesaler serves as the intermediary, the number of contacts is reduced from 100 to 25: five contact lines between the manufacturers and the wholesaler, and 20 contact lines between the wholesaler and the retailers. Reducing the number of necessary contacts brings more efficiency into the distribution system by eliminating duplicate efforts in ordering, processing, shipping, etc.

Intermediaries provide a second benefit by bridging the gap between the assortment of goods and services generated by producers and those in demand from consumers. Manufacturers typically produce large quantities of a few similar products, while consumers want small quantities of many different products. In order to smooth the flow of goods and services, intermediaries perform such functions as sorting, accumulation, allocation, and creating assortments. In sorting, intermediaries take a supply of different items and sort them into similar groupings. Accumulation means that intermediaries bring together items from a number of different sources to create a larger supply for their customers. Intermediaries allocate products by breaking down a homogeneous supply into smaller units for resale. Finally, they build up an assortment of products to give their customers a wider selection.

A third benefit provided by intermediaries is that they help reduce the cost of distribution by making transactions routine. Exchanging relationships can be standardized in terms of lot size, frequency of delivery and payment, and communications. Seller and buyer no longer have to bargain over every transaction. As transactions become more routine, the costs associated with those transactions are reduced.

The use of intermediaries also aids the search processes of both buyers and sellers. Producers are searching to determine their customers' needs, while customers are searching for certain products and services. A degree of uncertainty in both search processes can be reduced by using channels of distribution. For example, consumers are more likely to find what they are looking for when they shop at wholesale or retail institutions organized by separate lines of trade, such as grocery, hardware, and clothing stores. In addition, producers can make some of their commonly used products more widely available by placing them in many different retail outlets, so that consumers are more likely to find them at the right time.

4. Physical distribution

Physical distribution is the set of activities concerned with efficient movement of finished goods from the end of the production operation to the consumer. Physical distribution takes place within numerous wholesaling and retailing distribution channels, and includes such important decision areas as customer service, inventory control, materials handling, protective packaging, order procession, transportation, warehouse site selection, and warehousing. Physical distribution is part of a larger process called "distribution," which includes wholesale and retail marketing, as well as the physical movement of products. Physical distribution activities have recently received increasing attention from business managers. This is due in large part to the fact that these functions often represent almost half of the total marketing costs of a product. The importance of physical distribution is also based on its relevance to customer satisfaction. By storing goods in convenient locations for shipment to wholesalers and retailers, and by creating fast, reliable means of moving the goods, business owners can help assure continued success in a rapidly changing, competitive global market.

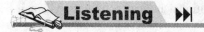

Listening ▶▶|

Conversation

Tapescript

Interviewer:	Dr. Merrifield is an advisor for wholesale distribution companies. As we all know e-commerce is rapidly changing our traditional concept of distribution strategy. Dr. Merrifield, do you see e-commerce as a threat or an opportunity to current distribution channels?
Merrifield:	I think the answer depends on your perspective and your channel position. If you play to win big, you pray for these types of revolutionary opportunities. If you play to protect what you have, then it's a huge threat.
Interviewer:	How about channel intermediaries? I guess they must respond quickly to the changes in today's distribution industry.
Merrifield:	Yeah, you bet it is. Channel intermediaries must be reactive to the changes in channel frameworks that are usually dictated by manufacturers and occasionally by powerful end-users. Intermediaries that adapt quickly and smoothly will excel at the expense of those who don't.
Interviewer:	Many industry insiders forecast e-channel will take away more and more business from distributors in all the B2B and dotcom clamors. I wonder what you would say about this.

Merrifield:	I'm afraid I wouldn't say that. In spite of all of the B2B and dotcom noise about online exchanges taking volume away from distributors, most of these exchanges will get very little share of physical sales.
Interviewer:	You mean physical distribution?
Merrifield:	Yes. Physical distribution exists primarily because of the freight, bundling, local processing and time sensitivity properties of the goods.
Interviewer:	How will e-commerce change the landscape of physical distributors in the, say, in the next five years?
Merrifield:	As I see it, channels will experience a significant net shrinkage of inventory, people and paper-work intensity.
Interviewer:	But don't you think traditional distribution channels are still playing a big role today?
Merrifield:	I see what you mean, but the only reason channels are as big as they are today is due to informational poverty and poor lines of communication between end-users and producers. As organizations begin to capture, store and make available more real-time information to channels, many traditional human activities will melt away.
Interviewer:	Oh, I remember you have mentioned the case of Wal-Mart in your newly published book *Electronic Commerce for Distribution Channels*.
Merrifield:	Yes, exactly. As Wal-Mart has proven for over 12 years, if manufacturers can get better real-time approximations of channel inventory and endpoint consumption, then they can significantly reduce total channel inventory.
Interviewer:	Then what advice would you give to distributors and other types of intermediaries to survive and prosper in the e-world?
Merrifield:	The first I'd like to say is, er, don't panic. Channel ecosystems are far more complex and flexible than even the players that are in the channels understand. B2B dotcom invaders will do far less, far more slowly than the hype would lead everyone to believe.
Interviewer:	So we only tell those distributors: Hey, guys. Take it easy. They are just bragging.
Merrifield:	No, I don't mean that. It is evident that a revolution is at hand. Don't resist it. Embrace it.

I. Listen to the conversation and choose the best answers to the questions you hear.

1. What is Dr. Merrifield?   (D)

2. According to Dr. Merrifield, to whom is e-commerce a huge threat?   (B)

3. How will e-commerce affect current distribution channels?   (A)

4. Which of the following is true about current distribution channels?   (A)

5. What can be concluded from the interview?   (D)

II. Listen to the conversation again and answer the following questions with what you hear.

1. What is the conversation mainly about?

   The impact of e-commerce on current distribution channels.

2. According to Dr. Merrifield, under what circumstances will e-commerce be a threat to current distribution channels?

   If you play to protect what you have and fight the progress, e-commerce is a huge threat to current distribution channels.

3. Who usually controls distribution channel frameworks today?

   Manufacturers and occasionally some powerful end-users.

4. What is the primary reason for the existence of physical distribution?

   Physical distribution exists primarily because of the freight, bundling, local processing and time sensitivity properties of the goods.

5. What change will e-commerce bring to the physical distribution channels in the next five years?

   Physical distribution channels will experience a significant net shrinkage of inventory, people and paper-work intensity.

6. Why are traditional distribution channels as big as they are today?

   It is due to informational poverty and poor lines of communication between end-users and producers.

7. What does the case of Wal-Mart prove?

   If manufacturers can get better real-time approximations of channel inventory and end-point consumption, then they can significantly reduce total channel inventory.

8. Why does Dr. Merrifield advise distributors and channel intermediaries not to feel panic at the advent of e-world?

   Because channel ecosystems are far more complex and flexible than even the players that are in the channels understand. B2B dotcom invaders will do far less, far more slowly than the hype would lead everyone to believe.

Passage

● ●

Tapescript

Retailing involves selling products and services to consumers for their personal or family use. Department stores, like Burdines and Macy's, discount stores like Wal-Mart and K-Mart, and specialty stores like The Gap, Zales Jewelers and Toys R Us, are all examples of retail stores. Service providers, like dentists, hotels and hair salons, and on-line stores, like Amazon.com, are also retailers.

As the final link between consumers and manufacturers, retailers are a vital part of the business world. Retailers add value to products by making it easier for manufactures to sell and consumers to buy. It would be very costly and time consuming for you to locate, contact and make a purchase from the manufacturer every time you wanted to buy a candy bar, a sweater or a bar of soap. Similarly, it would be very costly for the manufactures of these products to locate and distribute them to consumers individually. By bringing multitudes of manufacturers and consumers together at a single point, retailers make it possible for products to be sold, and, consequently, business to be done.

Retailers also provide services that make it less risky and more fun to buy products. They have salespeople on hand who can answer questions, may offer credit, and display products so that consumers know what is available and can see it before buying. In addition, retailers may provide many extra services, from personal shopping to gift wrapping to delivery, that increase the value of products and services to consumers.

Advances in technology, like the Internet, have helped make retailing an even more challenging and exciting field in recent years. The nature of the business and the way retailing is done are currently undergoing fundamental changes. However, retailing in some form will always be necessary. For example, even though the Internet is beginning to make it possible for manufacturers to sell directly to consumers, the very vastness of cyberspace will still make it very difficult for a consumer to purchase every product he or she uses directly. On-line retailers, like Amazon.com, bring together assortments of products for consumers to buy in the same way that bricks-and-mortar retailers do.

In addition, traditional retailers with physical stores will continue to be necessary. Of course, retailers who offer personal services, like hair styling, will need to have face-to-face interaction with the consumer. But even with products, consumers often want to see, touch and try them before they buy. Or, they may want products immediately and won't want to wait for them to be shipped. Also, and perhaps most importantly, in many cases the experience of visiting the retailer is an important part of the purchase. Everything that the retailer can do to make the shopping experience pleasurable and fun can help ensure that customers come back.

I. Listen to the passage and decide whether the following statements are true or false. Write T for true and F for false in the brackets.

1. (F)　2. (T)　3. (T)　4. (T)　5. (F)　6. (F)　7. (F)　8. (F)

II. Listen to the passage again and complete the notes with what you hear.

Examples of retail stores	• (1) <u>department stores</u>, like Burdines and Macy's • (2) <u>discount stores</u>, like Wal-Mart and K-Mart • (3) <u>specialty stores</u>, like The Gap, Zales Jewelers and Toys R Us • (4) <u>service providers</u>, like dentists, hotels and hair salons • (5) <u>on-line stores</u>, like Amazon.com
Function of retailing	• adding value to products by (6) <u>making it easier for manufacturers to sell and consumers to buy</u> • providing services that (7) <u>make it less risky and more fun to buy products</u>
Services retailers provide	• (8) <u>having salespeople on hand to answer questions</u> • (9) <u>offering credit</u> • displaying products so that (10) <u>consumers know what is available and can see it before buying</u> • providing many extra services, from personal shopping to (11)<u>gift wrapping</u> to delivery
Impact of Internet on retailing	• making retailing (12) <u>an even more challenging and exciting field</u> • bringing fundamental changes to (13) <u>the nature of the business and the way retailing is done</u> • enabling manufacturers to (14) <u>sell directly to consumers</u>
Reasons for the existence of traditional retailing	• Retailers offering personal services will need to have (15) <u>face-to-face interaction with the consumer</u>. • Consumers often want to (16) <u>see, touch and try products</u> before they buy. • Consumers may want products immediately and won't want to (17) <u>wait for them to be shipped</u>. • (18) <u>The experience of visiting the retailer</u> is an important part of the purchase.

Further Listening

Short Recordings

Tapescript

Item 1

BRUSSELS — The European Commission has rejected Microsoft's offer to settle its case by putting competitors' software on CD-ROMs sold with computers, a source familiar with the situation said Tuesday. The Commission believed the CD-ROMs distributed with new computers would get little use and would be an ineffective channel for distribution. According to a draft decision, the Commission has decided that Microsoft abused its dominant position and curbed competition by tying its Media Player program — used for playing music and videos — to its Windows operating system. The Commission has been considering an order which would tell Microsoft to unbundle Media Player from Windows, which the firm insists would wreck the system.

Microsoft Corporation, the world's No. 1 software company, provides a variety of products and services, including its Windows operating systems and Office software suite. The company has expanded into markets such as video game consoles, interactive television and Internet access. With its core markets maturing, Microsoft is targeting services for growth, looking to transforming its software applications into Web-based services for enterprises and consumers.

Item 2

NEW YORK — Shares of major tobacco companies rose sharply on Monday following a favorable court decision. The judge in the US Justice Department's $280 billion racketeering lawsuit against major tobacco companies on Friday agreed to allow an appeals court to review one of her decisions, Altria Group Inc.'s Philip Morris USA unit said. The nation's largest tobacco maker said US District Judge Gladys Kessler will let a court review her decision to allow the government to pursue its bid to force the companies to give up profits they earned in the past. The suit filed by the Clinton administration in 1999 accuses tobacco companies of deliberately misleading the public about the risks of smoking in a conspiracy going back to the 1950s.

Altria Group, Inc. is formerly known as Philip Morris Companies Inc. The Group's principal activities are to manufacture and market various consumer products, including cigarettes, foods and beverages. The Group's activities are carried out through its subsidiaries Phillip Morris USA Inc, Phillip Morris International Inc and Kraft Foods Inc. Phillip Morris USA Inc manufactures and markets cigarettes including brands like Marlboro, Virginia Slims and Parliament. Phillip Morris International Inc manufactures and sells tobacco products (mainly cigarettes) internationally. Kraft Foods Inc manufactures branded foods and beverages, which include grocery products, snacks, beverages, cheese and convenient meals.

Item 3

JOHANNESBURG — South African lawyers are suing entertainment conglomerate Walt Disney Co. for infringement of copyright on "The Lion Sleeps Tonight," lawyers said Friday. The song earned an estimated $15 million in royalties since it was written by Zulu migrant worker

Solomon Linda in 1939, and featured in Walt Disney's "Lion King" movies. However, Linda's impoverished family has only received about $15,000. Linda sold the worldwide copyright of the song to a local firm, but under British laws in effect at the time, those rights should have reverted to his heirs 25 years after his death in 1962. This means Linda's surviving three daughters and 10 grandchildren were entitled to a share of royalties from the song, which has since been recorded by at least 150 musicians.

Disney (Walt) Company's principal activity is to provide entertainment and information. The Group operates in four business segments: Media Networks, Parks and Resorts, Studio Entertainment and Consumer Products. The Media Networks segment includes the operations of ABC Television Network and ABC Radio Networks, which has affiliated stations providing coverage to the United States television households. The Parks and Resorts segment operates the Walt Disney World Resort in Florida and the Disneyland Resort in California. The Studio Entertainment segment produces and acquires live-action and animated motion pictures for distribution to the theatrical, home video and television markets. The Consumer Products segment licenses the name Walt Disney, as well as the Group's characters, visual and literary properties.

Item 4

NEW YORK — Eastman Kodak Co., the No. 1 maker of photographic film, said Tuesday it has filed suit against Japan's Sony Corp. alleging that the consumer electronics company infringed 10 of Kodak's patents related to digital photography. In a suit filed in a New York Federal Court, Rochester, New York-based Kodak alleged that Sony's products use technology invented by Kodak. Kodak, which is undergoing a tough transition toward digital products amid the decline of its film business, and Sony are among the leaders in sales of digital cameras, which do not use film and record images on computer chips and built-in memory cards. The lawsuit follows the failure of talks between the companies that Kodak hoped would produce a licensing pact.

Sony Corporation's principal activities are to develop, design, manufacture and sell electronic equipment, instruments and devices for consumer and industrial markets. The Group also manufactures and markets home-use game consoles and software. The Group operates through six segments — *Electronics*: Manufactures and sells audio-visual, informational and communicative equipment, instruments and devices; *Game*: Develops and sells PlayStation and PlayStation 2 game consoles and related software; *Music*: Manufactures and distributes recorded music in all commercial formats and musical genres; *Pictures*: Develops, produces and manufactures image-based software; *Financial services*: Represents insurance-related underwriting business and *Other segment*: Consists of various operating activities including Internet-related services and advertising agency.

Eastman Kodak Co. (KODAK) is the world leader in helping people take, share, enhance, preserve, print and enjoy pictures — for memories, for information, for entertainment. The company is organized into these key businesses: Digital & Film Imaging Systems — providing consumers, professional photographers and the motion picture industry with digital and traditional products and services; Health Imaging — supplying the healthcare industry with traditional and digital image capture, output and information management products and services; Graphic Communications — printing products, systems, networks and services for the printing and publishing industry, including commercial print shops and high-end on-demand color printing; Commercial Imaging — offering image capture, output and storage products and services to business and government; and Display & Components — delivering image display and capture devices for products such as digital cameras and scanners.

Item 5

LOS ANGELES — Twentieth Century Fox sued longtime distribution partner Virgin Entertainment Group on Monday, claiming that Virgin had not paid for shipments of DVDs and videocassettes of Fox films since October. The lawsuit, filed in Los Angeles Superior Court, said Fox has had an agreement since 1996 to sell videos and DVDs to Virgin to sell through its Virgin Megastores movie and CD retail chain. The Los Angeles-based Virgin Entertainment Group is an affiliate of Virgin Group Ltd., owned by British billionaire Richard Branson. According to the lawsuit, Virgin Entertainment owes more than $400,000 on products shipped as recently as last month. Fox asked a judge to order the company to pay the tab as well as interest and an unspecified amount of damages.

Fox Entertainment Group Inc.'s principal activities are carried out through four segments: *Filmed entertainment:* Produces and acquires live-action and animated motion pictures for distribution and licensing to the entertainment media. In addition, it also produces original television programming in the United States and Canada. *Television stations*: Broadcasts television stations in the United States. *Television broadcast network*: Includes broadcasting of network programming in the United States. *Cable network programming*: Produces and licenses programming, which is distributed through cable television systems and direct broadcast satellite (DBS) operators and professional sports team ownership.

Virgin Entertainment owns and operates about 25 Virgin Megastores in the US and Canada. The stores offer music, DVDs, books, and video games. Its virginmega.com website is run through a partnership with Amazon.com.

I. In this section, you will hear five short recordings. For each piece, decide for what each company has got involved in a lawsuit.

1. Microsoft Corp. ....C............   A. Tax evasion
2. Altria Group Inc. ....F............   B. Accounting fraud
3. Walt Disney Co. ....G............   C. Antitrust violations
4. Sony Corp. ....D............   D. Patent infringement
5. Virgin Entertainment ....E............   E. Outstanding payment

F. Consumer rights charges

G. Copyright infringement

H. Gender discrimination

II. Listen to the five recordings again and decide whether the following statements are true or false. Write T for true and F for false in the brackets.

1. (F) 2. (T) 3. (T) 4. (F) 5. (F) 6. (T) 7. (T) 8. (T) 9. (F) 10. (F)

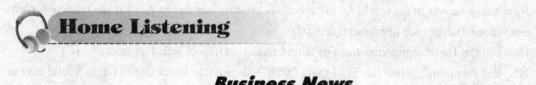

Home Listening

Business News

Tapescript

Oil prices edged higher Tuesday after ministers from the Organization of Petroleum Exporting Countries (OPEC) agreed to reduce output.

OPEC ministers have decided to stop producing more than their quota of 24.5 million barrels per day, effective immediately. The ministers also moved to lower the output quota by one million barrels per day, beginning April 1.

Some of the ministers said the two-step cutback is aimed at keeping oil prices steady while demand for oil is expected to decline as spring comes to the northern hemisphere.

With current demand high, OPEC countries have been exceeding production ceilings by an estimated 1.5 million barrels per day. If the cuts announced Tuesday are implemented, they would amount to a 10 percent reduction in OPEC's oil production.

But economic analyst Jim Steel, who is director of research at Refco Securities in New York, said the decision may not be so easy to implement. "The important statement I think is their attempt to rein in that production, and that, I think, is going to be very difficult because historically the crude oil prices are very high and it's very difficult for OPEC to cut when the price incentive to keep producing is so strong with oil in the $30 and above range."

Oil prices have surpassed OPEC's $22 to $28 a barrel price range in recent months, and rose again on Tuesday following the announcement of the production cuts.

Mr. Steel said the elevated price of oil, combined with the decrease in output that OPEC plans for April, may encourage other oil producers to increase their production. "We're going to see slowly increasing output from Iraq, and also we're going to see increased output from other non-OPEC countries, particularly in the Caspian. Russia is going to continue to produce, because these prices are very, very high and what OPEC has to realize is the incentive to produce outside of OPEC because of these high prices."

In Washington, a White House spokesman responded to OPEC's decision on Tuesday, saying President Bush hopes the cartel does not take any action that would hurt the US economy.

Listen to the business news report and choose the best answers to the questions you hear.

1. What had been OPEC countries' daily oil output before the production cuts were announced Tuesday?   (D)

2. How many barrels of oil would OPEC countries produce per day in April if the reduction plans announced Tuesday are implemented?   (C)

3. How did the Tuesday announcement of output reduction impact world oil prices?   (C)

4. Why did economic analyst Jim Steel think OPEC's decision to lower output might not be easy to implement?   (D)

5. Which of the following countries is likely to be benefited from OPEC's decision to reduce oil output?   (B)

Unit 8

International Trade

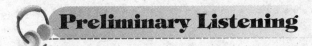

Preliminary Listening

Dictation

Listen to the following short paragraph and fill in the blanks with what you hear.

International trade is the exchange of goods and services across international boundaries or territories. In most countries, it represents (1) <u>a significant share of GDP</u>. Trading activities are directly related to (2) <u>an improved quality of life</u> for the citizens of nations involved in international trade. While international trade has been present throughout much of history, (3) <u>its economic, social, and political importance</u> has been on the rise in recent centuries. Industrialization, (4) <u>advanced transportation</u>, globalization, multinational corporations, and outsourcing are all having a major impact. Free trade zones, (5) <u>export subsidies and return of product tax</u> are often used to encourage export. However, to (6) <u>protect infant industry</u>, and (7) <u>prevent domestic markets from being occupied</u> by foreign products, governments often resort to (8) <u>various tariff and non-tariff barriers</u> to discourage import.

Listening & Speaking

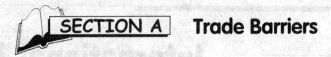

SECTION A **Trade Barriers**

Pre-listening ▶▶

Background Information

1. Comparative advantage and absolute advantage

Under the principle of absolute advantage, developed by Adam Smith, one country can produce more output per unit of productive input than another. A country has an absolute advantage over another in producing a product if it can produce that product using fewer resources than another country. For example, if one unit of labor in Scotland can produce 80 units of wool or 20 units of wine; while in Spain one unit of labor makes 50 units of wool or 75 units of wine, then Scotland has an absolute advantage in producing wool and Spain has an absolute advantage in producing wine. Scotland can get more wine with its labor by specializing in wool and trading the wool for Spanish wine, while Spain can benefit by trading wine for wool. (Adam Smith, Wealth of Nations, Book IV, Ch. 2) The benefits to nations from trading are the same as to individuals: trade permits specialization, which allows resources to be used more productively. Limitations to the theory may exist if there is single kind of utility. The very fact that people want food and shelter already indicates that multiple utilities are present in human desire. The moment the model expands from one product to multiple goods, the absolute may turn to a comparative advantage. However, pure labor arbitrage, where one country exploits the cheap labor of another, would be a case of absolute advantage that is not mutually beneficial. The principle of comparative advantage, generally attributed to David Ricardo, extends the range of possible mutually beneficial exchanges. It is not necessary to have an absolute advantage to gain from trade, only a comparative advantage. This means that one needs only to be able to make something at a lower cost, in terms of other goods sacrificed, to oneself to gain from trade. With comparative advantage, even if one country has an absolute advantage in every type of output, the disadvantaged country can benefit from specializing in and exporting the product(s) with the largest opportunity cost for the other country. Comparative advantage is a key economic concept in the study of free trade.

2. Protectionism

Protectionism is the economic policy of restraining trade between nations, through methods such as tariffs on imported goods, restrictive quotas, a variety of restrictive government regulations designed to discourage imports and anti-dumping laws in an attempt to protect domestic industries in a particular nation from foreign take-over or competition. This is closely aligned with anti-globalization, and contrasts with free trade, where no artificial barriers to entry are instituted. Businesses and living wages are protected by restricting or regulating trade between foreign nations.

- Subsidies: to protect existing businesses from risk associated with change, such as costs of labor, materials, etc.
- Protective Tariffs: to increase the price of a foreign competitor's goods, including restrictive quotas, and anti-dumping measures, on par or higher than domestic prices.
- Quotas: to prevent dumping of cheaper foreign goods that would overwhelm the market.
- Tax cuts: to alleviate the burdens of social and business costs.
- Intervention: to use state power to bolster an economic entity.
- Trade restriction.
- Exchange rate.

Protectionism is the economic means to achieve the political goal of an independent nation. The opposite of protectionism, free trade, is the economic means to achieve the political goal of interdependent nations. Recent examples of protectionism in first world countries are typically motivated by the desire to protect the livelihoods of individuals in politically important domestic industries. Whereas formerly blue-collar jobs were being lost to foreign competition, in recent years there has been a renewed discussion of protectionism due to offshore outsourcing and the loss of white-collar jobs. Some may feel that better job choice is more important than lower goods costs. Whether protectionism provides such a tradeoff between jobs and prices has not yet reached a consensus with economists. Some point out that free-trade has not benefited those in manufacturing, and that service-sector jobs, such as store clerk, do not pay as well as manufacturing used to.

3. Reasons for international trade

There are numerous reasons that countries engage in international trade. Some countries are deficient in critical raw materials, such as lumber or oil. To make up for these various deficiencies, countries must engage in international trade to obtain the resources necessary to produce the goods and/or services desired by their citizens. In addition to trading for raw materials, nations also exchange a wide variety of processed foods and finished products. Each country has its own specialties that are based on its economy and the skills of its citizens. Three common specialty classifications are capital, labor, and land. Capital-intensive products, such as cars and trucks, heavy construction equipment, and industrial machinery, are produced by nations that have a highly developed industrial base. Japan is an example of a highly developed industrial nation that produces large quantities of high-quality cars for export around the world. Another reason Japan has adapted to producing capital-intensive products is that it is an island nation; there is little land available for land-intensive product production. Labor-intensive commodities, such as clothing, shoes, or other consumer goods, are produced in countries that have relatively low labor costs and relatively modern production facilities. China, Indonesia, and the Philippines are examples of countries that produce many labor-intensive products. Products that require large tracts of land, such as cattle production and wheat farming, are examples of land-intensive commodities. Countries that do not have large tracts of land normally purchase land-intensive products from countries that do have vast amounts of suitable land. The United States, for example, is one of the leading exporters of wheat. The combination of advanced farming technology, skilled farmers, and large tracts of suitable farmland in the Midwest and the Great Plains makes the mass production of wheat possible. Over time a nation's work force will change, and thus the goods and services that nation produces and exports will change. Nations that train their workers for future roles can minimize the difficulty of making a transition to a new, dominant market. The United States, for example, was the dominant world manufacturer from the end of World War II until the early 1970s. But, beginning in the 1970s, other countries started to produce finished products more cheaply and efficiently than the United States, causing US manufacturing output and exports to drop significantly. However, rapid growth in computer technology began to provide a major export for the United States.

4. Factors influencing international trade

Political environment. Each country varies regarding international trade and relocation of foreign plants on its native soil. Some countries openly court foreign companies and encourage them to invest in their country by offering reduced taxes or some other investment incentives. Other countries impose strict regulations that can cause large companies to leave and open a plant in a country that provides more favorable operating conditions. When a company decides to conduct business in another country, it should also consider the political stability of the host country's government. Unstable leadership can create significant problems in recouping profits if the government falls of the host country and/or changes its policy towards foreign trade and investment. Another key aspect of international trade is paying for a product in a foreign currency. This practice can create potential problems for a company, since any currency is subject to price fluctuation. A company could lose money if the value of the foreign currency is reduced before it can be exchanged into the desired currency.

Economic environment. An important factor influencing international trade is taxes. Of the different taxes that can be applied to imported goods, the most common is a tariff. A country can have several reasons for imposing a tariff. For example, a revenue tariff may be applied to an imported product that is also produced domestically. The primary reason for this type of tariff is to generate revenue that can be used later by the government for a variety of purposes. This tariff is normally set at a low level and is usually not considered a threat to international trade. When domestic manufacturers in a particular industry are at a disadvantage, the government can impose what is called a protective tariff. This type of tariff is designed to make foreign products more expensive than domestic products and, as a result, protect domestic companies. A protective tariff is normally very popular with the affected domestic companies and their workers because they benefit most directly from it. In retaliation, a country that is affected by a protective tariff will frequently enact a tariff of its own on a product from the original tariff enacting country. Another form of a trade barrier that a country can employ to protect domestic companies is an import quota, which strictly limits the amount of a particular product that a foreign country can export to the quota-enacting country. The power of import quotas has diminished because foreign manufacturers have started building plants in the countries to which they had previously exported in order to avoid such regulations. A government can also use a non-tariff barrier to help protect domestic companies. A non-tariff barrier usually refers to government requirements for licenses, permits, or significant amounts of paperwork in order to allow imports into its country. This tactic often increases the price of the imported product, slows down delivery, and creates frustration for the exporting country. The end goal is that many foreign companies will not bother to export their products to those markets because of the added cost and aggravation.

Cultural environment. Before a corporation begins exporting products to other countries, it must first examine the norms, taboos, and values of those countries. This information can be critical to the successful introduction of a product into a particular country and will influence how it is sold and/or marketed. Business professionals also need to be aware of foreign customs regarding standard business practices. Thus, before businesspeople travel overseas, they must be given training on how to conduct business in the country to which they are traveling. Business professionals also run into another practice that occurs in some countries — bribery. The practice of bribery is common in several countries and is considered a normal business practice. If the bribe is not paid to a businessperson from a country where bribery is expected, a transaction is unlikely to occur. Laws in some countries prohibit businesspeople from paying or accepting bribes. As a result, navigating this legal and cultural thicket must be done very carefully in order to maintain full compliance with the law.

Listening ▶▶

Conversation

Tapescript

Interviewer:	Environment and trade is a challenging issue that the World Trade Organization (WTO) has to tackle. Dr. Douglas, many environmental advocacy organizations feel the WTO's rules have put a straitjacket on efforts to protect the environment by restrictions on harmful trade. What does your study show?
Interviewee:	As you know, WTO rules clearly permit countries to put up trade barriers for environmental reasons. The questions we tried to answer are: how widely are such sanctions applied, for what products, and what are their effects? Of 4,917 products we examined in world trade, we found only 1,171 that do not face any environmentally-related trade barriers (ETBs). The 3,746 other products — that do face barriers in at least one importing country — accounted for 88% of world merchandise trade in 1999.
Interviewer:	That seems an awful lot.
Interviewee:	We are not suggesting that 88% of products traded internationally directly face such barriers. The value of trade directly affected by ETBs, in fact, is US$679 billion — 13% of world trade. Of the 3,746 products I mentioned, 86% of the value of world exports bypasses these barriers. That means exporters focus their shipments on markets free of restrictions.
Interviewer:	But are these really environmentally-related measures? Developing countries have complained — some formally to WTO — that some industrial nations are using environmental protection to impose disguised protectionism.
Interviewee:	We took a practical view. It does not really matter for the exporter whether injury to the environment is truly ascertained or whether a measure is protectionism in disguise. What matters is whether traders can export.
Interviewer:	Then, Dr. Douglas, where were the ETBs usually found?
Interviewee:	Peaks of ETB protection appeared in particular for food items, and for plants and cut flowers.
Interviewer:	And the most affected product?
Interviewee:	Boneless bovine cuts — US$5.2 billion from US$5.4 billion of international trade: a coverage ratio of 97%. However, the peaks are not limited to agricultural products. Large automobiles are the major non-agricultural product in our listing. Trucks, smaller automobiles and motor vehicle parts appear prominently in other

ETB bands.

Interviewer:	I see. What are the other major products affected, Dr. Douglas?
Interviewee:	We have listed 100 in all. The most prominent are coniferous lumber, natural gas, footwear, medicines and telephones.
Interviewer:	These products do not seem to fall into the usual interpretation of environmentally sensitive products.
Interviewee:	We needed to look at the whole range of environmentally-related trade barriers, that is, all the reasons that could be invoked — meaning measures introduced by an importing country to protect the health and safety of wildlife, plants, animals and humans as well as the environment generally — all of which are possible under WTO rules.
Interviewer:	Dr. Douglas, according to your study, who is most affected by these ETBs?
Interviewee:	The implications from our study are quite clear: exporters from the 49 least developed countries are significantly more exposed to ETBs than those from any other group. These poorest countries of the poor may have to face even tougher hurdles in the future as a result of growing environmental concern worldwide.

I. Listen to the conversation and choose the best answers to the questions you hear.

1. What do many environmental advocacy organizations think of the WTO's rules?   (A)
2. Which of the following are NOT mentioned as the major products affected by environmentally-related trade barriers?   (D)
3. According to Dr. Douglas' study, who are most affected by environmentally-related trade barriers?   (B)
4. Which of the following is NOT covered in the interview?   (B)
5. What can be concluded from the interview?   (D)

II. Listen to the conversation again and complete the notes with what you hear.

Environmentally-related Trade Barriers (ETBs)

How widely are ETBs applied:
- ❑   (1) 1,171 out of 4,917 products examined do not face any ETBs.
- ❑   (2) 3,746 other products face ETBs in at least one importing country, accounting for (3) 88% of world merchandise trade in 1999.

❑ Trade value directly affected by ETBs amounts to (4) <u>US$679 billion</u> or (5) <u>13%</u> of world trade.

What products are affected by ETBs:

❑ Peaks of ETB protection are for (6) <u>food items, plants and cut flowers</u>.
❑ Most affected products are (7) <u>boneless bovine cuts</u>.
❑ Major non-agricultural products affected are (8) <u>large automobiles</u>.
❑ Other major products affected include trucks, (9) <u>smaller automobiles</u>, (10) <u>motor vehicle parts</u>, coniferous lumber, (11) <u>natural gas</u>, (12) <u>footwear</u>, (13) <u>medicines and telephones</u>.

What reasons could be invoked to impose ETBs:

To protect (14) <u>the health and safety of wildlife, plants, animals and humans as well as the environment generally</u>.

Who is most affected by ETBs:

(15) <u>Exporters from the 49 least developed countries</u>.

Passage

Tapescript

Any glance at the "International Trade" section of a business or economics textbook will tell you that free trade has advantages for all — higher total output and higher standards of living being the broadly cited benefits. The theory of comparative and absolute advantage with the often-used examples of wheat and wine seem to clearly demonstrate such benefits. Then why do countries impose restrictions on trade? The answer is very simple: the primary reason is to protect domestic workers from competition abroad. The basis for the decision is mainly political although there is some economic basis for protectionism.

In the United States, President George W. Bush applied this technique to offer support to workers in the steel industry in the Midwest of the USA. The industry was complaining that foreign steel producers were "dumping" cheap steel onto the US market rendering US steel producers uncompetitive. Textbook reasons for imposing some form of trade barrier often quote "protecting an infant industry" as a reason and explain that such protection offers the industry an opportunity to be able to grow and to be able to compete on an equal basis when the trade barrier is removed. Nice and convenient in theory but not quite so easy in practice.

Bush took the decision to impose a tariff on steel imports into the US amounting to 30%; his decision pleased the steel producers but has angered the steel users. Steel is used for a whole host of industrial applications from chemical manufacture to road building. Steel users in the US therefore faced a choice: continue buying from foreign suppliers and pay a higher price or buy from the US producers. On the face of it the second option looks to be the best but US steel producers took advantage of the protection they had been afforded to raise their prices.

Steel is a product that is used in a wide variety of different industries for many different purposes. So how do businesses react to this — they try to find a way round the problem. They are rearranging their supply chain and rather than manufacturing component parts in the US, they are transferring the work to Canada. The tariff does not affect steel imports landing in Canada and so getting a Canadian company to manufacture the component and then ship it to the US helps to keep costs low and avoids having to pay the tariff. The impact in manufacturing jobs in steel-using businesses in the US though is evident; if the work is transferred to Canada there is no longer a need for the workers in the US. An attempt to solve a problem in one sector by interfering in the market creates problems elsewhere. The question has to be: what is the balance of the costs and benefits, not just in the short term but also in the long term, for all interested parties?

I. Listen to the passage and choose the best answers to the questions you hear.

1. What do the often-used examples of wheat and wine show?   (A)
2. What is the major reason for governments to impose restrictions on trade?   (D)
3. Under what circumstances did President Bush decide to impose a tariff on steel imports?   (C)
4. Who would attack President Bush's protectionism policy on steel products?   (A)
5. Which of the following would be the outcome of Bush's protectionism policy?   (D)
6. What can be concluded from the passage?   (B)

II. Listen to the passage again and answer the following questions with what you hear.

1. What are the widely quoted benefits of free trade?
   Higher total output and higher standards of living.
2. What was the US steel industry complaining about?
   Foreign steel producers were "dumping" cheap steel onto the US market rendering US steel producers uncompetitive.
3. What opportunity does trade protectionism theoretically offer?
   An opportunity for infant industries to be able to grow and to be able to compete on an equal basis when the trade barrier is removed.

4. What choice did the US steel users face when President Bush decided to impose a steel import tariff amounting to 30%?

<u>To continue buying from foreign suppliers and pay a higher price or buy from the US producers.</u>

5. How did steel-consuming businesses react to President Bush's policy of imposing heavy steel import tariff?

<u>Finding a way round the problem by rearranging their supply chain and transferring manufacturing work to Canada.</u>

6. How can US steel-using businesses benefit by transferring their manufacturing jobs to Canada?

<u>Keeping costs low and avoiding having to pay the tariff.</u>

7. How would the imposition of tariff on steel imports affect manufacturing jobs in US steel-using businesses?

<u>The work would be transferred to Canada and there would no longer be a need for the workers in the US.</u>

8. What is essential when governments attempt to interfere in the market?

<u>To balance the costs and benefits, not just in the short term but also in the long term, for all interested parties.</u>

SECTION B   Trade Regulation

Pre-listening ▶▶

Background Information

1. World Trade Organization

The World Trade Organization (WTO) is an international organization designed to supervise and liberalize international trade. The WTO came into being on January 1, 1995, and is the successor to the General Agreement on Tariffs and Trade (GATT), which was created in 1947, and continued to operate for almost five decades as a de facto international organization. The World Trade Organization deals with the rules of trade between nations at a near-global level; it is responsible for negotiating and implementing new trade agreements, and is in charge of policing member countries' adherence to all the WTO agreements, signed by the bulk of the world's trading nations and ratified in their parliaments. Most of the WTO's current work comes from the 1986–1994 negotiations called the Uruguay Round, and earlier negotiations under the GATT. The organization is currently the host to new negotiations, under the Doha Development Agenda (DDA) launched in 2001. The WTO is governed by a Ministerial Conference, which meets every two years; a General Council, which implements the conference's policy decisions and is responsible for day-to-day administration; and a director-general, who is appointed by the Ministerial Conference. The WTO's headquarters are in Geneva, Switzerland.

2. ISO

The International Organization for Standardization, widely known as ISO, is an international standard-setting body composed of representatives from various national standards organizations. Founded on 23 February 1947, the organization promulgates world-wide industrial and commercial standards. It is headquartered in Geneva, Switzerland. While ISO defines itself as a non-governmental organization, its ability to set standards that often become law, either through treaties or national standards, makes it more powerful than most NGOs. In practice, ISO acts as a consortium with strong links to governments. The organization's logos in its two official languages, English and French, include the letters ISO, and it is usually referred to by these letters. ISO is not, however, an acronym for the organization's full name in either official language. Rather, the organization adopted ISO based on the Greek word *isos*, which means equal. Recognizing that the organization's initials would be different in different languages, the organization's founders chose ISO as the universal short form of its name. This, in itself, reflects the aim of the organization: to equalize and standardize across cultures.

3. Regulation of international trade

Traditionally trade was regulated through bilateral treaties between two nations. For centuries under the belief in Mercantilism most nations had high tariffs and many restrictions on international trade. In the years since the Second World War, controversial multilateral treaties like the GATT and World Trade Organization have attempted to create a globally regulated trade structure. These trade agreements have often resulted in protest and discontent with claims of unfair trade that is not mutually beneficial. Free trade is usually most strongly supported by the most economically powerful nations, though they often engage in selective protectionism for those industries which are strategically important such as the protective tariffs applied to agriculture by the United States and Europe. During recessions there is often strong domestic pressure to increase tariffs to protect domestic industries. The regulation of international trade is done through the World Trade Organization at the global level, and through several other regional arrangements such as MERCOSUR in South America, NAFTA between the United States, Canada and Mexico, and the European Union between 27 independent states.

Listening ▶▶

Conversation

Tapescript

Interviewer:	Well, Mr. Minister, you know that in 2000, the euro slumped and the oil price hiked. How do these factors influence the global trade?
Interviewee:	Despite these unfavorable and unsteady factors, major developed nations and many developing countries saw vigorous economic growth, and many countries in North America, Western Europe and Southeast Asia reported significant improvement in their financial situations.
Interviewer:	Could you please analyze the major characteristics the international trade has shown during its steady growth?
Interviewee:	The global trade has shown three characteristics. First, the proportion of commodities with a high scientific and technological level and high added value has increased constantly. Second, computer, financial, telecommunications and other most vigorous sectors have promoted international service trade with a growth rate exceeding that of commodity trade. Third, e-commerce has been extensively applied in international trade.
Interviewer:	Could you make it more specific with figures?
Interviewee:	For example, trade of IT products has grown by 20 percent annually, accounting for 12 percent of the total global commodity trade volume at present. And according to a report released by the United Nations a short time ago, e-commerce would rise to US$377 billion in 2000.
Interviewer:	China's foreign trade has successfully relieved the negative impacts of the Asian financial crisis and recorded a rapid growth of imports and exports in 2000. Could you give a brief account of the general situation of China's foreign trade in 2000?
Interviewee:	According to statistics of the customs, in 2000 China's import and export volume totaled US$474.3 billion, up 31.5 percent on the previous year. Export rose by 27.8 percent to US$249.2 billion and import by 35.8 percent to US$225.1 billion, creating a trade surplus of US$24.1 billion. The goal set by the Ninth Five-Year Plan (1996–2000) to reach an import and export volume of US$400 billion was met ahead of schedule.
Interviewer:	China is implementing the west development strategy. China's central and western regions have weaker infrastructure facilities and a lower level of opening-up compared

with coastal areas. Please tell us any of your ideas about this point.

Interviewee: The investment environment in central and western regions needs to be improved. To make a breakthrough and greater progress in foreign capital attraction, the central and western regions should not simply copy the policies of coastal areas. Instead, they must take measures suited to local conditions, display their unique advantages, create new ideas and new patterns, and adopt more active and effective measures to further expand opening-up.

Interviewer: As the Minister of the Foreign Trade and Economic Cooperation Work, could you make an analysis about the future background of China's foreign trade and economic cooperation?

Interviewee: Generally speaking, China's foreign trade and economic cooperation work faces sound internal and external environments for development. Global economy and trade are expected to maintain a certain growth rate, and China's national economy will continue to maintain fairly rapid development. However, there are many uncertain factors that will affect and restrain the development of China's foreign trade and economic cooperation.

I. Listen to the conversation and decide whether the following statements are true or false. Write T for true and F for false in the brackets.

1.(F) 2.(T) 3.(F) 4.(T) 5.(F) 6.(T) 7.(F) 8.(T) 9.(T) 10.(F)

II. Listen to the conversation again and complete the following notes with what you hear.

Brief account of international trade in 2000

Unfavorable factors influencing the global trade in 2000:
- ☐ (1) the slump of euro
- ☐ (2) the rise of oil price

Major characteristics of the international trade in 2000:
- ☐ steady increase of commodities with (3) a high scientific and technological level and high added value
- ☐ rapid growth of (4) international service trade promoted by computer, financial, telecommunications and other most vigorous sectors
- ☐ extensive application of (5) e-commerce in international trade

Customs statistics of China's imports and exports in 2000:

❑ total import and export volume: (6) US$474.3 billion

❑ export volume: (7) US$249.2 billion

❑ import volume: (8) US$225.1 billion

❑ export increase rate: 27.8%

❑ import increase rate: (9) 35.8%

❑ trade surplus volume: (10) US$24.1 billion

Future development environment of China's foreign trade:

❑ global economy and trade are expected to (11) maintain a certain growth rate

❑ China's national economy will continue to (12) maintain fairly rapid development

❑ many uncertain factors may affect and restrain the development

Passage

Tapescript

ISO has made great contributions toward foreign trade. As we know, standards have always been closely connected with trade, that is, the exchange of goods or services between supplier and customer. For example, agreement on weights and dimensions has for many hundreds of years made life easier for buyer and seller engaged in such simple exchanges as buying bread or pasta.

ISO standards are developed within nearly 190 technical committees, each of which deals with a specific area of technology. ISO has requested each committee to develop a business plan to guide its work program. The objectives are to require the technical committee to analyze conditions and trends in the market sector which it serves and explicitly to link its work program with the sector's requirements.

The growth in the volume of world trade continues to outstrip that of world production. Markets are becoming global. More and more, the supply chains which bring goods from producer to consumer link economic players across borders. International Standards facilitate this cross-border trade.

Businesses and customers stand to reap the maximum benefits when International Standards for products and services are implemented on a sufficiently broad scale to make technologies compatible worldwide.

Suppliers are then able to save money by offering one product based on internationally standardized specifications on markets everywhere, thus avoiding expensive and wasteful modifications and separate production runs necessary to meet different national requirements. Customers, in turn, find that their choice of products is widened to include offerings from around the world which nevertheless conform to adequate levels of quality, reliability and safety. In addition, customers should benefit from reduced prices brought about by competition between suppliers.

In addition to developing International Standards for products, services, systems and materials, ISO facilitates world trade by its standards and guides for what is called "conformity assessment". Conformity assessment is the process of evaluating products, services, systems, processes or materials against standards, regulations or other specifications. ISO standards and guides for conformity assessment encourage best practice and consistency internationally.

At present, ISO is developing some new Internet-based standardization projects. ISO is making more and more use of information and communication technologies, including the Internet, to speed up standardization, drive down costs and communicate with our customers and stakeholders.

I. Listen to the passage and decide whether the following statements are true or false. Write T for true and F for false in the brackets.

1. (F)　2. (F)　3. (T)　4. (F)　5. (T)　6. (T)　7. (F)　8. (F)　9. (F)　10. (T)

II. Listen to the passage again and complete the following notes with what you hear.

ISO & Foreign Trade

The contributions made by ISO to foreign trade

ISO facilitates world trade, encourages best practice and consistency internationally by developing:

❑　(1) international standards for products, services, systems and materials
❑　guides for conformity assessment, the process of evaluating (2) products, services, systems, processes or materials against standards, regulations or other specifications

The development of ISO standards

ISO standards are developed by its technical committees, each of which is required:

❑　to develop (3) a business plan to guide its work program
❑　to analyze (4) conditions and trends in the market sector which it serves
❑　to link (5) its work program explicitly with the sector's requirements

The benefits of implementing ISO standards

For suppliers:

☐ to save money by (6) <u>offering one product based on internationally standardized specifications on markets everywhere</u>

☐ to avoid (7) <u>expensive and wasteful modifications</u> and (8) <u>separate production runs necessary to meet different national requirements</u>

For customers:

☐ to obtain access to widened choice of products, including offerings from around the world which (9) <u>conform to adequate levels of quality, reliability and safety</u>

☐ to enjoy (10) <u>reduced prices brought about by competition between suppliers</u>

The impact of emerging technologies on ISO

Information and communication technologies are used by ISO:

☐ to (11) <u>speed up standardization</u>

☐ to drive down costs

☐ to (12) <u>communicate with customers and stakeholders</u>

Further Listening

Short Recordings

Tapescript

Item 1

It is a restriction invariably imposed by the government to prevent free trade among countries. The popular trade restrictions are tariffs, import quotas, and assorted non-tariff barriers. An occasional embargo will be even thrown into this mix. Its primary use is to restrict imports from entering the country. By restricting imports, domestic producers of the restricted goods are protected from competition and are even subsidized through higher prices. Consumers, though, get the short end of this stick with higher prices and a limited choice of goods.

Item 2

It refers to a condition in which a nation's imports are greater than exports. In other words, a country is buying more stuff from foreigners than foreigners are buying from domestic producers. It is usually thought to be bad for a country. For this reason, some countries seek to improve this condition by establishing trade barriers on imports, reducing the exchange rate in such a way that exports are less expensive and imports more expensive, or invading foreign countries with sizable armies.

Item 3

Unlike tariffs, import quotas, and other non-tariff barriers that protect domestic producers from competition, it is intended to punish the export destination country. One of the most famous cases in recent decades was the oil embargo that several middle-eastern countries imposed on the United States in the 1970s. This caused higher gasoline prices in the United States, created all sorts of havoc for the economy, and pretty much achieved the punishment objective. The United States is also prone to throw it up here or there when another country acts against its political wishes.

Item 4

It is a limit on the importation of a particular good brought into one country from another country. It, for example, would stipulate something like only X million pounds of Swiss cheese can be imported into the United States from Switzerland each year. Such a limit is a popular type of non-tariff barrier imposed by countries throughout the world, competing with tariffs as the number one trade restriction. The general justification for it is to protect domestic firms and industries from unfair competition by foreign companies.

Item 5

It is a tax usually imposed on imports, but occasionally on exports too, very rarely, of course. This is one form of trade barrier that is intended to restrict imports into a country. Unlike non-tariff barriers and quotas that increase prices and thus increase revenue received by domestic producers, it generates revenue for the government. Most economists who spend their waking hours pondering the plight of foreign trade contend that the best way to restrict trade, if that's what you want to do, is through this way.

I. In this section, you will hear five short recordings. For each piece, decide which foreign trade term the speaker is talking about.

1. _____E_____	A. Tariff
2. _____F_____	B. Embargo
3. _____B_____	C. Non-tariff barrier
4. _____D_____	D. Import quota
	E. Trade barrier

5. _____A_____

F. Trade deficit

G. Trade surplus

H. Antidumping duty

II. Listen to the five recordings again and decide whether the following statements are true or false. Write T for true and F for false in the brackets.

1.（T） 2.（F） 3.（F） 4.（F） 5.（T） 6.（F） 7.（T） 8.（F）

Home Listening

Business News

Tapescript

Japan and Southeast Asian countries have wrapped up a summit in Tokyo, pledging to create an East Asia economic community that includes free-trade agreements and aid. Japan also agreed to sign a non-aggression treaty with the 10 members of the Association of Southeast Asian Nations or ASEAN.

Japan and the 10-member ASEAN group unveiled ambitious plans for the creation of an East-Asian community.

In a joint declaration, signed after a two-day summit in Tokyo, the leaders of Japan and ASEAN promised to improve regional economic and security cooperation and to aim to establish a free-trade zone within 10 years.

To that end, Japan announced Thursday it would start talks early next year with the Philippines, Malaysia, and Thailand on setting up bilateral free-trade agreements.

Japan is already Southeast Asia's second-largest trading partner — with trade last year totaling more than $120 billion.

At the end of the summit, President Megawati Sukarnoputri of Indonesia — the current ASEAN chair — told reporters globalization creates both challenges and opportunities, which require greater regional unity in Asia.

"Although our relationship is in a good state, nevertheless, the dynamic global and regional and other environments require ASEAN and Japan to work together even more closely. We note a desire to consolidate our cooperation in the political and security fields."

Tokyo showed its support of these goals by promising to sign ASEAN's non-aggression pact in which all of its members promise to respect each other's sovereignty and territorial integrity. China and India have also agreed to sign a treaty.

Japanese Prime Minister Junichiro Koizumi also pledged $3 billion in new aid to Southeast Asia. Half will go to developing the Mekong River region — which flows through Thailand, Cambodia, Laos, Vietnam, and Burma. The remainder will be divided between those countries and the other five ASEAN member-states: Brunei, Indonesia, the Philippines, Singapore and Malaysia.

Japan announced it would continue to earmark 30 percent of its vast foreign aid budget for ASEAN countries.

In their joint declaration, Japan and Southeast Asia also promised to work closely to fight terrorism, piracy, and human trafficking.

Listen to the business news report and complete the following notes with what you hear.

ASEAN Summit In Tokyo	
Achievements at the ASEAN summit	Japan and Southeast Asian countries have pledged: ➢ to create (1) <u>an East Asia economic community</u> that includes free-trade agreements and aid; ➢ to sign a non-aggression pact in which all the ASEAN members promise to (2) <u>respect each other's sovereignty and territorial integrity</u>.
Joint declaration by Japan & Southeast Asian countries	In a joint declaration signed after a two-day summit in Tokyo, the leaders of Japan and ASEAN promised: ➢ to improve (3) <u>regional economic and security cooperation</u>; ➢ to aim to establish (4) <u>a free-trade zone within 10 years</u>; ➢ to work closely to fight (5) <u>terrorism, piracy, and human trafficking</u>.
Bilateral trade between Japan & Southeast Asian countries	➢ Japan is Southeast Asia's second-largest trading partner — with trade last year totaling (6) <u>more than $120 billion</u>. ➢ Japan would start talks early next year with the Philippines, Malaysia, and Thailand on (7) <u>setting up bilateral free-trade agreements</u>.
Comments by ASEAN chair on Japan-Southeast Asia relationship	➢ Globalization creates both challenges and opportunities, which require (8) <u>greater regional unity in Asia</u>. ➢ Although Japan-ASEAN relationship is in a good state, the dynamic global and regional and other environments require ASEAN and Japan to (9) <u>work together even more closely</u>. ➢ Both Japan and Southeast Asian countries note a desire to (10) <u>consolidate their cooperation</u> in the political and security fields.

continued

Japan's aid to Southeast Asia	Japan pledged (11) <u>$3 billion</u> in new aid to Southeast Asia. ➤ Half will go to (12) <u>developing the Mekong River region</u> — which flows through (13) <u>Thailand, Cambodia, Laos, Vietnam, and Burma</u>. ➤ The remainder will be divided between the above countries and the other ASEAN member states: (14) <u>Brunei, Indonesia, the Philippines, Singapore and Malaysia</u>. ➤ Japan would continue to commit (15) <u>30 percent of its vast foreign aid budget</u> to ASEAN countries.

Unit 9

Insurance

Dictation

Listen to the following short paragraph and fill in the blanks with what you hear.

Insurance is a form of risk management primarily used to (1) <u>hedge against the risk of a contingent loss</u>. It protects society from the consequences of financial loss from (2) <u>death, accidents, sicknesses, damage to property</u>, and injury caused to others. The person seeking to transfer risk, the insured (policyholder), pays a relatively small amount, the premium, to an insurance company, the insurer, which issues an insurance policy in which the insurer agrees to (3) <u>reimburse the insured for any losses covered by the policy</u>. Insurance is the process of (4) <u>spreading the risk of economic loss</u> among as many as possible subject to the same kind of risk and is based on (5) <u>the laws of probability and large numbers</u>. There are many perils that society faces, some natural (e.g., (6) <u>earthquakes, hurricanes, tornados, flood, drought</u>), some human (e.g., (7) <u>arson, theft, fraud, vandalism, pollution, terrorism</u>), and some economic (e.g. inflation, obsolescence, recessions). Insurers are able to provide (8) <u>coverage for virtually any predictable loss</u>.

Listening & Speaking

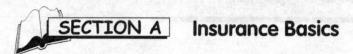

SECTION A　Insurance Basics

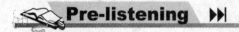

Pre-listening ▶▶

Background Information

1. Insurance basics

The term insurance describes any measure taken for protection against risks. When insurance takes the form of a contract in an insurance policy, it is subject to requirements in statutes, administrative agency regulations, and court decisions. By redistributing risk among a large number of people, insurance reduces losses from accidents incurred by an individual. In return for a specified payment (premium), the insurer undertakes to pay the insured or his beneficiary a specified amount of money in the event that the insured suffers loss through the occurrence of an event covered by the insurance contract (policy). By pooling both the financial contributions and the risks of a large number of policyholders, the insurer is able to absorb losses much more easily than is the uninsured individual. When an insured suffers a loss or damage that is covered in the policy, the insured can collect on the proceeds of the policy by filing a claim, or request for coverage, with the insurance company. The company then decides whether to pay the claim. The recipient of any proceeds from the policy is called the beneficiary. The beneficiary can be the insured person, or other persons designated by the insured. Insurers may offer insurance to any individual able to pay, or they may contract with members of a group (e.g., employees of a firm) to offer special rates for group insurance. Marine insurance, covering ships and voyages, is the oldest form of insurance; Fire insurance arose in the 17th century, and other forms of property insurance became common with the spread of industrialization in the 19th century. It is now possible to insure almost any kind of property, including homes, businesses, motor vehicles, and goods in transit. Insurance is vital to a free enterprise economy. It protects society from the consequences of financial loss from death, accidents, sicknesses, damage to property, and injury caused to others. Many persons are willing to pay a small amount for protection against certain risks because that protection provides valuable peace of mind.

2. Insurance business

The business of insurance is sustained by a complex system of risk analysis. Generally, this analysis involves anticipating the likelihood of a particular loss and charging enough in premiums to guarantee that insured losses can be paid. Insurance companies collect the premiums for a certain type of insurance policy and use them to pay the few individuals who suffer losses that are insured by that type of policy. The key functions of an insurer are marketing, underwriting, claims (investigation and payment of legitimate claims as well as defending against illegitimate claims), loss control, reinsurance, actuarial, collection of premiums, drafting of insurance contracts to conform to statutory law, and the investing of funds. Underwriters are expert in identifying, understanding, evaluating, and selecting risks. Actuaries play a unique and critical role in the insurance process: they price the product (the premium) and establish the reserves. The primary goal of an insurer is to underwrite profitably. Disciplined underwriting combined with sound investing and asset or liability management enables an insurer to meet its obligations to both policyholders and stockholders. Underwriting combines many skills — investigative, accounting, financial, and psychological. While some lines of business (e.g., homeowners, auto) are underwritten manually or class rated, many large commercial property and casualty risks are judgment rated, relying on the underwriter's skill, experience and intuition.

3. Insurance policy

Insurance policy is an insurance contract specifying what risks are insured and what premiums must be paid to keep the policy in force. Policies also spell out deductibles and other terms. Policies for life insurance specify whose life is insured and which beneficiaries will receive the insurance proceeds. Homeowner's insurance policies specify which property and casualty perils are covered. Health insurance policies detail which medical procedures, drugs, and devices are reimbursed. Auto insurance policies describe the conditions under which car owners will be covered in case of accidents, theft, or other damage to their cars. Disability policies specify the qualifying conditions of disability and how long payments will continue. Business insurance policies describe which liabilities are reimbursable. The policy is the written document that both the insured and the insurance company refer to when determining whether or not a claim is covered. The insurance policy varies among states and class of business; however, there are common features.

❑ Declaration Page: names the policyholder, describes the property or liability to be insured, type of coverage, and policy limits.

❑ Insuring Agreement: describes parties' responsibilities during the policy term.

❑ Conditions of the Policy: details coverage and requirements in event of a loss.

❑ Exclusions: describes types of property and losses not covered.

4. Top insurance companies

中国人民保险公司	The People's Insurance Company of China
中国人寿保险公司	China Life Insurance (Group) Company
中国平安保险公司	Ping An Insurance Company of China
中国太平洋保险公司	China Pacific Insurance (Group) Co., Ltd.
中宏人寿保险有限公司	Manulife-Sinochen Life Insurance Co., Ltd.
太平洋安泰人寿保险有限公司	Pacific-Antna Life Insurance Company Ltd.
安联大众人寿保险有限公司	Allianz-Dazhong Life Insurance Co., Ltd.
金盛人寿保险有限公司	AXA-Minmetals Life Insurance Co., Ltd.
日本住友生命	Sumitomo Life Insurance
英国伦敦劳合社	Corporation of Lloyd's
法国安盛公司	AXA
德国安联公司	Allianz
荷兰国际集团	Ing Group
英国皇家太阳联合保险集团	Royal & Sun Alliance Insurance Group
瑞士苏黎士金融服务	Zurich Financial Services

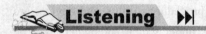 **Listing** ▶▶▶

Conversation

Tapescript

Interviewer: Mr. Howard, executive director and founder of the Insurance Consumer Advocate Network, knows about insurance and knows just about every trick by insurance companies. Mr. Howard, you spent 40 years in the insurance claims field, didn't you?

Howard: Yeah. Since 1965, I worked as an adjustor and insurance advocate and retired in 1994, but not for long. I was sick and tired of watching Oprah, and then one of my sons showed me the power of the Internet. I turned off Oprah and have been online ever since.

Interviewer: I guess Oprah would feel rather upset about it, but luckily we consumers have got the Insurance Consumer Advocate Network as a result. How did the idea of having a website to help insurance consumers occur to you?

Howard: It dawned on me that folks everywhere can be helped. I used to train adjustors for insurance companies and now I train consumers who in turn educate adjustors.

Interviewer: And how does your website help the consumers?

Howard: The whole point of our website is to teach consumers what questions to ask their insurance companies, what answers they have a right to expect and where to turn in their local areas if they don't get the right answers. We encourage consumers to go online to our website and we keep records of complaint ratios and rate comparisons from one company to another. You can see which companies are providing competitive rates and then look at the survey of consumer complaints. If you find a company that has reasonable rates and rare complaints, this is a good one to consider.

Interviewer: Mr. Howard, what can the consumer do if wronged by an insurance company?

Howard: The first thing to understand is that an insurance policy is a contract containing terms and conditions and rights and obligations of both parties. One of the obligations not specified in the policy is that the insurance company has to put the financial interest of the policy holder ahead of the insurance company's interests.

Interviewer: What if the insurance company puts its interests ahead of the policy holder's?

Howard: If that happens, this is a breach of contract. If the insurance company puts its financial interests ahead of the policy holder's as a usual and customary practice, that constitutes bad faith. In a breach of contract, the policy holder can pursue money for breach of contract, actual damages and compensatory damages. If the court determines that the insurance company intended wrongful conduct, it will be punished. Then the wronged party is entitled to the above plus punitive damages. Punitive damages are intended to discourage this kind of future misconduct.

Interviewer: How often are punitive damages awarded?

Howard: It isn't uncommon for punitive damages to be awarded. For example, State Farm Insurance Company was sued for bad faith in one of their regions and punitive damages were awarded for $50 million. It was alleged that State Farm violated rights of their policy holders by putting premium refunds due to the policy holders into offshore bank accounts to the tune of $35–50 billion!

Interviewer: So State Farm got caught. Did they admit they were withholding the refunds?

> **Howard:** As a matter of fact, State Farm didn't deny they were withholding the refunds. Rather, they referred to the money as policy holders' security accounts, and said they were holding them in trust. Interestingly enough, the money was used to buy some banks that were consolidated into State Farm banks. Stockholders were members of State Farm and policy holders were encouraged to borrow money from these banks. The bottom line: policy holders were borrowing their own money and paying interest for the privilege of borrowing their own money.
>
> **Interviewer:** I'm just wondering how these insurance companies can get away with it.
>
> **Howard:** They stay in business because they can. The insurance industry has been abusing customers as a matter of practice. But I believe consumers are reading about these lawsuits against insurance companies and becoming savvier about insurance-related topics now, especially with more websites such as ours.

I. Listen to the dialogue and choose the best answers to the questions you hear.

1. What can be learned about Mr. Howard? (A)

2. What does Mr. Howard's website teach consumers? (B)

3. According to Mr. Howard, what is a good insurance company for consumers to consider? (C)

4. What is the wronged party entitled to if the court determines that the insurance company intended wrongful conduct? (C)

5. What can be concluded from the dialogue? (D)

II. Listen to the dialogue again and decide whether the following statements are true or false. Write T for true and F for false in the brackets.

1.（F） 2.（F） 3.（T） 4.（F） 5.（T） 6.（F） 7.（F） 8.（T） 9.（T） 10.（T）

Passage

Tapescript

Insurance is the sharing of risks. Nearly everyone is exposed to risk of some sort. The house owner, for example, knows that his property can be damaged by fire; the ship owner knows that his vessel may be lost at sea; the breadwinner knows that he may die at an early age and leave his family the poorer. On the other hand, not every house is damaged by fire and not every vessel is lost at sea. If these persons each put a small sum into a pool, there will be enough to meet the needs of the few who do suffer loss. In other words, the losses of the few are met from the contributions of the many. This is the basis of insurance. Those who pay the contribution are known as "insured" and those who administer the pool of contributions as "insurers".

Not all risks lend themselves to being covered by insurance. Broadly speaking, the ordinary risks of business and speculation cannot be covered. The risks that buyers will not buy goods at the prices offered can not be insured against even if they can be estimated.

The legal basis of all insurance is the "policy". This is a printed form of contract on paper of the best quality. It states that in return for the regular payment by the insured of a named sum of money, called the "premium", the insurer will pay a sum of money or compensation for loss, if the risk or event insured against actually happens. The wording of policies often seems very old-fashioned, but there is a sound reason for this. Over a large number of years many law cases have been brought to clear up the meanings of doubtful phrases in policies. The law courts, in their judgments, have given these phrases a definite and indisputable meaning, and to avoid future disputes the phrases have continued to be used in policies even when they have passed out of the normal use of speech.

The business of insurance is sustained by a complex system of risk analysis. Generally, this analysis involves anticipating the likelihood of a particular loss and charging enough in premiums to guarantee that insured losses can be paid. The key functions of an insurer are marketing, underwriting, claims, loss control, reinsurance, actuarial, collection of premiums, drafting of insurance contracts to conform to law, and the investing of funds.

Because the insurance market has many sellers and buyers, little product differentiation, and freedom of entry and exit, it is highly competitive. Insurance companies seek to operate more efficiently and improve their communication and distribution systems. Combining insurance with other financial products and services is perceived to provide better sources for customers. Nowadays the insurance industry continues to explore new distribution systems, including the Internet and formation of alliances with banks and other financial services organizations in an effort to become more efficient and focused on the customer, who today places as much importance on service and convenience, as on price.

I. Listen to the passage and choose the best answers to the questions you hear.

1. What is said to be the basis of insurance?　(A)
2. According to the passage, which of the following risks can not be insured against?　(C)
3. Why does the wording of insurance policies often seem very old-fashioned?　(B)
4. What accounts for the high competitiveness of the insurance market?　(B)
5. Which of the following statements is true?　(D)

II. Listen to the passage again and complete the following notes with what you hear.

Possible risks people are exposed to:

❑ house owner: (1) <u>his property can be damaged by the fire</u>

❑ ship owner:　(2) <u>his vessel may be lost at sea</u>

❑ breadwinner: (3) <u>he may die at an early age and leave his family the poorer</u>

Risk analysis in the insurance business involves:

❑ anticipating (4) <u>the likelihood of a particular loss</u>

❑ charging (5) <u>enough in premiums to guarantee that insured losses can be paid</u>

Key functions of an insurer include:

❑ marketing

❑ (6) <u>underwriting</u>

❑ claims

❑ (7)<u>loss control</u>

❑ reinsurance

❑ actuarial

❑ (8) <u>collection of premiums</u>

❑ (9) <u>drafting of insurance contracts to conform to law</u>

❑ investing of funds

Ways for insurance companies to operate more efficiently:

❑ combining (10) <u>insurance with other financial products and services</u>

❑ exploring (11) <u>new distribution systems, including the Internet</u>

❑ forming (12) <u>alliances with banks and other financial services organizations</u>

SECTION B | Insurance Types

Pre-listening ▶▶│

Background Information

1. Choosing right insurance policies

Any risk that can be quantified can potentially be insured. An insurance policy will set out in detail what perils are covered by the policy and what are not. A single policy may cover risks in one or more of the categories. For example, auto insurance would typically cover both property risk (covering the risk of theft or damage to the car) and liability risk (covering legal claims from causing an accident). A homeowner's insurance policy in the US typically includes property insurance covering damage to the home and the owner's belongings, liability insurance covering certain legal claims against the owner, and even a small amount of health insurance for medical expenses of guests who are injured on the owner's property. Protecting your most important assets is an important step in creating a solid personal financial plan. The right insurance policies will go a long way toward helping you safeguard your earning power and your possessions. The following are policies that you shouldn't do without.

Long-term Disability Insurance. The prospect of long-term disability is so frightening that some people simply choose to ignore it. While we all hope that, "Nothing will happen to me," relying on hope to protect your future earning power is simply not a good idea. Instead, choose a disability policy that provides enough coverage to enable you to continue your current lifestyle even if you can no longer continue working.

Life Insurance. Life insurance protects the people that are financially dependent on you. If your parents, spouse, children or other loved ones would face financial hardship if you died, life insurance should be high on your list of required insurance policies. Think about how much you earn each year (and the number of years you plan to remain employed) and purchase a policy that will replace that income in the event of your untimely demise.

Health Insurance. The soaring cost of medical care makes health insurance a necessity. Even a simple visit to the family doctor can result in a hefty bill. Injuries that require surgery can quickly rack up five-figure costs. Although the ever-increasing cost of health insurance is a financial burden for just about everyone, the potential cost of not having coverage is much higher.

Home Insurance. Replacing your home is an expensive proposition. Having the right home insurance can make the process less difficult. When shopping for a policy, look for one that covers replacement of the structure and contents in addition to the cost of living somewhere else while your home is repaired. Also, be sure the policy provides adequate coverage for the cost of any liability for injuries that occur on your property.

Automobile Insurance. Some level of automobile liability insurance is required by law in most localities. Even if you are not required to have it, automobile liability insurance is something you shouldn't skip. If you are involved in an accident and someone is injured or their property is damaged, you could be subject to a lawsuit that could cost you everything you own. Accidents happen quickly and the results are often tragic — having no automobile liability insurance or purchasing only the minimum required coverage saves you only a small amount of money and puts everything else that you own at risk.

In addition to the policies listed above, business owners need business insurance. Liability coverage in a litigation-happy society could be the difference between a long and prosperous endeavor or a trip to bankruptcy court. Insurance policies come in a wide variety of shapes and sizes and boast many different features, benefits and prices. Shop carefully, read the policies and talk to the salesperson to be certain that you understand the coverage and the cost. Make sure the policies that you purchase are adequate for your needs, and don't sign on the dotted line until you are happy with the purchase.

2. Business owner's policy (BOP)

A business owner's policy (BOP) has been compared to a homeowner's policy for business. BOPs were first developed in the 1970s and have become a very popular form of insurance for small to medium sized businesses. BOPs combine some of the basic coverages needed by a typical small business into a standard package at a premium that is generally less than would be required to purchase these coverages separately. Business owners also like the simplified nature of the package as opposed to buying a collection of small policies. The efficiency also appeals to insurance companies and allows them to offer a lower premium for the package. Most of the coverages that are needed by small and medium sized businesses, with the exception of auto and worker's compensation, are generally included. This not only simplifies the process of buying the basic insurance coverages, but often gives a lower premium for businesses that qualify for a BOP. Business owner's policies basically consist of property coverage, liability coverage and some additional types of coverage that most businesses require. Optional coverages can also be added to meet specific needs of the business. Typically, a BOP policy includes:

❑ Property insurance (covering buildings, equipment and inventory);

❑ Business interruption insurance (covering losses that cause you to shut operations or reduce production for a time), which can provide money to offset lost profits or to pay continuing expenses (typically for up to a year for insured losses);

❑ Casualty or liability protection (covering harm done by the employees or products to other people or their property);

❑ Crime insurance (covering loss of money or securities resulting from burglaries or robberies or destruction) as well as losses from employee theft or embezzlement;

❑ Liability insurance covering lawsuits arising from accidents (as when someone trips and falls on your business's property) or when you sell a product that damages the customer's property or you are accused of offenses such as slander, copyright or invasion of privacy;

❑ Vehicle coverage for rented or borrowed vehicles.

A number of other coverages such as flood insurance or earthquake insurance or owned vehicle coverage and specialized liabilities are generally not included in BOPs. Some of these may be available separately for extra premiums. One of the distinguishing features of BOPs is that most automatically include business income and extra expense coverage (subject to some limitations).

3. General liability and property package

General liability and property package coverage is the most basic type of commercial insurance and is limited to liability claims of bodily injury or property damage. Coverage is provided for accidents on your premises or at your customer's location. Some client contracts also refer to these policies as Comprehensive Commercial Liability. It is important to remember that these policies exclude errors and omissions type claims related to the delivery of your professional services. Typically offered as a general liability and property package policy, coverage is also provided for theft or destruction of your company's computer hardware and software and other assets (see property coverage) such as office furnishings and equipment up to a specified amount. Business Liability insurance protects your business against financial loss resulting from claims of injury or damage caused to others by you or your employees.

❑ *Automatic Additional Insured Coverage* is automatically provided when required in a written contract, agreement or permit.

❑ *Personal and Advertising Injury* covers you for certain offenses you or your employees commit in the course of your business, such as libel, slander, disparagement, or copyright infringement in your advertisements.

❑ *Employment Practices Liability* covers claims, including legal defense costs, for certain employment-related lawsuits brought against you by your employees or job applicants ($5,000 limit where available).

❑ *Defense Costs* pays legal expenses for certain liability claims brought against your business regardless of who's at fault.

❑ *Medical Expenses* pays the applicable medical costs if someone is injured and needs medical treatment due to an accident on your premises.

❏ *Premises and Operations Liability* provides coverage for bodily injury and property damage sustained by others at your premises or as a result of your business's operations.

❏ *Tenant's Liability* protects your business against claims of damage due to fire or other covered losses caused by you to premises that you rent.

Listening ▶▶|

Conversation

Tapescript

Professor:	As we know, cargo transport insurance is an indispensable part of the import and export practice now. It protects the interests of both importers and exporters from possible financial losses by risks during the transit of goods.
Student:	Risks in cargo transport are of various kinds and different risks mean different losses. I guess they have to be covered by different insurance clauses.
Professor:	Exactly. And further, different insurance clauses mean different premiums. So a good understanding of various risks and losses is necessary for us to effect insurance.
Student:	Then what risks do importers and exporters usually have for transactions?
Professor:	One of the risks involved in an export or import transaction is that of losses or damages to goods during their transportation owing to storms, traffic accidents and so on.
Student:	Thus, exporters or importers have to get their goods insured in case such damages occur, don't they?
Professor:	Yes. In most cases, full protection from these risks can be provided through special cargo transport insurance, such as ocean transportation insurance, overland transportation insurance and air transportation insurance. Protection can be provided to cover all transport risks from the time the goods leave the seller's warehouse or factory until they reach the final destination stipulated by the foreign buyer. Such insurance provides the means to repay the cargo owners for any losses or damages that occur during the transportation of the goods.
Student:	If such losses do happen, will the carrier be legally called upon to make payment?
Professor:	No. If the goods are insured, the insurance company will be responsible for the losses and compensate the insured according to their agreement.
Student:	What is the deciding factor in the question as to who needs transportation insurance?

Professor: It's insurable interest. Generally speaking, insurable interest depends on whether a company will benefit from the safe arrival of the carrier and its cargo or whether the company will be hurt by the loss, damage or delay of the cargo.

Student: In that way, not only the owners of the carriers and cargoes have such an interest, but also may certain non-owners. It is vital for businesses to have their goods insured.

Professor: Absolutely. The reliability of the transportation carrier in international trade is severely limited. So shipments on ocean-going vessels are invariably covered by marine cargo transport insurance. When a CIF is quoted to a buyer the exporter must furnish marine insurance.

Student: One more question. Is the regular form of open or floating policy used for marine insurance also used for insurance of air cargo?

Professor: Yes, but air transport insurance requires a special rider, which is attached to the open policy. If the exporter makes regular shipments by air, it is to his or her advantage to obtain an open policy covering all shipments. Such a policy is able to be arranged to cover door-to-door shipments from exporter to importer.

I. Listen to the conversation and decide whether the following statements are true or false. Write T for true and F for false in the brackets.

1.（T） 2.（F） 3.（F） 4.（F） 5.（F） 6.（T） 7.（F） 8.（T）

II. Listen to the conversation again and complete the notes with what you hear.

Cargo Transport Insurance

Importance of cargo transport insurance:

❑ Being an indispensable part of the import and export practice now

❑ Protecting the interests of importers and exporters from (1) <u>possible financial losses by risks during the transit of goods</u>

Types of cargo transport insurance:

❑ Ocean transportation insurance

❑ (2) <u>Overland transportation insurance</u>

❑ Air transportation insurance

Coverage by cargo transport insurance:

- ☐ · Covering all transport risks from the time (3) <u>the goods leave the seller's warehouse or factory</u> until (4) <u>they reach the final destination stipulated by the foreign buyer</u>
- ☐ Providing the means to (5) <u>repay the cargo owners for any losses or damages that occur during the transit of goods</u>

Factor deciding who needs cargo transport insurance:

The factor deciding who needs transportation insurance is (6) <u>insurable interest</u>, which depends on whether (7) <u>a company will benefit from the safe arrival of the carrier and its cargo</u> or whether (8) <u>the company will be hurt by the loss, damage or delay of the cargo</u>

Legal documents used in cargo transport insurance:

- ☐ (9) <u>Regular form of open or floating policy</u> is used for both marine and air cargo insurance.
- ☐ (10) <u>A special rider attached to the open policy</u> is required in air transport insurance.

Passage

Tapescript

Together, public and private insurers issue four main types of insurance: property, liability, health, and life. Nearly every homeowner and business in the United States has some form of property insurance. Property insurance covers losses resulting from physical damage to real estate or personal property. This damage may result from fire, lightning, wind, hail, explosion, theft, vandalism, or other destructive forces.

To protect themselves if they are held responsible for damage to persons or to the property of other people, individuals and businesses often buy liability insurance. For example, supermarkets may be sued by customers who get injured in cluttered aisles or who ingest bad food. Automobile insurance is the most commonly issued liability insurance, accounting for $60 billion in premiums paid to insurers each year.

There is no way to insure the health of a business, but insuring the health of employees is a major cost to US companies. Health insurance covers medical and hospital care expenses as well as loss of income resulting from injury or disease.

Another major employee-benefit expense for most firms, life insurance is the most common form of insurance issued. In addition to this group coverage, many people buy additional life insurance to provide for their families in case of their premature death.

There are three basic forms of life insurance. Most companies provide employees with term insurance. It provides protection for a specified number of years, after which the protection ends. For example, a $50,000, 20-year term policy pays the face amount to a beneficiary if the insured dies during those 20 years. If the insured survives beyond 20 years, the coverage ends and no further premiums or benefits are paid. Term insurance is most useful to younger families who need financial protection against the early deaths of working members. But term life has no savings value.

In contrast, whole life insurance is a combination of insurance protection and savings. In addition to buying insurance coverage, a portion of the premiums builds up as savings. As a result, whole life is more expensive than term insurance. Insured individuals who decide to cancel their policies are entitled to receive the accumulated savings of the policy. If the insured dies while the policy is in force, the beneficiary receives the face amount of the policy, just as with term policies.

Endowment policies are even more savings-oriented and expensive than whole life. These policies are written for a fixed term, such as 30 years or until age 65. If insured individuals survive, they receive the entire face amount of the policy. Otherwise, the face value is paid to the beneficiaries.

I. Listen to the passage and choose the best answer to complete each of the following sentences.

1. B   2. D   3. C   4. A   5. B   6. A

II. Listen to the passage again and complete the notes with what you hear.

Insurance Types	Main Coverage or Features	
Property insurance	Covering losses resulting from (1) <u>physical damage to real estate or personal property</u>, which may result from (2) <u>fire, lightning, wind, hail, explosion, theft, vandalism, or other destructive forces</u>	
Liability insurance	Covering losses if individuals and businesses are held responsible for (3) <u>damage to persons or to the property of other people</u>	
Health insurance	Covering (4) <u>medical and hospital care expenses as well as loss of income resulting from injury or disease</u>	
Life insurance	Term	✧ Providing protection for (5) <u>a specified number of years</u> ✧ Being most useful to younger families who (6) <u>need financial protection against the early deaths of working members</u> ✧ Offering no savings value

continued

Insurance Types		Main Coverage or Features
Life insurance	Whole	✧ Offering a combination of (7) <u>insurance protection and savings</u> ✧ The insured individuals being entitled to (8) <u>receive the accumulated savings of the policy</u> if they decide to cancel their policies ✧ The beneficiary receiving the face amount of the policy if (9) <u>the insured dies while the policy is in force</u>
	Endowment	✧ Being more (10) <u>savings-oriented and expensive</u> than whole life ✧ Being written for a fixed term ✧ (11) <u>The insured receiving the entire face amount of the policy</u> if the insured survives ✧ (12) <u>The face value being paid to the beneficiaries</u> if the insured dies

Further Listening

Short Recordings

Tapescript

Item 1

WASHINGTON — The Supreme Court refused Wednesday to overturn a nearly $70 million judgment against the maker of Scotch tape in a monopoly case. A jury had ordered 3M to pay damages to a Pittsburgh-based company, LePage's Inc., which specialized in making store-brand tapes for big retailers. An appeals court said St. Paul-based 3M lured away LePage's customers by offering bundled rebates that retailers could collect only by selling multiple 3M product lines. LePage's had sued 3M, claiming it lost business from some of its largest customers because of the rebate program involving payments as high as $1 million to retailers who agreed not to buy from competitors.

3M Company is a diversified technology company with a global presence in the following markets: healthcare, industrial, display and graphics, consumer and office, safety, security and protection services, electronics, telecommunications and electrical and transportation. 3M products are sold directly to users and through numerous wholesalers, retailers, jobbers, distributors and dealers in a wide variety of trades in many countries worldwide.

Item 2

TOKYO — Software giant Microsoft Corp. received a warning from Japan's antitrust regulators about unfair business practices Tuesday, but the decision did not carry the heavy fines the US firm was given in Europe. Japan's Fair Trade Commission (FTC) said Microsoft should scrap a provision in its licensing contracts with PC makers that prevents them from filing patent infringement suits if they find Microsoft's Windows software contains features similar to their own technology. The FTC believes there is a high probability that the provision would discourage PC makers from developing their own technology for added value.

Item 3

NEW YORK — The dominance of America Online's Instant Messenger service is raising antitrust concerns in the government's review of its proposed merger with Time Warner. The Federal Trade Commission is examining the inability of competitors such as Microsoft to connect to AOL's Instant Messenger network as one of handful of antitrust concerns related to the merger. AOL controls 90 percent of the IM market and only allows registered users to communicate over its network. While the merger would not increase the combined company's share of the IM market, government officials are concerned that such leadership combined with the potential broadband Internet reach of New York-based Time Warner could raise antitrust concerns.

America Online, the Internet division of Time Warner (previously AOL Time Warner), is the world's largest Internet access provider. The AOL proprietary network offers content, communication tools, and online shopping, among other services.

Time Warner Inc., formerly known as AOL Time Warner Inc., is a media and entertainment company. It classifies its business interests into five fundamental areas: America Online, Inc., consisting principally of interactive services; Cable, consisting principally of interests in cable systems providing video and high-speed data services; Filmed Entertainment, consisting principally of feature film, television and home video production and distribution; Networks, consisting principally of cable television and broadcast networks, and Publishing, consisting principally of magazine and book publishing.

Item 4

NEW YORK — The US Justice Department, fresh from its antitrust victory in breaking up Microsoft Corp., has now set its sights on San Francisco-based Visa, and N.Y.-based MasterCard, which together own 80 percent of the total US credit card market compared with rivals Discover and American Express, both based in New York. The Justice Department alleges the two credit networks quash competition through an exclusion policy with their member banks. The policy prohibits member banks from issuing competitors' cards. The Justice Department is seeking an end to the practice because it is intended to severely restrict competition by depriving American Express and Discover of the ability to sell network services to people who are potential customers.

Visa USA, headquartered in San Francisco CA, is an association of nearly 14,000 Member financial institutions that comprise the US operations of the world's leading payment brand and largest payment system. Globally, nearly 21,000 financial institutions issue more than 1 billion Visa-branded cards, accounting for $2.5 trillion in annual transaction volume.

MasterCard is the US's #2 payment system and is owned by its 25,000 financial institution members worldwide. It markets the MasterCard (credit and debit cards) and Maestro (debit cards) brands, provides the transaction authorization network, and collects fees from members. Its cards are accepted at more than 22 million locations around the world..

Discover Financial Services, a business unit of Morgan Stanley Dean Witter & Co. operates the Discover® Card brands. With approximately 4 million merchant and cash access locations, Discover is the largest independent credit card network in the United States.

American Express is known primarily for its credit cards today, and it is also (and above all) the leading financial service provider in the travel sector. Who, for example, has never heard of its famous Traveler's Checks? It also has two other strings to its bow — firstly financial services through the American Express Corporation and American Express Financial Advisors, and secondly banking services which mainly specialized in the management of the group's financial products and asset management.

Item 5

NEW YORK — The Federal Trade Commission Monday voted to file an antitrust suit against Intel Corp., accusing the semiconductor giant of abusing its monopoly power in the microprocessor market. The complaint filed by the FTC seeks to stop Intel from using its dominance to withhold key information from companies that have legal disputes with Intel. Intel contended it is within its legal rights when it withholds technical information from other companies. "By its administrative complaint, the commission apparently questions whether Intel has the legal right to assert its intellectual property rights as a defense to an attack on its core microprocessor business," Intel said in a statement.

Intel, the world's leading semi-conductor manufacturer, is over and above all known for its microprocessors, the "chips" which are found in 80% of the world's computers. Intel's activities are divided into three divisions, with the Architecture Business Group and its microprocessors accounting for more than 4/5 of its business. There is also the Networking and Communications Group for networks and their components, and finally the Wireless Communications and Computing Group which makes communications devices and instruments as well as mobile telephone, Flash memory, and embedded processors. Always at the cutting edge of research, Intel is constantly trying to push back the physical limits that electronic design sets.

I. In this section, you will hear five short recordings. For each piece, decide for what each company is accused of antitrust violations.

1. 3M Co.	............D............	A. Exclusionary rule
2. Microsoft	............F............	B. Patent infringement
3. AOL	............G............	C. Company corruption
4. Visa & MasterCard	............A............	D. Bundled discount programs
5. Intel	............E............	E. Withholding key information
		F. Disputable contract stipulation
		G. Dominance of Internet access
		H. Intellectual property right violation

II. Listen to the five recordings again and choose the best answers to the questions you hear.

1. What can be learned about 3M Co.?   (D)
2. Which of the following is true about software giant Microsoft Corp.?   (B)
3. Why are federal government officials concerned about AOL's merger with Time Warner?   (D)
4. What can't be said about the US Justice Department?   (D)
5. How does Intel respond to the FTC's complaint?   (C)

Home Listening

Business News

Tapescript

The European Union says what it calls Europe's disappointing economy is starting to pick up, but that unemployment is expected to get worse next year. The EU's executive commission is also warning France and Germany that they risk violating the bloc's budget deficit limits for a fourth straight year in 2005 unless they change policies.

The EU's Stability and Growth Pact requires the 12 members of the bloc that use the euro single currency to keep their public deficits under three percent of gross domestic product.

But France and Germany have flouted those rules for two straight years, announced that they will do so again next year and, according to the European Commission, are on track to do so in 2005.

The Commission's semi-annual report on the euro-zone economy says Portugal, too, is likely to go over the deficit limits next year, and that Italy will do so in 2005.

The French and German governments have argued that the EU's budget rules should be more flexible in hard economic times, when job creation and economic pump-priming should take precedence over belt-tightening.

But the Commission says short-term economic stimulus plans should not come at the expense of long-term structural reforms designed to make the euro-zone more competitive with the United States. The Commission is taking particular aim at France and, theoretically, could recommend that the French government be fined for breaching the limits.

Looking at the euro-zone economy as a whole, the Commission's report says growth will be no more than 0.4 percent in 2003. When Britain, Denmark and Sweden — the three countries that do not use the euro — are included, that figure rises to 0.8 percent.

The report blames the EU's weak economic performance on uncertainties about the price of oil stemming from the war in Iraq, the decline in stock markets and worries about jobs and pensions.

And even though it says the euro-zone and the EU as a whole should return to average growth next year, thanks in part to encouraging signals from the US and Asian economies, the Commission warns that joblessness will probably increase next year and not improve until 2005.

It also warns that the euro's rise this year against the dollar poses risks for the competitiveness of European goods on world markets.

Listen to the business news report and choose the best answers to the questions you hear.

1. Which of the EU members is least likely to exceed the deficit limits in 2004?   (A)

2. What can be learned about the EU's limit on public deficits?   (D)

3. Which of the EU member countries has not yet adopted the European single currency?   (C)

4. What is held responsible for the EU's disappointing economic performance?   (D)

5. Which of the following is true according to the news report?   (B)

Unit **10**

Transportation

Listen to the following short paragraph and fill in the blanks with what you hear.

Transportation concerns the movement of products from a source — such as a plant, factory, or work-shop — to a destination — such as (1) <u>a warehouse, customer, or retail store</u>. Transportation may take place via (2) <u>air, water, rail, road, pipeline, or cable routes</u>, using planes, boats, trains, trucks, and telecommunications equipment as the means of transportation. Transportation costs generally depend upon (3) <u>the distance between the source and the destination</u>, the means of transportation chosen, and (4) <u>the size and quantity of the product to be shipped</u>. The means of transportation chosen will affect decisions regarding (5) <u>the location of a business or facility</u>, (6) <u>the form of packing used for products</u> and (7) <u>the size or frequency of shipments made</u>. Although transportation costs may be reduced by sending larger shipments less frequently, it is also necessary to consider (8) <u>the costs of holding extra inventory</u>.

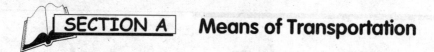

Listening & Speaking

| SECTION A | Means of Transportation |

Pre-listening ▶▶

Background Information

1. Mode of transport

Mode of transport (or means of transport or transport mode or transport modality or form of transport) is a general term for the different kinds of transport facilities that are often used to transport people or cargo. Where more than one mode of transport is used for a journey, the journey can be described as multi-modal. For each mode, there are several means of transport. Here are some examples of modes of transport.

- ❑ Animal-powered transport   carriage, sled, wagon, coach, dogcart …
- ❑ Aviation   aircraft, airship, glider, helicopter …
- ❑ Human-powered transport   bicycle, rickshaw, tricycle …
- ❑ Ship transport   boat, ship, submarine, liner …
- ❑ Rail transport   cable car, metro, tram, train …
- ❑ Road transport   bus, car, motorcycle, truck …
- ❑ Other   escalator, elevator, meglev（磁悬浮）train, pipeline …

Worldwide, the most widely used modes for passenger transport are the automobile, followed by buses, air, railways, and urban rail. The most widely used modes for freight transport are sea, followed by road, railways, oil pipelines and inland navigation.

2. Basic means of freight transportation

There are five basic means of transporting products utilized by manufacturers and distributors: airplane, truck, train, ship, or pipeline. Many distribution networks consist of a combination of these means of transportation. For example, oil may be pumped through a pipeline to a waiting ship for transport to a refinery, and from there transferred to trucks that transport gasoline to retailers or heating oil to consumers. All of these transportation choices contain advantages and drawbacks.

Air transport. Air transportation offers the advantage of speed and can be used for long-distance transport. However, air is also the most expensive means of transportation, so it is generally used only for smaller items of relatively high value — such as electronic equipment — and items for which the speed of arrival is important — such as perishable goods. Another disadvantage associated with air transportation is its lack of accessibility; since a plane cannot ordinarily be pulled up to a loading dock, it is necessary to bring products to and from the airport by truck. Air cargo remains a comparatively small segment of total freight transportation volume when measured by tonnage. But access to air transportation is expected to become increasingly important since a growing number of customers (such as hospitals and electronic manufacturers) depend upon "just in time" delivery systems as well as the increasing number of high-tech industries (such as computer manufacturers) adopting the "build-to-order" strategy. These trends, coupled with increased pressure on consumer goods manufacturers to deliver products quickly to meet customer expectations and reduce inventory and other supply chain costs, are expected to fuel the demand for expedited services. Accordingly, competition is heating up among the major air cargo and express carriers who are building specialized hubs to handle larger aircraft and major sorting facilities.

Trucks. Accessible and ideally suited for transporting goods over short distances, trucks are the dominant means of inland shipping in most countries.

Railways. Trains are ideally suited for shipping bulk products, and can be adapted to meet specific product needs through the use of specialized cars, i.e., tankers for liquids, refrigerated cars for perishables, and cars fitted with ramps for automobiles. Rail transportation is typically used for long-distance shipping. Less expensive than air transportation, it offers about the same delivery speed as trucks over long distances and exceeds transport speeds via marine waterways.

Water transport. Water transportation is the least expensive and slowest mode of freight transport. It is generally used to transport heavy products over long distances when speed is not an issue. Although accessibility is a problem with ships — because they are necessarily limited to coastal area or major inland waterways — piggybacking is possible using either trucks or rail cars. The main advantage of water transportation is that it can move products all over the world.

Pipeline facilities. Most pipeline transportation systems are privately owned. Generally used for transport of petroleum products, they can also be used to deliver certain products (chemicals, slurry coal, etc.) of other companies.

3. Transportation in business

The goal for any business owner is to minimize transportation costs while also meeting demand for products. Transportation costs generally depend upon the distance between the source and the destination, the means of transportation chosen, and the size and quantity of the product to be shipped. In many cases, there are several sources and many destinations for the same product, which adds a significant level of complexity to the problem of minimizing transportation costs.

The decisions a business owner must make regarding transportation of products are closely related to a number of other distribution issues. For example, the accessibility of suitable means of transportation factors into decisions regarding where best to locate a business or facility. The means of transportation chosen will also affect decisions regarding the form of packing used for products and the size or frequency of shipments made. Although transportation costs may be reduced by sending larger shipments less frequently, it is also necessary to consider the costs of holding extra inventory. The interrelationship of these decisions means that successful planning and scheduling can help business owners to save on transportation costs.

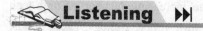

Listening ▶▶

Conversation

....

Tapescript

Operator:	Hello, China Ocean Shipping Agency, Can I help you?
Client:	Hello, could you put me through to the shipping department, please?
Clerk:	Hello, shipping department, what can I do for you?
Client:	I'd like to book shipping space with Maersk Line service to San Francisco.
Clerk:	Oh, I see. When will you effect the shipment?
Client:	According to the contract, the shipment must be effected prior to March 12th. Is there any space available?
Clerk:	Wait a moment. Let me check it for you. Er … here, yes. There's a vessel named "Mild Sea" going to Western America on March 10th.
Client:	How old is the ship? Our client requires that any ship built before 1989 should not apply to this shipment.
Clerk:	Hmm, well, it's a new ship built in 2001.
Client:	That's great. In this case, I'd like to book two forty-feet containers.
Clerk:	No problem. May I have your consignee's full name and address, so I can fill out the Shipping Order?
Client:	Oh, it's Vertex International Trading Corporation. V-E-R-T-E-X, Vertex.
Clerk:	OK. Vertex International Trading Corporation. Address, please?
Client:	1453 Mission Street, San Francisco, CA 94103, United States.
Clerk:	Mission Street?
Client:	Yes, M-I-S-S-I-O-N, Mission Street.
Clerk:	(A little slowly) Vertex International Trading Corporation at 1453 Mission Street, San Francisco, CA 94103, USA. Is that right?

Client:	Perfect!
Clerk:	Thank you. Are there any other parties to be informed of the cargo's arrival?
Client:	No. Just the company mentioned above. By the way, I'd like to know the container number, so I can notify my client earlier.
Clerk:	OK. Container numbers are MSKL257289 and MSKL354890. Now, what kinds of commodity to be shipped?
Client:	Shoes, leather shoes in 1248 cartons. During the shipment they should be strictly kept away from damp and pressure.
Clerk:	Don't worry. We'll make corresponding marks on the package. Can you tell me the gross weight and measurement for the sake of storage?
Client:	OK, let me see. The cargo weighs 42984.7 kilograms with 102.437 cubic meters.
Clerk:	Thank you. I'll fax you the Shipping Order. If you confirm all the items, please sign it, so that I can arrange the shipment as quickly as we can.
Client:	I will. Thank you.

I. Listen to the conversation and choose the best answers to the questions you hear.

1. When should the cargo be shipped according to the contract?   (C)
2. What is required of the shipping vessel by the client?   (B)
3. Who is to be informed of the cargo's arrival?   (C)
4. How will the clerk send the Shipping Order to the client?   (A)
5. Which of the following is NOT mentioned in the conversation?   (B)

II. Listen to the conversation again and complete the Bill of Lading with what you hear.

BILL OF LADING

PENAVICO

S/O No.

SNLL0054812

Shipper

Shanghai Jiahua International Inc.

8–15 F. Baishu Mansion   1230–1240 Zhongshan Road N. 1, Shanghai

Tel: (86) 21–66862506   Fax: (86) 21–66868742

Consignee

Vertex International Trading Corporation

1453 Mission Street, San Francisco, CA 94103, USA.

Tel: (415) 863-1506　　Fax: (415) 863-1508

Notify Party

Same as consignee

Pre-carriage by	**Place of Receipt**
Jincheng Logistics company	Shanghai

Ocean Vessel	**Voy. No.**	**Port of Loading**
Mild Sea	V. 0060E	Shanghai Port

Port of Discharge	**Place of Delivery**
San Francisco	San Francisco

Particulars Furnished by the Shipper

Container No.	No. of Containers or Packages	Description of Goods	Gross Weight	Measurement
MSKL 257289 MSKL 354890	two 40' containers 1248 cartons	Leather shoes	42984.7KGS	102.437M^3
Prepaid at	**Payable at**		**Place of Issue** Shanghai	
Total Prepaid	**No. of Original B/L** Three (3)			
Special Requirement	Strictly kept away from damp and pressure			

Passage

Tapescript

The cost of physically moving a product is the highest cost faced by many manufacturers. Thus, cost is certainly a major factor in choosing a transportation method. But manufacturers must also consider the nature of their product, the distance it must travel, how quickly it must be received, and customers' wants and needs. The difference in cost among trucks, railroads, planes, ships, and pipelines is directly related to the speed of delivery.

The advantages of trucks include flexibility, fast service, and dependability. Because breakage is normally less than by railroad, trucked goods need less packing. Trucks are a particularly good choice for short-distance distribution and more expensive products. Large furniture and appliance retailers in major cities, for example, use trucks to shuttle merchandise between their stores and make deliveries to customers. Trucks, however, can be delayed by bad weather. They also are limited in the volume they can carry in a single load.

Railroads have been the backbone of transportation system. They now are used primarily to transport heavy, bulky items such as cars, steel and coal. To regain market share, railroads have expanded their services to include faster delivery times and piggy-back service, which places semitrailers on railcars. Piggy-back service alone can save shippers up to one-half of the transportation costs of trucking goods.

Air is the fastest available transportation mode. Other advantages include greatly reduced costs in packing, handling, unpacking, and final preparations necessary for sale to the customer. Also inventory carrying costs can be reduced by eliminating the need to store certain commodities. Fresh fish, for example, can be flown to restaurants each day, thus avoiding the risk of spoilage that comes with packaging and storing a supply of fish. However, air freight is the most expensive form of transportation.

Of all the transportation modes available, water transportation is the least expensive. The network of internal waterways, locks, rivers, and lakes allow water carriers to reach areas throughout the world. Unfortunately, water transportation is also the slowest way to ship. Boats and barges are thus utilized for extremely heavy, bulky materials and products where transit times are unimportant. Manufacturers are using water carriers more often, however, since many ships are now specially constructed to load and store large standardized containers.

Like water transportation, pipelines are slow in terms of overall delivery time. They are also very inflexible, being built to travel only one route. But they do provide a constant flow of the product and are unaffected by weather conditions. Traditionally, this delivery system has transported liquids and gases.

For many years, companies that transported goods specialized in one transportation method. But in recent years, this pattern has changed. Large railroad companies are merging with trucking, air, and shipping lines. Their goal is to offer customers complete, simplified source-to-destination delivery by whatever combination of transportation methods is needed to get the job done.

I. Listen to the passage and choose the best answers to the questions you hear.

1. What is the highest cost faced by many manufacturers?   (C)
2. What must manufacturers take into consideration in choosing a transportation method?   (D)
3. How can piggy-back service benefit the shippers?   (A)
4. What is the cheapest mode of transportation?   (B)
5. What can be inferred from the passage?   (A)

II. Listen to the passage again and complete the table with what you hear.

Transport Means	Products suitable for Transport	Advantages	Disadvantages
Trucks	A particularly good choice for (1) <u>short-distance distribution and more expensive products</u>	Including (2) <u>flexibility, fast service, and dependability</u>; Requiring less packing	Can be delayed by bad weather; Limited in (3) <u>the volume to be carried in a single load</u>
Railroads	Used primarily to transport (4) <u>heavy, bulky items</u>		
Airplanes		Fastest available transportation mode; Reduced costs in (5) <u>packing, handling, unpacking, and final preparations necessary for sale to the customer</u>; Reduced inventory cost	(6) <u>Most expensive form of transportation</u>
Ships	Used for (7) <u>extremely heavy, bulky materials and products where transit times are unimportant</u>	(8) <u>Least expensive transportation mode</u>	Slowest way to ship
Pipelines	Built to transport (9) <u>liquids and gases</u>	Providing (10) <u>a constant flow of the product</u>; Unaffected by (11) <u>weather conditions</u>	Slow in terms of (12) <u>overall delivery time</u>; Inflexible, being built to travel only one route

SECTION B **Sea Transportation**

Pre-listening ▶▶

Background Information

1. Sea transportation

Sea transportation is primarily used for the carriage of people and non-perishable goods, generally referred to as cargo. Although the historic importance of sea travel for passengers has decreased, due to the rise of commercial aviation, it is still very effective for short trips and pleasure cruises. While slower than air transport, modern sea transport is a highly effective method of moving large quantities of non-perishable goods. Transport by water is significantly less costly than transport by air for transcontinental shipping. Ship transport is used for a variety of unpackaged raw materials ranging from chemicals, petroleum products, and bulk cargo such as coal, iron ore, cereals, bauxite, and so forth. Sea transport remains the largest carrier of freight in the world. About 80% of all of the world's international trade is carried on the oceans. The growth of industrial potential, reduction of an international division of labor, strengthening of economic ties between the countries on different continents, the increase of the volume of foreign trade, and the discovery of new marine mineral deposits give rise to a steady increase in ocean cargo transportation. The comparatively inexpensive, almost limitless characteristics of sea transport and the greater overall dimensions of transported freight, make it a truly global pathway.

2. Containerization

Containerization is a system of intermodal freight transport using standard shipping containers that can be loaded and sealed intact onto container ships, railroad cars, planes, and trucks. The concept of containerization is considered as the key innovation in the field of logistics which has revolutionized freight handling in the twentieth century. There are five common standard lengths, 20-ft (6.1 m), 40-ft (12.2 m), 45-ft (13.7 m), 48-ft (14.6 m), and 53-ft (16.2 m). The 20-ft container is the most common container worldwide, but the 40-ft container is increasingly replacing it, particularly since costs tend to be per container and not per foot. Container capacity is measured in twenty-foot equivalent units (TEU, or sometimes teu). An equivalent unit is a measure of containerized cargo capacity equal to one standard 20-ft (length) × 8 ft (width) × 8.6 ft (height) container. In metric units this is 6.10 m (length) × 2.44 m (width) × 2.59 m (height), or approximately 38.5 m³. Most containers today are of the 40-ft (12.2 m) variety and are known as 40-foot containers. This is equivalent to 2 TEU. Two TEU are equivalent to one forty-foot equivalent unit (FEU). The maximum gross mass for a 20-ft dry cargo container is 24,000 kg, and for a 40-ft, it is 30,480 kg. Allowing for the tare mass of the container, the maximum payload mass is there reduced to approximately 21,800 kg for 20-ft, and 26,680 kg for 40-ft containers.

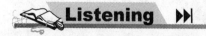 **Listening** ▶▶|

Conversation

Tapescript

| **Mr. Wilson:** | Ms. Chen, shall we move on and discuss the packing? |

Ms. Chen:	Very well. You know, we have definite ways of packing various garments. As to blouses, we use a polythene wrapper for each article, all ready for window display.
Mr. Wilson:	Good. A wrapping that catches the eye will certainly help push the sales. With competition from similar garment producers, the merchandise must not only be of good value but also look attractive.
Ms. Chen:	You are right. We'll see to it that the blouses appeal to the eye as well as to the purse.
Mr. Wilson:	What about the outer packing?
Ms. Chen:	We'll pack them 10 dozen to one carton, gross weight around 25 kilos a carton.
Mr. Wilson:	Cartons?
Ms. Chen:	Yes, corrugated cardboard boxes.
Mr. Wilson:	Could you use wooden cases instead?
Ms. Chen:	Why should we use wooden cases?
Mr. Wilson:	I'm afraid the cardboard boxes are not strong enough for such a heavy load.
Ms. Chen:	The cartons are comparatively light and therefore easy to handle. They won't be stowed with the heavy cargo. The stevedores will see to that. Besides, we'll reinforce the cartons with straps.
Mr. Wilson:	That sounds reassuring, but the goods are to be transshipped at Hamburg or London. If the boxes are moved about on an open wharf, the dampness or rain may get into them. This would make the blouses spotted or ruined.
Ms. Chen:	I think there is no need to worry about that. The cartons are lined with plastic sheets and thus are water-proof. As the boxes are made of cardboard, they will be handled with care.
Mr. Wilson:	Well, I don't want to take any chances. Besides, cartons are easy to be cut open, and this increases the risk of pilferage.
Ms. Chen:	Tampering with cartons is easily detected. I should say this rather discourages any possible pilferage.
Mr. Wilson:	Maybe you have got a point here, but I'm afraid in case of damage or pilferage, the insurance company will refuse compensation on the ground of improper packing, or packing improper for sea voyage.
Ms. Chen:	But cartons are quite seaworthy. They are widely used in our shipments to continental ports.
Mr. Wilson:	Well, I can understand your position, but …
Ms. Chen:	OK. I think we will use wooden cases if you insist, but I'm afraid the charge for packing will be considerably higher, and it slows down delivery.
Mr. Wilson:	Well, I'll call home immediately for instruction on this matter.
Ms. Chen:	Please do. I'll be waiting for your reply.

I. Listen to the conversation and decide whether the following statements are true or false. Write T for true and F for false in the brackets.

1. (F)   2. (F)   3. (T)   4. (T)   5. (T)   6. (T)   7. (T)   8. (F)   9. (F)   10. (F)

II. Listen to the conversation again and complete the notes with what you hear.

Ms. Chen		Mr. Wilson
Suggestion: • packing the blouses with (1) <u>a polythene wrapper</u> Reason: • a definite way of packing blouses	**inside packing**	Response: Affirmative Reasons: • looking attractive • (2) <u>helping push the sales</u>
Suggestions: • packing the blouses (3) <u>10 dozen to one corrugated cardboard carton</u> • stowing cartons separate from the heavy cargo • (4) <u>reinforcing cartons with straps</u> • (5) <u>lining cartons with plastic sheets</u> • handling cartons with care • Reasons: • cartons being comparatively light and (6) <u>therefore easy to handle</u> • pilferage discouraged with easy detection of carton tampering • cartons being quite sea worthy and (7) <u>widely used in sea transportation</u> • wooden cases incurring (8) <u>higher charge and slower delivery</u>	**outside packing**	Response: Negative Reasons: • (9) <u>cartons being not strong enough for a heavy load</u> • blouses being (10) <u>spotted or ruined by the dampness and rain</u> in transshipment • increased risk of pilferage because (11) <u>cartons are easy to be cut open</u> • possible trouble with insurance compensation on the ground of (12) <u>packing improper for sea voyage</u> • Suggestion: • using wooden case

Passage

Tapescript

Since the container ship came into being, big ports throughout the world have undergone a revolution: cargo delivery has speeded up. What's more, big ports have changed completely in their appearance. Docks and ships look quite different nowadays. Instead of forests of tall thin cranes lifting pallets, we see a few huge heavily built transporter cranes lifting big steel boxes. Instead of hundreds of stevedores working in the holds and on the quayside we see no men at all; we just see huge machines. Instead of long warehouses at the dockside, we see open spaces with stacks of boxes. The ships themselves look like huge steel tanks with lots of smaller tanks stacked in them.

Containers are steel boxes of different sizes but usually 8 by 8 by 20 or 40 feet that is 2.4 by 2.4 by 5.9 or 12 meters. But all containers are of the same width and height. This is limited by the width of roads. Containerization has brought great revolution into ocean shipping.

With container ships, handling at docks can be done mostly by machines. Ships designed with special guide structure in their hold can receive the containers. With container ships, very few stevedores are needed. A traditional ship took one hundred men, three to four weeks to unload and load. A container ship of the same size takes twelve to fifteen men, three to four days. Unloading and loading a container ship is very fast and time spent in port is much shorter. Goods can be delivered more quickly by fewer ships. With container ships, packing can be done in the suppliers' factories. Containers needn't be opened except for customs inspection until they reach the customers. With container ships, warehouses are unnecessary. Containers are water-proof and can be stacked by straddle carriers outside in the rain. Refrigerated containers can be connected to electrical plant at the dockside and in the ship. In addition, container ships are the only way in which a cargo can be shipped in different modes of transportation without massive handling.

With so many advantages mentioned, it is undoubted that the containerization is the trend for international transportation. However, the capital cost of containerizing ports is enormous. So the majority of ports still use traditional methods.

I. Listen to the passage and choose the best answers to the questions you hear.

1. How has the container ship revolutionized international transportation?   (A)

2. Why do all containers have the same width and height?   (C)

3. Why has containerization not been adopted by the majority of ports throughout the world?   (B)

4. Which of the following statements is true according to the passage?   (B)

5. What can be inferred from the passage?   (D)

II. Listen to the passage again and complete the notes with what you hear.

Advantages of Container Ships

Advantages of container ships include:
- ❏ (1) <u>Handling at docks can be done mostly by machines</u>;
- ❏ (2) <u>Very few stevedores are needed</u>;
- ❏ (3) <u>Unloading and loading a container ship is very fast and time spent in port is much shorter</u>;
- ❏ (4) <u>Packing can be done in the suppliers' factories</u>;
- ❏ (5) <u>Warehouses are unnecessary</u>;
- ❏ Containers are water-proof and can be (6) <u>stacked by straddle carriers outside in the rain</u>;
- ❏ Refrigerated containers can be (7) <u>connected to electrical plant at the dockside and in the ship</u>;
- ❏ Container ships enable a cargo to be shipped (8) <u>in different modes of transportation without massive handling</u>.

Further Listening

Short Recordings

Tapescript

Item 1

BRUSSELS — The European Union slapped Microsoft Corp. with a record fine Wednesday and ordered the world's largest software company to take immediate steps to stop some of its competitive practices. The EU executive said Microsoft must act within four months to change the way it does business in Europe "because the illegal behavior is still going on". The European Commission — the enforcer of EU competition law — levied a record fine of €497.2 million, or $611.8 million, and ordered the unbundling of Windows Media Player within 90 days. The Commission characterized Windows, which runs on more than 95 percent of all personal computers, as a "near monopoly".

Item 2

SEATTLE — Boeing Co. will pay between $40.6 million and $72.5 million to settle a class-action lawsuit brought by women alleging they were mistreated based on their gender, the No. 2 jet maker said on Friday. A Seattle judge gave preliminary approval to the settlement — including changes in the way Boeing evaluates workers for pay raises and promotions — between the company and a plaintiffs group that could number as many as 29,000. The case was first brought in February 2000 by female employees who claimed Boeing tolerated sexual intimidation and improper advances in the workplace and paid women less than men doing the same jobs as far back as 1997.

Item 3

NEW YORK — Mazda Motors of America was hit with a $5.25 million civil penalty Thursday for deceptive television advertising two years ago about its car lease offers, the largest fine ever imposed by the Federal Trade Commission in a consumer protection case. Among the violations listed by the FTC, Mazda reportedly showed lease cost disclosures required under the agreement in print that was too small and unreadable, and left them on the screen of its television ads for too short a time. "This substantial penalty should send a strong signal to everyone in the automobile industry — manufacturers, dealers and advertising agencies — that important leasing information cannot be buried in fine print," said Jodie Bernstein, the director of the FTC's bureau of consumer protection.

Mazda Motor Corporation, Japan's fifth-largest automaker — behind Toyota, Nissan, Honda, and Mitsubishi — makes cars, minivans, pickup trucks, and commercial vehicles. Models sold by Mazda in the US include sedans, minivans (MPV), sports cars, and pickup trucks. Operating from two Japanese and 17 international manufacturing plants, Mazda sells some 330,000 vehicles annually in Japan, and more than 630,000 abroad. Ford Motor owns a controlling 33% of Mazda.

Item 4

NEW YORK — Beverly Enterprises Inc., the largest US nursing home chain, agreed Thursday to pay a $175 million fine and give up 10 of its nursing homes to settle federal charges of Medicare fraud. It is the largest government settlement ever in a nursing home case. The Justice Department said Beverly submitted phony documents that inflated the number of hours nurses spent caring for Medicare patients at 10 nursing homes in California and elsewhere. Beverly will pay $170 million in a civil settlement — $25 million within 30 days, and the rest to be deducted from Medicare reimbursements over eight years. The company's California subsidiary will pay about $5 million in criminal fines.

Beverly Enterprises, Inc. is engaged in providing healthcare services, including the operation of nursing facilities, assisted living centers, hospice and home care centers, outpatient clinics and rehabilitation therapy services. As of December 31, 2003, the Company operated 373 nursing facilities with a total of 39,435 licensed beds in the United States. Its nursing facilities are located in 24 states and the District of Columbia and range in capacity from 24 to 355 licensed beds.

Item 5

COLUMBUS, Ohio — De Beers pleaded guilty on Tuesday in federal court to a decade-old price-fixing charge, freeing the world's dominant diamond producer to compete directly in the lucrative US market. The South African diamond concern was fined the maximum $10 million under the terms of the plea agreement. De Beers had previously refused to acknowledge US jurisdiction. But the company's stance left representatives of the 124-year-old De Beers, a dominant force in the global $55 billion diamond industry, subject to arrest if they set foot in the United States, the world's biggest diamond market. It also forced De Beers to use intermediaries to sell in the United States, where more than half of the world's diamonds are purchased.

De Beers Consolidated Mines Limited (DBCM) controls the South African mining interests of De Beers, the world's largest diamond miner and marketer. The company's mines in South Africa produce about 12 million carats of the sparkly gem every year. DBCM and sister company De Beers Centenary were taken private in 2001 under DE BEERS SA, a holding company owned by South Africa's Anglo American and the Oppenheimer family (45% each). Nicky Oppenheimer, grandson of Anglo American's founder, heads the De Beers operations.

I. In this section, you will hear five short recordings. For each piece, decide for what each company was imposed heavy penalties.

1. Microsoft	C	A. Credit fraud
2. Boeing Co.	E	B. Medicare fraud
3. Mazda Motors	F	C. Antitrust violations
4. Beverly Enterprises	B	D. Patent infringement
5. De Beers	G	E. Sex discrimination
		F. Misleading advertising
		G. Price fixing accusation
		H. Government illegal aid

II. Listen to the five recordings again and choose the best answers to the questions you hear.

1. What did the European Union order Microsoft Corp. to do?   (B)
2. Which of the following is included in the charges against Boeing Co.?   (A)
3. What is the FTC's main purpose of giving Mazda a substantial penalty?   (C)

4. How will Beverly settle the $175 million fine payment?　(D)

5. Which of the following is NOT true about De Beers?　(B)

Home Listening

Business News

Tapescript

Finance ministers from many of the more than 180 member-countries of the International Monetary Fund (IMF) and World Bank are meeting in Washington to discuss global economic developments.

For Ghana's finance minister Yaw Osafo-Maafo the most important issues are debt and the price of oil. His West African country has been registering significant economic growth in recent years and has had its foreign debt cut in half. Despite that, said Mr. Osafo-Maafo, Ghanaians remain very poor and now they have endured an economic shock in the form of a doubling of gasoline prices.

Substantive decisions are not expected at the meetings. Instead there will be wide ranging discussion on problems of economic policy, the economic outlook and developing country debt.

World Bank President James Wolfensohn said that the recovering world economy is good news, but he added that the benefits of growth are uneven with poor countries like Ghana paying a heavy price for this year's sharp increase in oil prices. Mr. Wolfensohn wants the meetings to focus on global poverty.

"We frankly believe that you can't have peace and stability unless you deal with the question of poverty," he noted. "But it is not at the moment a hot button issue. A lot of people talk about it but there is not tremendous action."

It was 60 years ago that the World Bank and International Monetary Fund were created at a war-time financial conference at which over 30 countries participated. Anne Krueger, the acting head of the IMF, said that the two organizations have promoted global financial stability during six decades of significant progress.

"We've had a growth of international trade," she said. "We've had a liberalization of trade which has spurred that growth. We've had living standards, life expectancies — any measure you name — not just incomes, life expectancies, education attainments going up."

The IMF itself is in transition as a new managing director is in the process of being named. He is expected to be the outgoing Spanish finance minister Rodrigo Rato. Horst Koehler, the first German to head the fund, resigned last month to accept the nomination to become Germany's state president.

Listen to the business news report and choose the best answers to the questions you hear.

1. Which issue is covered in the discussion at the World Bank and IMF Finance Ministers' meeting in Washington?   (B)

2. What seems to be World Bank President's greatest concern at the meeting?   (C)

3. According to the acting chief of the IMF, what is one of the most significant achievements made by the World Bank and IMF?   (C)

4. Who is the former IMF managing director?   (B)

5. Which of the following can be learned from the news report?   (C)

Unit 11

Agencies

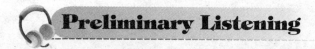

Preliminary Listening

Dictation

Listen to the following short paragraph and fill in the blanks with what you hear.

A company can use different avenues to sell its products overseas. Direct exporting provides (1) <u>more control over the export process</u>, potentially higher profits, and (2) <u>a closer relationship to the overseas marketplace</u>. However, the company needs to devote (3) <u>more time, personnel, and other corporate resources</u> than are needed in indirect exporting, which provides a way to penetrate foreign markets without getting involved in (4) <u>the complexities and risks of exporting</u>. Several types of intermediary companies provide (5) <u>a range of indirect exporting services</u>. One of them is import export agencies, which act as a matchmaker between manufacturers in one country and (6) <u>wholesalers, importers and buyers in another country</u>. They earn revenue through (7) <u>an agreed commission on each sale</u>, usually in an agreed territory, and sometimes in (8) <u>a particular product or market sector</u> in which they have knowledge and expertise.

Listening & Speaking

| SECTION A | **Agency Appointment** |

Pre-listening ▶▶

Background Information

1. **Choosing how to enter overseas markets**

When selling overseas, you can sell your product or service directly to customers or use an intermediary. You may decide a mix of these approaches is best for your business. There is no "one size fits all" solution. You should consider the implications of each method in terms of:

❑ the direct and indirect costs, such as investment in an overseas operation, or the heavy discounts often demanded by distributors;

❑ how much control you'll retain over how your product is sold, and how much you'll need to delegate to partners or intermediaries;

❑ which export-related risks you'll have to bear, such as exchange-rate fluctuations, non-payment risks, longer trading cycles and delays due to documentation problems.

An intermediary may be able to handle issues such as paperwork, shipping and warehousing. However, you will have less direct control. Selling directly may give you more control, but you will have to bear higher costs. To make the right decision, you should investigate your new market and how your product will fit into it. Consider the following questions.

❑ What's your priority — minimizing potential costs or controlling the process?

❑ Do you have the market knowledge (and language skills) to make contacts and generate sales?

❑ Do you have the time and money to invest in setting up a local branch or subsidiary?

❑ Are there restrictions on the way you can enter the market? For example, some countries may insist you form a joint venture with a local business.

❑ What is appropriate for your product? If it requires specialist after-sales support, selling through an intermediary may not be suitable.

❑ What are the usual distribution channels for products like yours in the target market?

Answering these questions will help you with the strategic planning for entering overseas markets.

2. Using an overseas agent

A sales agent acts on your behalf in the overseas market and is paid a commission for any sales they make. The key benefit of using an overseas sales agent is that you get the advantage of their extensive knowledge of the target market. However, while there are clear benefits, agency relationships can have their downsides too.

Advantages

❑ Provides predictable sales costs. The manufacturer and agent agree in advance on a set commission which remains the same for the life of the agreement in good times or bad. Knowing up front that your cost of sales is a fixed percentage of the unit price eliminates many planning and pricing headaches.

❑ Lowers sales costs. You avoid the recruitment, training and payroll costs of using your own employees to enter an overseas market. You avoid the cost of automobile and travel expenses, insurance benefits, stock and profit sharing plans, sick leave, vacation and holiday pay and per diem expenses as well.

❑ Reduces administrative overhead. With an outside sales force, the constantly escalating costs of administrating sales payroll and furnishing various administrative services for sales employees is reduced significantly or eliminated.

❑ Eliminates cost of training and turnover in sales personnel. Whenever you hire new sales employees you start paying them immediately, but they don't start paying off for you until much later, if at all. There is no way to recover the sales that they miss during all these transitions. But you can avoid losing them by using a trained and established sales force for hire.

❑ Gives immediate access to the market. With the agency, manufacturers have an experienced sales team in the territory immediately. The agency people are familiar with the area and have a number of good prospects who they feel would be ready to consider your product line. They should already have solid relationships with potential buyers — it might take you some time to build up your own contacts.

❑ Provides a highly experienced, more aggressive sales force. Most agents are well trained and were a sales manager or a senior salesperson before going on their own to work for an agency. Since there is no base salary to rely on, agents can't afford to slack off at any time.

❑ Provides a broader sales context for your product. Because the agent sells several related but non-competing product lines, he is in a position to expose you to a wider variety of prospects and customers. By doing this he often finds applications for your products which would be missed by the single-line salesperson.

❑ Adds marketing flexibility at less cost. Sales agents can increase your volume by selling outside your present marketing territory — and you pay them a commission only when they produce. Agents can also sell a new line without conflicting with your present sales organization.

❑ Increases sales. It has been estimated that the individual agent sells approximately 70% more than the average company salesman — due in part, no doubt, to his independent status and a greater need to succeed.

Disadvantages:

❑ Agents tend to deal in a variety of related or even unrelated products. One cannot expect an agent to concentrate solely on a recently introduced product, and many opportunities may be lost due to the agent's inability to explore all likely options.

❑ Agents may insist on a sole agency contract and then not obtain any sales, with the result that the exporting company cannot enter the market itself or appoint another agent, and thus lose many sales opportunities.

❑ Agents receive commission on all sales achieved. The products with the highest percentage of total commission will obviously attract the attention and efforts of the agent and any slow moving product lines offering limited or irregular commission may be neglected or even totally ignored after a certain period of time.

❑ Agents are unlikely to be able to exploit the potential of overseas markets fully, due to the nature and limitations of their operations.

❑ After-sales service can be difficult when selling through agent.

❑ You may lose some control over marketing and brand image, compared with entering the market yourself.

❑ The activities of agents may not be totally ethical or marketing orientated. Marketing organizations may seek a long term relationship with a group of customers, while agents may settle for one-off commissions. Any adverse reactions from the product users may have an adverse long term effect on the reputation of the products which could make future growth extremely problematic if not impossible.

3. Contracting with overseas agents

Make sure any agreement with an agent is formalized in a clear written contract. This will reduce the chances of disagreements or problems arising later. It's worth seeking expert advice, for example, from a lawyer with trade-related experience. The following are the key points the contract should cover.

❑ Parties — the names and addresses of the businesses involved, and the nature of the relationship.

❑ Products — a clear description of your goods.

❑ Territory — the geographic area within which the agent or distributor will sell your goods.

❑ Exclusivity — will they have sole rights to sell your goods?

❑ Exceptions to exclusivity — for example, can you sell direct to customers you already have in the market?

- □ Pricing — what price will you receive from a distributor for your goods? What price will an agent charge their customers?
- □ Commission — what commission will an agent receive?
- □ Payment terms — when will payments be made, in what currency, and at what exchange rate?
- □ Period — set a termination date for the agreement, and include clear provisions for ending the agreement before that date.
- □ Confidentiality — make sure that sensitive information about your business or products is protected.
- □ Intellectual property — what rights will the agent have to use your business name, brand names, trade marks, etc.?
- □ After-sales care — for example, product liability, insurance and warranties. Who is responsible at each stage of the trading process?
- □ Marketing — what promotional activities will support your products and who will pay for them?
- □ Rights — ensure that rights you assign can't be transferred to a third party.
- □ Jurisdiction — which country's rules will apply to the contract? This can affect the employment, performance and termination provisions of agency contracts.

If you are contracting with an overseas agent, you may also want to set clear weekly or monthly sales targets that are realistic and measurable. The action to be taken if these targets are not met should also be dealt with in the contract. If you can't agree on terms with your agent, or if a contractual dispute arises, consider resolving the issue through the International Chamber of Commerce (ICC) International Court of Arbitration or a similar body.

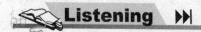 **Listening** ▶▶

Conversation

Tapescript

Mr. Clinton:	Ms. Zhang, I'm really very pleased that we have been able to strike a quick deal this time.
Ms. Zhang:	So are we, Mr. Clinton. We wish to express our gratitude for your close cooperation in this business. As a matter of fact, I didn't expect that you could conclude such a substantial business with us. That's nearly twice as big as that of last year.
Mr. Clinton:	To be frank, your products, either sports jackets and trousers or women's suits,

have met with the approval of our clients. They are very popular in our market for their reliable quality.

Ms. Zhang: Do they have any comments on the style and colors?

Mr. Clinton: Yes, they find the style and colors are quite to their taste.

Ms. Zhang: We've heard of similar comments from other European companies, too.

Mr. Clinton: By the way, may I know the possibility of handling as an agent of the goods you are exporting now? You know we are commanding an extensive domestic market in this line.

Ms. Zhang: Well, we highly appreciate your good intention and your efforts in pushing the sales of our textile products. Yet, in regard to your request for an agency arrangement, I'm afraid it's still too early for us to come into the matter.

Mr. Clinton: Early? Why, Ms. Zhang, the business between us two parties has been going on very smoothly and growing rapidly.

Ms. Zhang: That's true, Mr. Clinton. Business between us has been increased year by year. However, according to our records, the total amount of your orders in the last two years was quite moderate. The year before last in particular, you placed a very careful order. All these do not warrant an agency appointment.

Mr. Clinton: Ms. Zhang, do you mean you still have doubt in our sales ability?

Ms. Zhang: No, we have full confidence in your sales ability. But you should at least let us know your market connections, the effectiveness of your sales organization and your technical ability to handle the goods to be marketed.

Mr. Clinton: Well, as you know, our company is specialized in this line of business for years. We have more than ten sales representatives, who are on the road all the year round, covering the whole of the north European market.

Ms. Zhang: Do you have any middleman or sell direct to the retailers?

Mr. Clinton: Through years of efforts, we have set up effective channels of distribution and we canvass the retailers direct without any middleman.

Ms. Zhang: That's good. If you could pursue your efforts in building a large turnover, we shall be glad to consider your proposal of an agency agreement.

Mr. Clinton: Please be assured of that. By the way, what commission can we enjoy?

Ms. Zhang: Generally speaking, commission is paid in proportion to the size of the order.

Mr. Clinton: That is the general principle. But what's the commission rate on this specific class of merchandise?

Ms. Zhang: As far as this class of merchandise is concerned, commission is usually granted at the rate of 3% or so.

Mr. Clinton: Well, Ms. Zhang, I wish to draw your attention. Your competitors, to be concrete, the Japanese exporters, are now offering a much higher rate of commission.

Ms. Zhang: I was informed. However, in order to help you start business in this line, we will grant you exceptionally a 3.5% to 4% commission.

Mr. Clinton: That's acceptable. Then how do you work out the commission?

Ms. Zhang: It is our usual practice to work out all commissions on FOB value. In other words, your commission will be calculated on the basis of invoice value after the deduction of freight and insurance.

Mr. Clinton: I see. That's very clear. When can we enter into an agency agreement?

Ms. Zhang: Let's say the day after tomorrow. I'll have to get it prepared.

Mr. Clinton: OK. See you then.

I. Listen to the conversation and choose the best answers to the questions you hear.

1. What is beyond the expectation of Ms. Zhang, the exporter?   (D)

2. For what are the exporter's products popular in the importer's market?   (C)

3. Why does the exporter think it still too early to establish the agency with the importer?   (B)

4. What determines the commission rate that can be enjoyed by the importer?   (A)

5. What can be concluded from the conversation?   (D)

II. Listen to the conversation again and complete the following notes with what you hear.

A Proposal for Agency

Products to be handled:
- textile products including (1) <u>sports jackets, trousers and women's suits</u>

What the exporter is concerned about:
- the importer's market connections
- (2) <u>the effectiveness of the importer's sales organization</u>
- (3) <u>the importer's technical ability to handle the goods to be marketed</u>

What is prerequisite to an agency appointment:
- (4) <u>Whether the importer is able to build a large turnover.</u>

What is to the advantage of the importer:
The importer
- having concluded a substantial business with the exporter
- (5) <u>commanding an extensive domestic market in this line</u>
- enjoying a smooth and rapidly growing business with the exporter

- (6) <u>specializing in this line of business for years</u>
- boasting a strong sales force
- (7) <u>having set up effective channels of distribution</u>
- (8) <u>selling direct to the retailers without any middleman</u>

What is to the disadvantage of the importer:

- (9) <u>The total amount of orders placed by the importer in the last two years</u> is too moderate to warrant an agency appointment.

About commission:

- General principle to pay commission:
  (10) <u>in proportion to the size of the order</u>
- Specific commission rate on textile products:
  usually at the rate of 3% or so
- Favorable commission granted to help start business:
  (11) <u>an exceptional 3.5% to 4% commission</u>
- Usual practice to calculate commission:
  all commissions will be calculated on the basis of (12) <u>FOB value/invoice value after the deduction of freight and insurance</u>

Passage

Tapescript

A vast amount of international trade is handled not only by direct negotiation between buyers and sellers but also by means of agencies. An important reason for appointing a foreign agent is his knowledge of local conditions and of the market in which he will operate. He knows what goods are best suited to his area and what prices the market will bear. In developing foreign trade, agents and intermediaries often play a very important role.

As far as buying and selling is concerned, there are mainly two types of agents: general agent and sole agent or exclusive agent.

A general agent may be a firm or a person who acts under some degree of instructions from the principals to sell or to buy goods on the best terms obtainable. He charges a "commission" for his services under some kind of agreement or contract.

Similar to a general agent, a sole agent may be a firm or a person who acts exclusively for one foreign principal with exclusive agency rights to sell on a commission basis certain commodities in a certain area under some kind of agreement or contract.

The first step in choosing an agent is to make sure whether the firm or person to be appointed has sufficient means to develop the trade and whether the firm or person has reliable connection in the designated area.

The terms of agency are sometimes set out in correspondence between the parties, but where dealings are on a large scale, a formal agreement may be desirable. Matters to be covered may include all, or some of the following: (1) the nature and duration of the agency, e.g. sole agency or agency merely for transmitting orders and so on; (2) the territory to be covered; (3) the duties of agent and principal; (4) the method of purchase and sale, e.g., whether the agent is to buy for his own account or "on consignment".

There are other types of agencies with varying degrees of authority. Brokers negotiate sales and purchase contracts for buyers and sellers, without rights of their own in the goods. Factors have authority to sell in their own name for the principal, to receive payment, and to sell at times and prices which they consider advisable. Fruits, agricultural products and raw materials are often handled by factors and brokers. Forwarding agents carry out all the duties connected with collecting and delivering the goods. The services of forwarding agents are particularly valuable in foreign trade because of the complicated arrangements that have to be made.

I. Listen to the passage and choose the best answers to the questions you hear.

1. What is an important reason for appointing a foreign agent?   (D)
2. Who negotiate sales and purchase contracts for buyers and sellers but have no rights of their own in the goods?   (A)
3. Which of the following products is often handled by factors and brokers?   (A)
4. Which of the following statements is true?   (B)
5. What can be learned from the passage?   (C)

II. Listen to the passage again and complete the following notes with what you hear.

Types of agents:
- ❑ general agent — acting (1) <u>under some degree of instructions from the principals</u> to sell or to buy goods on the best terms obtainable
- ❑ sole (exclusive) agent — acting exclusively for one foreign principal with (2) <u>exclusive agency rights to sell certain commodities</u>
- ❑ brokers — negotiating (3) <u>sales and purchase contracts for buyers and sellers</u>, without rights of their own in the goods

❑ factors — having authority to (4) <u>sell in their own name for the principal</u>, to receive payment, and to (5) <u>sell at times and prices which they consider advisable</u>

❑ forwarding agents — carrying out duties connected with (6) <u>collecting and delivering the goods</u>

First step in choosing an agent:

To make sure whether the firm or person to be appointed has

❑ (7) <u>sufficient means to develop the trade</u>

❑ (8) <u>reliable connection in the designated area</u>

Major terms covered in an agency agreement:

❑ (9) <u>the nature and duration of the agency</u>

❑ (10) <u>the territory to be covered</u>

❑ (11) <u>the duties of agent and principal</u>

❑ (12) <u>the method of purchase and sale</u>

SECTION B **Import-Export Agent**

Pre-listening ▶▶|

Background Information

1. What an import-export agent does

The import and export of goods is a great way of looking for more business opportunities in more markets. Import-export agents have the potential to earn a lot from the transactions that they facilitate. Aside from this, the work of being an import-export agent requires little financial investment. A good head for organizing matters, an ability to sell with diplomacy and tact and the right amount of determination are the only traits an import-export agent needs to be able to handle the type of work that this job entails. He searches for business opportunities, looking for contacts in trade directories. He makes it easier for manufacturers and companies to reach a worldwide market. One of the important things an import-export agent needs to do is to make sure that he keeps himself abreast of trends, laws, and any policy regarding trade, business and manufacturing in different countries. Having a feel for the market will make it easier to understand his clients. Matching the foreign markets and manufacturers with the domestic manufacturers and companies with each other is a crucial part of the work of an import-export agent. He contacts foreign distributors that will purchase the goods. He gets a signed contract with a domestic manufacturer from which you will get this order. The foreign distributor may make arrangements regarding shipping or freight forwarding and the agent need not worry any more about these matters. If this is not the case, the extra cost of getting the merchandise is incorporated together with his commission into the price of the goods. These terms are agreed upon before any exchange takes place.

2. Choosing which intermediary to work with

The most important thing is that an agent or distributor has proven experience in your target market. But there are many other factors to consider:

❑ Are they well located, with the geographical coverage you need?

❑ Are they well established in the market, and how do they compare with their own competition?

❑ Look at the product lines they currently sell — will your product fit in well?

❑ Ask about their strategy for the next five years — does it fit well with your objectives in the market?

❑ How large and experienced is their sales team? Is it well managed and given effective incentives?

❑ Can they provide you with market research to feed into your sales forecasts?

❑ Do they have the warehousing, servicing and other facilities you're looking for?

It's also important to look into their financial standing to ensure you're dealing with a reputable business that can be relied upon to pay you. This can be more difficult with overseas businesses.

3. Criteria to evaluate import-export agents

Finding a suitable agent is not always an easy task. Unfortunately, while there are several individuals who may operate as "import-export agents", they may not have the experience, skills, or the drive to actually become successful agents. It is essential, therefore, that you find an agent that can prove to you that they have the background to do the work for you. Agents have to be evaluated very carefully before they are appointed and the following screening criteria are strongly recommended.

❑ Agent's human and physical resources: particularly important where the agent must use a sales force and physically distribute the product.

❑ Years of experience: in a particular industry or with particular products.

❑ Agent's overall reputation.

❑ Financial stability.

Never appoint a sole agency unless the agency is guaranteeing some success within a specific period or is willing to market in a manner agreed in writing. Never sign an agency agreement that does not clearly indicate the way in which the exporting company (the principal) and agency will settle disagreements between them. Evaluate how much commission the agent may reasonably expect over a year and then determine if your company could obtain more customers through sending salespeople abroad or by advertising in the country.

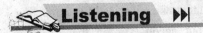

Listening ▶▶

Conversation

Tapescript

Ms. Lin:	Good afternoon, Mr. Mason. Have you received your firm's confirmation?
Mr. Mason:	Good afternoon, Ms. Lin. Yes, I've got the OK to go ahead. Now shall we discuss other details of the agency agreement?
Ms. Lin:	All right. The territory to be covered of the sole agency will be the whole of Europe.
Mr. Mason:	Agreed. Then what would be the term of agency? I mean the time period?
Ms. Lin:	Two years, commencing on 1st January next year and renewable for a further period of two years if both parties agree.
Mr. Mason:	That's fine. What about commission?
Ms. Lin:	We usually allow a commission of 4% on the invoice value.
Mr. Mason:	I feel 4% is really out of the question. Ms. Lin, you know that in the business of table cloths in the European market you have fierce competition from other Asian countries. We've got to spend a considerable amount of money on publicity to canvass business for you. I'm afraid that 4% won't leave us much. If you put the advertising expenses on your account I think we could accept this 4% commission rate.
Ms. Lin:	Generally speaking, Mr. Mason, we don't take advertising expenses. Our price is worked out according to the costing. If we put advertising expenses on our account, it means an increase in our price.
Mr. Mason:	Ms. Lin, I'm afraid I have to tell you that your competitors are now offering a much higher commission.
Ms. Lin:	Well, Mr. Mason, to our mutual benefit we shall allow 2% of your sales to be appropriated for advertising purposes.
Mr. Mason:	If you can do no better, we can't but agree to 4% commission and 2% of the sales

for advertising.

Ms. Lin: I'm glad to hear that. I think the draft for the agreement can be ready tomorrow.

Mr. Mason: That's great. Ms. Lin, before drawing up the agreement for signature we'd like to reiterate the main points upon which we have reached agreement so far. First, we act as your sole agent in the Europe market for a period of two years and the term of agency will be extended automatically for another two years upon expiration unless notice is given to the contrary. Secondly, you pay us a commission of 4% on our sales of your products and another 2% of the sales for advertising …

Ms. Lin: You are perfectly right. By the way, you must undertake not to sell the competing products of other manufacturers either on your account or on that of other suppliers. In addition, you must render monthly statements of sales and honor drafts we draw on you. As soon as you receive your firm's confirmation we'll make out a formal one.

Mr. Mason: That'll be fine. I'm looking forward to a happy and successful working relationship with you.

I. Listen to the conversation and decide whether the following statements are true or false. Write T for true and F for false in the brackets.

1. (F) 2. (T) 3. (F) 4. (F) 5. (T) 6. (F) 7. (F) 8. (T) 9. (T) 10. (T)

II. Listen to the conversation again and complete the following notes with what you hear.

Major Terms Included in the Agency Agreement	
Nature of the agency	(1) <u>sole agency</u>
Commodity concerned	(2) <u>table cloth</u>
Territory to be covered	(3) <u>the whole of Europe</u>
Term of agency	two years, commencing on (4) <u>1st January next year</u> and renewable for (5) <u>a further period of two years</u> if both parties agree
Commission rate	*Supplier's usual practice:* (6) <u>4% on the invoice value</u> *Agent's reason for refusal:* • the agent having to (7) <u>spend a considerable amount of money on publicity</u> • the supplier's competitors offering (8) <u>a much higher commission</u> *Final agreement reached by both supplier and agent:* (9) <u>4% commission and 2% of the sales for advertising</u>

continued

Major Terms Included in the Agency Agreement	
Other terms & conditions	During the validity of the agreement, the agent must • undertake not to (10) <u>sell the competing products of other manufacturers</u> either on the agent's account or on that of other suppliers • (11) <u>render monthly statements of sales to the supplier</u> • (12) <u>honor drafts the supplier draws on the agent</u>

Passage

Tapescript

Michelle Freeman, sole proprietor of Freeman Import Company, describes a typical day in the life of an Import/Export agent.

7:00 am   If you deal with companies based in the Far East and you want to talk to them by telephone or receive a quick answer then it is important once or twice a week to start early or stay up late in order to catch them. I am an early riser so I often make a few calls and send a few emails before breakfast. I have a completely fitted out home office with all the latest technology. I use it together with a digital camera to send and receive photographs of products.

8:00 am   Breakfast with my family. Take the kids to school. Take the dog for a walk. Read the papers. I am always on the look out for new product ideas. It is wonderful working at home — the one downside is everyone thinks you are available for doing chores. I know some Import/Export agents who like to go on buying expeditions overseas — but I hate travel and I hate hotels.

10:00 am   Start work in earnest. I usually devote my mornings to marketing, my afternoons to administration. However, the post brings several cheques so I spend an hour doing my accounts, writing out some invoices, and filling in the bankbook. Most of my commission is paid by direct transfer into either my US dollar or sterling account which saves me a lot of time.

11:00 am   A manufacturer I have never dealt with before has sent me a box of thirty clock radios. He wants me to act for him in the UK. I spend an hour testing his product and after deciding that it is of good quality and would work well in the market, I create a fact sheet describing its features and setting out the price and delivery details. I aim to make at least 15% on everything I sell. His product offers good value for money and I know it is going to be popular. I e-mail him a copy of my standard terms and conditions asking him to sign a copy and fax it back within 48 hours. Five minutes later the fax comes through even though he is in a time zone nine hours ahead of the UK!

Midday   After a break for coffee I draw up an initial list of possible customers for the clock radios. Nowadays, I have my own list of customers but there are plenty of reference sources when you are starting out. I decide to fax my fact sheet to about one hundred wholesalers — offering them a free sample on a first come, first served basis. Thanks to the computer I can send the one hundred faxes in a matter of minutes. I don't deal much by telephone and I rarely make a sales visit — though I do take my best customers out to nice meals every few months.

1:30 pm   Stop for lunch. Walk the dog. Kids come home from school, so I stop to have a cup of tea with them.

4:00 pm   Back in the office. Process orders for other products I sell. A few messages get left on my answering machine. I pool smaller orders together to make up whole containers. Although this may mean a slight delay for my customers they are happy to wait because it means they can order less but still benefit from a rock bottom price.

5:00 pm   Send all my orders off to the manufacturers I represent. Most now have email — but some have to be faxed. It takes me half an hour. Deal with a telephone call from a wholesaler looking for electric kettles. Promise to send him details and prices within 24 hours and immediately send off an e-mail to a dozen possible suppliers in China.

6:00 pm   Call it quits for the day! A few inquiries have already come in for the new clock radio so before I turn off the computer I run out name and address labels. First thing tomorrow morning I'll post off samples.

I. Listen to the passage and choose the best answers to the questions you hear.

1. What does Michelle think is the disadvantage of working at home?   (B)
2. What does Michelle usually deal with in the morning?   (B)
3. What does Michelle think of the clock radios newly sent to him?   (A)
4. Which of the following is on George's schedule that day?   (D)
5. Which of the following statements is true according to the passage?   (A)
6. What can be learned from the passage?   (C)

II. Listen to the passage again and complete the following notes with what you hear.

A day in the life of an Import/Export agent

7:00 am
- (1) Making a few calls and sending a few emails before breakfast

8:00 am
- Having breakfast with the family

- Taking the kids to school and the dog for a walk
- (2) <u>Reading the papers for new product ideas</u>

10:00 am
- Doing the accounts
- (3) <u>Writing out some invoices</u>
- Filling in the bankbook

11:00 am
- Testing a newly-sent product (clock radios)
- (4) <u>Creating a fact sheet which describes the new product's features</u>
- (5) <u>Setting out the price and delivery details</u>
- (6) <u>Emailing the manufacturer a copy of his standard terms and conditions</u>

Midday
- Having a coffee break
- (7) <u>Drawing up an initial list of potential customers for the new product</u>
- (8) <u>Faxing the fact sheet to the wholesalers</u> and offering them a free sample

1:30 pm
- Stopping for lunch
- Walking the dog
- Having a cup of tea with the kids

4:00 pm
- (9) <u>Processing orders for other products he sells</u>
- Dealing with a few messages left on the answering machine
- (10) <u>Pooling smaller orders together to make up whole containers</u>

5:00 pm
- Sending all the orders off to the manufacturers he represents
- (11) <u>Dealing with a telephone call from a wholesaler looking for electric kettles</u> and promising to send him details and prices within 24 hours
- (12) <u>Sending off an email to a dozen possible suppliers in China</u>

6:00 pm
- Running out name and address labels for posting off samples

Further Listening

Short Recordings

Tapescript

Item 1

NEW YORK — Procter & Gamble's $7 billion acquisition of German hair care firm Wella on Tuesday is perhaps a clear signal that the company's new mission is to champion shampoo and hair color over detergent and diapers. Analysts said it's not surprising that the maker of such consumer products as Tide detergent, Crest toothpaste and Pampers diapers is keen on strengthening its health and beauty business. The global market for hair care products reached sales of $27 billion in 2001, with North and South America the biggest markets, accounting for 40 percent of the total. P&G bought the Clairol hair care business for $4.95 billion in 2001 and the Clairol acquisition made it the global leader in the consumer hair care market over L'Oreal.

The Procter & Gamble Company (P&G) is the #1 US maker of household products, courting more market share and billion-dollar brands. P&G's products now fall into three categories: global beauty care; global health, baby, and family care; and global household care. P&G also makes pet food and water filters and produces soap operas: Sixteen of P&G's brands are billion-dollar sellers (Actonel, Always/Whisper, Ariel, Bounty, Charmin, Crest, Downy/Lenor, Folgers, Head & Shoulders, Iams, Olay, Pampers, Pantene, Pringles, Tide, and Wella). P&G bought hair care giant Clairol from Bristol-Myers Squibb in 2001 and well-groomed Wella in 2003.

Item 2

NEW YORK — Seagram Co. Ltd.'s conversion from a Canadian juice and liquor firm to a Hollywood powerhouse took a giant step forward Thursday with its $10.6 billion purchase of music recording giant PolyGram N.V. The move catapults Seagram to the top of the charts for the music industry and represents a historic shift for the Canadian beverage company — which for the first time will derive a majority of its operating income from entertainment businesses. To help finance the acquisition, Seagram will issue a maximum of about 47.9 million common shares valued at approximately $2 billion. As a result of the transaction, Seagram's entertainment assets now constitute nearly 75 percent of overall earnings before interest, taxes, depreciation and amortization.

PolyGram N.V. is involved in the creation, acquisition and production of recorded music which it markets and distributes in the form of compact discs, music cassettes, record albums, digital compact cassettes, video tapes and laser disks. The company is also active in music publishing and the production of films and television programming. PolyGram is one of the world's largest recorded music companies. Its labels in the popular music sector include Motown, Mercury, Polydor, Vertigo, Fontana, A&M, Island and Verve, while the company's classical music business includes the labels Decca, Deutsche Grammophone and Philips Classics. PolyGram is also the world's third largest music publisher, with rights to some 250,000 song titles. In the area of filmed entertainment PolyGram launched Gramercy Pictures in 1993, which is a film distribution joint venture with Universal Pictures.

Item 3

NEW YORK — Financial services giant Citigroup Inc. is buying lending powerhouse Associates First Capital Corp. for $29.5 billion in stock, seeking to stabilize earnings and expand its global presence in the consumer finance arena. The deal announced yesterday will give Citigroup control of the largest publicly traded finance company in the United States and the fifth-largest consumer finance company in Japan. In addition, Associates First's vast lending operations represent a steady and predictable stream of earnings, as opposed to the often volatile profits generated by Citigroup's investment banking business, which will rise and fall based on the US stock and bond markets.

Citigroup, the preeminent global financial services company which has 200 million customer accounts and does business in more than 100 countries, provides consumers, corporations, governments and institutions with a broad range of financial products and services, including consumer banking and credit, corporate and investment banking, insurance, securities brokerage, and asset management. Major brand names under Citigroup's trademark red umbrella include Citibank, CitiFinancial, Primerica, Smith Barney, Banamex, And Travelers Life and Annuity.

Item 4

NEW YORK — Dexia, Europe's largest municipal lender, announced on Tuesday two acquisitions worth almost $4 billion, which are moves aimed at making the Belgian-French bank group a major player in global public finance and European banking. Dexia, which has assets of more than $230 billion, said it would buy US-based Financial Security Assurance Holding (FSA) for $76 a share or a total price of $2.6 billion. Dexia's chief executive officer, Pierre Richard, said the merger, which is expected to close in the second quarter, marked a major step for the group. A combination of Dexia and FSA will create a global leader in public finance and specialized financing for corporations. In the US, Dexia's financial backing will further enhance FSA's ability to compete successfully in the municipal and asset-backed insurance sectors.

Dexia came about as the result of a merger between Credit Local de France and Crédit Communal de Belgique in 1996. Dexia's main area of business is financing local administration authorities. In this niche market Dexia is a European leader with an impressive market share in Belgium and in France. Dexia is keen to accelerate its expansion on to the international arena with an acquisition policy that will lead it establishing further activities and enhancing its development in the United States, the Benelux countries, Switzerland, and the United Kingdom.

Item 5

NEW YORK — The proposed buyout of the MediaOne cable company by long-distance titan AT&T is widely expected to blur the lines that still divide local and long distance service providers. It also will bring to bear the all-inclusive service offerings that long-distance companies have promised consumers for years. Industry insiders predict consumers will be able to purchase a low-cost package of Internet, long-distance, local and cable services from AT&T in one to two years. AT&T spokesman Mark Siegel confirmed the all-in-one service packages are expected to be rolled out over the "next several years". The plan is to enable consumers to receive cable, local phone service, long distance and high-speed Internet access over a single line, he said.

I. In this section, you will hear five short recordings. For each piece, decide what each company mainly aims to achieve through acquisition.

1. P & G	C	A. Offer one-stop service
2. Seagram	B	B. Shift to new business
3. Citigroup	F	C. Solidify its core business
4. Dexia	E	D. Refocus on information technology
5. AT&T	A	E. Achieve global business leadership
		F. Ensure reliable business revenues
		G. Monopolize international market
		H. Diversify investment portfolio

II. Listen to the five recordings again and choose the best answers to the questions you hear.

1. Which of the following is true about Procter & Gamble?   (C)

2. How will Seagram Co. Ltd. finance its purchase of music recording giant PolyGram N.V.?   (B)

3. What will happen to Citigroup after its acquisition of Associates First Capital Corp.?   (C)

4. How can Financial Security Assurance Holding (FSA) benefit from Dexia's acquisition?   (D)

5. Which sector was AT&T traditionally engaged in?   (B)

Home Listening

Business News

Tapescript

The Russian government has seized a controlling interest in Russia's largest oil company, Yukos, a few days after arresting the firm's chief executive. The development sent Russian stocks tumbling for the second time in days.

The Russian stock market, already jittery over the weekend arrest of Yukos Chief Executive Mikhail Khodorkovsky, fell sharply Thursday, after Russian prosecutors seized a majority of shares in the huge Russian oil company.

Moscow's MICEX index recorded losses of more than eight percent, and Yukos shares closed down 14 percent, after dropping 20 percent on Monday.

Yukos Spokesman Alexander Shadrin says prosecutors seized more than 50 percent of the company's shares in a move he called a gross violation of the Russian criminal code and Constitution. Mr. Shadrin told Russia's Interfax news agency that the shares seized do not have any connection to Yukos chief Mikhail Khodorkovsky. But the prosecutor's office claimed otherwise, in a brief statement confirming the move on Thursday.

Despite what some see as an escalation of hostilities between the Kremlin and big business, Mr. Shadrin says Yukos executives remain optimistic.

Mr. Shadrin says nothing bad can happen to the shares, as, he says, Russian law prevents them from being sold to third-parties. He also maintains that Yukos shareholders still have a right to take part in voting, and that it is still possible to recover a profit.

Word of the seizure came as President Putin was meeting at the Kremlin with leading Russian and foreign investors, who are growing increasingly wary of events surrounding the Yukos affair. The meeting had been long planned, and it was not clear if the latest actions against Yukos were discussed.

But Mr. Putin made clear earlier this week that he will not engage in any negotiations over the Yukos affair, as requested by Russian big business interests. •

He has also sided with the prosecutors in the arrest of Mr. Khodorkovsky, saying it was within the framework of Russian law.

Russian secret police arrested and jailed Mr. Khodorkovsky last week on seven charges of tax evasion and fraud. At least two other senior Yukos officials are under investigation, and Russian prosecutors have raided the offices of Yukos-affiliated companies over the past four months.

Listen to the business news report and decide whether the following statements are true or false. Write T for true and F for false in the brackets.

1. (T) 2. (T) 3. (F) 4. (F) 5. (F) 6. (T) 7. (T) 8. (T) 9. (T) 10. (F)

Unit 12

Securities

Dictation

Listen to the following short paragraph and fill in the blanks with what you hear.

Securities are instruments representing (1) <u>ownership, a debt agreement, or the rights to ownership</u>. They include (2) <u>shares of corporate stock or mutual funds</u>, (3) <u>bonds issued by corporations or governmental agencies</u>, stock options or other options, limited partnership units and (4) <u>various other formal investment instruments</u> that are negotiable and fungible. Unlike the banking world, where (5) <u>deposits are guaranteed by the government</u>, stocks, bonds and other securities can lose value. There are (6) <u>no guarantees in the securities markets</u>. That's why investing should not be a spectator sport; indeed, the principal way for investors to protect the money they put into the securities markets is to (7) <u>do research and ask questions</u>. Only through the steady flow of (8) <u>timely, comprehensive and accurate information</u> can people make sound investment decisions in today's securities markets.

Listening & Speaking

SECTION A **Market Regulation**

Pre-listening ▶▶

Background Information

1. Mutual fund

A mutual fund is an investment vehicle which is comprised of a pool of funds collected from many investors for the purpose of investing in securities such as stocks, bonds, money market securities and similar assets. Mutual funds are operated by money mangers, who invest the fund's capital and attempt to produce capital gains and income for the fund's investors. A mutual fund's portfolio is structured and maintained to match the investment objectives stated in its prospectus. One of the main advantages of a mutual fund is that it gives small investors access to a well-diversified portfolio of equities, bonds and other securities, which would be quite difficult (if not impossible) to create with a small amount of capital. Each shareholder participates proportionally in the gain or loss of the fund. Mutual fund units, or shares, are issued and can typically be purchased or redeemed as needed at the current net asset value per share.

2. Stock option

A privilege, sold by one party to another, that gives the buyer the right, but not the obligation, to buy or sell a stock at an agreed-upon price within a certain period or on a specific date. Stock option plans are often used to compensate corporate managers and other employees for specific services.

3. Limited partnership units

Limited partnership units represent interests in a partnership consisting of a general partner, who manages the partnership, and limited partners, who provide the investment capital. The liability of limited partners is generally limited to their initial investment, provided that they do not become involved in management. Limited partnerships will typically invest in a specific industry sector (such as real estate or oil and gas) and often provide for some tax benefits to "flow through" from the partnership to the limited partners.

4. Investment portfolio

Well-diversified portfolios — containing various mixes of stocks, bonds, mutual funds, cash equivalents like Treasury bills or money funds, and sometimes other types of investments — can help iron out a lot of the ups and downs in investing. Diversification helps protect against risk by spreading your investments around instead of investing in only one area. For example, you can balance cash investments and money market funds with stocks, bonds, and stock or bond mutual funds. You can buy stocks of small growth companies while also investing in blue chips, which are the stocks of large, well-established companies. Often when the return is down in one area, it's balanced by a positive performance in another. You may also want to evaluate your assets and realign the investment mix from time to time. For example, if some stocks increase in value, they will make up a larger percentage of your portfolio. To keep the balance, you may want to decrease your stock holdings and increase your bond or cash holdings. Finding the right portfolio mix depends on your assets, your age, and your risk tolerance. Asset allocation means dividing your portfolio among investment categories according to a particular formula. One allocation model, for example, would put 60% of your investment capital in stocks, 30% in bonds, and the remaining 10% in cash. No single portfolio is ideal for everyone. While a stock-heavy portfolio may tend to grow faster over time, the value also fluctuates more. It may also produce losses in some years. And you don't have to stick to the same model throughout your investing career. Many experts suggest that young people put 80% or more of their investments in stock and stock mutual funds. People nearing retirement, on the other hand, might want more of their assets in income-producing investments, such as US Treasuries or high-rated corporate bonds. Asset allocation can make a real difference in portfolio performance over an extended period.

5. W. R. Grace & Co. (Grace)

W. R. Grace & Co. (Grace), a US multinational corporation established in 1854, is a leading global supplier of catalysts and silica products, specialty construction chemicals and building materials, and container protection products. Grace operates in two business segments: Davison Chemicals and Performance Chemicals. Davison Chemicals manufactures catalysts and silica-based products. Performance Chemicals produces specialty construction chemicals, including performance-enhancing concrete admixtures, cement additives and additives for masonry products; specialty building materials, including fireproofing and waterproofing materials and systems, and sealants and coatings for packaging that protect food and beverages from bacteria and other contaminants, extend shelf life and preserve flavor.

6. Waste Management, Inc. (WMI)

Waste Management, Inc.(WMI) is a provider of integrated waste services in North America. Through its subsidiaries, the company provides collection, transfer, recycling and resource recovery and disposal services. WMI is also a developer, operator and owner of waste-to-energy facilities in the United States. The Company's customers include commercial, industrial, municipal and residential customers, other waste management companies, electric utilities and governmental entities throughout the United States, Puerto Rico and Canada. The Company manages its operations through seven operating groups, five of which are organized by geographic area and the other two of which are organized by function.

Listening ▶▶

Conversation

Tapescript

Interviewer: Concerned that the quality of financial information available to investors might be compromised by companies who use the same firms for consulting and audits, the government is considering rules that will mandate disclosure of such relationships. Today we will talk with Securities & Exchange Commission Chairman Arthur Levitt about this issue. Currently there is a new rule regarding auditor independence. Mr. Levitt, I wonder if you could explain what the interest of individual investors might be in this rule.

Levitt: Well, today the reliability of the numbers that are reported to investors is absolutely critical. When we see a statement that falls short by a penny or two of expectations, stocks drop by 30, 40, and 50%.

Interviewer: So regulators as well as investors must keep a close eye on what's going on down there at the accounting firms, I guess.

Levitt: Yeah. Accounting firms in the past derived most of their money from auditing, and all public companies by law must be audited by a CPA. Today, there has been a dramatic change and accounting firms derive more than half of their money from non-audit services. Therefore, it's critical that investors know whether the audits of companies are impacted by fees paid to their auditor that is much greater than the audit fee.

Interviewer: Yes, I can imagine. So comes the new rule for auditor independence, I suppose.

Levitt: Well, this rule would call for disclosure and it would also eliminate conflicts that an auditor would have in performing certain consulting services for an audit client. I can think of no rule or regulation that has a greater significance on public confidence in our markets than this question of auditor independence.

Interviewer: Now up to this point in time, my understanding is that the accounting profession has countered the initiatives undertaken by your office regarding this rule, with the argument that there is no "smoking gun" existing that shows any audit has been negatively affected, even if there exists the possibility. What's your response to that argument?

Levitt: Well, I would rather take action when there is the smell of smoke rather than when there's a full-blown fire. We are seeing more evidence of audit failures today than almost any other time in the history of the commission. We are seeing more evidence of managed numbers by companies that have such an economic hold on their auditors that they are unwilling to stand up for the shareholders. We have brought a large number of cases involving audit failures — cases such as W.R. Grace and Waste Management — to mention just a few. I've headed enough audit committees to understand the hold that corporations very often have on their auditors, so I don't accept "the smoking gun argument" one single bit.

Interviewer: And in the specific cases that you mentioned, were those instances of the presence of auditing and advisory relationship mixed together?

Levitt: Those were cases where there was an advisory and auditing relationship mixed together. For instance, let's say that an auditor provides a consulting service for an American company and that consulting activity fails. Consider this conflict. The auditor would appropriately say, "Let's write off $100 million." The company would say, "Hey, wait a second. We paid you $100 million for this project. You can't say that we've got to write it off in one year and kill our earnings." So there is an inherent conflict in the performance of audit and non-audit services — and that's one of the things this rule gets at.

I. Listen to the conversation and decide whether the following statements are true or false. Write T for true and F for false in the brackets.

1.(T) 2.(F) 3.(T) 4.(T) 5.(F) 6.(F) 7.(F) 8.(F) 9.(F) 10.(T)

II. Listen to the conversation again and answer the following questions with what you hear.

1. What's the difference between today's accounting firms and those in the past?
   Accounting firms in the past derived most of their money from auditing, while today's accounting firms derive more than half of their money from non-audit services.
2. Why do the SEC and government call for disclosure of mixed auditing and advisory relationship?
   Because it is essential for investors to know whether the audits of companies are handled properly or not and such disclosure would also eliminate conflicts incurred by an auditor performing certain consulting services for an audit client.

3. Why are some auditors unwilling to stand up for the shareholders?

Because the companies, to which auditors provide consultancy, have an economic hold on them.

4. What is Mr. Levitt's purpose of mentioning cases such as W. R. Grace and Waste Management?

Those cases are instances of auditing and advisory relationship getting mixed together. By mentioning those cases, Mr. Levitt provided us with evidence that the said auditing failures do exist.

5. What does the last illustration cited by Mr. Levitt signify?

It signifies that there is an inherent conflict in the performance of advisory services as well as the audit so it is justifiable to enforce the rule for auditor independence.

Passage

Tapescript

There are several reasons for a company to issue stock rather than debt. The first is that it believes its stock price is inflated, and it can raise money by issuing stock. The second is when the projects for which the money is being raised may not generate predictable cash flows in the immediate future. A simple example of this is a startup company. The owners of startups generally will issue stock rather than take on debt because their ventures will probably not generate predictable cash flows, which is needed to make regular debt payments, and also so that the risk of the venture is diffused among the company's shareholders. A third reason for a company to raise money by selling equity is that it wants to change its debt-to-equity ratio. This ratio in part determines a company's bond rating. If a company's bond rating is poor because it is struggling with large debts, they may decide to issue equity to pay down the debt.

When a company believes the stock is undervalued and believes it can make money by investing in itself, the company would buy back the stock. This can happen in a variety of situations. For example, if a company has suffered some decreased earnings because of an inherently cyclical industry (such as the semiconductor industry), and believes its stock price is unjustifiably low, it will buy back its own stock. On other occasions, a company will buy back its stock if investors are driving down the price precipitously. In this situation, the company is attempting to send a signal to the market that it is optimistic that its falling stock price is not justified. It's saying: "We know more than anyone else about our company. We are buying our stock back. Do you really think our stock price should be this low?"

An investor that wants the upside potential of equity but wants to minimize risk would buy preferred stock. The investor would receive steady dividends from the preferred stock that are more assured than the dividends from common stock. The preferred stock owner gets a superior right to the company's assets if the company should go bankrupt. A corporation would invest in preferred stock because the dividends on preferred stock are taxed at a lower rate than the interest rates on bonds.

Different investors have different strategies. Some look for undervalued stocks, others for stocks with growth potential and yet others for stocks with steady performance. A strategy could also be focused on the long-term or short-term, and be more risky or less risky. Whatever your investing strategy is, you should be able to articulate these attributes.

I. Listen to the passage and decide whether the following statements are true or false. Write T for true and F for false in the brackets.

1. (T) 2. (T) 3. (F) 4. (T) 5. (T) 6. (F) 7. (F) 8. (T)

II. Listen to the passage again and complete the notes with what you hear.

Stock Investment Know-how

When to issue stock:
- ☐ when (1) a company believes its stock price is inflated
- ☐ when (2) the projects for which the money is being raised may not generate predictable cash flows in the immediate future
- ☐ when (3) a company wants to change its debt-to-equity ratio

When to buy back stock:
- ☐ when a company believes (4) the stock is undervalued and it can make money by investing in itself

This can happen in situations:
- ➢ if (5) a company has suffered some decreased earnings because of an inherently cyclical industry, and believes its stock price is unjustifiably low
- ➢ if (6) investors are driving down the price precipitously and the company is attempting to send a signal to the market that it is optimistic that its falling stock price is not justified

Why to invest in preferred stock:

- ☐ (7) the investor would receive steady dividends from the preferred stock
- ☐ (8) the preferred stock owner gets a superior right to the company's assets if the company should go bankrupt
- ☐ (9) the dividends on preferred stock are taxed at a lower rate than the interest rates on bonds

What stocks to invest in:

Investors look for stocks that are

- ☐ (10) undervalued
- ☐ (11) with growth potential
- ☐ (12) with steady performance

SECTION B   **Investor Protection**

Pre-listening ▶▶

Background Information

1. The stock exchange

A stock exchange or a share market is a corporation or mutual organization that provides facilities for stockbrokers and traders, to trade company stocks and other securities. Stock exchanges also provide facilities for the issue and redemption of securities, as well as other financial instruments and capital events including the payment of income and dividends. To be able to trade a security on a certain stock exchange, it has to be listed there. The initial offering of stocks and bonds to investors is by definition done in the primary market and subsequent trading is done in the secondary market. Usually there is a local & central location at least for record keeping, but trade is less and less linked to such a physical place, as modern markets are electronic networks, which gives them advantages of speed and cost of transactions. Increasingly more and more stock exchanges are part of a global market for securities.

2. Risks of stock investment

Stock prices fluctuate widely, in marked contrast to the stability of bank deposits or bonds. This is something that could affect not only the individual investor or household, but also the economy on a large scale. In order to minimize the risks of financial market imbalances, it is important that there be a well thought-out legislative, regulatory, and supervisory infrastructure that functions properly, smoothly, and honestly. Today both opportunities and risks for the individual investor have been amplified many times over. Because a considerable part of the stock market is comprised of non-professional investors, sometimes the market tends to react irrationally to economic news, even if that news has no real effect on the technical value of securities itself. Therefore, the stock market can be swayed tremendously in either direction by press releases, rumors and mass panic. Furthermore, the stock market comprises a large amount of speculative analysts, who have no substantial money or financial interest in the market, but make market predictions and suggestions regardless. Over the short-term, stocks and other securities can be battered or buoyed by any number of fast market-changing events, turning the stock market in a generally-dangerous-and-difficult-to-predict environment for those people whose lack of financial investment skills and time does not permit reading the technical signs of the market. Investors may temporarily pull financial prices away from their long-term trend level and thus over-reactions may occur — so that excessive optimism may drive prices unduly high or excessive pessimism may drive prices unduly low.

3. Stock investment strategies

One of the many things people always want to know about the stock market is, "How do I make money by investing?" There are many different approaches; two basic methods are classified as either fundamental analysis or technical analysis. Fundamental analysis refers to analyzing companies by their financial statements. Technical analysis studies price actions in markets through the use of charts and quantitative techniques to attempt to forecast price trends regardless of the company's financial prospects. Additionally, many choose to invest via the index method. In this method, one holds a weighted or unweighted portfolio consisting of the entire stock market or some segment of the stock market. The principal aim of this strategy is to maximize diversification, minimize taxes from too frequent trading, and ride the general trend of the stock market. Finally, one may trade based on inside information, which is known as insider trading. However, this is illegal in most jurisdictions (i.e., in most developed world stock markets).

4. Roles played by the Stock Exchange

❑ Raising capital for businesses. The Stock Exchange provides companies with the facility to raise capital for expansion through selling shares to the investing public.

❑ Mobilizing savings for investment. When people draw their savings and invest in shares, it leads to a more rational allocation of resources because funds, which could have been consumed, or kept in idle deposits with banks, are mobilized and redirected to promote business activity, resulting in a stronger economic growth and higher productivity levels.

- Facilitating company growth. Companies view acquisitions as an opportunity to expand product lines, increase distribution channels, hedge against volatility, increase its market share, or acquire other necessary business assets. A takeover bid or a merger agreement through the stock market is one of the simplest and most common ways to company growing by acquisition or fusion.

- Redistributing wealth. By giving a wide spectrum of people a chance to buy shares and therefore become part-owners (shareholders) of profitable enterprises, the stock market helps to reduce large income inequalities. Both casual and professional stock investors through stock price rise and dividends get a chance to share in the profits of promising businesses that were set up by other people.

- Improving corporate governance. By having a wide and varied scope of owners, companies generally tend to improve on their management standards and efficiency in order to satisfy the demands of these shareholders and the more stringent rules for public corporations by public stock exchanges and the government. It is alleged that public companies (companies that are owned by shareholders who are members of the general public and trade shares on public exchanges) tend to have better management records than privately-held companies (those companies where shares are not publicly traded, often owned by the company founders and/or their families and heirs, or otherwise by a small group of investors).

- Creating investment opportunities for small investors. As opposed to other businesses that require huge capital outlay, investing in shares is open to both the large and small stock investors because a person buys the number of shares they can afford. Therefore the Stock Exchange provides an extra source of income to small savers.

- Government raising capital for development projects. Governments at various levels may decide to borrow money in order to finance infrastructure projects such as sewage and water treatment works or housing estates by selling another category of securities known as bonds. These bonds can be raised through the Stock Exchange whereby members of the public buy them, thus loaning money to the government.

- Being barometer of the economy. At the stock exchange, share prices rise and fall depending, largely, on market forces. Share prices tend to rise or remain stable when companies and the economy in general show signs of stability and growth. An economic recession, depression, or financial crisis could eventually lead to a stock market crash. Therefore the movement of share prices and in general of the stock indexes can be an indicator of the general trend in the economy.

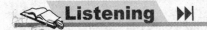
Listening ▶▶

Conversation

Tapescript

Interviewer: Like many exchanges around the world, the Australian Stock Exchange (ASX) has to grapple with the split roles of a private company and a regulator. In this interview with ASX chief executive Richard Humphry, we focus on the watchdog role of the exchange and the need for tougher controls. Mr. Humphry, how powerful do you see yourself as a regulator?

Richard: The ASX is a private company, not a government agency. It has only the powers of referral to the Australian Securities and Investment Commission (ASIC) and the power to suspend the company if it thinks it is necessary. As we have a license to run a market, we must ensure that market is orderly. That is really the basic motivation that drives us to have listing rules and rules governing brokers, business rules. In the event that we are unsatisfied with answers or responses we will take action but that action does not extend to prosecutions. The action must be simply a referral to the ASIC, who are the government regulators for this area.

Interviewer: Are the laws which you govern with good enough, or could they be strengthened?

Richard: I think the corporation's law is deficient in the sense that the penalties seem to range from a slap on the wrist at one end to a jail sentence at the other. I have been a strong supporter of the chairman of ASIC, who is calling for an introduction of fines between those two extremes. I think for many companies where there has been a clear case of inappropriate behavior it should be appropriate that there be some sort of fine levied on them.

Interviewer: The ASX seems to give out daily queries about irregular trades, yet there have only been two convictions for insider trading. How do you explain that?

Richard: It goes to the heart of the issue of corporation's law and why the chairman of ASIC is calling for fines for companies. I think the way the law is structured at the moment makes it difficult for ASIC to secure a conviction because of the mechanisms that they are required to go through. There needs to be a more flexible approach to the way in which we handle penalties or sanctions.

Interviewer: Do you suspect there is a lot more insider trading going on that isn't being found?

Richard: Well, at the moment there are certainly some instances of it, but it isn't as widespread as people think.

Interviewer:	Is it only two cases?
Richard:	That is the two cases of successful prosecution by ASIC. I'm not sure it's two; it could be more. They've been quite successful lately with some of their prosecutions but the number of referrals that go across from ASX is a different matter.
Interviewer:	How many have you referred in the last 12 months?
Richard:	The number of queries that we've raised would be numbered from probably around one to two a week that go across. These are issues that we think require some attention. It is important to understand that many queries that go on with companies are not driven by any inappropriate behavior. We're simply looking for clarification because we think the market may not have sufficient information.

I. Listen to the conversation and choose the best answers to the questions you hear.

1. Why does ASX have to refer irregularity cases to the ASIC for prosecution?　(B)
2. What is ASX NOT authorized to do?　(C)
3. What does ASX chief executive think of the current governing laws?　(B)
4. What does the chairman of ASIC call for?　(D)
5. What makes it difficult for ASIC to secure a conviction?　(B)

II. Listen to the conversation again and decide whether the following statements are true or false. Write T for true and F for false in the brackets.

1. (F)　2. (F)　3. (T)　4. (T)　5. (F)　6. (T)　7. (T)　8. (T)

Passage

Tapescript

The primary mission of the US Securities and Exchange Commission (SEC) is to protect investors and maintain the integrity of the securities markets. As more and more first-time investors turn to the markets to help secure their futures, pay for homes, and send children to college, these goals are more compelling than ever.

The laws and rules that govern the securities industry in the United States derive from a simple and straightforward concept: all investors, whether large institutions or private individuals, should have access to certain basic facts about an investment prior to buying it. To achieve this, the SEC requires public companies to disclose meaningful financial and other information to the public, which provides a common pool of knowledge for all investors to use to judge for themselves if a company's securities are a good investment. The SEC also oversees other key participants in the securities world, including stock exchanges, broker-dealers, investment advisors, mutual funds, and public utility holding companies.

Crucial to the SEC's effectiveness is its enforcement authority. Each year the SEC brings between 400–500 civil enforcement actions against individuals and companies that break the securities laws. Typical infractions include insider trading, accounting fraud, and providing false or misleading information about securities and the companies that issue them.

Fighting securities fraud, however, requires teamwork. At the heart of effective investor protection is an educated and careful investor. The SEC offers the public a wealth of educational information on its Internet website at www.sec.gov.

Before the Great Crash of 1929, there was little support for federal regulation of the securities markets. This was particularly true during the post-World War I surge of securities activity. Tempted by promises of "rags to riches" transformations and easy credit, most investors gave little thought to the dangers inherent in uncontrolled market operation. When the stock market crashed in October 1929, the fortunes of countless investors were lost. Banks also lost great sums of money in the Crash because they had invested heavily in the markets.

With the Crash and ensuing depression, public confidence in the markets plummeted. There was a consensus that for the economy to recover, the public's faith in the capital markets needed to be restored. Congress held hearings to identify the problems and search for solutions.

Based on the findings in these hearings, Congress passed securities laws designed to restore investor confidence in capital markets by providing more structure and government oversight. The main purposes of these laws can be reduced to two common-sense notions.

Companies publicly offering securities for investment must tell the public the truth about their businesses, the securities they are selling, and the risks involved in investing. People who sell and trade securities must treat investors fairly and honestly, putting investors' interests first.

Monitoring the securities industry requires a highly coordinated effort. Congress established the Securities and Exchange Commission in 1934 to enforce the newly-passed securities laws, to promote stability in the markets and, most importantly, to protect investors.

I. Listen to the passage and choose the best answers to the questions you hear.

1. What is NOT supposed to be the SEC's responsibility?   (B)
2. What is of critical importance to the SEC's effectiveness?   (C)
3. What is the key to effective investor protection?   (A)
4. What does the passage say about the Great Crash?   (C)
5. Which of the following statements is NOT true according to the passage?   (D)
6. What can be learned about the SEC?   (C)

II. Listen to the passage again and complete the notes with what you hear.

Get to Know SEC

When SEC was established:
- ❑ (1) <u>in 1934</u>

Why SEC was established:
- ❑ to (2) <u>enforce the newly-passed securities laws</u>
- ❑ to (3) <u>promote stability in the markets</u>
- ❑ to protect investors

What SEC's primary mission is:
- ❑ to (4) <u>protect investors and maintain the integrity of the securities markets</u>

Why investors turn to the securities markets:
- ❑ to help (5) <u>secure their futures, pay for homes, and send children to college</u>

What concept guides American securities laws & rules:
- ❑ (6) <u>all investors should have access to certain basic facts about an investment prior to buying it</u>

How SEC secures investors' equal access to information:
- ❑ SEC requires public companies to (7) <u>disclose meaningful financial and other information to the public.</u>
- ❑ SEC oversees (8) <u>key participants in the securities world.</u>

What typical infractions SEC deals with:
- ❑ (9) <u>insider trading, accounting fraud, and providing false or misleading information about securities and the companies that issue them</u>

What SEC does to educate investors:
- ❑ SEC offers the public (10) <u>a wealth of educational information on its Internet website at www.sec.gov.</u>

Further Listening

Short Recordings

Tapescript

Item 1

FRANKFURT — German sporting goods maker Adidas-Salomon is not planning to buy smaller US rival Reebok, an industry source said Tuesday amid market talk that a bid was pending. Traders at three German banks had said that Adidas shares had got a lift from the takeover talk. "There are rumors circulating in the market that Adidas wants to buy Reebok," said one dealer, explaining a rise that made the stock a top gainer on Germany's blue-chip DAX index. Shares in Reebok were up as much as 2 percent in early trading. Adidas has been struggling to keep up with a fast-changing North American market where it competes head-on with global titan Nike.

Adidas-Salomon, based at Herzogenaurach in Germany, is second on the world sporting goods market. Because, in addition to those famous shoes with their three stripes, Adidas also offers a range of clothing and sports apparel marketed under different brand names. There is Salomon for skiing, snowboarding, ski boots, skateboards, in-line skates and hiking equipment. A range of golf accessories, clothing, clubs and balls is available from TaylorMade-Adidas Golf. Then there is Mavic for cycling, Bonfire for winter sports equipment. And we must not forget the leading brand, Adidas, for footwear of course, but also for all its sportswear, balls and bags.

Reebok International Ltd. is a global company that designs and markets sports and fitness products, including footwear, apparel and accessories. It also designs and markets casual footwear, apparel and accessories for non-athletic use. The Company also pursues opportunities to license its trademarks and other intellectual property to third parties for use on equipment, apparel, accessories, sporting goods, health clubs and related products and services.

Nike is the world's #1 shoemaker and controls over 20% of the US athletic shoe market. The company designs and sells shoes for a variety of sports, including baseball, cheerleading, golf, volleyball, and wrestling. Nike also sells Cole Haan dress and casual shoes and a line of athletic apparel and equipment. Nike sells its products throughout the US and in about 200 other countries. Chairman, CEO, and co-founder Phil Knight owns more than 80% of the firm.

Item 2

SAN FRANCISCO — PepsiCo Inc., the world's second-largest soft drink maker, said it expects strong first-quarter results on higher revenue and said it would spend more than $2.5 billion on stock buybacks this year. The New York-based maker of Pepsi soft drinks and Frito-Lay snack foods, also said Monday after the close that it plans to raise its annual dividend by 44 percent to 92 cents a share, and said its board has authorized an additional $7 billion stock repurchase plan for the next three years. The news pushed shares of PepsiCo $1.09, or 2.1 percent, higher at $53.30 in early afternoon trading on Tuesday.

Pepsico Inc.'s principal activity is to manufacture, market and sell salty, convenient, sweet and grain-based snacks, carbonated and non-carbonated beverages and foods. The Group operates in three divisions: Snacks business provides a varied line of snacks, which includes Lay's potato chips, Doritos flavored tortilla chips, Cheetos cheese flavored snacks, etc. Beverages business manufactures concentrates, fountain syrups and finished goods for Pepsi, Diet Pepsi, Pepsi One, Mountain Dew, Mug, Tropicana Pure Premium, etc. Food business manufactures cereals, rice, pasta and other branded products, which includes Quaker oatmeal, Cap'n Crunch and Life ready-to-eat cereals, Rice-A-Roni, etc. The Group operates in United States, Canada and 170 other countries.

Frito-Lay Inc. is the undisputed chip champ of North America. The company makes some of the best-known and top-selling snack-food brands, including Cheetos, Doritos, Fritos, Lay's, Rold Gold, Ruffles, SunChips, and Tostitos. Frito-Lay also makes Grandma's cookies, Funyuns onion-flavored rings, Cracker Jack candy-coated popcorn, and Smartfood popcorn. The company's WOW! line of chips are made with the fat substitute olestra. In 2004 parent Pepsico restructured its divisions such that Frito-Lay now only reports North American snack food sales (which are about two-thirds of Pepsi's total sales). International snack sales are now reported by Pepsi's International division.

Item 3

MOSCOW — Shares in Russian oil company Yukos extended their end-week rally Monday after officials gave the company a month to pay a $3.4 billion back-tax bill — longer than some had expected. Yukos shares rallied by up to 17.6 percent at the open before easing back slightly, with the breathing space won by the company to pay its tax debts. Trading was later suspended for an hour with shares ahead by 12.6 percent on the session at 128.40 roubles, or $4.41. There were several suspensions last week amid volatile trade driven by fears that officials collecting Yukos' tax debt for 2000 would sell off core asset and that Russia's biggest oil firm was on the verge of collapse.

Yukos, Russia's second largest oil concern (behind LUKOIL) has turned its vast oil resources in cold Siberia into cold cash. The oil producer, which also has assets in the Volga region, has proved reserves of 13.7 billion barrels of oil and 7.8 trillion cu. ft. of gas. YUKOS operates five refineries and more than 1,200 gas stations across Russia, and is eyeing exploration opportunities in Kazakhstan and Africa. YUKOS was led by entrepreneur and 44%-owner Mikhail Khodorkovsky. However, he was arrested for alleged tax fraud in 2003 and resigned. That year, YUKOS bid to buy Sibneft, Russia's fifth-largest oil producer, fell through. In 2004 the company was charged with not paying $3.4 billion in back taxes.

Item 4

CHICAGO — Gillette Co. on Thursday said profit rose 26 percent as its battery-powered M3Power men's razor, Venus Divine women's razor and other higher-priced new products lifted sales. But shares fell as much as 5 percent on disappointment that the world's largest maker of blades and batteries, whose profit beat analysts' consensus estimates by a penny a share, did not exceed Wall Street forecasts by a wider margin, analysts said. Boston-based Gillette, which also makes Duracell batteries and Oral-B toothbrushes, posted second-quarter profit of $426 million, or 42 cents a share, compared with $338 million, or 33 cents a share, a year ago.

Gillette, the world's No. 1 maker of shaving supplies, is best known for its razors and blades (Sensor, Trac II, and the premium-priced Mach3 and M3Power), but Gillette is also a leading producer of batteries (Duracell). The company also offers products for dental care (Braun and Oral-B brands), toiletries (Right Guard), and electric shavers (Braun). Warren Buffett's Berkshire Hathaway and FMR Corp. own about 9% apiece of Gillette.

Item 5

NEW YORK — Intel Corp., the world's largest maker of microprocessors, said it will replace up to one million circuit boards that could cause computers to intermittently freeze or reboot. The cost of replacing the circuit boards could hit hundreds of millions of dollars, depending on how many users decide to have them replaced. The defect could turn out to be the most embarrassing one since the late 1994 controversy over a flaw in the company's Pentium microprocessors that caused incorrect answers to some division problems. In late-day trading, Intel's stock was down 6.8 percent, while the entire Nasdaq was down about 3.8 percent.

I. In this section, you will hear five short recordings. For each piece, decide why the shares of each company fluctuate.

1. Adidas-Salomon	E	A. Drop in quarterly profits
2. PepsiCo	B	B. News of stock buyback
3. Yukos	D	C. Launch of new products
4. Gillette	H	D. Postponement of tax paying
5. Intel	G	E. Speculation on a takeover bid
		F. Rumors of pending bankruptcy

G. Replacement of defective products

H. Earnings below market expectations

II. Listen to the five recordings again and choose the best answers to the questions you hear.

1. What can be learned about Adidas-Salomon?   (C)

2. How much would PepsiCo Inc. spend on the four-year stock repurchase?   (C)

3. Which of the following is NOT true about Yukos shares?   (B)

4. What did Wall Street analysts forecast Gillette's second-quarter profit to be?   (D)

5. What can be concluded from the last news item?   (C)

Home Listening

Business News

Tapescript

Asia's major markets were volatile this week. Analysts say worries over the Iraq situation made investors cautious early in the week, but stronger than expected economic data prompted a mid-week rally in Asian stocks.

According to analysts, investors in Asian equities were taking profits on gains made over the past few months, but were also on edge over the apparent deterioration of stability in Iraq this week.

Sean Darby, an investment strategist with Nomura Securities，says markets went through a correction as investors re-evaluated their risks.

"The economic data has actually surprised possibly more on the upside so in contrast to the market performance, those data points have actually been very good. But the markets have over-reached themselves and the news from Iraq started to unsettle some international investors."

Mr. Darby says investors are worried about damage to Asian exporters from a weaker US dollar. For example, prices of US consumer goods manufactured in Japan and South Korea could become more expensive as the Japanese yen and South Korean won appreciate against the dollar.

Japan's market felt the pinch, with the Nikkei 225 finishing Friday at 10,167, more than four percent lower than a week ago. But despite worries, South Korea's Kospi index reached a 17-month high this week. By Friday morning, however, the rally had subsided and the Kospi closed at 809, gaining just more than a half point on the week.

Early-week selling on Hong Kong's stock market was also short-lived, when the Hang Seng index surged by more than two percent on Thursday. The Hang Seng ended at 12,203 Friday, 12 points lower than a week ago.

Despite the correction this week, Mr. Darby predicts investors will continue to move assets back into Hong Kong shares.

"Hong Kong has had an unusual performance because the interest rates here have actually been going down and the reason for that is there's been very strong inflow of portfolios into Hong Kong."

Taipei's Taiex index recovered from selling earlier in the week and closed Friday 12 points down from last week's end at 6,044.

Listen to the business news report and complete the notes with what you hear.

Asian Stocks		
General Performance	Asia's major markets were volatile this week: ➤ Early in the week — (1) <u>Worries over the Iraq situation</u> made investors cautious. ➤ Mid in the week — (2) <u>Stronger than expected economic data</u> prompted a rally.	
Performance in Major Asian Stock Markets	Nikkei 225	Japan's Nikkei 225 ended Friday at (3) <u>10,167</u>, more than four percent lower than a week ago. Reason(s) for the pressure in Japan's market: Investors are worried about (4) <u>damage to Asian exporters</u> as the Japanese yen and South Korean won increase in value against (5) <u>the weaker US dollar</u>.
	Kospi	South Korea's Kospi index reached (6) <u>a 17-month high</u> this week. By Friday morning, however, the rally had subsided and the Kospi closed at (7) <u>809</u>, gaining just more than (8) <u>a half point</u> on the week.
	Hang Seng	Hong Kong's Hang Seng index surged by more than two percent on Thursday but ended at (9) <u>12,203</u> Friday, 12 points lower than a week ago. Reason(s) for the unusual performance in Hong Kong market — (10) <u>strong inflow of portfolios</u> into Hong Kong keeps Hong Kong's (11) <u>interest rates going down</u>.
	Taiex	Taipei's Taiex index recovered from selling earlier in the week and closed Friday 12 points down from last week's end at (12) <u>6,044</u>.